29. JUL. 1999

-2. NOV. 1999

29. MAY 2000

26. JUN. 2000

13. OCT 2000
23. JUL. 2001

-5. NOV. 2001

-4. JAN 2002

21. MAY 2002

19. APR 2002

09. AUG. 02

22. APR

FB

23. AUG 05

02 SEP 05

1 8 SEP 2017

MACNEILL, A.   F

MORAY COUNCIL
DEPARTMENT OF TECHNICAL AND
LEISURE SERVICES

00 59 64 52

This item should be returned
on or before the latest date
shown above to the library
from which it was borrowed.
A fine may be charged for
overdue items.

D1433375

DOUBLE-BLIND

Also by Alastair MacNeill

MOONBLOOD

DOUBLE-BLIND

Alastair MacNeill

VICTOR GOLLANCZ

LONDON

First published in Great Britain 1997
by Victor Gollancz
An imprint of the Cassell Group
Wellington House, 125 Strand, London WC2R OBB

© Alastair MacNeill 1997

The right of Alastair MacNeill to be identified as author of
this work has been asserted by him in accordance with
the Copyright, Designs and Patents Act, 1988.

A catalogue record for this book is
available from the British Library.

ISBN 0 575 06499 4

596452

MORAY COUNCIL
Department of Technical
& Leisure Services

F

Typeset by Rowland Phototypesetting Ltd,
Bury St Edmunds, Suffolk
Printed in Great Britain by St Edmundsbury Press Ltd,
Bury St Edmunds, Suffolk

All rights reserved. No part of this publication may be
reproduced or transmitted in any form or by any means,
electronic or mechanical including photocopying,
recording or any information storage or retrieval system,
without prior permission in writing from the publishers.

This book is sold subject to the condition that it shall not,
by way of trade or otherwise, be lent, resold, hired out, or
otherwise circulated without the publisher's prior consent
in any form of binding or cover other than that in which it
is published and without a similar condition including this
condition being imposed on the subsequent purchaser.

97 98 99   5 4 3 2 1

double-blind: denoting an experiment in which the identities of the control group are known neither to the subjects nor the experimenters

PREFACE

'Betcha can't.'

'Betcha I can.'

Two sisters. Eight years old. Each the mirror image of the other. The only discernible difference between them that afternoon, as they stood at the foot of the expansive garden at the back of their parents' spacious double-storey house, was in their clothes. One was wearing a pale blue dress with white socks and black sandals. The picture of childlike innocence. The other had on a pair of faded dungarees over a grubby white T-shirt. She was barefoot. The quintessential tomboy. The one in the dungarees held out her catapult and pointed to the two tin cans on the wall twenty feet away from where they stood. It was with some reluctance that her sister took it. She had never fired a catapult in her life, but was determined not to lose face in front of her sister.

'Can't, can't, can't!' the tomboy chanted mockingly, as she danced around her sister.

'Can too,' came the defensive reply.

'Can too,' the tomboy mimicked. 'Betcha my pocket money you can't hit either of those cans. Betcha, betcha—'

'You're on,' her sister cut in defiantly.

The tomboy pulled the quarter that her mother had given her earlier that morning from the oversized pocket of her dungarees and held it out in her palm. Her sister removed a tiny purse from the side pocket of her dress, opened it and took out her quarter too. Both coins were placed on the stone bench behind them. The tomboy selected a suitable small pebble from a nearby flower-bed and gave it to the other, who cupped it in the sling then took a step forward and aimed at the larger of the two cans. She drew back the elastic and held the sling between her thumb and forefinger.

Behind, her sister had suddenly gone quiet and instinctively she glanced over her shoulder. The tomboy was down on one knee, her eyes focused on the cans, the tip of her tongue protruding between her lips in an image of intense concentration. Her eyes flickered up, a questioning look on her face. Her sister turned her attention back to the cans and, moments later, let fly the pebble.

'Missed, missed, missed!' the tomboy exclaimed and clapped her hands. She hurried over to the bench, scooped up the two coins, and slipped them into her pocket. It was at that moment she saw the dove settle on the edge of the bird bath at the top end of the garden. She snatched the catapult from her sister's hand and, after searching in vain for a suitable projectile, she dug her hand into her pocket and removed one of the quarters, which she inserted into the leather sling. She moved cautiously forwards and paused when she was within range of the dove. Then she raised the catapult to eye level, but as she was about to fire it her sister came up behind her and grabbed the crook of her arm. The missile hurtled from the sling, narrowly missing the bird – which took flight – and smashed through the bottom corner of the kitchen window. The girls stared in horror at the shattered window. Then the tomboy shoved the catapult into her startled sister's hand and darted from sight behind an adjacent hedge.

'Stop right there!'

The furious voice came from the house. The remaining sister looked from the catapult in her upturned palm to her mother standing on the back porch, her face red with rage. 'It – it wasn't me, Mommy,' she stammered nervously as her mother marched across the lawn.

'Then what's that in your hand?'

'Mel did it. Honestly. Then she ran off.'

'It's always your sister, isn't it? Never you.'

'I didn't do it, Mommy,' came the fearful reply. Tears trickled down her cheeks.

'Where's your sister?' No reply. 'Melissa, where are you? Melissa?'

Moments later the tomboy hurried into view from behind the hedge, her eyes wide and questioning. 'What is it, Mommy?' she asked, breathlessly.

'Where have you been?'

'I was playing down by the river.'

'What's your sister doing with your catapult?'

'I lent it to her before I went down to the river. She said she wanted to shoot at those cans at the bottom of the garden.'

'That's not true,' her sister blurted out between sobs. 'It's not true, Mommy.'

'Then whose is this?' their mother asked, holding up the quarter she had retrieved from the kitchen floor.

'It's not mine,' Melissa said innocently, taking the other quarter from the pocket of her dungarees.

'She bet me my pocket money I couldn't hit those cans,' her sister said in desperation.

'Why are you trying to get me into trouble, sis?' Melissa said, her voice laced with hurt and disbelief. 'I wasn't even here.'

'She's the one who's in trouble,' their mother announced sharply, then jabbed her thumb towards the house. 'Inside, young lady.'

'But I told you—'

'Now!' her mother snapped, then grabbed her daughter's wrist and led her towards the door.

Melissa slipped the quarter back into her pocket, sniggered

gleefully to herself at her sister's misfortune, and there was an extra skip in her step as she headed off in the direction of the river.

ONE

Sunday

The pistol was aimed at her heart. Yet there was no fear in her eyes as she looked up slowly from the barrel of the 10mm Glock automatic to the face of the man holding it. Mid-thirties. Ice-blue eyes. Rich tan. Cropped brown hair. He held her stare momentarily then a faint smile tugged at the corners of his mouth and he slipped the weapon back into the custom-made inside-the-waistband holster concealed beneath his loose-fitting white linen suit and stepped aside to let her enter the room.

Melissa Wade wiped her hand across her clammy forehead then stepped into the room, careful to avoid any contact with him. 'I'm sorry if the gun startled you, but you just can't be too careful these days,' he said, closing the door after her. There was no apology in his voice.

'It didn't. It's hot tonight.' Which was true. It was midsummer in Mexico City. Daytime temperatures sweltered uncomfortably in the high thirties; at night they dropped significantly, but the damp, sticky humidity invariably prevailed until the air was cleansed by the onset of a welcome thunderstorm. Rain had been predicted for six. It was now eight. Again the forecasters had got it wrong. But that didn't surprise her. Even the weather wasn't punctual in Mexico. She crossed to the curtains, tugged one back, and noticed a figure standing in the street below. He was wearing a dark suit, similar to the one worn by the armed man she had encountered in the lobby when she arrived at the hotel, and guessed that others would be strategically positioned around the periphery of the building.

She focused on the reflection of the man standing behind her. Rumour had it that James Doyle had been responsible, either directly or from his own specific orders, for some two hundred murders in the past four years since he had become the right-hand man of Juan and Ramón Salcido, the brothers who presided over the most powerful – and brutal – of the six main drug cartels in Mexico. But it *was* only a rumour. She would have put the figure closer to four hundred. And even that was only a conservative estimate.

'I take it you weren't followed here tonight?' Doyle asked.

She let the curtain fall. 'What do you think?'

'If the DEA were ever to find out that you were working for us—'

'They won't,' she cut in sharply.

The DEA. The Drug Enforcement Administration – the United States government's élite anti-narcotics police force, a sub-division of the US Justice Department, which fell directly under the control of the Attorney General in Washington.

'Did you bring it with you?'

She took a computer disk from her pocket and tossed it on to the bed. He fed it into the laptop computer he had brought with him and a dozen names, each with an accompanying address and contact number, appeared on the screen. All were informers who worked for a rival cartel in Tijuana in the north of the country. The fact that Doyle already knew all but two of the names was of little concern to him. The disk had been merely a gesture of goodwill on her part.

'That's just a sample of what's on offer,' she said from the window. 'Do you still want to go ahead with the deal?'

'When?'

'Let's make it in a week's time. Next Sunday. I'm due to fly back to the States tomorrow. I'll be in New York for a couple of days so I'll be able to copy the program on to disk from our central data bank while I'm there.'

'Which would give us the names of every informer and every undercover federal agent currently working with the DEA both in Mexico and Colombia,' Doyle said, knowing that that kind of inside information would give the Salcidos a distinct advantage in the bitter power struggle constantly raging between the country's main narco-cartels.

'And in return you'll pay me ten million dollars in small, cut diamonds,' she told him.

'That's what we agreed,' Doyle said. 'Where and when next Sunday?'

'Why not meet here again? Same room. Say, ten o'clock in the morning?'

'That's fine by me. I'll book the room before I leave.' Doyle ejected the disk from the computer and held it up towards her. 'Can I keep this?'

'Sure,' she replied. 'It's no use to me.'

Doyle pocketed it and switched off the computer. 'You know that the DEA will never stop looking for you once they realize what you've done.'

'Except that I'll already have a ten-million-dollar head start. That kind of money can buy me a lot of time.' She crossed to the door then paused to look round at him. 'And remember, come alone on Sunday. If I see any of your goons, the deal's off. I'm sure I wouldn't have much difficulty in finding another buyer, even at such short notice. After all, the names of many of your informants will be on the disk too.'

Doyle smiled fleetingly at her but his eyes remained cold. 'If I didn't know better, Agent Wade, I'd almost be inclined to think you didn't trust me.'

'Whatever gave you that idea?' With that she left the room and closed the door behind her.

* * *

Thirty-four years old. Five foot four. Shoulder-length black hair. 'Honey-tanned' complexion (inherited from my Spanish mother). Brown eyes. Slim. Attractive.

That was how Laura Wade had described herself in the application form for a national dating agency that she had filled in for fun, then promptly torn up, a couple of months back at her apartment in New York. Melissa had been with her at the time. It could have been about either of them. Physically they were identical twins. Yet that was where the similarity ended. Whereas Laura had picked *shy, reliable, considerate* and *conventional* as her four main personality traits, Melissa would have chosen *brash, extrovert, adventurous* and *unconventional* to describe herself. Men were almost always drawn to their dusky looks, but whereas they could get within range of Laura before she abruptly shut them out Melissa's assured self-confidence had them scampering back to the pseudo-sanctuary of their male friends. Not that she was in the least bit interested in any of the weasels who skulked obsequiously in her shadow. It was only when she met her match that she was prepared to start making concessions – but even then they were always on her terms . . .

It had been that same self-confidence that had first brought her to the attention of the DEA while she had been working as a UC – an undercover cop – with the Narcotics Bureau in Brooklyn. Now, six years later, she was regarded as one of the DEA's most experienced special agents, having worked extensively as a UC in the States, as well as in Bolivia and Colombia before her cover was 'burnt' by an informer while working on a deal in Medellín. She was immediately pulled out of Colombia for her own protection. Her days as a UC were over. There was talk of her being given a desk job in Washington when Tom Kellerman, the DEA's chief officer in Mexico – and her former supervisor in Bolivia – had requested her to head up a specialist unit to investigate the activities of the Salcido cartel. She was given a deadline of eighteen months to accumulate enough evidence to bring Juan and Ramón Salcido to justice. A similar operation had been tried twice before but on both occasions the head of the newly appointed task force had been murdered within weeks of arriving in Mexico. Melissa had no desire to make it three in a row. With that in mind, she had chosen a different approach. One that would benefit both parties immediately . . . but only one in the long term.

For the past eight months she had been passing on inside information to Doyle and for which she had been paid handsomely in untraceable US dollars. And in six days' time she was going to play her final hand – then get out fast before all hell broke loose around her . . .

She pulled into the driveway of the house in the modest suburb of San Angel where she had lived since taking up her position in Mexico City. Switching off the engine, she got out of the car and went into the house where she deactivated the alarm system, kicked off her ankle boots, went through to the lounge and switched on the television. Although fluent in Spanish, she ignored the local news and turned to CNN International for the latest global bulletin. She poured herself a shot of bourbon but as she slumped into a chair the telephone rang. She groaned then reached behind her for the cordless handset. Her mood changed when the caller identified himself as the man over whom she had 'accidentally' spilled red wine at a tedious cocktail party the previous weekend at the American Embassy. She remembered him well, having handed over her unlisted home number as consolation for her apparent clumsiness. A strikingly handsome self-made millionaire, younger than her, with a penchant for fine wines and expensive restaurants. Yes, she would have dinner with him at the exclusive Hacienda de Los Morales. Yes, she would meet him there in an hour's time. Yes, she was looking forward to seeing him again.

She replaced the handset and smiled contentedly to herself. A perfect end to her day . . .

TWO

Monday

Melissa Wade had become disillusioned with the DEA. She knew that, with the limited resources at their disposal, the DEA could never hope to stem the tide of drugs constantly washing over the bloodied streets of America. The root of the problem could be traced back to countries in Asia and South America where local peasants could earn ten times as much from a single coca crop as from traditional farming. The local drug syndicates would offer them extended credit against their crop, as well as providing them with free fertilizers and equipment. And they always had a ready buyer for their produce, which wasn't always so with the more traditional foodstuffs. Those who chose not to farm coca were subjected to intimidation and violence for daring to challenge the power of the drug cartels. They got little protection from the local police, many of whom already subsidized their meagre wages with narco-bribes. And the vast profits made from drug trafficking went further than that. They could easily buy a sympathetic politician – and if enough of them stood in an election, the balance of a government could even tilt in favour of the omnipotent cartels.

Despite numerous requests for more financial aid from Capitol Hill to fight the problem abroad, Melissa knew that the DEA were still chronically underfunded – and understaffed. But Congress, ever-sensitive to growing public unease over the drug menace, expected – and demanded – results from the DEA.

When they weren't forthcoming the White House was quick to deflect any criticism from the government by instigating yet another reshuffle of the DEA's hierarchy. But without more funds, it was a token gesture. That, though, had never bothered the politicians on Capitol Hill. It bought them more time – until the next reshuffle . . .

Ten months earlier Mark Braithwaite, a former high-ranking spook at Langley, had been brought in as the latest administrator of the DEA. It had been a controversial appointment, considering the tense relationship between the two camps after the DEA had accused the CIA of colluding with the drug-lords of the notorious 'Golden Triangle' in south-east Asia by allowing them to smuggle heroin into Europe in return for information on the Communist threat in the region. Langley had vehemently denied the allegations but the DEA had never been convinced of their innocence. The White House had specifically chosen Braithwaite in an attempt to end the feud between the two agencies but he had never been fully accepted, or trusted, by those working under him.

Melissa had taken an instant dislike to him. One of the first things he had done on taking office was appoint Bob Fulton, then the DEA's chief officer in Mexico, as its new divisional head in New York. Fulton's deputy, and intelligence chief in Mexico, Tom Kellerman, had been promoted in his place. Kellerman had wanted Melissa brought in as his new intelligence chief but Braithwaite refused and approved Kellerman's second choice, a younger agent with considerably less field experience. Melissa believed that she had been overlooked because she was a woman but without proof to back up her suspicions, she could do nothing about it. It had left her feeling bitter towards the DEA in general, and Braithwaite in particular. Not that she had ever let her emotions surface in front of him. She would never have given him the satisfaction of knowing just how much it still hurt . . .

Both Braithwaite and Tom Kellerman were waiting for her

when she entered the office on the fifth floor of the DEA's New York headquarters on the corner of 11th Avenue and West 57th Street. She had come straight from the airport and acknowledged Braithwaite with a nod.

Mid-fifties; grey hair and matching suit; nondescript features. A typical faceless bureaucrat, she thought disdainfully. Her eyes softened when she smiled at Kellerman. Thirty-nine, with tousled black hair and a genial personality, he was handsome in a rugged, outdoors way. His were the kind of looks that invariably drew admiring glances from women, and envy from men. Yet there was nothing conceited about him. If anything, he was too self-effacing, especially around women. Or so she had told him enough times in the seven years they had known each other. But that was his way and he wasn't going to change. He was totally career-minded and regarded anything else as little more than a distraction. Which was why he had chosen to sacrifice his marriage to further himself within the DEA. She had always liked Tom Kellerman . . .

'How was the flight from Mexico City?' Kellerman asked.

'Don't ask.' She snorted. 'I had this guy sitting next to me who was determined to tell me his whole life story and it got to the point where the thought of the plane going down over the Gulf of Mexico began to take on a certain appeal.'

Kellerman smiled. Braithwaite remained impassive. 'Sit down, Agent Wade,' he said brusquely, and gestured to the second chair in front of his desk.

'Well, what happened last night?' Kellerman asked. The levity was over. This was business.

'Doyle took the bait,' she replied. 'The deal will go ahead, as planned, on Sunday.'

'I knew he'd go for it!' Kellerman punched his fist into his palm. 'And the moment he hands over the diamonds, we've got him.'

'As long as there's no slip-up on the day,' Braithwaite said.

Melissa bit back her anger. She knew that the comment had

been directed at her. It had been unnecessary, but typical of Braithwaite. She noticed Kellerman watching her and read the look of caution in his eyes, but she said, 'I've been running with Operation Checkmate for eight months now, sir. Nothing's going to go wrong at this stage. You have my word on that.'

Braithwaite remained silent. His face gave away nothing.

'Melissa's got every angle covered,' Kellerman said, breaking the uneasy silence that had suddenly descended over the room. 'She won't make a mistake. My only concern is the INCD, the Mexican anti-narcotics unit. We don't have any jurisdiction over there, so they'll have to make the arrest after Doyle's taken possession of the disk. If they screw up, Doyle walks. You can be sure of that.'

'As you know, I've been in close contact with my opposite number in the INCD ever since the two of you first hatched this plan,' Braithwaite said. 'I have every confidence in them.'

'Then we've got him – as long as the extradition warrant holds up under scrutiny,' Melissa said. 'You can be sure that the Salcidos will bring in some of the country's top lawyers to contest it.'

'There may not be an extradition treaty between Mexico and the United States at present, Agent Wade, but this deal was agreed at the highest level of government,' Braithwaite replied, enraged that she should question his plans. 'The Justice Department in Washington covered every eventuality when they drew up the extradition papers. There aren't any loopholes. Doyle will be back in Florida by the middle of next week. Then it'll be up to him whether he stands trial for the murder of the policeman he shot in Miami five years ago. It would carry the mandatory death penalty were he convicted. Unless, of course, he were to choose to cheat the electric chair and start a new life under the Witness Protection Program by agreeing to co-operate with us to bring the Salcidos to justice. Which, after all, is the whole point of Operation Checkmate.'

'What if he decides to take his chances in court?' Melissa asked.

'Would you, given the choice?' Braithwaite retorted.

'We've been through this before, Melissa,' Kellerman told her.

'I know, but it's still the one aspect of Checkmate that's been left to chance,' she replied. 'What if he doesn't go for the deal?'

'I have every confidence he will,' Braithwaite said, reaching for a folder on his desk, 'otherwise I would never have sanctioned this operation in the first place. You just do your part, Agent Wade, and leave the rest to us.'

'Is that supposed to reassure me?' she asked sardonically.

'I think we've taken up enough of the administrator's time,' Kellerman said, and got to his feet.

'You don't like me, do you, Agent Wade?' Braithwaite said candidly. 'You think that I purposely overlooked you for promotion because I'm some kind of misogynistic dinosaur. Have you ever thought that your obvious contempt for authority may have played a major part in my decision? I realize, of course, that you revel in this image you've created for yourself as some kind of loose cannon, and I have to admit you do have your admirers in the DEA hierarchy. But I'm not one of them. And I never will be – not until you lose the attitude. Think about it, Agent Wade.'

'What for? We both know that you've got no intention of ever promoting me. Because if you did, it would be as good as admitting that you'd been wrong all along. And that would really stick in your craw, wouldn't it?'

Kellerman grabbed her arm and propelled her towards the door. He yanked it open, shoved her into the corridor, and led her away from Braithwaite's office. 'What the hell was that all about?' he snapped. 'Well?' he demanded, when she remained silent.

'I don't have to take that kind of shit from him,' she retorted defensively.

'This is exactly what he was talking about,' Kellerman shot back. 'Your contempt for authority.'

'You've been my superior for as long as we've known each other. Have I ever shown any disrespect towards you? No, because you've earned my respect. He hasn't. And he never will. The guy's an asshole. We both know that.'

'There you go again.'

'It's true, though. OK, so I've got an attitude problem. I admit that. But I also know that I'm damn good at what I do. And, although he'd never say it to my face, Braithwaite knows that too. Because if he didn't, he'd have pulled the plug on me when my review came up earlier this year. So if promotion means having to play footsie with suits like Braithwaite – fuck them. They can shove it, as far as I'm concerned.'

'I'm sure he'll be relieved to hear that,' Kellerman replied, but the anger had already left him. She spoke her mind, but what she said was only the truth, which was why she generally got away with it.

'Come on, you can buy me a drink before we go our separate ways,' she said.

'Pass. I've got another meeting in . . .' he paused to look at his watch and pulled a face '. . . five minutes ago. At least it's only Bob Fulton. He's never on time anyway.'

'Tell him hi from me.'

'Sure,' Kellerman replied. 'Are you staying with your sister?'

'I always stay with Laura when I'm in New York. It's the only time we ever get to see each other these days.'

'You can tell her hi from me.'

'But you don't even know her,' Melissa said, with a puzzled frown.

'I feel as if I do. After all, you two are identical twins.'

'Looks can be deceptive,' she replied.

'You never talk much about your sister, do you?'

'I thought you said you had a meeting with Bob Fulton five minutes ago?'

'I can take a hint. I'll see you at JFK Wednesday afternoon.'

'Yeah, sure,' she replied absently, then called after him as he walked off, 'And, Tom, thanks.'

'What for?' he asked, surprised, looking back at her.

'For having always been there for me. I know I haven't always been the easiest person to work with but your friendship's meant a lot to me over the years. I just wanted you to know that.'

'It's not like you to be sentimental. What's brought this on?'

She gave a quick shrug. 'It needed to be said, that's all. No big deal.'

He watched her walk to the elevator. As the doors parted in front of her, she glanced at him and he could have sworn he saw a look of sadness flash through her eyes. Then she was gone.

It was raining when Melissa emerged from the building. Her first thought was to hail a cab to take her to Laura's apartment, above the dental practice she shared with her partner, Raquel Vasquez, in El Barrio – better known as Spanish Harlem. Melissa liked Raquel: she had been a good friend to Laura ever since they had first met at university.

It was then that Melissa spotted the yellow cab waiting for the lights to change at the intersection on the opposite side of the street. It was available, a rarity in rush-hour traffic. She looked round furtively, hoping that nobody else had seen it, then the lights changed and, her arm flailing frantically in the air, she ran towards it. For a moment she thought the driver hadn't seen her as the cab drove straight past, but it stopped twenty yards further on and she hurried towards it only to see a couple in their early twenties scramble into the back.

Melissa stood despondently on the kerb. There was a bar on the opposite side of the street – it didn't look particularly appealing from the outside, she thought, but it would provide a temporary sanctuary from the driving rain. She darted over, through the stationary cars, pushed open the door and went in.

It looked even less appealing from the inside: a scattering of tables against the wall opposite the counter and a single pool table at the back of the room. The walls were adorned with faded black-and-white photographs of long-forgotten sporting personalities. She counted ten customers, all male and, apart from the two playing pool, all sitting alone. She could feel their eyes following her as she crossed to the counter and sat down.

'What'll it be?' the barman asked, getting off a stool to serve her.

'Bourbon, straight up.'

'You look like you got caught in the rain,' the barman said, as he poured her drink.

'That's observant,' she riposted sharply as she handed him a ten-dollar bill.

The barman eyed her then picked up the money and crossed to the till. He returned with her change and sat down again to continue watching the replay of a recent Knicks victory at Madison Square Gardens.

Melissa knew there had been no need to snap at him like that but she wasn't in the mood for small-talk. She sank the bourbon in one gulp then saw in the mirror behind the counter that the man on her right was staring at her, a salacious smile on his puffy, unshaven face. She turned her head and glared at him. He immediately looked away.

She suddenly recalled Tom Kellerman's words, 'You never talk much about your sister, do you?' No, she didn't. She had always been protective of Laura. It went back to their childhood. Laura had been painfully shy at school, the perfect target for the bullies – until Melissa intervened. Nobody picked on her sister without answering to her. Yet as children they had never been close. They had had different interests, different friends, different lives: all they had ever had in common were their identical features. They had grown closer as adults, but there was still an emotional chasm between them. Melissa doubted that it would ever be crossed. Yet it suited them like that: they were both fiercely independent and the fact that they weren't just another typical set of identical twins appealed to their strong sense of individuality.

'Barman, another shot for the lady.'

The voice startled Melissa and she focused on the reflection of the man standing behind her. When she arrived he had been sitting at one of the tables. Although she could smell the alcohol on his breath, she could see he wasn't drunk. Just damn irritating. She put her hand over her empty glass when the barman tried to refill it.

'Come on, have a drink with me,' the man urged. 'I'm buying.'

'If I'd wanted another drink, I'd have paid for it myself,' Melissa said, then slipped off the stool.

As she was about to leave the man grabbed her arm. 'Come on, you'll get soaked out there. Just one drink. That's all.'

'I'd rather take my chances,' she retorted, shrugging off his hand.

'What's your problem?' the man demanded, blocking her escape.

The time for diplomacy was over. Melissa slammed the heel of her boot savagely into his shin. He cried out in anguish and as he doubled over in pain she grabbed a handful of his hair and cracked his forehead down against the edge of the counter. He collapsed, unconscious, at her feet, knocking over several stools as he fell. 'I'd say he'd had enough, wouldn't you?' she said to the startled barman then, pocketing her change, left the bar to find a cab.

El Barrio, to the south of Harlem and inhabited by a predominantly Hispanic community, is one of New York City's worst slum areas. Fear, intimidation and distrust pervade its atmosphere and the streets are lined with burnt-out vehicles and vandalized, unoccupied buildings. Of the other boroughs in the city, only the South Bronx has a worse crime record.

The dental practice was in a converted two-storey house, sandwiched between a laundromat and a newly opened hair salon, situated on Park Avenue, close to La Marqueta – a five-block street market in one of the least salubrious parts of the neighbourhood. It had been burgled several times by junkies looking for drugs. An alarm had been installed after the first break-in, but had made no difference. Each time it went off Laura wisely remained locked in her apartment until the police arrived, when the intruders had long gone.

By the time the cab pulled up in front of the building it had stopped raining but it was still dark and overcast. Melissa paid the driver then got out. She opened the front door, which led directly into the waiting room. The receptionist, a young Hispanic woman, glanced up and smiled fleetingly before returning her attention to the dog-eared appointment book on the counter in front of her. 'A moment, Dr Wade, let me just change this appointment before I forget,' she said in Spanish.

'I'm not Dr Wade, I'm her sister,' Melissa replied in Spanish: both sisters were bilingual.

The receptionist stared at her. 'I'm sorry,' she said, 'it's just that, well . . .'

'We look exactly alike.' Melissa finished the sentence for her. 'Don't worry, it happens all the time. You're new here, aren't you?'

'I started last week.'

'Melissa?' a voice said from behind her. Raquel Vasquez crossed to where she was standing and shook her hand warmly. She was a dumpy woman in her mid-thirties with short black hair and a chubby face offset by the large glasses she wore. 'Laura said you were coming in from Mexico today. How was the flight?'

'Don't ask,' Melissa replied.

'Come on through to the back room,' Raquel said. 'Laura's with a patient right now. It's just a routine filling. She shouldn't be long.'

'I see you've got a new receptionist. What happened to Mañuela?'

'She's pregnant – again,' Raquel said, rolling her eyes.

'Number seven if you please.' They entered a sparsely furnished room to which Laura and Raquel could retreat between patients for a few draws on a cigarette or a cup of coffee. 'You want coffee? I've just made some.'

'Thanks,' Melissa said, sitting down in the nearest of the two armchairs. 'How are Ben and the kids?'

'Good,' Raquel said. 'Milk, no sugar. Right?' Melissa nodded. 'Ben got a promotion a couple of months back.'

'Laura told me about it. He's doing well and I'm glad – he deserves it with the amount of overtime he puts in. And what about Abby and little Chloe?'

'Abby started school this year. Chloe's not so little any more. She'll be three next month. She's going to be the smart one of the family, I can tell.' Raquel moved to the door. 'I'll let Laura know you're here.'

'No need,' said a voice and Laura appeared in the doorway.

'Hey, sis, how's it going?' Melissa said, got up and hugged her sister.

'Overworked, but what's new?'

'How long are you going to be?' Melissa asked. 'I thought we could go out for a meal then maybe take in a movie.'

'Can't do, Mel, not tonight,' Laura said, with an apologetic smile. 'I've got to finish my paperwork. I was hoping to have it done before you got here, but it didn't work out that way. Sorry.'

'Oh, come on, Laura, Melissa's only here for a couple of days,' Raquel said. 'The paperwork can wait.'

'No, Laura's right,' Melissa replied, coming to her sister's defence. 'It's best to get it done. I'm the worst when it comes to paperwork. I'm never up to date. At least one of us is conscientious.'

'I'll definitely get it finished tonight,' Laura promised. 'The practice is closed tomorrow so we'll have the whole day to spend together. And tomorrow night we can go out for a meal. My treat.'

'You're on,' Melissa said. 'Perhaps it's just as well, really. I've got to go see a few friends while I'm here in New York anyway. I'll do it tonight. Leave you in peace.'

'D'you want to borrow my car?' Laura asked.

'Yeah, that would be great. Thanks.'

'You know where the keys are. There's a spare for the apartment on the bunch.'

'I'll probably need it. God knows what time I'll be back.' Melissa moved to the door and put a hand lightly on Raquel's arm. 'Good to see you again.' Then she looked at Laura. 'I'll have a quick bath then I'd better get going. Don't bother waiting up for me.'

'I won't,' Laura said.

Raquel waited until Melissa had disappeared then looked at her watch and groaned. 'Well, I guess we'd better get back to work.'

'You know what they say – no rest for the wicked,' Laura replied.

'Chance would be a fine thing,' Raquel retorted good-humouredly.

'Hmm, it would, wouldn't it?' Laura muttered thoughtfully to herself as she followed Raquel from the room.

THREE

Laura woke with a start. Momentarily disoriented, her first thought was that someone had again broken into the surgery. But reason prevailed: the alarm was silent. She peered at the illuminated face of the clock on the bedside table: 2.47 a.m.

The sound of the doorbell jolted her upright. She got out of bed and pulled on her robe, securing it tightly round her waist. Having learnt to take no chances, especially at that time of night, she opened the top drawer of the bedside table and removed the small Colt .380 automatic that Melissa had insisted she buy after the first break-in. She had since joined a gun club on the Upper East Side and now regarded herself a reasonable shot. The doorbell rang again, longer this time, more urgently. She didn't switch on the light as she made her way along the hallway to the front door where she peered tentatively through the spy-hole. It was a man she had never seen before. Unshaven. Tousled black hair. Leather jacket. Sweatshirt. Unease flooded through her. 'Who is it?' she called, forcing herself to sound confident. It wasn't how she was feeling.

'It's Tom Kellerman. Melissa, is that you?'

'No. I'm her sister.'

'Dr Wade, I work with Melissa at the DEA. If you look through the spy-hole, you'll see that I'm holding up my ID badge.'

Laura peered through it at the laminated card. She had heard

28

of Tom Kellerman – Melissa had mentioned him. She drew back the two heavy bolts then opened the door on the chain and asked him to pass her the card. Satisfied that it was authentic, she removed the chain and opened the door.

'Is Melissa here?' Kellerman asked.

'I assume so,' Laura replied. 'She went out last night to see some friends. She took my car. I didn't hear her come back, though. But I went to bed quite early. She's probably asleep.'

'Could you check for me?' Kellerman said, and saw the uncertainty on her face. 'Please, it's very important.'

Laura heard the anxiety in his voice. 'Is something wrong?' she asked hesitantly.

'Please, Dr Wade, see if she's back,' Kellerman insisted.

Laura went to a door further down the hall and looked into the darkened room. Melissa's blue holdall was still on the bed where she had left it. 'She's not back,' Laura said. 'Something's happened, hasn't it?'

'There's been an accident,' Kellerman said, 'but we don't know yet whether Melissa was involved. That's why I'm here.'

'I don't understand – what d'you mean, you don't know whether she was involved?'

'Earlier this evening your car was found at the foot of an embankment near the Passaic Expressway on the outskirts of Hackensack. It was completely burnt-out. A body was recovered from the scene, but it's burnt beyond recognition.' Kellerman grabbed Laura's arm as her legs buckled. 'I think it's best if you were to sit down, Dr Wade. Where's the lounge?'

'I'll ... I'll be all right,' she said, shakily, and rubbed a trembling hand over her ashen face.

Kellerman switched on the hall light, pushed open the door behind him and found, to his relief, that it led into the lounge. He helped her to the nearest armchair then sat down on the edge of the sofa opposite. 'Can I get you a drink?' he asked.

'No, thank you,' she replied in a barely audible voice. 'Do you have a cigarette?'

'I don't smoke,' Kellerman replied. It was almost an apology.

'Doesn't matter. I've got some around here somewhere,' she said, looking around absently. Kellerman saw the pack, beside her lighter on the mantelpiece. He handed them to her. Her hands shook as she pulled out a cigarette and pushed it between her lips.

'We don't know yet whether it is Melissa,' Kellerman said.

'Who else could it be?' She was struggling to hold back the tears. 'I told you, she took my car to go visit some friends. It has to be her. You know that as well as I do.'

'We won't know for sure until we can make a positive identification.' Kellerman handed Laura his handkerchief. 'You were Melissa's dentist, weren't you?'

Laura wiped her eyes. 'Yes, ever since I graduated. Mel was my first patient. She insisted on it. And you didn't argue with Mel.'

'Don't I know,' Kellerman said.

'I've got her dental chart in my office downstairs,' Laura said. 'I'll get it for you.'

'Would you like me to come with you?' Kellerman asked.

'No,' she replied, then stubbed out her cigarette. 'But thank you all the same. I won't be long.'

She returned a couple of minutes later carrying a cardboard folder in her hand. He could see that she had been crying. She handed it to him. 'Her complete dental history's in there. You'll let me know the results of the post-mortem as soon as you hear them?'

'Yes, of course,' Kellerman assured her. 'Is there someone you'd like me to call to come over and be with you tonight? At least until you know the outcome of the post-mortem.'

'I already know the outcome. And if you're honest with yourself, so do you.' Laura brushed away fresh tears. 'I'd prefer to be alone right now.'

Kellerman removed a notebook from his pocket, wrote a number on the first page, tore it out and handed it to her. 'That's the number of my cellular phone. Please don't hesitate to call should you need anything.'

'Thank you,' Laura said softly. 'How did the police know to call the DEA if the body was so badly burnt?'

'Melissa's ID was found at the scene of the crash,' Kellerman replied. 'The local cops rang us when they found it. It's routine.'

'And you still think there could be any doubt about the identity of the body?' she asked, opening the door for him.

He didn't say anything. He knew she was right. He left without another word.

'It's her,' Braithwaite said to Kellerman. 'The forensic orthodontist made a positive identification from the chart you got from her sister earlier this morning.'

'It was really only a question of confirming what we already knew,' Kellerman said, then moved to the window behind Braithwaite's desk and watched the early-morning traffic cascading down 11th Avenue. 'I still can't believe it. Not Melissa. Not after everything we've been through together over the years.'

'Including Operation Checkmate,' Braithwaite said. He picked up the folder in front of him then slapped it back on the desk. 'Our one chance to bring down the Salcido cartel. Gone. I don't believe it!'

'Is that all Melissa's death means to you?' Kellerman turned away from the window.

'Frankly, yes,' Braithwaite replied bluntly, then swivelled his chair to face Kellerman. 'I know you held Agent Wade in high esteem—'

'It was more than that,' Kellerman cut in. 'She was also a good friend.'

'And I'm sorry for your loss,' Braithwaite said, without sounding it. 'But I can't afford the luxury of befriending the operatives. I have to evaluate them solely in terms of results. I realize that may sound insensitive at a time like this, but the fact remains that Agent Wade was our only link to Doyle. Without her, the deal can't go ahead on Sunday. Which means that Operation Checkmate is dead in the water, allowing the Salcido cartel to continue its activities with impunity. And that's what I'll have to explain to the Attorney General later today. He, in turn, will have to inform the White House. I don't think the President will be too pleased, do you?'

Kellerman returned to his chair and sat down. He cupped his hands over his nose and mouth and stared at the floor for some time. Then he looked up at Braithwaite. 'There is another possibility.'

'Go on,' Braithwaite said.

'We could use Laura Wade.'

Braithwaite folded his arms across his chest without taking his eyes off Kellerman's face. 'Her sister?' he said at length.

'Her identical twin sister,' Kellerman corrected him.

'Out of the question!' Braithwaite barked. 'Christ! If anything were to happen to her while she was working for us we'd be crucified by the press. And rightly so. The answer is no.'

'Why should anything happen to her?' Kellerman countered. 'All she would have to do is meet Doyle on Sunday and hand over the disk. He'd never suspect a thing. It's got to be worth a try, surely?'

'And what if word of Agent Wade's death were to leak back to Doyle before Sunday?' Braithwaite challenged.

'The forensic orthodontist only confirmed Melissa's death a few minutes ago. It's not as if it's been released to the press yet. We could hold it back for another week. That way Laura Wade's name need never appear in any of the reports. As for the Attorney General and the White House, Melissa completed the operation before she died. That would leave you in the clear.'

Braithwaite pondered the implications of Kellerman's idea. Then he shook his head. 'No, I still say it's too risky.'

'We're this close to cracking the biggest drug cartel in Mexico,' Kellerman said, indicating with his thumb and forefinger. 'We're never going to get another chance like this. We both know that. All Laura Wade would have to do is hand over the disk, take the diamonds and leave. Then the INCD would move in and arrest Doyle. Where's the risk in that?'

Braithwaite reached for his cigarettes and lit one. 'And how do you intend to persuade Laura Wade to go along with this?'

'All I can do is ask her.'

'And all she can do is say no.'

'More than likely. But I won't know that unless I ask her.'

'I still say it's too risky. What do you know about Laura Wade?'

'Nothing, other than that she's a dentist,' Kellerman replied, 'but there's sure to be something about her in Melissa's personnel file.'

'I'll take a look,' Braithwaite conceded.

'I told Dr Wade that I'd call her once the results of the post-mortem were through,' Kellerman said, getting to his feet.

'I'll see you back here in half an hour,' Braithwaite said, then took a long drag on his cigarette. 'By then I'll have read through Agent Wade's file and I'll give you my final answer.'

Kellerman hung up, rubbed his hands slowly over his face. There were aspects of his job that he hated – and having to break the news to a relative that an agent had been killed was at the top of the list. He'd had enough experience of it and it never got any easier. Words were so hollow at a time like that. But Laura Wade had been remarkably calm and in a way he could understand that. He had just confirmed what she had known all along – what they had both known all along.

But how could he ask her to see through Operation Checkmate in Melissa's place? And expect an answer before he flew back to Mexico the following day. What right did he have to intrude on her grief? He knew that, if he were in her shoes, he would say no.

He called up Melissa's personnel file on the computer and

her ID photo appeared on the screen. The likeness between the two sisters was almost eerie. Laura Wade's hair was longer, but other than that he couldn't tell them apart. He worked through the file until he came to her family background. He knew that her parents had been killed in a light plane crash three years earlier while on holiday in Spain and Melissa had taken their deaths hard. Then he arrived at the section on Laura. It appeared to be fairly standard stuff: graduated from NYU ten years ago as one of the top three students in her year. Worked at an exclusive private dental practice in the affluent Riverdale area of the Bronx. Married Jefferson Harvey, a doctor at Bellevue. Now divorced.

To his surprise, he discovered that information relating to the period after the divorce and until she went into partnership with Raquel Vasquez in El Barrio had been classified by a former DEA administrator. As a chief of operations, Kellerman had the necessary clearance code to access it. He punched in his security code and the missing data came up on the screen.

Once he had read it he knew exactly what Braithwaite's answer would be . . .

'No.'

'You can't condemn her for what happened in the past,' Kellerman remonstrated.

'Laura Wade's an alcoholic, for Christ's sake,' Braithwaite said.

'She *was* an alcoholic,' Kellerman corrected him. 'According to Melissa's file, she's been on the wagon now for the last two years.'

'An alcoholic can lapse at any time. They're never cured. All it needs is one drink to start them off again.' Braithwaite tossed the print-out on to the table. 'And you want to push her into a highly pressurized situation at a time when she's at her most vulnerable. That's exactly what could trigger her off.'

'I'd be watching her every step of the way. And if she looked like she might crack, I'd abort the operation and pull her out.' Kellerman sat forward in his chair. 'But this is all just speculation. Chances are she's going to say no anyway.'

'I want to smash the Salcido cartel just as much as you do, Tom,' Braithwaite said, 'but using Laura Wade would be too much of a risk. Especially with what we now know about her. I'm sorry, I can't authorize it.'

Kellerman stared at his feet then looked up slowly at Braithwaite. 'What if this conversation never took place? What if I were to approach Laura Wade without your knowledge or your permission? That way if she agreed to help me and anything were to go wrong in Mexico, you'd be in the clear. It would be my head on the block. Not yours.'

Braithwaite held Kellerman's stare as he lit a cigarette and exhaled the smoke out of the corner of his mouth. 'Theoretically speaking, if this conversation never took place, how can I be expected to comment on what you've just said?'

Kellerman smiled and got to his feet.

'Tom,' Braithwaite called after him, 'you know that if this backfires you're on your own. And there'd be no way back for you after that. I'd see to that personally. I have to protect the good name of the DEA at all costs. I hope you understand that.'

'Then I guess I'd better make sure it goes according to plan,' Kellerman said. 'But first I've got to convince Laura Wade of that. And somehow I don't think that's going to be very easy.'

'Mr Kellerman, I wasn't expecting to see you again . . . well, at least, not so soon,' Laura said, when she opened the door of her apartment.

Kellerman could see by the redness around her eyes that she had been crying. But there were no tears now. She had taken a few moments between asking who it was when he had first rung the bell and opening the door. He guessed she had used the time to compose herself. 'I know this must be a particularly difficult time for you right now, but there's something I'd like to talk to you about. If you feel up to talking, that is.'

'Yes, of course. Please, won't you come in?' Laura stepped aside to allow him past her. 'We can talk in the kitchen,' she said.

He hadn't smelt alcohol on her breath as she passed him. And if there was ever a time when she might have been tempted to turn to the bottle for solace, it would have been during those last harrowing hours. That had to be a good sign.

'Mr Kellerman?' she called.

'Sorry, I was miles away,' he replied, with a rueful smile then followed her into the kitchen. 'I tried the door downstairs when I arrived, but it was locked. I take it you've closed until further notice?'

'No, we're always closed on a Wednesday. That's because we work all day Saturday. It was Raquel's idea.' Laura glanced round at Kellerman as she filled the kettle. 'Raquel Vasquez. My partner. Her husband works a half day on Wednesdays. It allows them to spend a bit of time together, away from the kids.' She waved at the pine table in the corner of the room. 'Won't you sit down?'

Kellerman selected the furthest chair, so that he would be facing Laura, and looked around the kitchen. No sign of any alcohol. 'I'm sorry I couldn't have come here in person this morning to give you the results of the post-mortem. Telephones are always so impersonal. But this is the first chance I've had to get away from the office.'

'I'm glad you came,' Laura said softly, then switched on the kettle before sitting down opposite him. 'Do you mind if I smoke?'

'Please, go ahead,' Kellerman replied. 'Have you told anyone yet about Melissa's death?'

Laura lowered her eyes, then shook her head. 'I don't know many people in New York any more. I guess Raquel's my only real friend here now. I thought about phoning her, but I knew she'd have been round straight away. And I didn't want any company this morning. I just needed some time to myself. I'll ring her later this afternoon.'

The fact that none of her friends knew of Melissa's death was a blessing as far as Kellerman was concerned. It was imperative that as few people knew the truth as possible. At least until after Sunday.

'Mel held you in high regard,' Laura said, interrupting his thoughts. 'Not that she ever said it in so many words. She was never big on compliments, as I'm sure you know. But you're the only person she ever spoke about when it came to work.'

'The feeling was mutual, Dr Wade,' Kellerman replied.

'Laura, please.'

'Did she talk much to you about work?'

'No. Very rarely. She never discussed any cases with me. But I do remember she was thrilled when she found out she was being posted to Mexico.' Laura's eyes went to the kettle as it came to the boil then flittered back to Kellerman. 'Do you mind if I ask you something . . . about you and Mel?'

'Was there ever anything between us?' Kellerman replied, and saw in her eyes that he had anticipated her question correctly. It wasn't the first time he had been called upon to answer it. 'No, although a lot of people in the DEA didn't believe that. It was a purely platonic friendship. Nothing more.'

Laura got up and switched off the kettle. 'How do you take your coffee?'

'Milk. No sugar.'

She handed him a mug and sat down with hers. She took a sip. 'You said there was something you wanted to talk to me about.'

He put his coffee on the coaster in front of him and turned it round as he struggled to express himself. 'This is harder than I thought it was going to be,' he said finally.

'You're not going to tell me that Mel was involved in something illegal, are you? Because I won't believe it. Not Mel.'

'No, it's nothing like that,' Kellerman assured her. 'I guess I better just cut to the quick here. We need your help, Laura. Melissa was working on a sensitive operation at the time of her death. In fact, it was almost complete. But she was the key to its success. Without her, it won't work. What we want is for you to impersonate Melissa. It would just be the once and you'd be in no danger.'

Laura ground out her cigarette in the ashtray. 'I think you should go,' she said, in a barely audible voice.

'I realize how insensitive—'

'Mel's only been dead a few hours and all you can think about is completing some operation she was working on,' Laura interrupted angrily. 'Is that all she meant to you? No, don't say anything,' she said, raising a hand to silence him before he could speak, 'I don't want to hear it. Just go, please. Go.'

'At least hear me out, that's all I ask. If only for Melissa's sake. I'm not talking about arresting some two-bit drug dealer here. This was the biggest operation that either of us had ever worked on, and it was Melissa's brainchild from the start. If we can see it through to its completion, we have every chance of bringing down the most powerful drug cartel in Mexico. And we're only one step away now. Please, hear me out. That's all I ask. And if you still don't want to get involved, then I'll leave and you won't hear from me again. You have my word on that.'

'Very well.' Laura lit another cigarette.

Kellerman opened his attaché case and removed a folder. 'I don't know how much you know about the drugs trade, but at present between fifty and seventy per cent of all Colombian cocaine smuggled into this country passes through Mexico. And of the six major narco-cartels operating in Mexico, the Salcido cartel handles almost a half of that traffic. It is run by two brothers, Juan and Ramón Salcido, and it's believed that some time in the last couple of years they struck an exclusive deal with the Cali cartel in Colombia to handle all their cocaine shipments routed through Mexico. Melissa was brought in to break the cartel's stranglehold and deliver the Salcidos to justice. These surveillance pictures of the two brothers were taken recently by one of our agents in Mexico City.' He took two enlarged colour photographs from the folder and pushed them across the table to Laura.

In the first a short, balding man with pock-marked cheeks was standing beside a black BMW. He was staring straight at the camera, as if he knew he was being photographed. Three men – she assumed they were bodyguards – were positioned close to him, each looking in a different direction. The man in the second picture was distinctly photogenic. He reminded her of one of those suave Latin film stars of the fifties – not her type, but she had to admit that he was good-looking. He was standing in the doorway of a restaurant, deep in conversation with a strikingly beautiful blonde whose hand was resting lightly on his arm. There was nobody else in the shot.

'That's Ramón Salcido,' Kellerman said, tapping the first photograph. 'Thirty-nine years old. Unmarried.' He indicated the man in the second photograph. 'Juan Salcido. The older brother by four years. That's his wife, Katrine, with him. She's German. Both brothers are graduates of the University of Mexico. Ramón Salcido has a degree in mineralogy and is widely regarded as one of the most eminent gemmologists in Central America. He has a specialist knowledge of diamonds and owns a chain of jewellery stores across the country. Juan Salcido has a degree in engineering – he's the director of Mex-Freight, the largest freight company in Mexico. They're not your typical drug barons. They use their legitimate businesses to give themselves an air of respectability – as well as using them to launder the proceeds of their lucrative drug deals with the Cali cartel. They own several private banks in the Caribbean where most of the money is eventually deposited after first being washed through safe havens like Pakistan, Panama and many of the eastern bloc countries. I use the word "own" in a liberal sense, because these banks are nothing more than a brass plaque in a registered office. Anyone can buy a fully chartered private bank in any number of Caribbean countries for under ten thousand dollars. And as there's no control on the amount of money entering or leaving these countries, nobody knows the brothers' true worth. Their legitimate businesses are worth about five hundred million dollars. That much we know from public accounts. We estimate that the exclusive deal they made with the Cali cartel is worth in the region of a billion dollars a year, but that's only an educated guess.'

He removed a third photograph from the folder and handed it to her. 'That's James Doyle. He's a former sergeant in the Special Forces who turned to crime after he was cashiered from his unit. He shot and killed a policeman during a failed bank robbery in Miami five years ago. He fled to Mexico, knowing there was no extradition treaty between the two countries, and got a job as a bodyguard to an American who was illegally smuggling wetbacks across the border. That's when he first came to the attention of the Salcidos who offered him a job with the cartel. He's now officially in charge of security for their legitimate business enterprises. Unofficially, he's their link with the Cali cartel. Not only does he make all the deals with the Colombians, but he also handles the arrangements to have the drug shipments routed through Mexico and into the States. He runs the operation for them. And that makes him a very powerful figure in their organization.

'But he's still wanted for murder in Florida and if he were ever to return there he'd be arrested and put on trial for murder. And, if found guilty, he'd receive the death sentence. It was with this in mind that Melissa first came to me a year ago with an idea. If we could get Doyle back on US soil, we could offer him immunity from prosecution if he were to help us put the Salcidos behind bars for life. The Attorney General was naturally enthusiastic about the idea but it meant that, as there was no extradition treaty between the two countries, the White House would have to bring pressure on the Mexican government to extradite Doyle. To cut a long story short, the Mexican government agreed, albeit reluctantly, but only if criminal charges could be brought against him in Mexico. So Melissa and I put together a deal, which was approved by the Attorney General. It's called Operation Checkmate. We implemented it eight months ago when Melissa first approached Doyle, offering to sell him some information about a forthcoming DEA operation against the cartel. Of course, Doyle suspected a trap and wanted nothing to do with her. The information turned out to be accurate and the cartel lost a valuable shipment of cocaine destined for the streets of Los Angeles. Had he acted on her information, the shipment could have been rerouted and saved. That's when he made some discreet enquiries about her and discovered that she was in financial difficulties and couldn't make ends meet on her salary. That's the disinformation we'd already circulated in the underworld. The next time she offered him information, he was more receptive. He took it on board and again it proved accurate. Of course we were loath to let any of these shipments enter the US, but we had to give credibility to her cover. And it worked. Doyle, with the backing of both Salcidos, began to rely on her for inside information. And they paid her well for it. It dispelled his initial fears that it was some kind of trap – after all, she was the one providing all the information. There was nothing to incriminate him or the cartel.

'At the end of last month I had another rumour circulated that the DEA suspected one of their agents of passing classified information to the Salcido cartel. That's when Melissa played her final ace. She told Doyle that she was going to jump ship before she was caught – and offered to sell him a copy of a classified DEA file that contained the names of all the undercover cops as well as all the known police and cartel informers in both Colombia and Mexico. In return she wanted ten million dollars in small, cut diamonds – which we knew Ramón Salcido could get hold of without any trouble. And when Doyle handed over the diamonds in exchange for the computer disk, containing the classified file, the Mexican anti-narcotics unit would arrest him and he'd be put on the next flight to Miami.

'At least that was the idea. Melissa met Doyle on Sunday night and they agreed to conclude the deal next Sunday. So you can see our predicament. Unless Doyle has the disk on him, the INCD have no grounds to arrest him. Which is why I'm here. You're our only chance now of salvaging Operation Checkmate. All you'd have to do is give the disk to Doyle and take the diamonds from him in return. And, as I said to you earlier, you'd be perfectly safe. Doyle would only be arrested after you'd already left the area.' He replaced the photographs in the folder. 'Well, would you be willing to help us?'

'I can't,' she replied, then added quickly, 'It's not because I'm worried that anything might happen to me, I just don't believe I could pull it off. Not right now. I realize how important this operation is to the DEA but I'd only let you down. And I don't want to do that.'

'I'm not so sure you would. And I'm willing to take that chance. Question is, are you?'

'Why do I get the feeling I'm being manoeuvred into some kind of emotional corner?'

'No, you're not.' Kellerman closed the folder and pushed it across the table to her. 'The full details of Operation Checkmate are in there. I'll call you again in the morning, once you've had a chance to read through it.' He stood up. 'Oh, and there is one other thing. I'd be grateful if you were to keep Melissa's death to yourself – at least for the time being. We won't be releasing any information about the accident until after I've spoken to you in the morning. You've got the number of my cellular phone, should you want to talk to me before then. Call anytime, day or night. It doesn't matter.'

'What do I tell Raquel in the morning?'

'That all depends on what you've decided to do. If you do have a change of heart – and I hope you will after you've read through the folder – then it's imperative that you don't tell her about your sister's death. If not, tell her the truth. It'll come out soon enough if we have to abort the operation.'

'More subtle pressure,' Laura said, but there was no malice in her voice. She opened the door. 'I'll read the folder, but I'm not making any promises. Just remember that.'

'I will.'

She waited until he had gone down the metal stairs leading to the alley at the side of the building, then closed and locked the front door. She took a key from her pocket and paused outside the spare room before inserting it in the lock and opening the door. 'Get away from the window. What if he sees you?' she hissed, as she entered the room.

'Then he'll think it's you,' Melissa replied.

'Except we're wearing different clothes.'

'As if he'd notice! He's a man,' Melissa retorted, then grinned broadly as she turned away from the window. 'You were great. I heard everything you said through the bug I planted in the kitchen last night. You even had me thinking I was dead.'

'It wasn't that difficult. I just kept thinking back to how I felt after Mom and Dad died.' Laura sat on the edge of the bed and smiled thoughtfully to herself. 'You were right about one thing, though. He's cute, all right.'

'I told you you'd like him. Just your type, sis.'

'Yeah, right,' Laura muttered.

'Oh, so you do like him?' Melissa said, with a mischievous grin when Laura's cheeks flushed lightly.

'Of course not. I hardly know him.'

'The instant denial. That's a sure sign of guilt.' Melissa chuckled softly, then moved to the door. 'I'm ready for coffee.'

'I had some with Tom.'

'Tom? I didn't hear him say you could call him by his first name.'

'Cut it out, Mel,' Laura retorted irritably.

'You just make sure you keep your distance from him,' Melissa said, her face serious suddenly as she levelled a warning finger at her sister. 'This is business. The fun comes later. Remember that.'

'And just what the hell's *that* supposed to mean?' Laura snapped indignantly. 'I'm not the one who lures guys into bed for some meaningless one-night stand.'

'That's a cheap shot.'

'But true.'

'At least I have a sex life. Which is more than can be said about you since your divorce. Then again, from what I understand it wasn't that different when you *were* married,' was Melissa's parting shot before she left the room.

Laura had a suitably caustic reply lined up as she stormed after her sister, but she stopped abruptly in front of the kitchen door. What would it achieve? More acrimony? It wasn't worth it. She thought about going into the kitchen to make peace with her sister but they both needed to cool off. And, anyway, why should she make the first move? Mel had started it. Let her make the opening gambit . . .

She went into the lounge, sat down on the sofa and switched on the CD player. She didn't know what disc she had left in the tray but instantly recognized the distinctive opening bars of Van Halen's 'Runnin' With The Devil'. Moments later the music erupted from the wall-mounted loudspeakers. She had been a rock junkie since her teens and liked to think of herself secretly as a closet head-banger, knowing it was the closest she would ever get to being a rock 'n' roll rebel. The thought brought a smile to her lips and she closed her eyes, allowing herself to be drawn into the music.

It hadn't been difficult to help Mel fake her own death. Not that she knew everything that had happened the previous night – and neither did she want to – but her own part had been vital to its success. During her time as a UC with the NYPD, and later with the Narcotics Bureau, Mel had made a number of dubious contacts at several of the city's main hospitals and late the previous afternoon she had paid an unscrupulous mortuary attendant $3000 in cash for a recently deceased Jane Doe, in her mid-thirties, who'd been brought in earlier that day. The attendant had personally handled all the routine paperwork to cover his tracks. Mel had removed the body in a hire van, which she had parked in the alley beside the practice, and once the last of the patients had left and Raquel had gone home, Laura had made a dental chart of Jane Doe's teeth. The whole episode had sickened her, but it had to be done for the scam to work. She had replaced Mel's dental chart with Jane Doe's, then burnt Mel's. Laura had no idea how Melissa had staged the accident or how she had ensured that the body was so badly burnt. And she didn't want to know. She had done her part.

The next phase of the plan was for her to agree, albeit reluctantly, to help the DEA when Kellerman rang her the next day. Posing as Mel, she would fly with him that afternoon to Mexico City. She had suggested that Mel take her place on the flight – it wasn't as if Kellerman would know the difference – but Mel already had her own plans to re-enter Mexico unnoticed. She would return there later that evening, in disguise and using a false passport, and book into the Hotel Canada, where she had been due to meet Doyle on Sunday. Laura would remain at Mel's house in San Angel until then when Mel would make her counter-move . . . and, if all went according to plan, the two of them would be safely out of the country by nightfall with the diamonds. A fifty-fifty split with no comebacks. New identities. New lives. That was the part that had finally won her over.

'I don't know how you can listen to that racket.'

The voice startled Laura and she opened her eyes to see Melissa standing in the doorway, a mug in her hand. 'It's a hell of a lot better than that mawkish country music you listen . . .' She trailed off when she saw her sister's teasing smile. It was her way of making the first move and Laura understood that. She turned down the volume. 'I'm sorry I had a go at you just now. I guess my nerves are just a bit raw.'

'So what's my excuse?' Melissa said, then sat beside her. 'What

45

you said was true. I do use guys. And, what's more, I get a real kick out of it. What else can I say? But what I said about your marriage was unforgivable. I know the hell you went through when you were married to that bastard.'

'It's water under the bridge now,' Laura said.

'Is it?' Melissa asked, raising her eyebrows.

'I'm not still in love with Jefferson, if that's what you're implying. Christ, I'd have to be some kind of masochist to still be in love with a guy who was screwing around for the whole of our marriage.'

'I know you're not. But you think that because you weren't able to satisfy him, it would be the same with any guy and that's why you've been so reluctant to get involved in another relationship. It wasn't your fault, sis. It never was. The bastard was screwing around long before you two got married.'

'What's brought this on all of a sudden?'

'You're going to have the chance to start afresh, away from this shit-hole. A new life. I want you to be able to enjoy it.'

'Are you kidding? If I can't get some kind of enjoyment out of five million dollars then there's really got to be something wrong with me.'

'Remember, money can't buy you happiness,' Melissa said, 'but it can go a hell of a long way to help get over the disappointment.'

'True,' Laura agreed.

'Are you going to miss this place?' Melissa asked.

'Not the place, no. The thought of getting out of Spanish Harlem was the main reason why I decided to come in with you. No more living in constant fear of being mugged every time I go shopping. No more lying awake in bed worrying about whether the practice is going to be burgled that night. Believe me, I won't miss any of that. I'll miss Raquel, though. I already feel guilty about leaving her without even so much as a goodbye. She was the only one who was prepared to give me a job after I gave up the booze. I owe her a lot.'

'So send her a couple of diamonds, if that'll help to ease your conscience.'

'You're all heart, Mel, you know that? And what about you? Will you miss the DEA?'

'No.' But Melissa sat forward slowly, her arms resting on her knees. 'Well, maybe just a bit. I've made some good friends there over the years.'

'Tom Kellerman?'

'Yeah, Tom for one. I've lost count of the number of times I overstepped the mark only to have him pull me back from the brink of disciplinary action. The fact that I'm still in the job is primarily thanks to him. But, having said that, I can't afford to let sentiment get in the way. We're going to pull this off. You mark my words. We're going to do it.'

'And then the fun and games will really start.'

'More than you can ever imagine, sis,' Melissa replied, thoughtfully. 'More than you can ever imagine.'

FOUR

Wednesday

'Are you sure you want to do this?'

'No,' Laura replied bluntly. She was sitting opposite Kellerman in the lounge of her apartment. 'No, I'm not,' she repeated, 'but if I don't all Mel's hard work will have been for nothing.'

'I appreciate your honesty,' Kellerman said. 'I'm glad you've had a change of heart. We're certainly grateful to you.'

'I don't want your gratitude. I'm not doing this for you or for the DEA. I'm doing it for Mel. I realize now how important the operation was to her. She'd obviously put a lot of time and effort into taking it this far. I know she'd have wanted me to do it.' Laura took a cigarette from the packet on the small coffee table beside her and lit it. 'So what happens now?'

'Melissa and I were due to fly back to Mexico City this afternoon. And Doyle will know that. So it's imperative that we stick to the plan. I've got all the relevant travel documents at the hotel. All you'll need is Melissa's passport. It's probably in her holdall.'

'I guess so,' Laura replied. 'I haven't been able to go through it yet. One step at a time.'

'If you want me to look—'

'No,' Laura cut in. Melissa was in the spare bedroom, listening in to their conversation on a pair of headphones. 'Thanks anyway, but sooner or later I've got to face up to going through her things.'

'What will happen about work?'

48

'I had to tell Raquel what happened. I've asked her not to say anything until Mel's death has been officially released next week. As far as anyone else is concerned, I had to go away at short notice for personal reasons. She's agreed to see as many of my patients as she can over the next few days. The others will be given new appointments for when I get back. That won't be a problem.'

'You know that you're going to have to get your hair cut before we go.'

'I've already made an appointment. I'll take a recent photo of Mel with me so that they can get the length right. Actually, my hair's only a few inches longer than Mel's was. I'm surprised you noticed. Mel even said—' She stopped abruptly and cursed herself silently for allowing her guard down so easily. But she felt at ease in his company. It was the first time she had acknowledged that and it unnerved her. It meant she was going to have to be extra vigilant around him. He was watching her, waiting for her to finish what she had started to say. 'It was just something Mel used to say about men – that they don't always notice things about women. Like their clothes. Or a particular hairstyle. Little things that another woman would notice right away.'

'I think there's a degree of truth in that. It only struck me because I was specifically looking for differences between the two of you.' He sat back slowly in the chair. 'I take it I haven't overlooked anything?'

'Nothing that anyone other than Mel and I would notice. Even our parents couldn't always tell us apart, especially when we were kids and dressed in identical clothes. Wearing identical clothes never bothered me that much. But Mel always hated it. She finally rebelled against it when we were six. I guess she just developed her own identity that bit earlier than I did.' Laura stubbed out her cigarette in the ashtray beside her. 'You'll have to excuse me. I've still got things to do. What time do you want me to meet you at JFK?'

'I'll come by and fetch you,' Kellerman offered.

'Thanks, but I'll make my own arrangements to get there. After all, Mel would have, wouldn't she?'

'You've got a point there. The flight leaves at three o'clock this afternoon. American Airlines. Let's meet at one o'clock at the check-in counter.'

'I'll be there – or, rather, Mel will be.'

'You've got my number if you need me before then,' Kellerman said.

Laura saw him out. The moment she closed the door she exhaled deeply then pressed her back against the wall, her head tilted, her eyes closed. Another mistake like the one she had almost let slip earlier could prove costly. She had to keep him at arm's length. It was the only way she was going to get through it.

'Not good, but at least you stopped yourself before you could do any real damage. You covered it well, though.'

'I shouldn't have needed to, should I?' Laura said bitterly, opening her eyes to look at Melissa who had emerged from the spare bedroom.

'You're allowing yourself to get drawn to him, aren't you?'

'No, I'm not,' Laura replied defensively. 'It was just a slip of the tongue, that's all.'

'This is me you're talking to now,' Melissa said sharply. 'I know you better than anyone else. And I can see what's happening.'

'Nothing's happening!'

'No? Normally when you're around men you don't know you're hard pressed to string two words together. Now, suddenly, you're telling Tom about your childhood. The last time you did that was when you were all starry-eyed after you'd just met Jefferson.'

'You're overreacting. Sure Tom's good-looking, but that doesn't mean I'm attracted to him. Do you honestly think I'd jeopardize my chances of getting out of here once and for all just because of a man? Because if you do, you don't know me as well as you think.'

'I hope you're right.'

Laura watched her disappear into the spare room. It wasn't like her to become so defensive with Melissa. But then it wasn't like her to lie to her either . . .

Laura arrived at JFK half an hour before she was due to meet Kellerman. She was wearing a pair of jeans, a baggy sweatshirt and the New York Knicks cap Melissa had given to her before she left the apartment. Melissa rarely went anywhere without it. She looked for Kellerman at the check-in counter, didn't see him, and decided to go outside the terminal building for a cigarette.

Just what the hell are you playing at? How many times had she asked herself that in the past few hours? Everything had been going so well until she had met Tom Kellerman. There had been an instant attraction, at least from her side, which she'd had to conceal behind a pretence of grief. She thought she had managed to mask it well, except that Mel had seen through it right away. Did that mean Kellerman had picked up on it too? Somehow she doubted it. After all, Mel knew her better than anyone. But it worried her. Why had she allowed her emotions to surface so easily? Especially at a time like that. It would have been easy to pass it off as nerves – or the uncertainty about what lay ahead. Only she knew it went deeper than that. She had always been the more emotional of the two sisters. Although Mel was the extrovert, she had always been able to hide her feelings behind her outgoing personality. Laura hid hers by retreating further into her shell. But when she met someone she felt at ease with, she tended to discard the shell, which left her exposed. Her only defence then was words. And that meant she talked too much.

Get back into your shell and stay there. Don't let him get any closer. It was easier said than done. Yet if she didn't, she knew that she could ruin everything. There was no turning back now. She was in this as much as her sister. If Mel was caught, she would go down with her. And that would mean jail. *Isn't that incentive enough to draw back from him while you still can?*

'You're going to have to give that up, you know – at least in public.'

Laura turned round sharply and found Kellerman standing behind her near the entrance to the terminal. 'I'm sorry, I was miles away,' she stammered, struggling to regain her composure. 'What did you say?'

'That you're going to have to stop smoking in public once we reach Mexico City,' Kellerman said, gesturing to her cigarette. 'Melissa didn't smoke.'

'Don't I know? She was always on at me about it,' Laura said, dropping her stub and crushing it out under her heel. 'Didn't work, though.'

Kellerman handed Melissa's flight ticket to her. 'Are you ready to check in?'

'Sure,' Laura replied, tugging the Knicks cap over her head.

'I see you're a Knicks fan, like Melissa,' Kellerman said as they walked along the concourse.

'No, this is Mel's. I found it in her holdall. I know she liked to wear it.'

They arrived at the check-in counter and Kellerman motioned for Laura to approach the desk first. 'After you . . . Melissa.'

Laura paused momentarily then stepped forward and placed the ticket, together with Melissa's passport, on the desk.

Melissa had made only one change to her appearance on her last visit to New York when she had had the photograph taken for her false passport. She had coiled her hair up on her head, secured it in a net and worn a page-boy style blonde wig, which had been stored in a drawer in Laura's spare bedroom until she flew out of the country.

She could have sworn that she had packed it in her hand

luggage but when she had been looking for something else in her bag on the way to the airport she realized that it wasn't there. Fortunately, there was time to go back for it. But she was pissed that she could have made such a basic error. Was she getting too confident?

The thought still lingered in her mind as she pulled up opposite the practice. She looked at her watch. It had already gone seven o'clock. She knew that Raquel and Laura normally closed at five thirty. The front door was shut and the curtains had been drawn across the waiting-room window. The building appeared to be in darkness.

She got out, hurried across the street and into the alley at the side of the building. The lower-ground window overlooking the alley was in darkness. Raquel's office. Even though she was satisfied that Raquel had left, she climbed the metal steps silently to Laura's second-floor apartment. She unlocked the door and slipped into the dark hall then made her way to the spare bedroom and crossed to the chest of drawers beside the window. She peered down into the alley. It was deserted but, not taking any chances, she reached out to draw the curtains. Her arm caught a porcelain figurine, which toppled off the chest and smashed on the wooden floor, shattering the silence. Her eyes went to the open door and she remained motionless for several seconds, not daring to draw breath for fear that the sound might give her away, then she chuckled to herself. She couldn't believe how nervy she was. Opening the top drawer, she removed the blonde wig and moved quickly to the door.

'Who's there?' a voice challenged from the hall.

Melissa's heart missed a beat. It was Raquel! She pressed herself against the wall then moved her head fractionally to try to look into the hallway.

'I know there's someone in here,' Raquel continued. 'I'm armed so come out now!'

Melissa had no way of knowing if Raquel was bluffing. Laura had a gun. Why wouldn't Raquel have one too, especially in this neighbourhood? She thought of passing herself off as Laura, but dismissed the idea. There was another option . . .

'Raquel, is that you?' she called out, but didn't move.

'Who's there?'

'It's Melissa. I'm coming out. For God's sake, don't shoot.' Silence. 'Raquel, did you hear me? It's Melissa.'

'Melissa's dead.'

'No, I'm not. It's a long story. I'm going to step out into the hall with my hands up. Just don't shoot.' A moment later the hall was bathed in light. She stuffed the blonde wig underneath her denim jacket which she zipped up before stepping out hesitantly into the light, her hands raised in front of her.

Raquel's eyes widened in disbelief. 'I don't believe it. Laura said that you . . . were dead.'

'I still could be if that were to go off accidentally,' Melissa said, nodding towards the Ruger 9mm in Raquel's hand.

Raquel lowered the weapon. 'What about the car crash? Laura said that your body could only be identified from your dental records.'

'As I said, Raquel, it's a long story. It was all a ruse. But don't worry – it was sanctioned by the DEA.'

'And Laura was involved?'

'She had to be for it to work,' Melissa said. She gestured to the open lounge door. 'Let's talk in there. I'll tell you what I can but a lot of this is still classified for the time being.'

As Raquel reached out to switch on the light Melissa clamped a hand on either side of her face and jerked her head savagely to one side, snapping her neck. The Ruger clattered to the floor and Melissa laid Raquel's body carefully on the carpet. She knew she should feel remorse, even guilt, for what she had just done. But at that moment she felt nothing. Had she really become so immune to death over the years? She pondered the question momentarily then pushed it from her mind without coming up with an answer. She checked for a pulse. None. She was about to pick up the gun when she stopped herself. She couldn't afford any slip-ups.

She went through to Laura's room and rummaged through her closet until she found a pair of gloves. Slipping them on, she returned to the hall to decide her next move. Make it look like an accident, as if she had fallen awkwardly and broken her neck. Down some stairs? Her first thought were the metal steps leading down to the alley. No, too public. The stairs to the practice? That made more sense. The door was still open. Melissa grabbed Raquel's body under the arms and dragged it along the carpet until she reached the top of the stairs. Hoisting the body upright, Melissa balanced it on the top step, then let it fall. She watched dispassionately as it tumbled down the stairs and landed in a crumpled heap at the bottom. She retrieved the Ruger, went downstairs and replaced it in the open safe in Raquel's office. She closed the safe door and spun the combination to lock it again.

She returned to the apartment, secured the door behind her, then removed Laura's gloves and replaced them in the closet, exactly as she had found them. Then she left the apartment, locking the front door behind her and, turning up the collar of her denim jacket against the cold night air, hurried across the road to her car.

Laura had spent most of the flight going through the file that Kellerman had given her to read shortly after they boarded the plane. It contained photographs and short biographies of the other DEA agents stationed at the American embassy in Mexico City. He had told her that it had been decided not to tell anyone there about Melissa's death until after the story was released to the press the following week. As far as they were concerned, Laura was Melissa. He had added that it was unlikely she would meet any of the agents – apart from Bill Walker, his deputy and Melissa's immediate superior, with whom Kellerman said tactfully Melissa hadn't always seen eye to eye. But Laura knew that Melissa disliked him intensely: she regarded him as a liability to the DEA's ongoing operations in Mexico – his incompetence had cost the lives of several local narcotics agents. But he had got results, and that was all that mattered to Washington. Laura knew, too, that Melissa suspected Kellerman felt the same way as she did about Walker.

'Why didn't they get on?' Laura asked. She wasn't making mischief. She was just interested to gauge his reaction.

If the question caught Kellerman by surprise, he didn't show it. Instead he said, noncommittally, 'It was just a clash of personalities. Bill can be stubborn and so could Melissa – as you well know. It was only natural that sparks would fly when they didn't agree. But there was nothing wrong with that. They spoke their minds, and I always respected them for that.'

'And what if I do come across Walker? How should I react to him?' She noticed his eyes flicker towards the darkness beyond the window, his obvious reluctance to say anything. 'I don't care if they were at each other's throats twenty-four hours a day,' she continued, 'but I need to know what to do should the situation arise. How else can I impersonate Mel with any conviction? Unless you intend to tell him the truth.'

'No,' Kellerman said tersely. He stared into the darkness for some time before he went on, 'I suppose you could say they tolerated each other. A strained cordiality would probably be the best way to describe it. Not that it fooled anyone. It had got to the point where I had Melissa reporting directly to me rather than to Bill. It was far from satisfactory, but it was the only way to keep the peace.'

'Did you do anything about it?'

'Let's just say Bill's in line for a lateral move back to Washington. Not that he knows about it – yet. But now that things have changed, maybe he'll stay on in Mexico after all.'

'You almost sound disappointed.'

'Do I?' Kellerman said, with a faint smile. 'I think I've said enough. Let's leave it at that, shall we?'

'Don't worry, I won't say anything to him. We haven't even met, and already I don't like him. I won't have any trouble slipping into character if I have to.'

Kellerman pointed out of the window at the panoply of glinting lights spread out in the distance like millions of tiny diamonds shimmering on a velvet backdrop. 'Welcome to Mexico City. With a population of some twenty-two million, it's regarded as the largest city in the world.'

'I can believe it,' Laura said in awe, gazing at the spectacle of light continually unfolding below her as far as the eye could see.

The safety-belt sign came on and moments later the captain announced that they were about to make their final descent into Benito Juárez International Airport. The temperature on the ground was a pleasant twelve degrees Celsius. Laura was alarmed at how low the 747 seemed to skim over the roofs of the houses as it came in to land but the pilot executed a perfect landing. After the aircraft had halted Kellerman unfastened his belt, took their hand luggage from the overhead compartment, and handed Laura her bag before leading the way to the exit. Laura was amazed at the sheer size of the terminal. It was almost like a self-contained city. After clearing passport control Kellerman collected a trolley for their suitcases and both pressed the green button at customs. Neither was stopped.

'I'll lead the way in my car to Melissa's house in San Angel,' Kellerman told her once they emerged into the concourse. 'You follow in her car.'

'Do you know where it's parked?' Laura asked.

'Yeah, the embassy has its own parking spaces that we use . . .'

'What is it?' Laura asked when Kellerman trailed off, following his gaze to a figure in a black tunic who was approaching them.

'He's an embassy driver. His name's Pedro. Melissa always called him Ped,' Kellerman told Laura. 'Question is, what's he doing here? I didn't order a driver to meet us.'

'Good evening, sir,' the driver said to Kellerman. He smiled at Laura and touched his cap. 'Agent Wade.'

'Hi, Ped,' Laura replied.

'What are you doing here, Pedro?' Kellerman demanded. 'I didn't ask to be met at the airport.'

'Agent Walker sent me, sir,' the driver told him.

'So what's the big panic?' Kellerman asked.

'I don't know, sir. My instructions were to drive you both back to the embassy as soon as you'd cleared customs. I'm parked outside. If you give me your keys, I'll arrange to have your own cars taken to the embassy.'

They handed over their keys and Kellerman dropped back with Laura as Pedro pushed the trolley towards the exit. 'I don't know what's going on, but it's got Bill worried. And that's not like him. You're going to have to play along, at least for the time being. Leave the talking to me.'

'It wouldn't be like Mel not to say anything,' Laura said.

Kellerman stopped abruptly and turned to her. 'Then fake tiredness. Or say you're not feeling too good. I don't want you blowing your cover the moment you get here by saying something out of turn. Ideally, I'd have preferred to have seen Bill alone. But you wouldn't know how to get to Melissa's house by yourself.'

'What do you *think* I'm going to say? I do know when to keep my mouth shut, you know. Please try to credit me with a little intelligence.'

'I guess I deserved that. I'm sorry, I didn't mean to sound patronizing. It's just I'm worried not knowing why Bill's acting this way.'

'There's only one way to find out,' Laura said.

Pedro had already loaded the suitcases into the trunk of the black Mercedes and was waiting for them by the open back door. Laura climbed in first and Kellerman got in after her. The door was closed behind them.

Kellerman activated the soundproof partition between the

front and back seats then used the car phone to dial Walker's private line. It was answered after the first ring. 'Bill, it's Tom. What's up?'

'I'd rather not discuss it over the phone.'

'This is a secure line,' Kellerman reminded him.

'Secure or not, I'd prefer to tell you in person when you get here.'

'I understand. We've just left the airport. Depending on the traffic, we should be with you in the next half an hour.'

'Fine. I'll bring you up to speed then.'

Kellerman replaced the handset then saw the uncertainty in Laura's face. He wanted to put her at her ease, but he couldn't even find the words to reassure himself.

Thirty-five minutes later the car pulled up outside the wrought-iron gates at the back of the American embassy – an unattractive, box-shaped building dwarfed beside the majestic splendour of the Sheraton Maria Isobel Hotel which rose up gracefully into the cloudless night sky. Their IDs were checked then the car was waved through. It pulled up beside a side door and Kellerman got out, followed quickly by Laura. Kellerman used a key card to access the door, which opened on to a flight of stairs. Closing it behind them, he led the way down to another door. Again he used the key card to gain entry to a deserted, black-and-white-tiled corridor illuminated by a row of bright fluorescent lights. He walked to one of the doors that lined one side of the corridor and knocked before entering.

The man who got up from behind the desk to greet him was in his early thirties, overweight, with oily skin and greasy black hair. It was the first time Laura had seen Bill Walker, but she could understand why Melissa found him so odious. His eyes went briefly to Laura. 'Hello, Melissa,' he said, as if in passing.

'Billy,' Laura said curtly. Out of the corner of her eye she saw Kellerman glance at her briefly before he sat down in one of the two chairs in front of Walker's desk. She knew immediately what she had done. Melissa called Walker 'Billy' when she wanted to annoy him. But her sister had told her that. Kellerman had never mentioned it. She cursed herself silently. Kellerman had been right – she should just keep her mouth shut. She sat down.

'OK, so what's this all about?' Kellerman asked Walker.

'So far it's only a rumour, but it comes from Benitez. And he's one of our most reliable CIs.' CI was DEA speak for a confidential informant. Walker's eyes went to Laura. 'I know he's your snitch. He asked for you but agreed to speak to me when I told him you were out of the country.'

'When was this?' Kellerman asked.

'He called earlier this evening. I met with him about an hour ago. Usual place. He told me there's a rumour doing the rounds about Hector Lacamara.'

'The Salcido cartel's senior accountant?' Kellerman said. Laura knew that had been for her benefit.

'The same. Word is, he's transferred fifty million dollars from several of the cartel's accounts in the Caribbean to an untraceable account that he'd already set up for himself, also probably somewhere in the Caribbean. Now he's on the run with his new mistress.' Walker paused to look at the sheet of paper in front of him. 'Carmen Lopez, a twenty-three-year-old nightclub singer he met last year. They were booked on a flight to Puerto Rico earlier this evening – that much we've been able to verify from the passenger manifest. Only they never got on the plane. According to Benitez, they were stopped at customs by an official on the cartel's payroll. Lacamara panicked and they fled from the airport, taking only their hand luggage with them. As I said, it's still only a rumour. What we do know for certain is that Lacamara left his office for lunch at one o'clock this afternoon and never returned. Doyle went to see Lacamara's wife earlier this evening. He was there for about twenty minutes. There's one more thing. Oscar Silva, the other senior partner in the firm, left work at five thirty this evening. Only he never arrived home. Although their firm handled all the Salcidos' business accounts, Lacamara and Silva were the only two who were involved in money-laundering. Which means that Silva could be in on it as well.'

'I'm not so sure about that,' Laura said, breaking the silence. 'Why wait those extra few hours before jumping ship? Why not just bail out with Lacamara? It seems like a big risk to take with so much at stake.'

Kellerman, initially horrified at Laura having ventured an opinion, found himself agreeing with her. 'Melissa's right. I'd be more inclined to think that he was intercepted on the way home by some of Doyle's goons and taken away for questioning. And if that's so, I don't hold out much hope for him. Even if he's innocent, he's going to be punished for allowing Lacamara to embezzle that kind of money from under his nose. No, we've got to concentrate on finding Lacamara. If we can get to him before the cartel's hit squads track him down, he'd be a vital witness in any future case against the Salcidos.'

'I'm ahead of you on that one,' Walker announced triumphantly, 'I've already been in touch with the INCD and told them to put out APBs on both Lacamara and Silva.'

'What would Lacamara's incentive be to testify against the cartel?' Laura asked. 'Would you want to co-operate with the authorities if you had fifty million dollars stashed away in an untraceable account in the Caribbean? What can you offer him? Immunity from prosecution? A new identity under the Witness Protection Program? It's not much of an incentive when you think about it, is it?'

Kellerman held back a smile. It was like listening to Melissa. Sharp. Incisive. And always quick to find fault with the small print. If he hadn't known better, he would have been inclined to think that Melissa had coached her. It was a good feeling. He just hoped she didn't become over-confident. Yet somehow he didn't think that would happen. Although Melissa had always been cocky and assertive, Laura was more careful, more thoughtful.

Kellerman got to his feet and paced the room before stopping in front of Walker's desk. 'If we have the slightest chance of reeling in Lacamara, then I'm prepared to take it at any cost. Put out the word on the street that the DEA would let Lacamara keep the money if he agreed to testify against the Salcidos.'

'You know as well as I do that Braithwaite would never go for that,' Walker said in disbelief.

'You put out the word and let me worry about him. That's my job. If Braithwaite wants Lacamara, then he's going to have to make some serious concessions to gain his trust. If we were to get Lacamara and Doyle to testify in court, we'd have a cast-iron case against the Salcidos. We're talking about their chief enforcer as well as their senior bookkeeper. We could put the cartel out of business permanently. That's got to be worth a few concessions on our part. If it's not, then I'll personally fly back to Washington and hand in my badge.'

'OK, I'll see to it that the word's on the street by morning,' Walker said.

'I want it on the street tonight,' Kellerman replied. 'The sooner Lacamara hears about it, the better.'

'Assuming he'll bite,' Laura pointed out.

'Agreed. But what have we got to lose?' Kellerman said.

'Chances are the cartel's hitmen will get to him first anyway,' Walker said.

'That's what I like about you, Bill, your perpetual optimism,' Kellerman said.

Walker noticed Laura smiling at his discomfort. 'It's true,' he said defensively. 'We don't have the kind of resources that they do. If we did, we wouldn't be fighting a losing battle out there.'

Kellerman gestured at the telephone by Walker's elbow. 'Find out if our cars have been brought back from the airport yet.'

Walker punched buttons, spoke briefly, hung up. 'They're parked out back. Pedro's got the keys.'

'Then I'm heading home. Tell the duty officer to keep me posted on any new developments that arise during the night. I'll be in early tomorrow morning. Melissa, you coming?' Kellerman held open the door for her, nodded in reply to Walker's 'Night, Tom', then closed it behind him. When they were out of earshot he placed a hand lightly on her arm. 'How did you know that Melissa called him Billy?'

Laura had been expecting the question. She had an answer ready. 'I didn't. I've got a friend in New York. He's also a dentist. Bill Johnson. We were at NYU together. I always call him Billy. I guess I just did it without thinking.'

She had been at NYU with Bill Johnson. He now practised in New York. Somewhere uptown, she thought. Only she hadn't spoken to him since her graduation. And she had never called him Billy. They made their way to the courtyard at the back of the embassy. Pedro, who was leaning against the railing, ground his cigarette underfoot and hurried over with the keys. Once he had gone, Laura turned to Kellerman. 'I know you told me to keep my mouth shut when we saw Walker, but I felt I had to contribute something to the conversation.'

'You were great,' Kellerman told her. 'Walker didn't suspect a thing.'

'That's hardly surprising,' Laura replied, making no attempt to hide her contempt. 'I can't believe that Mel was passed over for him.'

'Neither could a lot of other people,' Kellerman said, then handed her the keys to Melissa's car. 'I'll lead the way to the house. It's about a twenty-minute drive from here. Then I'm heading home. It's going to be a long day tomorrow.'

FIVE

Bob Smith was typical of the sort of guest Juan Salcido was entertaining that evening at his double-storey mansion in Lomas de Chapultepec, an exclusive residential area of Mexico City. He owned a small but reputable freight company in the United States. The annual turnover was moderate, but the company always remained in the black. It was exactly the type of company that interested the Salcidos.

Mex-Freight was never used to smuggle drugs into the United States and it had become a standard joke within the DEA – as well as among the local drug-enforcement agencies – that this was the main reason why it was now one of the most successful freight companies in Central America. The same couldn't be said for their rivals. Once a freight company had been targeted for drug shipment into the United States, one of a handful of trusted middlemen, who were answerable only to Doyle, would set about recruiting a number of employees from within the company, on generous wages to establish complete loyalty, whose job was to ensure that the shipment reached its destination safely. And if, as had happened on occasion in the past, an employee had a change of heart and went to the authorities, the name given by the middleman always turned out to be false and nothing connected Doyle to the operation. This not only protected him, but the Salcidos too. Only once had a middleman been convicted of bribery but he had gone to jail without giving any names. And, in return for his silence, the cartel had provided handsomely for his family.

'Can I tempt you to another glass of champagne?' Salcido asked, indicating the empty glass in Smith's hand.

'Well, one's normally my limit,' Smith replied, in a deep Texan drawl, 'before dinner, that is. Hell, after that, anything goes. But this is so good I think I might just take you up on that offer.'

'Excellent.' Salcido beckoned to a waiter, took a freshly filled glass from the tray, and handed it to Smith.

'Do you mind if we go out on to the balcony?' Smith asked. 'I only got a brief glimpse of your wonderful home when your driver brought me over here from the hotel.'

'Of course,' Salcido said, and led the way.

Smith whistled softly as he looked out over the vast, illuminated garden: a freshly mown lawn, bordered by carefully aligned rows of multicoloured blooms, led down to a swimming pool, whose crystal water shimmered invitingly in the soft reflection of the low-wattage underwater spotlights. He turned round and took in what he could see of the magnificent double-storey mansion with its vivid whitewashed walls and dusty-red tiled roof. 'This place must have sure set you back a few bucks.'

Salcido smiled politely. 'Let's put it this way. If you wanted to buy a house in this area of the city, you wouldn't be taken seriously if your opening bid was anything under two million dollars. And you'd be in illustrious company if you did choose to live in Chapultepec Park. Several of the country's leading politicians have houses here. As do many film stars. Even some Hollywood legends once lived here – John Wayne, for one. And Anthony Quinn still does.'

'We don't actually live here,' Katrine Salcido said from the doorway, then stepped out on to the balcony and crossed to where the two men were standing. 'I suppose you could call it our *pied-à-terre*. We use it mainly for entertaining – or Juan will sometimes use it if he's worked late and has to be at the office again early the following morning. We've got a ranch about thirty miles north of the city. It's a great place for our children to grow up. Back to nature.'

'This is my wife, Katrine,' Salcido said. 'Darling, this is Bob Smith. From Texas.'

'Where everything's bigger and better,' Katrine said, shaking Smith's extended hand.

'I'm not so sure any more, not after seeing this place,' Smith said, with a wide sweep of his arm.

Katrine smiled then glanced back inadvertently into the lounge, and noticed her brother-in-law looking at her. She felt goose-bumps crawl up her arms. She loathed Ramón. It was hard to believe that he and Juan were brothers. Juan was tall, handsome, charming and witty while Ramón was short and fat with few social graces and a vulgar, dissolute personality. He suffered from a severe form of discoid psoriasis – in which the skin became inflamed and covered with silvery scales – which was particularly bad on his chest and elbows and often left him in great physical discomfort. His nails were pitted and unsightly and in public he always wore white cotton gloves. He regularly told her how much he envied Juan for having a beautiful wife and two lovely children – and each time he did it left her wondering just how much of that envy had spilled over into a deep-rooted resentment of his brother's happiness. He always claimed that his condition meant that he could never form a meaningful relationship, but Katrine knew that wasn't the truth. Several times, at Juan's request, she had tried to set up Ramón with one of her friends but they had all found his deviant sexual practices both offensive and degrading, and wanted nothing more to do with him. It seemed that only the well-paid whores he had brought to him at his own mansion, also in Lomas de Chapultepec, were prepared to pander to his perversions.

The head waiter was approaching her. 'Excuse me, Mrs Salcido. The hors d'oeuvres are on the table.'

Juan demanded that all his staff speak English, even to him

66

or his wife, whenever they were entertaining foreign guests.

'Mr Salcido,' the head waiter continued, 'there's a phone call for you, sir. In the study.'

'Thank you.' Salcido put a hand lightly on his wife's arm. 'You'll have to excuse me, darling. I'll be along shortly.' He went back into the house, threaded a path through the small clusters of guests in the lounge, made his way to his study and closed the door. Sitting down behind the desk, he picked up the receiver. It was the only secure line in the house. 'Hello?'

'It's Doyle.'

'Any news of Lacamara?' Although Doyle spoke fluent Spanish, Salcido preferred to talk to him in English. That way there could be no misunderstandings when it came to carrying out his orders.

'Nothing.'

'I want him found, Doyle!' Salcido yelled, banging his fist on the desk.

'I've already got over a hundred men working on it round the clock.'

'Then bring in another hundred. I don't care how many men you use. But I want him found. You can also tell the police on our payroll to get off their fat asses and start earning their money.' Salcido lit a cigarette then sat back in his chair. His voice was calm when he spoke again. 'Where are you now?'

'I'm at the Workshop. Garcia and Peraya are here as well. We've got Oscar Silva with us.'

'Good. Find out if he knows anything.'

'He's been protesting innocence ever since we picked him up. I doubt he was in on it.'

'So do I, but I want you to make sure. What kind of book-keeper is he to let his partner embezzle fifty million dollars without even knowing he was doing it? There were supposed to have been safeguards in place to prevent this from ever happening. I want him tortured until he's screamed himself hoarse.

Then I want you to start all over again. I want him to suffer for every dollar that Lacamara's stolen from me.'

'He will,' Doyle assured him.

There was a knock at the door and Katrine peered into the room. Salcido gestured for her to enter. 'Keep me posted on any new developments,' he told Doyle, then severed the connection.

'Doyle?' Katrine asked. Her husband nodded. 'Any word on Lacamara?'

'Nothing yet.'

She pointed to the telephone on his desk. 'You've got a call waiting on line two.'

'Who is it?'

'Your daughter.'

Salcido looked at his watch. 'She should be in bed by now.'

'That's exactly what I told her. It seems that when Mrs Ortega told her it was bedtime, she announced that she wasn't going until she'd said goodnight to you.'

'Really?' Salcido picked up the receiver again. 'Sofia? . . . What's this I hear that you told Mrs Ortega you'd only go to bed after you'd said good night to me?' he asked sternly. 'Your mother and I said good night to you, and to your brother, before we left the ranch earlier this evening. And when we're not there, you're to do exactly as Mrs Ortega tells you. Is that clear? . . . She may be new, but that doesn't give you the right to take advantage of her like this. Now go to bed and stay there. I don't want to hear from Mrs Ortega that you've been naughty again . . . Good night, sweetheart.' Salcido hung up.

'I think you need to have a word with your daughter in the morning about this,' Katrine said, removing a hair from the lapel of his dinner jacket.

'Why is she always *my* daughter when she's been naughty?' Salcido asked.

'Because *my* daughter's never naughty. She takes after me in that respect.'

'Now why do I find that so hard to believe?' he said, with a teasing smile. She looped her hand through the crook of his arm and they made their way to the dining room.

Barely half a mile from the house in which Juan Salcido was entertaining his guests, a Spanish-styled villa stood on a hill overlooking the thousand-acre expanse of Bosque de Chapultepec – Chapultepec Park. The world-famous National Anthropology Museum could be seen from the top-floor windows. The villa was owned by the Salcidos, who had paid $4 million for it some years earlier when it had come on the market. Although it was periodically used to house visiting VIPs, its main function was as Doyle's interrogation base. It had once belonged to an eccentric American tycoon who, at the height of the Cold War, had converted the vast cellar beneath the house into a fully functional nuclear bunker. The bunker, which was now completely soundproofed, was nicknamed the Workshop and derived its name from the vast array of DIY tools housed there and used to torture prisoners. For security reasons, only three people other than the brothers and Katrine – Juan had no secrets from his wife – knew of its existence. Doyle was one and the other two had been with him when he had picked up Silva.

Peraya was Ramón Salcido's personal bodyguard. In his mid-thirties with the powerful physique of a professional bodybuilder, his black hair was combed back from a cruel face and secured in a ponytail. The second man was Juan Salcido's personal bodyguard, Garcia. He couldn't have been more different from Peraya: a former presidential bodyguard, he was in his early forties with an athletic build and an unsightly scar diagonally across his left temple where he had been shot during an attempted assassination. He had been unfairly blamed for the attempt on the President's life, and during his lengthy recuperation had developed a taste for cocaine that had ultimately cost him his job. Juan Salcido, who had listed the then President among his personal friends, offered Garcia a job. He helped wean him off drugs and, in the process, gave him back his dignity. Now Garcia was dedicated to him. Although Peraya had the more fearsome appearance, with his broad shoulders and bull neck, Doyle knew he wasn't in the same league as Garcia when it came to experience and professionalism. Over the years mutual respect between Garcia and Doyle had developed into a close friendship.

After he had finished speaking to Juan Salcido Doyle switched off his cellular phone. He was in a small office in the corner of the Workshop that had originally been the kitchen when the bunker was first built. One wall was now a two-way mirror and he could see the petrified Silva seated on a wooden chair in the centre of the concrete floor. He was sweating profusely and his eyes were screwed up against the bright fluorescent light on the ceiling directly above him. Garcia and Peraya were standing behind him. Doyle placed the phone on the table then came back into the Workshop.

'Did you speak to Señor Salcido?' Garcia asked him in English. Peraya preferred to communicate in Spanish but Garcia spoke English as often as he could to improve his grasp of the language.

Doyle beckoned the two men away from Silva and explained what had been discussed on the phone. He then crossed to where Silva was sitting, hauled him to his feet and spun him to face the back wall where three eight-foot wooden boards were bolted vertically to the wall. 'Do you know what we use those boards for, Oscar?' he asked Silva. No reply. 'Crucifixions. We can crucify three prisoners down here at any one time. And once they're immobilized, we can do anything we want to them. Peraya and I once worked in shifts to torture an informer continuously over a period of five days. There wasn't much left of him at the end. But he was still alive.' He yanked Silva round to face him again. 'Is that what you want to happen to you?'

'Please, no,' Silva begged.

'Then tell us what you know about the money Lacamara stole from the cartel, and none of this will be necessary.'

'I keep telling you, señor, I don't know anything. If I did, I would have already told you. I've always been loyal to the cartel. You must believe me. I don't know anything.'

'Then maybe we can help to jog your memory.' Doyle looked at Peraya. 'Strip him.'

Garcia twisted Silva's arms viciously behind his back while Peraya ripped off the man's clothes. Only when he was naked did Garcia let him go. Silva sank to his knees, his hands cupped over his crotch, but Peraya grabbed him and hauled him back to his feet. He pulled Silva's hands away from his groin and smiled contemptuously as he looked down at the man's exposed genitals. 'Don't worry. If they embarrass you so much we can easily remove them for you,' he whispered.

'Señor Doyle, I swear I don't know anything,' Silva whimpered then slowly sank to his knees again and clasped his hands as if in prayer. 'I beg you, please don't hurt me. Have mercy. I don't know anything. I don't know . . .' His voice trailed off as he broke down in tears, his body shuddering as he wept openly on the floor.

Doyle eyed Silva disdainfully then flicked his hand to the nearest board. Peraya half pulled, half dragged the man across the concrete floor and slammed him up against one of the boards. Garcia crossed to the row of metal cabinets mounted on the adjacent wall, opened one and removed a nail gun. Peraya forced Silva's left arm out flat against the board then Garcia grabbed his wrist, pressed the nozzle of the nail gun into his palm, and pulled the trigger. Silva screamed in agony as the nail ripped through his flesh, impaling his hand to the board. By the time they had nailed up his other hand he had drifted mercifully into unconsciousness. A pair of manacles secured his ankles to the foot of the board. A bottle of smelling salts brought him round and he was blindfolded. It was now only a question of how long he could survive at the skilled hands of his torturers . . .

Nine miles south of the city centre lies the former village of San Angel. It is now a beautiful suburb lined with cobbled streets and numerous old colonial mansions interspersed with blocks of more modern – and modestly priced – houses.

Kellerman pulled up outside a red-brick bungalow and gestured for Laura to park in the driveway. She came to a halt in front of the garage door. Leaving enough space for it to open, she switched off the engine and got out. A path led from the driveway to the veranda at the front of the house. She paused at the door to look at the neatly tended garden illuminated by the street light directly in front of the house. She knew that Mel would never have kept it that tidy. She hated gardening. Then again, they both did – it was one characteristic they hadn't inherited from their green-fingered mother.

Kellerman opened the door and punched in the code to silence the alarm. Switching on the hall light, he picked up the suitcase Laura had brought from the car and took it inside. Only then did he see that she was still standing on the veranda, a look of uncertainty on her face. 'Are you OK?' he asked.

'It's just that, well . . . this was Mel's house,' Laura replied shakily. It was important to keep up the role of the grieving sister but equally important not to overplay it. 'There's going to be a lot of memories here. But I guess I'm going to have to face them sooner or later.'

'I'd understand if you wanted to be on your own right now. I'll call you in the morning.'

'No,' she said firmly, then entered the house. 'Don't worry, I'm not going to break down on you. I did my crying back in New York. At least stay for coffee. Or a drink. I'm sure Mel must have had some booze here somewhere.'

'There's a drinks cabinet in the lounge,' Kellerman told her, 'but I'll settle for coffee.'

'Ah, could you point me in the direction of the kitchen?'

'Turn right at the end of the hall. It's the last door.' Kellerman picked up her suitcase. 'I'll put this in the bedroom for you.'

'The spare bedroom,' Laura said quickly.

'Sure,' he said.

She went through to the kitchen and she checked the fridge for milk. As she suspected – none. She found Kellerman in the lounge. 'I can only make you black coffee. There's no milk.'

'I'll have a drink then, but only a small one – I have to drive.' Kellerman crossed to the cabinet. 'What about you? All she's got in here is bourbon and brandy.'

'I'll just have a Diet Coke, thanks, if there is one,' Laura said.

'I'm sorry. I forgot you don't drink . . .' He realized he had just put his foot in it. In a big way.

'You also forgot to mention that you've been digging into my past.' She folded her arms across her chest and glared at him. 'I know that Mel would never have told you anything about my personal life, no matter how close you were. Obviously you've got it all written down on some file. So tell me, what else does it say about me? Come to think of it, I'm amazed that you even considered asking me to take Mel's place for such a sensitive operation. Aren't you worried that I'm going to crack at the first hurdle and hit the bottle again? Once a drunk, always a drunk. Isn't that what they say?'

'It's standard procedure to investigate every agent's background before they're assigned to the DEA. And that includes a routine check on their family as well.' The words sounded as hollow as they were insensitive.

'You never answered my question. What else does it say about me in my file?'

'It's all in the computer. I'll be glad to let you have a print-out in the morning.'

'So my whole life's on display for all to see at the DEA.'

'The section about your . . . drinking is classified. Only those in senior management have access to it.'

'That makes me feel so much better,' she retorted.

'Laura, if I didn't think you were up to this, I'd never have asked you to help. I know you've had your difficulties with alcohol. That can't be undone. But the fact that you beat it on your own shows a lot of character. And if there was ever a time when you might have been tempted to turn to the bottle for comfort, it would have been in the last couple of days. You didn't. You held firm. I'm not being patronizing when I say that Melissa would have been real proud of you. And she never mentioned to me that you had a drink problem. What she did talk about was your husband, Jefferson. To say that she disliked him would be an understatement.'

'That made two of us. Only I couldn't see it at the time.' Laura shook her head and sat down in the nearest armchair. 'Then again, I couldn't see much of anything at the time. Not with the amount of alcohol I was getting through every day.'

Kellerman took a can of Diet Coke from the fridge beneath the drinks cabinet and handed it to her with a glass. 'I know I should have told you that we had a file on you at the DEA. I'm sorry.'

'I suppose I should have guessed as much,' she said, then opened the can and poured half its contents into the glass. 'After all, Mel was working for a government agency.'

'I'm a bit surprised that she never told you herself,' Kellerman replied, helping himself to a shot of bourbon. 'She would have known about it.'

'As I told you in New York, Mel and I rarely discussed her work with the DEA. There were times when she'd come stay with me and sit by the window for hours on end, hardly saying a word. The first few times it happened I tried to find out what was troubling her, but all she would ever say was "Work". I learnt to leave her alone when she was in one of those moods.'

'I knew that side of her too. A lot of it stemmed from the problems she had with the suits in Washington. They didn't approve of her methods. She liked to take chances and they don't like that. They want everything done by the book. I'm the first to admit there were times when she sailed really close to the wind. Sometimes I thought she did it just to get their backs up.'

'You're a suit, so why didn't she feel the same way about you?'

'Believe me, Melissa and I had our fair share of fights over the years,' he said. 'But the major difference between me and most of the others is that I started out as a UC, like Melissa, working undercover in places like Bolivia, Colombia and Peru. Too many positions at senior-management level in Washington are filled by university graduates. They can put together a budget, and talk a good press conference, but not many would have the faintest idea about how to run a deep-cover operation. Sure, they'd know how to put it together in theory, but not in practice.

'Melissa would regularly submit a deal to them only for it to be turned down. That's when the sparks would fly. They either regarded it as too risky, or else the budget couldn't cover the kind of money she needed to buy the quantity of drugs on offer. They'd tell her to settle for a "bust-buy" operation, which means enticing the dealer to bring the drugs to a certain location where they would then be arrested. That's fine if you want to take down some two-bit street dealer, but it doesn't get us any closer to the narco-barons who run the major cartels. Every UC knows that. But try and explain that to Washington. They'd rather have guaranteed results on paper to show Congress than take a chance on working a major deal which could end in failure.'

'How much clout do you have with your superiors in Washington?'

'Not enough,' Kellerman replied grimly. He finished his bourbon and put the glass on the table. 'Well, you're going to have to excuse me. I need to get some sleep.'

'Will Lacamara's disappearance have any bearing on my meeting with Doyle on Sunday?' Laura asked.

'I can't see any reason why, at least not at this stage. Irrespective of what happens to Lacamara, the Salcidos will still want to get their hands on the disk. That kind of information would tilt the balance of power in their favour – and that's got to be a big incentive for them to see it through.'

'So what do you want me to do until Sunday?'

'Stay here,' Kellerman replied.

'I'm Mel now, remember? Why would I sit at home for the next four days? It doesn't make any sense.'

'But you're not. As far as anyone at the DEA is concerned, you're working out of town. Melissa often used to do that. She'd often be away from the embassy for days at a time. She'd check in with me and keep me up to speed on what she was doing. Not that anyone's going to ask anyway. We'll be too busy concentrating on trying to find Lacamara before Doyle does. I'll call you tomorrow and let you know what's going on.'

She walked with him to the door. 'One thing before you go. Could you give me the code for the alarm and show me how it works?'

She remained on the veranda until he had driven off then went back into the house and locked the door behind her. She returned to the lounge, switched on the television, and stared at the screen but her mind was elsewhere. In the car she'd had time to consider the implications of Lacamara's disappearance with $50 million of the cartel's money. If the DEA were to find Lacamara before Sunday, they would offer him immunity from prosecution in return for testifying against the Salcidos. Any deal they had intended to make with Doyle would assume less significance. Which would leave the scam in jeopardy. And failure to get her share of the diamonds would mean having to return to New York. She couldn't face that. She would rather die than have to spend one more day poking about in an endless succession of unhygienic mouths or lie awake one more night listening fearfully to every sound coming from the alley below her window.

Right now she desperately wanted to hear Mel's voice, but her sister was probably about to tuck into her in-flight meal, thirty thousand feet in the air, still several hours away from Mexico City. She switched off the television and flung the remote control down on the sofa. *What the hell's got into you? Since when have you ever needed to turn to Mel for comfort?* She had always

76

sorted out her own problems in the past. And this was no different . . .

She looked across at the drinks cabinet. She walked towards it, feeling as if she were moving in slow motion, and opened the doors. A quarter-full bottle of Jack Daniel's. A full bottle of Don Pedro brandy. She picked up the bourbon and turned it around in her hand until the label was facing her. Not that she needed to read it. She still knew every word on the label by heart. She opened the bottle, took a tall glass from the shelf above the cabinet, and emptied the contents into it. Then, picking up the brandy bottle in her other hand, she left the lounge, walked down the hall and paused outside the spare bedroom. Her eyes went from the double bed to the alcohol in her hands. A full glass and a spare bottle. It brought back a lot of memories. She continued on to the kitchen where she poured the bourbon down the sink. Then she opened the brandy and held it upside down over the plug hole until the bottle was empty. Then she rinsed out the glass and dropped the empty bottle in the bin.

'Old habits die hard,' she said to herself, then went through to the bathroom to relax in a long, hot bath before turning in for the night.

'Thank you for a most enjoyable evening,' Bob Smith said, shaking Juan Salcido's hand.

'I'm glad you could come,' Salcido replied, 'and I look forward to meeting with you again in the next few days to discuss further the business proposition I outlined to you earlier tonight.'

'I'm certainly interested, I can tell you that now.' Smith shook Katrine's hand. 'My compliments to you on the meal. It was certainly the best steak I've had in a very long time.'

'Thank you,' she said, forcing a smile. 'I'll be sure to pass on your compliments to our chef.'

'Ah, here's your driver,' Salcido said, gesturing to the black Mercedes as it pulled up at the foot of the stone steps leading down from the main entrance to the house.

Smith climbed into the car, his driver closed the door, got back behind the wheel and headed off down the driveway and out through the open wrought-iron gates. A security guard closed them.

'I thought he was never going to leave,' Salcido said, closing the front door.

'And did you notice how he thanked you for the evening, and thanked me for the meal – as if I actually prepared it myself,' Katrine Salcido snorted indignantly. 'I bet his wife's a timid, domesticated housewife who spends the whole day cooking and cleaning for him.'

'Has he gone?' Ramón Salcido asked, emerging from the lounge, clutching a drink.

Juan plucked the glass from his brother's hand. 'You've had enough. I don't care if he'd kept us up for the rest of the night, you don't use that kind of language in front of our guests.'

'It was all in Spanish,' Ramón replied. 'He didn't understand a fucking word I said.'

'I did. But, more importantly, so did the staff. I won't tolerate such behaviour in front of them. And it's time you went home, Ramón. We'll talk in the morning.'

'I'll go when I'm ready. But first I'm going to have another fucking drink. Just out of principle. You don't own me, brother.'

'That's the second time now that you've sworn in front of Katrine,' Juan said. 'Don't do it again.'

Ramón was about to say something but remained silent when he saw the look on his brother's face. He entered the lounge and snapped his fingers at the nearest steward. 'Have my car brought round to the front. And have a bottle of cognac put in the mini-bar for me.' He waited until the steward had scurried off in the direction of the kitchen to find the driver before turning back to his brother. 'I assume you have no objection to me having a drink on my way home?'

'You can do what you want in your own car,' Juan replied.

'I can, can't I?' Ramón wet his dry lips and shot a salacious glance in Katrine's direction. 'I think I'll pick up one of those whores who like it rough. Have a bit of fun tonight.'

'You're disgusting,' Katrine hissed contemptuously, and walked off.

'Excuse me, *patrón*,' the head waiter said uncertainly. 'There's a phone call for you in your study.'

Juan put a finger lightly on his brother's chest. 'Make sure you've gone by the time I get back,' he said, then went to his study and closed the door behind him. 'Hello?'

'It's Doyle.'

'Good news, I hope.' There was an uneasy silence at the other end of the line. Salcido sat down slowly on the edge of his chair. 'OK, what's happened?'

'Silva's dead,' Doyle said, then added quickly, 'It wasn't our fault. It was his heart.'

'Did he tell you anything useful before he died?'

'Nothing. But I never thought he was involved anyway.'

'Dispose of the body in the usual way. Then you may as well call it a night. Tell Peraya and Garcia to go home as well. You've all got an early start in the morning. I'll be up at five to take my morning run. I'll call you when I get back. Unless, of course, I get any news of Lacamara during the night. And you call me if you hear anything.'

'That goes without saying.' Another pause. 'How did the dinner party go tonight?'

'Good. You were right about the Texan. His company would be perfect to handle a future shipment into the States.'

'I'll send one of our middlemen to Dallas in the next few days to start making discreet enquiries about possible recruits among his workforce,' Doyle said.

'I'll leave that up to you.'

'I'm sorry about Silva,' Doyle said, after a moment's silence.

'Me too.' Salcido pushed another button on the telephone. It was answered by the head waiter in the lounge. 'Has my brother left yet?'

79

'Yes, *patrón*. Do you want me to have the car stopped?'

'No, let him go,' Salcido replied, 'and have my car brought round to the front now. It's been a long day. I'm ready to go home.'

SIX

Thursday

Her tooth had ached all night. She had tried taking painkillers, even resorted to a couple of shots of neat brandy. Nothing had worked. Why had she eaten that toffee? It wasn't even as if she particularly liked sweets. And the earliest time that Dr Raquel Vasquez could fit her in was eight o'clock the following morning . . .

The DJ on the radio announced that it was 7.41 a.m., the lights changed and she swung her car into Park Avenue.

The moment she saw the two patrol cars parked behind an ambulance further down the road she knew something was wrong, but it wasn't until she got closer that she realized a police cordon had blocked off the section of the street directly in front of the dental practice. She parked her car in an alley a block away from the cordon then grabbed her purse from the passenger seat and got out. She was in her late twenties with short bleached blonde hair and a pasty complexion. At six feet tall, with her large rose-framed glasses, she tended to catch the eye in a crowd. Perfect for a journalist. She was wearing an unflattering, loose-fitting dress, a baggy blouson and comfortable leather moccasins. The fact that she was fourteen weeks pregnant had had no bearing on her choice of clothes: she liked to dress down.

She wrapped her scarf round the lower half of her face to protect her tooth from the bracing wind and pushed her way through the scrimmage of onlookers to the front of the cordon. She was stopped by a uniformed patrolman when she tried to duck underneath the yellow tape.

'What's going on?' she demanded. 'I've got an appointment with Dr Vasquez this morning.'

'Dr Vasquez is dead,' the patrolman replied, indifferently.

The tips of her fingers went to her mouth and she inhaled sharply in disbelief, then screwed up her face in pain as the cold morning air seeped into her hollow tooth. 'How did it happen?' she asked.

'Dunno. The ME's in there now with the body.'

'Where's Dr Wade?'

'Dunno.'

She opened her purse and removed a press card which she proffered to him. 'My name's Justine Collins. I'm with the *New York Independent*. I know Dr Wade personally. I'd like to speak to her.'

'My orders are not to let anyone beyond the cordon.'

'Then can I speak to the detective in charge of the investigation?'

'There'll be a press conference later this morning at the precinct. I'm sure he'll be only too glad to answer your questions then.'

Justine looked across at the building. The front door was shut and guarded by another patrolman, and the curtains had been drawn across the waiting-room windows. Then she peered down the deserted alley at the side of the building, also cordoned off. She knew that Laura Wade lived in the apartment above the practice. If she could reach the apartment, there was a chance she could find out what had happened. Not that she regarded Laura Wade as a friend, she just knew her through Raquel Vasquez. It was a long shot. And there was no guarantee that Laura Wade would even speak to her.

She felt a sharp tug at the back of her jacket and turned to find herself face to face with a large black woman dressed in a thin cotton dress with an assortment of multicoloured bangles round her wrists. 'You a journalist?' the woman asked, in a strong Jamaican accent, and prodded a fleshy finger into Justine's chest.

'That's right.'

'I got a story for you, lady. You want to hear it?'

'A story?' Justine replied suspiciously, then winced and put her hand to her cheek as another stab of pain shot through her tooth.

'You all right?' the woman asked.

'I lost a filling yesterday.'

'Well, you sure come to the wrong place. You ain't gonna find no dentist here today.' The woman gave a deep belly laugh and her bangles jangled noisily. 'So, you want to hear my story?'

Justine shrugged – she had nothing to lose – and followed the woman to the opposite side of the street. 'So?'

'I already tell them police.' The woman stabbed a finger in the direction of the nearest patrol car. She jerked a thumb to a second-floor window in the building behind them. 'I live there. Seventeen years now. I see everything that happens around here. Some say I'm nosy. I don't care. I like to know what's going on.'

'And?' Justine prompted when the woman fell silent.

'Dr Wade's my dentist. I like her.'

'Yes, she seems like a nice person,' Justine agreed.

The woman paused as someone walked past them, before continuing. 'I don't sleep too well at night so I sit at my window. Drink a little and watch the people in the street. Well, Monday night I see Dr Wade go out in her car. About eight o'clock. I must have fallen asleep in my chair around eleven. I woke again about three. Soon after that I saw Dr Wade come back. Only she wasn't in her car no more. She was driving a different car. A red car. Her car is white. Well, you know, I didn't think much about it – until yesterday morning when I see her leave her apartment with a suitcase, like she was going away on holiday. There was a taxi waiting for her. She sees me sitting at the window and waves at me. She always waves to me when she sees me.

'Then last night, about half past seven, I was coming back from the shops and I saw the red car parked right here where we're standing. I'm about to go into my building when I see Dr Wade leaving her apartment. She comes down the steps then turns up the collar of her jacket and runs across the road to the car. I call out to her that it's a cold night to be out. You know, she just look straight at me. It's as if she's never seen me before. Then she gets in the car and drives away in a big hurry.'

'You said it was night time. Maybe she didn't recognize you.'

'I was standing in the doorway. There's always a light on in the lobby. And even if she didn't see me properly, she would have recognized my voice. Now them police say Dr Vasquez is dead. And Dr Wade is missing – or so I hear a policeman say on his radio.'

'Are you suggesting that Dr Wade killed her?' Justine asked.

'I just tell you what I know,' the woman said.

'Well, it's an . . . interesting story,' Justine conceded.

'How much you pay me?'

The question caught Justine by surprise. 'I didn't realize the story came at a price.'

'I gave you a good story. And all true. It's only right you pay me for it.'

'I never carry much money on me,' Justine told her. 'I've only got a couple of tens.'

'Twenty dollars?' the woman said, thought about it, then extended her hand towards Justine. 'I'll take it.'

Justine was about to protest but her tooth was killing her. She just wanted to get back into the warmth of her car. She pulled the two tens from her purse and the woman snatched them then strode off. 'Hey, what's your name?' Justine called after her. No reply. 'Hey . . .'

'That's Nora,' said the elderly man standing beside her. There was a faint smile on his lips. 'How much did you give her?'

'I don't think that's any of your business.' Justine bristled.

'Look, I don't care,' the man said. 'She'll just go and spend it on booze anyway. All she does is sit at her window and drink. Day and night. I heard her spin you that story. What are you, a journalist?'

'Yes,' Justine replied. 'Are you saying she made it all up?'

'All I'm saying is that Nora will do anything for a drink. Hell, everyone around here knows that.' He chuckled softly then walked away.

'Oh, great,' Justine muttered, as she headed back towards her car. 'Just great.'

'Dead?'

'I'm sorry, Laura. I really am,' Kellerman said.

Laura had taken a couple of sleeping tablets the previous night and had still been asleep when the phone had rung.

'What happened?' she asked, in a trembling voice, when she finally broke the lingering silence.

'The receptionist found her this morning when she arrived for work. She was lying at the foot of the stairs leading up to your apartment. Her neck was broken. There was no sign of a struggle, and all the doors and windows at the practice were locked. It appears as if she lost her footing on the stairs and fell awkwardly. A tragic accident, at least that's what the police seem to think. An autopsy's due to be carried out later today.'

'I still can't believe it,' Laura said, wiping away a tear. This time her emotion was genuine.

'I can't begin to imagine the hurt you must be feeling. First Melissa, now Raquel. I'd fully understand if you wanted to call this off and go back to New York.'

'No,' Laura replied sharply, as tears began to pour down her face. 'I said I was going to do this for Mel. And I'm determined to go through with it.' She sat back in the armchair and raked her hand through her dishevelled hair. 'What I don't understand is why Raquel would be going up to my apartment. It doesn't make any sense.'

'I only know what the NYPD told our New York office earlier this morning. They'll keep me informed on any new developments. The police naturally wanted to speak to you, especially as they've got an eye-witness who claims to have seen you leave your apartment around seven thirty last night, which was around the time that Raquel died.'

'But that's . . .' She trailed off and looked across at the framed photograph of Mel smiling down at her from the mantelpiece. Mel would have been at the airport at seven thirty. Wouldn't she?

'Crazy, I know,' Kellerman completed the sentence for her. 'The DEA has already been in touch with the NYPD. We didn't go into details as to your exact whereabouts, other than to say you were out of town at the time the eye-witness claims to have seen you leaving your apartment. We'll vouch for you, if necessary. But I doubt it'll come to that. According to the commissioner, the eye-witness is a woman who has a history of alcoholism and is well known to the local police. They think she was probably drunk at the time.'

'It sounds like Nora,' Laura said.

'I don't know her name.' He paused. 'Look, I'm kind of busy at the moment, but I can probably get an hour off around twelve. Would you like me to come over?'

'Thanks, but I'll be all right,' she replied.

'I understand. I'll drop by after work tonight. Around six. Assuming, of course, that nothing crops up before then.'

'I'd like that.' Laura replaced the handset then buried her face in her hands and sobbed uncontrollably.

The news of Raquel's death had devastated her. But even more appalling was the thought that Mel could have been involved. She wanted to believe that Nora had been drunk and had imagined it all. But what had Mel been doing at the apartment when she should have been at the airport – or at least on her way there? And what had Raquel been doing on the stairs leading up to her apartment? Had Raquel found Mel in the apartment? Laura felt a shiver run through her. Mel had promised her that nobody was going to get hurt. Now Raquel was dead.

She changed into a pair of jeans and a baggy white T-shirt then slipped on a pair of plimsolls and left the house. It was a bright sunny morning with only a hint of wispy cloud in the clear cerulean sky. She paused at the front gate to scan the length of the street. Mel had warned her that the house might be kept under surveillance, either by the DEA or by the cartel. Half a dozen cars were parked in the road. None appeared to be occupied. She stepped out on to the sidewalk and closed the gate behind her. A middle-aged man, stripped to the waist, was cutting the hedge on the opposite side of the street. He nodded in greeting. She smiled absently at him then walked to the public telephone: Mel had told her never to use the phone in the house if she wanted to contact her. She fed a coin into the slot then dialled Mel's cellular phone.

After a couple of rings Melissa answered. 'Hello?'

'Raquel's dead,' Laura blurted out. The only emotion in her voice now was raw, aggressive anger. 'You said nobody was going to get hurt.'

'My God! When did this happen?'

'You can cut the act, Mel. You were seen leaving my apartment last night around the time that Raquel supposedly fell down the stairs.'

There was a pause. 'Come to the hotel. Take two cabs to make sure you're not followed. Tell the first driver to take you to the National Palace. Then get another cab to bring you to the hotel. Use the city taxis. You can't miss them – they're everywhere. Yellow and white, or green and grey. Most are either Datsuns or VW Beetles. Follow the road for another hundred yards and you'll come out on to a main street. Flag one down.' The line went dead.

Laura hung up. Her hand was shaking. Suddenly she was very frightened.

Melissa was staying at the Hotel Canada under the name of Elaine Forman. It was the same hotel where she had agreed to meet Doyle.

'You weren't followed, were you?' Melissa demanded after she admitted Laura into the room and closed the door again behind her. Only then did she remove the blonde wig she had slipped over her own hair before answering the door.

'No,' Laura answered tersely.

'You want coffee?' Melissa asked, indicating the breakfast tray on the table.

'What I want is an explanation,' Laura replied. 'You told me that nobody was going to get hurt. That's why I agreed to go along with this in the first place. Now Raquel's dead—'

'I had no choice,' Melissa cut in angrily and held up the wig before tossing it on to the unmade bed. 'I left it at your apartment. Raquel walked in on me when I went back to get it. What could I do? The moment she saw me in your apartment, she already knew too much.'

'You could have passed yourself off as me,' Laura said.

'Too risky,' Melissa replied.

'Then you could have given her some spiel about us working together on a DEA operation and sworn her to silence. She wouldn't have said anything. Not Raquel. You didn't have to . . .' Laura tailed off into silence, struggling against tears.

Melissa sat down on the edge of the bed. When she spoke her voice was soft. 'I thought the world of Raquel. You know that. She pulled you back from the brink by taking you on as a partner after you'd dried out when no other dentist in New York wanted to know you. And you're right. She probably wouldn't have said anything but I couldn't afford to take that chance. Don't you see that? I had no choice. You've got to believe me, sis.'

'I don't know what to believe any more,' Laura said, as she moved to the window and looked out across the neighbouring rooftops.

Melissa, allowing herself a quick smile of satisfaction when she heard the tone of uncertainty harboured in Laura's voice, got up and crossed to her sister. She put an arm around Laura's shoulders. 'What do you think the DEA would do if they were to find out before Sunday that I'd faked my own death in New York? For a start, they'd abort the meet with Doyle. Then they'd arrest us. We'd go to jail. And if you think you had problems getting a job after you'd dried out, it would be nothing compared to the prejudice you'd encounter as an ex-con. We're in this together, sis. Don't forget that. And don't forget either that by Sunday night we're going to be ten million dollars richer. New identities. New lives. That's what this is all about, isn't it?'

'That's what I thought, until you murdered Raquel,' Laura shot back. Then she flung off Melissa's arm and went to sit down in the armchair in the corner of the room.

Melissa leant over her sister, her hands pressed firmly into the arms of the chair. 'Raquel's dead. There's nothing either of us can do to change that. But I can't stop you walking out of here and telling Tom Kellerman that you've had a change of heart and want out. It would leave me in a no-win situation, but you'd be on the next plane back to the States. Then what? Back to the dead end existence that you were so desperate to escape. Pulling teeth for another thirty years in some back-street ghetto. Is that what you want?'

'I've come this far and I intend to see it through,' Laura replied, holding her sister's gaze. 'And as for what happened to Raquel, that's something I'm going to have to live with for the rest of my life.'

'I think you'll find that five million dollars will do wonders for a troubled conscience,' Melissa said, with a smile, as she straightened up.

'Speak for yourself.'

Melissa poured herself some coffee. 'Who was the eye-witness?'

'If it's who I think it is, her name's Nora. She's a Jamaican. She claims that she called out to you, thinking it was me, but that you ignored her. According to Tom, the DEA have already told the NYPD that it couldn't have been me. And the local cops aren't taking what Nora said seriously because they know she's an alcoholic.'

'Looks like luck was with us this time,' Melissa said.

'I'm not so sure about that. Have you heard about Lacamara?' Laura asked.

'Yes, but how did you know?' Melissa replied in surprise.

Laura explained how she'd had to impersonate Melissa when they got to the embassy.

'So you met Billy, then?' Melissa snorted. 'I heard about Lacamara shortly after I arrived.'

'Benitez?' Laura asked.

'How do you know about him?' Melissa asked.

'Walker mentioned him.'

'No, it's not Benitez,' Melissa replied. 'Sure, he's my main CI here in Mexico City, but I can't risk using him now in case the DEA get to hear of it. I've got another CI that the DEA don't know anything about. Not as good as Benitez, but at least I know there won't be any comebacks with him.'

'According to Walker, Lacamara embezzling the cartel's money is still only a rumour at the moment,' Laura reminded her.

'It's no rumour, sis. You take my word for it. I know the Salcido cartel better than anyone else in the DEA. They don't panic easily but from what I've been told, Doyle's been running around like a headless chicken ever since Lacamara disappeared yesterday afternoon. That's not like him. I spoke to my CI less than an hour ago. Word is that the cartel's already put out a reward of a million pesos for Lacamara's capture. Which is great, if the cartel can get to him first. But there's no guarantee they will. The DEA will almost certainly match that figure if it means getting their hands on him. He's the cartel's bookkeeper. He knows where every cent of the drug money is hidden. That makes him an even bigger catch than Doyle.'

'Which could put the meeting with Doyle in jeopardy,' Laura added.

'It would certainly assume less significance if the DEA already had Lacamara, but they'd still go through with it. What would they have to lose? Doyle and Lacamara would be a dream team for the prosecution. Their testimony alone would put the Salcidos behind bars for life. No question of that.'

'So we don't have anything to worry about,' Laura said, with evident relief.

'Not exactly.'

'Mel, what is it?' Laura demanded when her sister fell silent.

'You know that, as part of Operation Checkmate, the DEA have been stringing along the cartel by having me pass on so-called "inside information" to Doyle. And all the money I received from the cartel was handed over to the DEA. Well, not all of it. I skimmed off a few thousand from each deal before I gave the money to Tom. The DEA never suspected a thing.' Melissa raised a hand before Laura could protest. 'I earned that money, sis. I was the one putting my ass on the line every time I met Doyle. If he'd suspected for one moment that I wasn't on the level, he'd have had me killed without a second thought – but not before torturing as much as he could out of me first. Lacamara was the cartel's paymaster. He'd know exactly how much Doyle paid me. And if the DEA were to find out before Sunday that I'd been taking a cut for myself, there'd be a lot of pressure from the Office of Professional Responsibility to abort the meet with Doyle. They're the DEA's equivalent of the military police. And just as unpleasant. I'd be suspended immediately pending a full inquiry.'

'But you're officially dead,' Laura reminded her.

'How many people know that? Tom would have had to clear it with Braithwaite before he brought you in. I doubt anyone else knows about the switch. They can't take that chance in case word of the deception were to leak back to the cartel. So as far as everyone else at the DEA is concerned, you are me. Which means Braithwaite would have to overrule the OPR if the operation was to be allowed to continue. And that would mean having to face a lot of awkward questions. That's how powerful these people are – they can even make life difficult for someone like Braithwaite. We can't take that chance, sis. Not when we're so close to pulling this off. That's why I've decided to go after Lacamara myself.'

'And what happens if you do find him first?' Laura asked.

'I'll kill him.'

'Why doesn't that surprise me?'

'Do you have a better idea?' Melissa countered. 'Because if you have, I'd be really interested to hear it.'

'I've got to get back to the house,' Laura said.

'We're in this together, sis,' Melissa called after her sister as she headed for the door. 'Whatever I have to do to ensure that everything goes according to plan on Sunday is as much for you as it is for me. Don't forget that.'

'Got a moment?'

Ethan Byrne looked up from his desk and smiled at Justine Collins whose head was poked round the door. 'Sure, come in,' he replied. A sharp, intuitive journalist in his late thirties, he had been prised away from his position as deputy editor on his hometown *Miami Herald* to become the first editor-in-chief of the *New York Independent*. Regarded in the industry as a quality broadsheet to rival the revered *New York Times* as well as the more jingoistic *USA Today*, the newspaper had gained a steady following among more liberal-minded New Yorkers. Although he had a reputation as a hard taskmaster, he was also approachable with an easy, outgoing disposition. Although he had no favourites in the newsroom, he had tremendous respect for Justine. He saw in her the same ruthless ambition that had pushed him to the top of his profession at a relatively early age and he had already earmarked her as a future editor in her own right. 'Sit down,' he said, pointing to the chair on the opposite side of his paper-strewn desk. 'How's the tooth?'

'Great,' she replied, prodding her cheek. 'You're a real lifesaver, Ethan. I don't know what I'd have done if you hadn't got your dentist to fit me in at such short notice. I really appreciate it.'

'It's the least I could do after what happened to yours. I sent Josh to the precinct in Spanish Harlem to cover the press conference.'

'I know. I spoke to him when I got back from the dentist.'

'Then you'll know that the police aren't as convinced as they were that it was an accident,' Byrne said.

'Josh said that the police have already eliminated Dr Vasquez's partner, Laura Wade, as a possible suspect. Except that I made a call of my own to a contact I have at the precinct in Spanish Harlem and I was told, off the record, that Laura Wade was never interviewed by the police. They haven't seen her since Raquel Vasquez's body was found this morning. Word is, the detective in charge of the investigation was told by the station commander not to pursue Laura Wade. No questions asked. Which suggests to me that the station commander got his orders directly from police headquarters.'

'Interesting,' Byrne said thoughtfully.

'Oh, it gets better,' she said, and explained about her conversation with the Jamaican woman at the crime scene. 'My first reaction was that I'd been ripped off. But then I made a few discreet enquiries of my own. Turns out Laura Wade has an identical twin, Melissa, who works for the DEA. She's now on the admin side, working as a senior case officer in Mexico, so I called an old colleague of mine in Mexico City, Felix Amador. He spent a couple of years on the *New York Post* while I was there. He said the word on the street is that the senior accountant for the Salcido drug cartel has gone on the run with his mistress after embezzling fifty million dollars. And guess who's in charge of monitoring the Salcido cartel?' She smiled triumphantly. 'That's right. Special Agent Melissa Wade. And she was here in New York only yesterday. Except that she has the perfect alibi. She was on a flight back to Mexico City when Raquel Vasquez died. At least, according to the passenger manifest she was. But what if it wasn't her, Ethan? What if it was her sister on that plane last night? What if Melissa Wade remained behind? It would account for her not recognizing the Jamaican woman as she left the apartment. Even if Laura Wade hadn't seen her, she'd have known the woman's voice. Believe me, it's distinctive.'

'The eye-witness is a lush. You said that yourself. What if she did make up the story just to get some money to buy herself a bottle of booze? It's got to be a possibility.'

'Of course it has, but what if she's on the level? It would throw up a lot of intriguing questions, wouldn't it?'

'I hear what you're saying, Justine, but you haven't given me a shred of evidence linking Melissa Wade to Raquel Vasquez's death. I think you're putting too much emphasis on what your eye-witness saw last night. All I can see is a series of random events with no apparent connection to each other.'

'At least let me run with it, Ethan. A few days, that's all.'

'Which would mean you flying out to Mexico to cover it.'

'I've already got a seat provisionally booked on an Aeroméxico flight later this afternoon,' she said, with a wry smile.

'I hardly think you're in any condition to go chasing after a story like that in the heat of Mexico, do you?'

'I haven't thrown up in over a week now.' She noticed the look of doubt on his face. 'I'm not just saying this to try to placate you, Ethan. If I didn't feel up to it, I wouldn't have taken it this far. I may have taken crazy risks in the past to get a scoop, but not this time. There's no story on earth that's worth risking the safety of my baby.' She grinned mischievously at him. 'And, anyway, Felix will be doing most of the legwork. So if he gets a story while I'm out there, we'll write it up together. He's working freelance so he'll sell it to the highest bidder in Mexico and we'll have the exclusive here in the States.'

'I want to see proof before I print anything. I also want a serious story. Nothing lightweight like a shabby tabloid exposé on this accountant and his mistress. That's not what this paper's about.'

'Your confidence in me is really touching, you know that?'

'It's not you I'm worried about,' Byrne replied.

'Felix has written leading articles for *Time* and *Newsweek* in the last couple of years. He's a damn good journalist, Ethan. Don't condemn him just because he spent some time on the *Post*. It was just work experience for him while he was here in the States, that's all.'

'When do you leave?'

'Four thirty, from JFK,' she replied.

Byrne looked at his watch. 'You're cutting it fine. You'd better go straight home and pack.'

'My suitcase is in the car. I just came up here to tell you that I was on my way.'

'It's nice to know that my authority still carries some weight around here,' Byrne said with a bemused smile. 'What if I'd said no?'

'You didn't,' she replied with a look of feigned innocence. 'Don't worry, I'll send you a postcard when I get there,' she quipped then got to her feet and moved to the door.

'I'll be expecting a lot more than that,' Byrne replied.

'You know you'll get it,' Justine called out over her shoulder as she left the room.

'I know,' Byrne said to himself as he stared at the door. Then the phone jangled on his desk, snapping him out of his reverie, and he quickly reached out a hand to answer it.

SEVEN

Laura didn't know how long she had been asleep – the layer of scum floating on the surface of her untouched coffee gave her no real indication. She stifled a yawn and glanced at the digital clock: 4.13 p.m. A couple of hours certainly. Possibly more. She had felt tired and listless ever since she arrived in Mexico City and knew it would take her another day or so to get acclimatized to the altitude. She swung her legs off the bed, went through to the bathroom, splashed cold water over her face, ran a brush through her hair, and picked up her sunglasses off the hall table on the way to the kitchen. Unlocking the back door, she slipped on the shades and then emerged out on to the patio and sat down in a deck-chair. With the sun beating down on her, she was tempted to close her eyes. But she dismissed the idea. She wasn't going to let that happen again.

Her thoughts returned to the uncomfortable meeting she'd had with Mel that morning. It was all she had been able to think about since leaving the hotel. The reality was that Raquel was dead. Admittedly, she had shed tears but the grief she felt had been overshadowed by her determination to see the scam through to the end. Had the anticipation of her share of the diamonds taken on more importance than the life of her best friend? She had yet to come up with an answer. And that frightened her.

Mel appeared to be out of control. She had killed Raquel.

Given the chance, she was going to kill Lacamara. How many more? *Whatever I have to do to ensure that everything goes according to plan on Sunday is as much for you as it is for me.* Her sister's parting words at the hotel still made Laura shudder. It made her an accomplice to murder. What's more, there was nothing she could do about it without jeopardizing the operation. That frightened her too.

She never wanted to go back to her old life in New York and would do anything to ensure that she never had to. But she knew that her conscience would catch up with her. And that frightened her most of all.

The phone rang inside the house. Laura jumped up and hurried through to the lounge to answer it.

'Hi, it's Tom Kellerman. I didn't get you out of the bath, did I?'

'No, why?'

'The phone's been ringing for ages. I was about to hang up and send out the cavalry to look for you.'

'I was sitting on the patio,' she replied. 'Has something happened?'

'No, I just thought I'd see how you were doing.'

'Bored.' She snorted. 'Any news of Lacamara?'

'No, nothing. But we're pretty sure he's still on the run, judging from the feedback we've been getting from our CIs. And as long as he's out there, we're still in with a chance of finding him.'

'You still coming over later?'

'That bored, eh?' Kellerman teased.

'I could do with the company.' Which was true, considering how vulnerable she was feeling.

'Me, too. I feel as if I'm banging my head against a brick wall here. I'll be there about seven.'

'Seven's good.'

'If you make a salad, I'll pick up a take-out on my way over.'

'Mel obviously told you about my cooking,' Laura quipped. 'So what exotic delicacy are you going to bring over?'

'You'll just have to wait and see.'

'Tacos. I might have guessed.'

'Not tacos, *quesadillas*,' Kellerman corrected her. 'Fried tortillas filled with melted cheese. Only they're not like the hard, crispy tortillas we get back home. These shells are still soft. That's the Mexican way. Two have got red *jalapeño* chillies in them. I wasn't sure whether you liked hot peppers or not.'

'Can't say I do,' she replied, bringing over the bowl of salad.

'That's all the more for me, then,' Kellerman said. He removed his jacket, draped it over the back of the chair, unfastened his top button and loosened his tie. Then, switching on the ceiling fan, he sat down opposite her at the table and removed the two spicy *quesadillas* from the box and put them on his plate. 'I could live on these things – sometimes I do, if I'm on a stake-out.'

'I thought you were a desk man.'

'Normally I am, but I still like to get out in the field – if I can. The problem is, my face is known to all the major players here in Mexico so that kind of limits what I can do. Of course I can't do any undercover work, but I can still be in on an important bust or a major surveillance operation. I get the impression that my superiors back in Washington think I should start acting more like a chief officer and less like a glorified UC. They're probably right. But I get them their quota of results and that seems to keep them happy enough.'

'Was your cover blown, like Mel's was when she was in Colombia?' Laura asked, helping herself to the salad.

'Yeah. I was working deep cover – that's when a UC goes undercover and adopts the identity of a criminal to be accepted at face value by their intended target. It may mean posing as a major buyer, or even infiltrating a cartel and working on the inside. The downside of it is that you're isolated – if you get into difficulties, you're on your own. You won't get any official backing from the DEA. I'd been working on the same deal for over a year and I'd managed to get close to one of the most powerful narco-barons in Peru. I wouldn't say he trusted me – these guys don't even trust themselves – but I'd made a lot of important contacts in the business through him.

'Well, it all came crashing down around my head one weekend when this guy was entertaining some pretty important *hombres* aboard his luxury yacht. Most of them were senior figures from the Medellín cartel in Colombia. Including one I'd helped put in jail some years earlier. Only I thought he'd been killed by a car bomb shortly after his release. At least, that's what my case officer had told me at the time. Although I'd grown a moustache and lightened the colour of my hair since I'd last seen him, he still recognized me. So there I was, a DEA officer outed in the middle of a hoods' convention.'

'What happened?'

'I was out of there faster than the speed of light.'

'But you said you were on board a yacht?'

'It was moored in the harbour at the time. Had it been at sea, I'd never have got away. I had an escape route set up and I was over the border into Chile by nightfall. The next day my case officer flew in to debrief me and the first thing I did when I saw him was slug him as hard as I could. The bastard let me walk on to that yacht without doing his homework properly. He was transferred to other duties. The narco-baron I'd conned had already put out a contract on me even before I'd left Peru but two days after my cover was burnt he was found dead in his swimming pool. His hands had been tied behind his back and he'd been shot through the back of his head. He'd paid the price for allowing the DEA to infiltrate the cartel.'

'And the contract?'

'As far as I know, it's still in circulation. But it's just one of several that have been put out on me over the years.'

'Has anyone ever tried to kill you?'

'Sure,' Kellerman replied, then picked up one of the *quesadillas* and took a bite.

'And that doesn't bother you?' Laura said, amazed.

'I guess it can be annoying,' he replied, between mouthfuls, 'but you have to learn to live with it. The alternative would be for me to go into hiding for the rest of my life. That's as good as admitting that they've won. I joined the DEA to fight these bastards, and I'm not about to run away at the first sign of trouble. Having said that, though, I'd hardly call myself a prize target. As far as the cartels in South and Central America are concerned, the DEA's little more than an ongoing irritation to them. We score the occasional success at their expense but they can replace a lost shipment of cocaine within a week. And that one *will* get through to its destination. The main threat to them comes from rival cartels. We're on the periphery with all the other law-enforcement agencies. And when you're talking about two hundred billion dollars a year being laundered by the various cartels around the world, that's exactly where we're going to remain until we can put in some serious money of our own to try to combat them. Only Congress won't sanction it. It's not a vote winner, not like tax cuts.'

'So what you're saying is that you're losing the war against drugs?' Laura asked.

'A little bit more every day,' Kellerman replied, grim-faced. 'And there's not a damn thing we can do about it.'

'That's a pretty frightening thought.'

'Especially if you've seen as much as I have over the years. And it can only get worse.' He fell silent as he ate his remaining *quesadillas*. Then he indicated the two on Laura's plate. 'What do you think?'

'Better than any taco I've had back in the States,' she replied, 'but they're very filling. I could have had them on their own, without the salad.'

'It's good salad,' Kellerman told her, and helped himself to more.

'Flatterer,' she said good-humouredly.

'No, I mean it. Hell, the closest I ever get to salad when I'm at home is scraping the fur off a bit of cheese that's been in the refrigerator too long.'

'Remind me never to come to your house for dinner.' Laura began on her third *quesadilla*. When she next looked up she saw that he was staring at her, with a faint smile. 'Why are you looking at me like that?'

'I still can't get over how alike you and Melissa are. It's like I'm sitting here with her again.'

'Did you come here often?'

'Often enough. We'd usually sit in here with the back door open and a bottle of bourbon on the table between us. Sometimes we'd talk about work. More often than not, though, we'd just sit here and shoot the breeze. A bit like we're doing now. Only . . . it's different with you.'

'In what way?' Laura asked, and put down her knife and fork.

'I feel more at ease with you. Melissa could get real heavy at times. If nothing else, she sure knew how to bitch . . .' He raised a hand in apology. 'I'm sorry. I shouldn't be talking about her like that. Not now.'

'I've already told you, I've done my crying. And I want to hear about you and Mel. Remember, this is a side of her I never got to see.'

'Well, she certainly liked to have her say,' he said, after swallowing his last mouthful. 'And it always seemed to turn heavy. Not that I did much of the talking, though. I left that to Melissa. Sometimes I got the impression that . . .'

'Tom?' she said, in exasperation, when he fell silent.

'I was going to say that I sometimes got the impression she was lonely. Sure, she was outgoing and liked a good time just as much as the next person, but I often wondered whether it was all a façade. She didn't have many friends out here. I think a lot of that had to do with her having such a dominant personality. People, particularly men, shied away from her.'

'But you didn't?'

'I was used to it. Remember, we'd worked together as UCs on several important deals over the years.'

'So you trusted her?'

'With my life – which happened every time we worked together. Melissa was the best UC I've ever known. No question of that.'

'She'd have liked that, coming from you,' Laura said, then took the plates across to the sink. 'Would you like coffee? I can't offer you a drink. I poured it all down the sink last night. I guess I still don't trust myself around booze. Better safe than sorry.'

'Coffee would be great, thanks.' He got up and opened the back door. The air was humid and muggy. He stepped out on to the patio and looked up at the night sky. 'I'd say we're due a thunderstorm any time now. They don't normally last long but they clear the air.' He turned to go back inside and instinctively put out a hand to prevent himself colliding with Laura, who had emerged silently on to the patio behind him. His hand lingered on her arm. She didn't move as she held his stare but when his hand came up to touch her face she turned sharply and went back into the kitchen. He followed her inside and closed the door.

'Milk, no sugar. Right?' she asked. The discomfort was obvious in her voice.

'Laura?' he said hesitantly, not even sure what he wanted to say.

'Here.' She thrust the mug aggressively towards him, forcing him to step back before he could take it.

His cellular phone rang. He put down the mug and removed the phone from the inside pocket of his jacket. 'Kellerman?' he said brusquely, then patted his jacket pockets but was unable to find his notepad. He cupped his hand over the mouthpiece and asked Laura, 'Can you get me a piece of paper?' She went through to the lounge and returned with the message pad that Melissa kept by her phone. 'OK, shoot,' he told the caller, and scribbled down an address. 'Have you told the INCD yet?' Pause. 'Get on to them right away. Tell them I want a dozen men assembled as quickly as possible. I'll meet them outside the hotel.' Another pause. 'No, you stay at the embassy in case any more information comes through, Bill.' He switched off the phone then slipped the paper into his shirt pocket.

'Lacamara?' Laura asked.

Kellerman nodded. 'Bill Walker had a tip-off from one of his CIs. And if we know about it, chances are Doyle will.'

'Tom, be careful.'

'You can count on it,' he replied, shrugging into his jacket. She heard the front door bang shut behind him and moments later the sound of a car engine.

She stood motionless in the kitchen. She didn't know what to think. Or, if she was honest with herself, she didn't want to think what she already knew. Mel had warned her not to get too close to him. But she'd thought she had the situation in hand. *Until now, that is*, she thought bitterly.

Her eyes focused on the message pad on the kitchen table. She picked it up, tilted it towards the light and was able to make out the indentation of Kellerman's handwriting on the top sheet. Suddenly she felt as if she were intruding on his privacy: the address had been given to him in confidence. But if the DEA were to get to Lacamara first, it could ruin everything. She knew what she had to do.

She tore off the top sheet and ran from the house, slamming the front door behind her. Every second was vital. She got into the car, reversed out of the driveway, swung the wheel violently and drove to the public telephone at the end of the street. She jumped out, leaving the engine idling. She dialled Melissa's cellular phone, then tapped her fingers impatiently on the side of the booth until it was answered. 'Tom's just got word from the embassy that Lacamara's been spotted. He left the house a couple of minutes ago to pick him up.'

'Do you know where he's headed?'

'It looks like . . . Tepotzotlán,' Laura replied, tilting the paper towards the overhead street light.

'Where in Tepotzotlán?'

'Room seventeen – Palacio Hotel. Do you know it?'

'No, but I'll find it.'

'Will you be able to get there before him?'

'Should do. Tepotzotlán's about a thirty-minute drive due north of Mexico City. San Angel, where you are, is to the south. I'm already in the city centre, so that makes me closer than Tom would have been when he set out. But he's already got a few minutes' start on me. Sis . . . you did well.' The line went dead.

Laura felt a prickle of conscience but she was quick to push it aside. Deal with it later. Along with the rest of her guilt. Then she replaced the handset and, as she walked back to the car, the first spots of rain began to fall.

By the time Melissa reached the outskirts of Tepotzotlán the downpour was over. The car's headlights picked out the silhouettes of two old men shuffling slowly along the side of the unlit road and she pulled over opposite them to ask for directions to the Palacio Hotel. One gave her an inane toothless smile. The second ambled slowly across the road and put a finger to his ear as he rested an arm on the roof of her car. She bit back her impatience and repeated the question. For a moment he said nothing and she was about to drive off when he nodded to himself then gave her the directions, gesticulating with his finger as if pointing out the route on an imaginary map. Once she got her bearings, she pulled away in a swirl of dust that engulfed the old man.

She followed his directions into the small, colonial town and past the main tourist attraction, the Colegio de San Francisco Javier, a magnificent Baroque church built by the Jesuits in the seventeenth century, and continued for another two blocks before turning down a narrow, ill-lit street. She slowed to a crawl as she scanned the crumbling buildings on either side of the street until she could see the grim, unlit façade of the Palacio Hotel on her right. After satisfying herself that neither Kellerman nor any local INCD agents had yet arrived, she drove on to the end of the street, cut the engine, then opened the glove compartment and removed her 10mm Smith & Wesson M1006 automatic and a silencer, both of which she had left in a locker at the airport before flying to New York earlier in the week. She pocketed the silencer and slipped the automatic into her concealed hip holster before getting out of the car. She was wearing a pair of baggy jeans, a loose-fitting sweatshirt, and her hair was hidden under a black peaked cap, tilted down to conceal her face.

She reached the alley at the side of the hotel and, once her eyes had adjusted to the gloom, made her way to the foot of the rusty fire escape. She eyed it uneasily: it had been secured originally to the side of the building but several of the bolts were loose and deep cracks ran down the unpainted wall. She shuddered to think what it might be like higher up. But it was her only access into the hotel, other than through the main entrance.

She slipped on a pair of black leather gloves then ran up the metal steps until she reached the first floor where she stepped into the corridor and closed the fire exit quietly behind her. Although she had no idea which floor the room was on, she would continue the search inside the hotel, floor by floor.

Luck was with her. She discovered a wall-mounted direction board further down the corridor, which pointed her in the right direction. On reaching the room, she took out her Smith & Wesson, screwed the silencer on to the barrel then, concealing it behind her leg, rapped twice on the door. No answer. She couldn't hear any noise coming from inside the room so she knocked again. Still no response. She pulled out the set of skeleton keys that she always carried and found one to unlock the door. She pushed it open and swept the room with the automatic. It was empty but still occupied, judging from the unmade bed and the two holdalls on the luggage rack.

She closed the door behind her and checked the cupboards. Nothing. Then she moved to the double doors leading out on to the small balcony and was about to push them open when she saw the two cars double-parked outside the hotel entrance. A man was standing beside one, a cigarette in his mouth. She recognized him as an INCD agent. Which meant that Kellerman and the other agents were already on their way up to the room. She had to get out. Fast.

Crossing to the door, she opened it a fraction and peered out into the corridor. It was deserted. She slipped out and made her way cautiously back towards the fire exit. She opened the door, stepped outside – and saw the silhouette of a man standing with his back to her at the mouth of the alley. Which left her with one choice: to climb up to the flat roof and hide there until it was safe to leave. She counted another three floors above her, then the roof.

She negotiated the steps to the second floor but before she could go any further she heard voices from behind the door. She pressed her back against the wall, her finger resting lightly on the trigger of the automatic. She heard one INCD agent ask another if he had checked his section of the floor. The answer was yes. Then the voices faded.

She glanced down at the man in the alley. He still had his back to her.

She reached the third floor, then the fourth when she heard voices again. This time they grew louder and then she heard the ominous sound of footsteps on the roof above.

Melissa knew she had only seconds before she was discovered. She stuffed the Smith & Wesson into the front of her jeans, clambered over the safety railing and eased herself down until her face was level with the walkway. Her legs were dangling precariously in the air but she swung them back and forth until she managed to lock her ankles round a strut underneath the stairs. Then she edged along the underside of the walkway until she was hidden.

The fire exit opened and two men came out. She could see the soles of their shoes through the perforations on the walkway. They remained there, talking, until the third man joined them from the roof. One dropped his cigarette butt but when he tried to crush it underfoot it slipped through one of the perforations and down the front of Melissa's sweatshirt. She bit back a yelp of pain and tried frantically to dislodge the burning ember. She lost her footing and the automatic slipped out of her belt. She gritted her teeth as it plummeted to the ground and clattered on to several discarded bottles in one of the overflowing refuse bins directly beneath the fire escape.

'What was that?' one of the men demanded.

Melissa's face was twisted in pain as the tip of the glowing cigarette seared into her flesh but she didn't dare move. The three men peered over the edge of the walkway as their colleague at the mouth of the alley played the beam of his torch over the bins. Suddenly a stray cat shot out from behind one and darted across the alley before it disappeared through a hole in the wall. The man laughed then switched off the torch.

The other three went down the fire escape then crossed to where he was standing. They spoke briefly then left him once more to his vigil. Melissa released one hand from the support and raked the cigarette butt out from under her sweatshirt. Then she eased her way along the underside of the walkway, climbed back over the railing and went the last few steps to the roof. Moving doubled over so as not to be seen from the road, she crossed to a door in the centre, made sure it was locked and slumped against the wall. Only then did she lift up the bottom edge of her sweatshirt and wince at the unsightly red weal on her skin. She looked at the illuminated dial on her watch. The INCD would be taking the room apart in an attempt to find some clue as to Lacamara's whereabouts. She had a feeling that she was going to be stuck on the roof for quite some time.

EIGHT

'What the fuck happened tonight?'

'The DEA got the drop on us,' Doyle said, his head bowed as he stood uncomfortably in front of Juan and Ramón Salcido, who were seated on two wooden chairs in the centre of the Workshop. The brothers had called the meeting when they had heard about the DEA-INCD raid on the hotel in Tepotzotlán earlier that evening.

'That's not good enough,' Ramón continued angrily, his face flushed with rage. 'What if the DEA had found Lacamara tonight and offered him immunity from prosecution in return for testifying against us? Where would that have left us?'

Doyle said nothing. He knew there was nothing he could say.

'What's more, we knew nothing about this until after the raid had already taken place,' Juan said bitterly. 'What kind of informers have you got working for you, Doyle? I was under the impression that we paid our sources better than any of the other cartels in Mexico. That's why we're supposed to have only the best on our payroll. And we pay them far more than the DEA can ever hope to pay their sources. So why did the DEA get the tip-off ahead of us? I want answers. And, if necessary, see to it that heads roll after tonight's fiasco. Nobody is indispensable to this organization.' He levelled a finger at Doyle. 'Lacamara's on the run again. That makes him vulnerable. And that can lead to mistakes. If he makes one, I want to be the first to know about it. Is that clear?'

'Perfectly,' Doyle replied.

'Then see to it,' Ramón said, gesturing at the door. He waited until Doyle had left the room then got up and gazed down at his brother. 'It looks like your man slipped up badly tonight.'

'*My* man?' Juan shot back.

'He's always been your man, and you know it.'

'He works for the cartel.'

'He works for you,' Ramón said. 'It doesn't bother me whether he likes me or not as long as he does his job properly. But he didn't tonight, did he? He hires the informers. So the buck stops with him when they fuck up. Agreed?'

'Agreed. And you can be sure that he'll find out what went wrong and deal with it accordingly.'

'As long as he doesn't let anything go wrong on Sunday too because if he doesn't get that disk—'

'Nothing's going to go wrong on Sunday,' Juan interrupted.

'Assuming that his sources don't screw up again. We might not be so lucky the next time. If Lacamara were ever to talk to the DEA, we could forget about the deal with Melissa Wade. We'd both be in jail.'

'Doyle won't let it happen again,' Juan insisted.

'I hope not. But to be on the safe side, I've already been in touch with one of my own sources. Someone Lacamara may turn to after what happened at the hotel tonight. And if he does, he'll be walking straight into a trap.'

'Who is this source?' Juan asked.

'That's my business.'

'*What?*'

'He works exclusively for me. Not the cartel. Now, if you'll excuse me, I'd better get back to the house in case they've tried to contact me while I've been here. If so, I'll call you. If not, we'll speak in the morning. Good night.'

*   *   *

'And I thought I was the only person you knew in Mexico.'

Justine Collins jumped and looked round. She put her hand to her heart. 'Felix, you scared the life out of me. How long have you been standing there?'

'I've just got here,' Felix Amador replied, kissing her cheek lightly. 'I'm sorry I'm late. So who were you talking to on the phone?'

'Ethan Byrne, my editor at the *Independent*. He told me to call him from the airport to let him know that I'd arrived safely. He's a bit concerned about me in my condition,' she said, patting her belly.

'And rightly so,' Amador replied. Then his face broke into a wide grin. 'So who's the lucky father? It's not that guy Rick you were dating the last time I saw you in New York?'

'Rick and I split up ages ago. As for the lucky father, he was out the door the moment I told him I was pregnant. Didn't want anything to do with the baby.'

'I'm sorry, Justine,' Amador said softly.

'I'm not. Good riddance, as far as I'm concerned. My baby and I will be just fine without him.'

'Somehow I can believe that,' Amador said, then retrieved her suitcase as she was about to pick it up. 'I'll carry that.'

'I can manage, you know,' she said, but she smiled. She cast an appraising look over him as they walked towards the exit. She didn't know his exact age but he was probably a couple of years older than her. He hadn't changed much since she had last seen him: he was still the dashing Lothario with his swarthy good looks and thick black hair that fell to his muscular shoulders. She had been one of the few women on the staff who had been more interested in his personality than his looks. But that had only been because she had been going steady at the time. Had she been single . . . well, things might have been different. She realized that he had seen her studying him and she flushed but he just grinned – he was used to it. There was a moment of uneasy silence then she asked, 'Are you sure you don't mind me staying at your place? I don't want to put you out.'

'How many times do I have to tell you? You're not putting me out. I invited you, didn't I? I could just as easily have booked you into a hotel. Now I don't want to hear another word about it. OK?'

'OK,' she replied.

They walked to where his car was parked and he put her cases in the trunk. 'I think you should ask me why I was late meeting you here tonight,' he said, opening the passenger door for her.

She gave him a quizzical look. 'So why *were* you late meeting me tonight?'

'Because I got a phone call just as I was about to leave the house. From Mexico's most wanted fugitive. Hector Lacamara.'

'You're joking! Why?'

'Because after I spoke to you this morning I put the word out on the street that I was prepared to help Lacamara and his mistress get out of the country, in return for an exclusive on the Salcido cartel. Earlier tonight the INCD raided a hotel where he and his mistress had been lying low since they fled from the airport yesterday. He's running scared now. He doesn't trust the DEA or the INCD. He says the cartel's infiltrated both organizations and that he'd be killed if he turned himself over to them. And with the cartel's hired guns breathing down his neck, he knows he's fast running out of options. I'm his last chance. It's ironic, really. Over the years I've written some of the most damaging exposés on the drug cartels in this country and now the paymaster of the biggest has turned to me for help.'

'So when do we meet him?' Justine asked, after Amador had got into the car beside her.

'*We?*' Amador asked, his hand hovering over the ignition key.

'Yes. We're working on this together. We agreed that. And I want to be in on any meeting you have with Lacamara.'

'He may not go for it.'

'Then convince him,' she replied. 'If you think for one minute that I've come out here just to sit around while you do the work, then you'd better think again.'

'You know you'll be credited as the co-author of any articles we write up together.'

'I don't want your charity, dammit!' Justine snapped fiercely.

'And how's your Spanish?' Amador asked, with a hint of sarcasm in his voice. 'I don't know if he speaks any English.'

'Then you can translate for both of us, can't you?'

Amador banged the steering wheel in frustration. 'It's like talking to a brick wall with you, Justine.'

'I'm not sure whether to take that as a compliment or not,' she replied, with a chuckle to diffuse the sudden tension between them. 'Have you got a plan to get Lacamara out of the country?'

'No, not yet,' Amador replied, more equably. 'I'll have to speak to him first.'

'That's where I could help. You'd have to arrange an escape route from inside the country. And if the Salcidos were to hear even the faintest whisper of what was being planned, they could intercept Lacamara before you had a chance to smuggle him out.'

'So where would you come in?' Amador asked.

'I'll contact my editor and get him to arrange everything from his side. And his only contact out here will be me. There's less chance of the Salcidos finding anything out that way. So, what do you say?'

'I guess it makes sense,' Amador conceded grudgingly. 'But I still don't know whether Lacamara will agree to see you as well. When I talked to him earlier, he insisted that I was alone. He said he'd call me later tonight to set it up.'

'Then what are we waiting for? He could be trying to ring you as we speak,' she said. 'C'mon, Felix. Let's go.'

'You know, the onset of motherhood hasn't mellowed you one little bit,' Amador said, with a weary half-smile as he started up the car. 'You're still as infuriating as ever.'

'Now that I *will* take as a compliment,' she replied.

He cast a despairing glance at her, then swung the car out of the parking space and headed towards the exit ramp.

The noise startled her. A shrill, pulsating sound, which seemed to emanate from under the magazines scattered across the coffee table. Laura moved the magazines, found a black clip-on beeper that had been concealed beneath them and deactivated it. Who was paging Mel? And why? She knew her best bet would be to call her sister and find out. It meant another trip to the pay phone at the bottom of the road but what choice did she have? It could be something important. Grabbing the car keys, she left the house and drove to the end of the street. She rang the number. There was no reply. Either Mel had left her phone behind when she had gone to Tepotztlán, or she had switched it off once she got there.

Laura drove back to the house. As she opened the front door she heard the beeper again. Hurrying through to the lounge, she switched it off. Whoever was trying to get in touch with Mel must want to speak to her urgently. What if it was an emergency? She knew she had to do something. Her only other option was to call Tom Kellerman. She rang his secure line at the embassy, even though she doubted that he would be back yet from Tepotztlán. She let it ring for some time and was about to hang up when it was answered.

'Tom?' she queried.

'Yes.'

'It's Laura.'

'Hey! I heard the phone ringing from the corridor. I ran to answer it. That's why I sound out of breath.'

'Did you get Lacamara?'

'No, he wasn't there. We've thrown a cordon around the hotel where he was staying in case he returns but I don't hold out much hope. So, what's up?'

Laura told him about the beeper.

'Shit!'

'Tom, what is it?' she demanded.

'Only one person uses that beeper. Doyle. He told Melissa to get it so that he could contact her in an emergency. The only time he ever used it before was when he was really pissed with her about something – usually if one of their drug shipments was intercepted by the DEA. He expected her to tip him off about everything.'

'Including the whereabouts of Lacamara,' Laura concluded.

'Yeah. It's my guess that he'll have been carpeted by the Salcidos because we almost got our hands on Lacamara tonight. And they wouldn't have known anything about it until we'd already hit the hotel. He's going to want to know why he wasn't tipped off in advance so that he could have got to Lacamara first.' Kellerman pondered. 'Frankly, I don't see any way out of this. You're going to have to meet Doyle, if only to clear the air.'

'Forget it!' Laura was horrified.

'It's the only way,' Kellerman told her.

'But I'd never be able to pull it off!'

'You fooled Bill Walker at the embassy,' he reminded her.

'That was Walker.' She snorted contemptuously. 'Anyone could pull the wool over his eyes.'

Kellerman chortled. 'There you go. You sound just like Melissa.'

'Oh, no, you're not going to get round me that easily.'

'It's best if I drive out to the house. We'll talk more when I get there.'

'You can talk all you like. I'm not doing it, Tom. End of story.'

'I can't believe you talked me into doing this.'

'I didn't,' Kellerman replied. 'You wouldn't be going through with it unless you felt comfortable posing as Melissa. And I wouldn't have blamed you if you'd decided not to.'

'Now you tell me,' she said. 'So what do I do first? Call Doyle?'

Kellerman nodded, then wrote down a number on the pad beside the telephone. 'That's the number of Doyle's cellular phone. He carries it everywhere with him.' He put a hand on her arm as she was about to reach for the telephone. 'Remember, Melissa despised him with a passion. And she never made any secret of that or of the fact that she was only in it for the money. So don't show any deference to him. He'll almost certainly want to meet you. Agree, but make sure it's on your terms.'

'And you say that Mel always called him Doyle?'

'On her good days,' Kellerman replied, with a grin.

Laura dialled the number then watched Kellerman slip on a pair of headphones to monitor the call. It rang a couple of times before it was answered. 'It's Melissa Wade,' she said abruptly. 'What do you want?'

'Nice of you to call,' Doyle said sarcastically.

'I don't have time for this, Doyle. What do you want?'

Kellerman gave her a thumbs-up.

'We need to meet,' Doyle told her.

'When?'

'Tomorrow morning. Early.'

Laura glanced at Kellerman. He shook his head and scribbled 'tonight' on the pad. 'I'm out of town tomorrow,' Laura said. 'It'll have to be tonight.'

'Tonight's difficult—'

'It's tonight or not at all,' she cut in quickly.

'OK,' Doyle retorted irritably. 'An hour. The usual place.'

The line went dead.

Kellerman removed the headphones. 'That was perfect.'

She held out her hands. They were trembling. 'And that was only on the phone. How am I going to pull this off when I come face to face with him?'

'You can do it,' Kellerman told her.

She looked less than convinced. 'I take it you know where "the usual place" is?'

'It's a bar about a mile from here.'

'A bar?' Laura exclaimed in horror.

'You're not going there to socialize. And if he offers you a drink, tell him where to go. That's what Melissa would have done.'

'Mel had that knack, especially with men. I don't.'

'You're going to be fine,' Kellerman said. Suddenly he reached out and took her hands in his. 'I'd never let anything happen to you, Laura, I swear it. You'll be wired up so I'll be able to hear everything from the car. If you get into any trouble, I'll be in there fast. If necessary, I'd take Doyle out without a moment's hesitation. And to hell with Operation Checkmate.'

'Thanks,' she said softly, then eased away her hands.

'But that's not going to be necessary because I know you'll do it without a hitch. I'd stake my career on that.'

'I could sure do with a shot of Dutch courage right now,' Laura said.

'Then what?' Kellerman asked, as he parked the car within sight of the bar.

'Then I'd probably have another. And another. And before I knew it, all the hard work I'd put into drying out over the last couple of years would have been in vain. But don't worry, that's not going to happen.'

'Doyle's already here. That's his white Mercedes in front of the bar. He's obsessively punctual. I guess it's a throwback to his years in the military. But don't worry, Melissa always kept him waiting. I think she got a real kick out of irritating him.'

'Mel got a real kick out of irritating most people,' Laura said.

'Say something to check whether the wire's working,' Kellerman said, then put on the headphones.

'Something to check whether the wire's working,' she replied.

'Very funny,' he said, pushing the headphones down around his neck. 'It's fine. Well, you'd better go in.'

'What happens when it's time to leave? I can hardly come back here. He'd see you.'

'He doesn't stand on ceremony. He'll say his piece then leave. He's not going to wait around for you.' Kellerman saw the uncertainty in her eyes. 'Like I said to you on the way here, play it by ear once you get inside. If you're not sure of an answer, don't give one. And let him do most of the talking.'

Laura took a deep breath. 'Go on then, wish me luck.'

'Go give 'em hell.'

She got out of the car and walked slowly towards the bar. *Just what the hell are you getting yourself into here?* This question had been plaguing her ever since she had agreed to meet Doyle. But Tom hadn't talked her into it. She could have said no. But she had to remain in character until Sunday. Then they would have the diamonds and it would be over. That had been her motivation. Selfish greed. And this recognition gave her renewed confidence.

She paused outside the bar, eyed it with distaste and was reaching for the door when it was flung open and a drunk stumbled out into the street. He stopped in front of her and stretched out a hand towards her. She shoved him away from her in disgust, and wiped her hand down the front of her T-shirt. Then she pushed open the door.

She was met with an overpowering stench of sweat and urine. No sooner had she stepped into the smoke-filled room than a hand squeezed her bottom. She swung round furiously, gave the culprit a mouthful in her choicest Spanish and forced her way through the drinkers towards the bar.

She saw Doyle sitting at a table at the far end of the room. Although all the other tables were full, there were three empty chairs at his table and no one was standing within ten feet of him. Whether this was out of respect or fear, she didn't know. When he noticed her he kicked out the chair opposite him.

'You're late . . . again,' he hissed as she sat down.

'What d'you want?' she demanded.

'Your usual, I believe,' Doyle said, pushing aside his bottle of beer to reveal a glass of bourbon. He pushed it across to her.

Her mind was racing. She couldn't drink it – even though she knew it would do wonders to ease her frayed nerves. But what to do? *Remain in character*, she reminded herself. What would Mel do in that situation? She despised the man. She wouldn't drink with him. So why had Doyle got her the drink? Did he always buy her a drink when they met at the bar? It didn't matter, she wasn't going to drink it. And that was final.

She pushed the glass back across the table and said defiantly, 'I didn't come here to shoot the breeze with you.'

Doyle dashed the glass against the wall. For a moment an eerie silence descended over the bar as all eyes turned towards them. He looked around coldly. 'Is there a problem?' he asked. The faces turned away and within seconds the noise level rose again. His eyes were focused now on Laura's face. 'The DEA got a tip-off about Lacamara tonight, didn't they? Why the fuck wasn't I told about it? That's what you're paid for.'

'Because I didn't know about it,' Laura replied. It was the answer Kellerman had told her to use. 'I wasn't on duty tonight. Walker was. He must have called the INCD. I only heard about it later.'

'What did they find in Lacamara's room?'

'As far as I know, nothing to indicate his present whereabouts.'

'*As far as I know* isn't good enough,' Doyle snarled. 'I want to know exactly what they found.'

'I'll make some enquiries,' she replied coldly.

'You do that, Agent Wade. Because if the DEA get to Lacamara, he'll take you down as quickly as he will the rest of us. So you see, it's as much in your interest as it is in ours to make sure we find him first.'

'I'd worked that one out for myself.'

'I also want to know who gave Walker the tip-off tonight.'

'Why? So you can kill him?'

'Just get me the name. And do it quickly. You'll be well paid for the information.' Doyle took a mouthful of beer then slammed the bottle down on the table. 'And it goes without saying that you'll call me the moment you hear anything about Lacamara. I don't care how insubstantial it is. Call me.'

'If I hear anything, you'll be the first to know,' Laura said.

Doyle got to his feet and walked out of the bar. Only then did she look down at her hands. They were steady. But, then, that didn't surprise her. Her instant dislike of Doyle had pushed aside any lingering fears she'd had when she first saw him.

She left the bar. The white Mercedes was gone. She walked back to Kellerman's car. He pushed open the passenger door for her. 'Well, how did I do?' she asked, getting in beside him.

'You handled it like a professional,' he replied.

'What about the information he wants from me?'

'I can easily get a list of everything the INCD found in Lacamara's room. There was nothing of interest in it anyway. As for the CI who tipped off Bill Walker, we'll play along and give him a name . . . We'll give him one of his own informers. That'll shake him.'

'Won't Doyle kill him?'

'What do you think?'

'But the informer's innocent,' Laura said.

'In this case, yes. But we know that the man whose name we're going to give him has been responsible for the deaths of several local narcotics agents. We've been looking for a way to take him out of circulation for some time now. This is the perfect opportunity.' Kellerman shot her a sidelong look and saw the look of disgust on her face. 'Welcome to the front line, Laura. No prisoner taken by either side.'

She shuddered then folded her arms tightly across her chest. Kellerman was silent for the rest of the journey back to the house.

'Hello?' Amador said, answering the telephone after the first ring.

'It's Lacamara.'

Amador looked at his watch. 'It's nearly midnight. I was expecting you to call a lot earlier than this.'

'Be at the entrance to the National Anthropology Museum in two hours' time. You'll be picked up from there.'

'I won't be alone,' Amador said, his eyes flicking across to Justine, who was sitting in the armchair opposite him. She stared intently at him, not understanding a word he was saying in Spanish.

'Then the deal's off!'

'Wait, wait,' Amador shouted into the mouthpiece. 'She's an American journalist. Her name's Justine Collins. I can vouch for her. She works for the *New York Independent*. Her editor's already agreed to arrange safe passage for you and Ms Lopez to a destination of your choice. It makes more sense than arranging it from this end. But first you'll need to show some goodwill. He's in it for a story, just like I am. I'm sure you can appreciate that.'

'When I bailed out, I took enough proof with me to put away some of the country's most influential politicians, judges and law-enforcement officers. I personally opened accounts for them in the Caribbean on behalf of the Salcidos. I'm not going to give you all the names – at least, not until Carmen and I are safe. But I'm prepared to let you have a sample up front, just enough to whet your appetite. Will that be enough *goodwill* for you?'

'As long as it can be verified,' Amador replied.

'That's your problem. But I'm sure you'll find a way.'

'I'm sure I will,' Amador said. 'We'll be waiting on the Paseo de la Reforma, outside the National Anthropology Museum, in two hours' time.'

'As an added precaution, a taxi will pick you up and take you on to another destination where Carmen will be waiting for you. If she's satisfied that you haven't been followed, she'll bring you to me.' The line went dead.

'Well?' Justine asked, when Amador replaced the handset.

'It's on. Two o'clock tomorrow morning.'

'Excellent. You know, I've got a good feeling about this.'

'Me, too,' Amador said, with a thoughtful smile. 'A real good feeling . . .'

NINE

'Where's the taxi?' Justine asked. 'It's already gone two o'clock.'

Amador didn't answer. He was constantly glancing around him, every shadow a potential threat. In the past few years he had written several articles for both local and international publications on the growing problem of crime. How ironic if he ended up as just another statistic on a police chart. He pushed the macabre thought from his mind. Something clattered to the ground behind him and he swung round to see a security guard pick up his nightstick, which he had dropped as he was crossing the spacious entrance plaza in front of the museum's illuminated façade. Amador cursed himself for being so edgy. But he felt vulnerable standing on the sidewalk at that time of night. Admittedly, the Paseo de la Reforma was one of the main roads in Mexico City, and it carried a steady flow of traffic throughout the night.

'Are you OK?' Justine asked, putting a hand lightly on his arm.

He grinned at her sheepishly. 'I'm sorry. It's just that I know this city. And standing around here at two o'clock in the morning wouldn't be recommended in any travel guide.'

'It looks like a taxi's going to stop,' she said.

The green and white Datsun pulled up and the driver bent his head to look through the open passenger window. 'Amador?' he asked, without appearing to address either of them.

'Yes,' Amador told him.

'I was told to pick you up from here,' the driver said, then jabbed his thumb over his shoulder. 'Get in.'

Amador held open the back door for Justine then climbed in after her. 'I hope you know where you're taking us,' he said to the driver, after he had closed the door.

The driver eyed him in the rear-view mirror then nodded. 'I was told you wouldn't know where you were going. I think you're going to be surprised when we get there.'

'So where exactly are we going?' Amador asked, as the driver pulled away from the kerb.

'Sorry, I can't tell you that,' the driver replied, with an apologetic smile. 'But it's been paid for already. With a handsome tip. All you have to do is sit back and enjoy the ride.'

'Here we are,' the driver said, pulling up at their destination.

'But we're back where we started,' Amador said in bewilderment, peering out at the National Anthropology Museum.

'I told you you'd be surprised,' the driver said. 'My instructions were to drive you around for fifteen minutes then bring you back to the museum. I've had some weird rides in my time but this has got to be the craziest yet. But who am I to complain? I was well paid to do it.'

Amador got out of the car and Justine followed. The taxi drove off.

'To make sure we weren't being tailed,' Amador said.

'I don't care if we're driven around in circles all night, just as long as we get a story at the end of it.' A white GM Cutlass slowed to a halt beside them. 'Looks like we've got company.'

The passenger window slid down. 'Get in,' a female voice ordered from behind the wheel. 'Hector's waiting for you.'

They got into the back and the driver looked round at Amador. 'My name's Carmen Lopez.'

She was in her early twenties with long black hair that framed a thin, angular face and there were dark sacs under her dull, expressionless eyes. Amador found himself wondering why Lacamara had risked so much for a woman like her. But he knew he was being unfair. Looks weren't everything.

'Does she speak Spanish?' The voice was as lifeless as the eyes.

'No,' Amador replied. 'Do you speak English?'

She shook her head.

'How did you know that the taxi wasn't being followed?' Amador asked.

'Because I was tailing it myself,' she replied. 'I have nothing more to say to either of you so I'd appreciate it if you didn't speak to me again.'

Then the car began to move.

Ten minutes later, after doubling back twice on to the Paseo de la Reforma, she turned the car into an unlit alley less than a mile from the museum. The headlights illuminated a row of metal bins against the wall and as she brought the car to a standstill a figure stepped out from behind one and strode briskly towards the passenger side. He was in his late forties with silver-grey hair, dressed in a pair of scruffy jeans and a V-necked sweater, unshaven, and carrying a black attaché case. The man got in beside her and she drove to the other end of the alley before pulling out into the street.

The man turned round in the passenger seat. 'I'm Hector Lacamara. I'm sorry about all this cloak-and-dagger stuff,' he said in faultless English, his eyes moving between the two figures seated in the back. 'It's just that after what happened earlier tonight, we have to be extra vigilant.'

'I didn't know you spoke English,' Amador said.

'I've travelled all round the world, laundering money for the cartel. English is the international language.' His eyes settled on Justine. 'You must be the American reporter.'

'Justine Collins, *New York Independent*,' she said.

'From what I'm told, it's a quality broadsheet,' Lacamara replied.

'We like to think so,' she replied. 'There's one question I have to ask you before we go any further.'

'You want to know why I've done this?' Lacamara said.

'Yes,' Justine replied.

'The truth is I've been thinking about getting out for the last couple of years now. You can't begin to imagine the pressure that comes with this kind of job. Everything has to be done in secret. You have to lie to your wife. Lie to your children. Lie to your friends. And you're always having to think about what you're going to say in case it incriminates you or one of the cartel's clients. In the end I felt like a machine. I couldn't be spontaneous any more. Then I met Carmen. My marriage was over by then anyway. Not that you could blame my wife. I wasn't a husband to her. She didn't know me any more. I was little more than a stranger living in her house. Carmen helped me realize that it was time to get out.'

'And you took fifty million dollars from the cartel before you left?' Amador said.

'It's closer to forty-seven million actually,' Lacamara corrected him. 'Not all in one lump sum, though. I've been skimming it off over the past twelve months. It was easy for me to cover my tracks with the amount of money in the cartel's accounts in the Caribbean and in the Far East. My partner had no idea what was happening. I heard that he went missing within hours of my own disappearance. Doyle will have had him tortured to find out if he knew anything. Then he'll have been killed.'

'You don't sound particularly bothered about that,' Justine said.

'You're wrong, Ms Collins. I liked Oscar. He was a brilliant accountant – better than me in many ways. But strangely naïve about life. I could never have confided in him. He just wouldn't have understood.'

'What about your family? Aren't you bothered about what might happen to them in retribution for what you did to the cartel?' Justine asked.

'My family will be perfectly safe, Ms Collins,' Lacamara told her, a hint of annoyance in his voice.

'You seem very sure of that,' she said.

'Juan Salcido is a man of honour. If someone crosses him, he goes after that person. Not their family. He only ever punishes those he believes are guilty. My wife and children have done nothing to him.'

'After you and Ms Lopez were recognized at the airport did you go straight to the Palacio Hotel in Tepotzotlán?' Amador asked after a moment's silence.

'We hadn't planned it. The fact that we drove north was irrelevant at the time. We knew that we had to get out of the city to give ourselves some time to rethink our strategy. Carmen saw the sign for the Palacio when we were driving through Tepotzotlán. The place was a real dive. Perfect to hide out for a day or so.'

'So where were you when the authorities raided the hotel earlier tonight?' Amador asked.

'We were out walking,' Lacamara replied, placing a hand lightly on Carmen's shoulder. 'We'd only left the hotel about ten minutes before they arrived. All we have now is this hired car and the clothes we're wearing.'

'And the attaché case,' Amador added.

'It hasn't been out of my sight since I left the office yesterday afternoon. There's enough evidence in there to send the Salcidos to jail for life.' Lacamara turned to Justine. 'As I said to Amador on the phone, I'm prepared to give you a few names up front, together with details of their accounts which I set up in the Caribbean. I've also got a number of incriminating photos of Doyle handing over cash to a senior member of the DEA at a number of different locations in the city. She's been passing on inside information to him for some time now. The photos were taken as an insurance policy in case she ever tried to back out of the deal. She's very important to the cartel. And they pay her well for her services.'

'Her name wouldn't be Melissa Wade, would it?' Justine asked.

A look of surprise flashed across Lacamara's face. 'How did you know?'

'An educated guess, that's all,' she replied.

Amador smiled faintly at her. There was a look of approval in his eyes. She had done her homework. She had come a long way from the naïve tabloid journalist he remembered from his days in New York. He had a feeling they would make a good team . . .

'How long will it take for you to verify the documents?' Lacamara asked Amador.

'I've got a couple of well-placed – and discreet – sources in the financial sector,' Amador replied. 'I'll contact them as soon as they open for business later this morning.'

Lacamara opened the attaché case and handed a folder to him. 'I think they'll find all the relevant information in there. I'll contact you at eleven tomorrow morning. Then every hour after that.'

'And in the meantime you're just going to drive around the city?' Justine said.

'That's really not your concern,' Lacamara told her. 'You just make sure that your editor keeps to his side of the bargain. Because without me you have no story.'

'He will,' Justine assured him.

Lacamara touched Carmen's arm and motioned her to pull over to the side of the road. 'We've brought you back to the Paseo de la Reforma. I'm sure you'll be able to find your way home from here.'

'I'll be expecting your call at eleven,' Amador said, then got out of the car.

Justine climbed out after him. The car drove off as soon as she had closed the door. Amador watched it until it had disappeared then flagged down an approaching taxi.

*   *   *

'Tom, it's Don Childs,' a voice announced, when Kellerman answered the phone moments after arriving at his office. Childs was the embassy's head of security. 'We've got a problem. Or, more to the point, you have.'

Kellerman sank back into his chair and rubbed his thumb and forefinger over his bloodshot eyes. He had had hardly any sleep the previous night. And it showed. 'Go on.' He sighed.

'Ever heard of an American journalist called Justine Collins?'

'Can't say I have. Why?'

'I've got her sitting in the main foyer. She wants to speak to Special Agent Wade. I've tried telling her that we don't have anyone by that name working here but she's not buying it. Not for one minute. She claims to have some photos that will be of interest to Special Agent Wade.'

'Did she show them to you?' Kellerman asked.

'She says she'll only show them to Special Agent Wade. And if she doesn't get to see her, she says she'll publish them anyway. And this is the bit I don't like. She claims that the photos would destroy Special Agent Wade's career in a heartbeat.'

'This is a great fucking start to my day,' Kellerman snapped. 'As if I don't already have enough to worry about.'

There was a pause at the other end of the line then, 'What do you want me to do about her?'

'You mean short of telling her to publish and be damned?' Kellerman tried to contain his rising anger. 'I'll have to come up and have a word with her. What else can I do?'

'I'll tell her you're on your way.'

Kellerman resisted the temptation to slam down the receiver. But his frustration was tempered by a feeling of unease. A journalist with photos that would have been of special interest to Melissa? Photos that could have destroyed her career? Melissa had never done anything illegal that could have backfired on her – at least not to the best of his knowledge. Which only left one alternative. They were photos of her meeting Doyle. But how could an American journalist have got hold of such incriminating evidence? And who had taken the photos? It was with a sense of trepidation that he made his way up to the main foyer. Childs pointed out Justine Collins to him.

'Ms Collins?' he asked, flashing his best smile at her.

'Who are you?' she demanded. 'I want to speak to Melissa Wade.'

'My name's Tom Kellerman. I'm the DEA's country attaché in Mexico.'

'What does that mean? That you're the head honcho around here?'

'I guess that's one way of putting it,' Kellerman replied, then gestured to the chair she had just vacated. 'Why don't we sit down and talk?'

'The only person I want to talk to is Melissa Wade,' she replied.

'I'm afraid that's not going to be possible.'

'I hope you're not going to insult me by reeling off the same tired line that your security chief gave me – "We don't have anyone by that name working here at the embassy."'

'That's standard procedure at any American embassy, Ms Collins. He was only doing his job.'

'So why can't I speak to her?'

'Because she's on assignment.'

'Can you get in touch with her?' Justine asked.

'In these kind of situations we keep phone silence from this end. She calls me when she has any new developments to report.'

'And, of course, you've got no idea when she'll ring you next?' Justine said, sarcasm in her voice.

'I'm afraid not,' Kellerman said, with an apologetic shrug. 'The chief security officer said that you had some photographs to show her. Perhaps I could be of some assistance?'

'As I told him, I'll only show them to Melissa Wade.'

'As you wish. If she does ring, I'll tell her that you called. Do you have a number where you can be reached?'

Justine took a notepad from her purse, wrote on it, then tore off the top sheet of paper and handed it to Kellerman. 'That's my cellular phone. And to be honest, Mr Kellerman, I don't buy any of this about you not being able to contact her. So you can tell her from me that she has until five o'clock this afternoon to make up her mind whether she wants to see me or not. If not, the *New York Independent* will publish the photos in the next couple of days. But naturally I'd prefer to give her the chance to put across her side of the story first. It's her choice.'

'I have to say I'm intrigued by these photos you claim to have—'

'Oh, I have them all right,' she cut in.

'And you say they could destroy her career?'

'Tell her to call me – before five,' she replied, then walked towards the main doors.

Kellerman crossed to where Childs was standing. 'I want her followed. Find out where she's staying. But that's all. My people will take it from there.'

'I'll get on to it right away.'

Kellerman returned to his basement office and dialled Melissa's house in San Angel. When Laura answered he said, 'Hi, it's Tom. We've got a problem. And we're going to need your help to straighten it out. I'm coming over to the house to brief you.'

'Not again.' She groaned.

'I'll be there in about half an hour,' he said.

'I only agreed to this on the understanding that all I'd have to do was meet Doyle on Sunday and give him a computer disk,' Laura said. 'Short and sweet. No risks, you said in New York. Only last night I had to meet with Doyle in some god-awful bar and now you want me to confront Justine Collins over these photographs. I know her, for God's sake. She was one of Raquel's regular patients. I even gave her a filling once when Raquel was away on vacation.'

'I know it's asking a lot, especially after last night, but if the photos are of Melissa meeting Doyle and they were published before Sunday, the cartel would call off the deal. There's no question of that. You have to convince her to hold back on publication – at least until after the weekend.'

'And how exactly am I supposed to do that?' Laura asked.

'Tell her you're flying back to New York early next week and that you'd be prepared to give her an exclusive interview then. But not before Wednesday. Give her some spiel about having to be debriefed first.'

'Only there won't be an interview because by Wednesday the DEA will have already released a press statement saying that Mel was . . .' Laura's voice tailed off as she turned away from Kellerman and put her hand over her face. *Be natural*, she told herself, *and don't overdo it.*

'Laura, are you OK?' he asked.

'I'm all right,' she said, studying his reflection in the window. 'I promised myself that I wouldn't cry any more. And I won't.'

Kellerman had been tempted to comfort her. It had been an instinctive – and impulsive – reaction. Now he was glad he hadn't. She wouldn't have thanked him for it. If anything, it could have made matters worse. For, in her own way, Laura was every bit as independent as Melissa.

'What if Justine doesn't buy it?' Laura went on.

'She's a journalist out for a story,' he replied. 'And you're offering her that story – if she agrees to wait an extra few days. Sure she could still go ahead and publish the photos but they'd carry a lot more punch if they had a lead story to accompany them. I think you'll find that she'll hold back until next week. It has to be worth her while.'

'She's bound to be suspicious when I fob her off.'

'Of course she will. But I don't see that she'll have much choice if she wants the story. And you have to convince her of that.'

'Easier said than done,' she muttered.

'You fooled Bill Walker into believing you were Melissa and Justine Collins never knew Melissa. I don't think you'll have any problem pulling it off.'

'So how do I set up the meeting?' she asked.

Kellerman took the sheet of paper from his pocket that Justine Collins had given to him and handed it to Laura. 'That's the number of her cellular phone. Call her now. The sooner we get this over with, the better.'

Laura picked up the phone, took a deep breath, then dialled the number.

Felix Amador was quick to answer his cellular phone without taking his eyes off the road as he drove through Centro, the nerve centre of the financial district in the heart of Mexico City. He listened, with mounting disbelief, as Justine told him about her morning, from her visit to the American embassy to the phone call she had received a few minutes earlier from Laura to set up a meeting at two o'clock that afternoon.

'What in God's name possessed you to go to the embassy?' he said, when she had finished.

'What are you so pissed about?' she retorted. 'Those photos are dynamite. And now I've got—'

'The DEA on your ass!' Amador roared. 'You'll have been tailed from the embassy and you'll have led them straight to my house. And *don't* look out the window!'

'I wasn't going to.'

'Now they'll know we're working together. And their sources will have already told them that I put out the word that I was prepared to help Lacamara skip the country in return for a story. Which means that they'll put Lacamara and the photos together pretty damn quickly.'

'Kellerman never saw the photos.'

'It doesn't matter. Kellerman's no fool. He'll have guessed what's in them.' Amador hit the horn when a taxi cut in front

132

of him then braked sharply for the lights. 'Why didn't you tell me what you were planning before I left the house this morning? You've put us in a real awkward situation now.'

'I want that story, Felix, and I'll do anything to get it,' Justine replied defiantly. 'Back home, the exposure of a corrupt DEA agent would be a far bigger scoop than some story about a Mexican accountant who's embezzled money from a drug cartel. And with her looks, it's guaranteed to hit the front page of every newspaper across the country. And that's what I'm after, Felix. Front-page recognition.'

'So Lacamara's already yesterday's news as far as you're concerned?'

'Of course not. The paper's still going to get him and his girlfriend out of the country. And once he's safe, we'll run his story.'

'You won't see either of them again until they're safely out of the country.'

'What are you talking about? Ethan asked me to babysit them until they're ready to leave.'

'Forget it, Justine. Your little stunt this morning means that from now on you're going to have to wait in the wings until the show's over. And you've only got yourself to blame. As I said, the DEA – or more likely the INCD – will already have my house under surveillance. And you can be sure that, from now on, you'll have a chaperon wherever you go. I'm damned if I'm going to have you lead them straight to Lacamara. I've got a safe house lined up where they can lie low until it's time for them to leave the country. I'll have to stay there too now because I certainly can't go home if it's under surveillance.'

'It's my paper that's getting them away, in case you've forgotten,' Justine said indignantly.

'I haven't forgotten. And I'm more than willing to speak to your editor and explain the situation to him. I think you'll find that he'll agree with me. You handle the Melissa Wade story and let me worry about Lacamara. When they're safely out of

Mexico, it'll be safe for me to return to my house. But not before.'

'I take it you'll keep me up to date on what's going on?' she asked. He was right to have blocked her out, and she knew it. Damn her impulsiveness. But on the plus side, she still had the Melissa Wade story all to herself.

'Of course I'll keep you up to date, although I won't be specific about my movements. Not over an open line.'

'Have you spoken to your source yet about the documents?' she asked.

'I'm on my way to see him now,' Amador replied.

'Keep me posted.'

'Likewise,' Amador said, then severed the connection and tossed the phone back on to the passenger seat.

The twelve-storey block of flats on the outskirts of Coyoacán, an affluent suburb thirteen miles south of Centro, had been condemned after the big earthquake of 1985. And, as with so many condemned buildings across the city, money hadn't been available to demolish them and rebuild. Instead they had been propped up with girders and stanchions, which had rusted from years of neglect.

Amador had never liked using the basement car park underneath the flats as a meeting place. The previous year a slab of concrete had crashed to the ground only feet away from where he had been standing. But his protests had been in vain. The meetings would continue there. He negotiated the ramp and as he turned into the parking bay he saw the black BMW. He pulled up beside it and, after switching off the engine, took the folder from the back seat and got out. His eyes went instinctively to the hole in the roof – he could have sworn it was larger than the last time he had been down here. Tentatively he approached the BMW but it was impossible to see anything behind the opaque black windows. One slid open and a spotless white-gloved hand beckoned him forward. Amador got into the back of the air-conditioned car then closed the door to maintain the cool, refreshing temperature.

'You're late!'

'I'm sorry, Señor, but the traffic—'

'Spare me your excuses, Amador,' Ramón Salcido broke in angrily. 'I don't like to be kept waiting, particularly not by an informer.'

'It won't happen again.'

'Are those the documents Lacamara gave you last night?' Salcido asked, pointing to the folder in Amador's lap.

'Yes,' Amador replied, and handed it to him.

Salcido opened the folder and leafed through the contents: inside were copies of three computer files that only Lacamara could have accessed with his personal security code. They contained details of the dates, as well as the exact amount, of each bribe that had been paid to three individuals, two prominent Mexican politicians and a former police chief in Tijuana. Also included was a record of which brother had authorized payment. Salcido knew that there were dozens more just like them, which Lacamara had carefully hidden in the firm's computer before going on the run, each as incriminating as the next, and that there was no way of locating them without the access codes. Which meant that capturing Lacamara alive was more important than ever. He turned over the last sheet of paper then shot a quizzical glance at Amador. 'I thought you said there were photographs of Doyle meeting Melissa Wade.'

Amador shifted uncomfortably on the seat. 'Justine must have removed them from the folder earlier this morning. I had no idea that she was going to take them, though. That's why I didn't think to check the folder before I left the house. I just assumed they would be there.'

'What did she want with them?' Salcido demanded. Amador recounted his recent conversation with Justine over the phone. 'Is there no limit to your incompetence?' Salcido said furiously, when he had finished. 'Fortunately Wade has as much to lose as the cartel, were those photographs to be published. She's sure to try to stall Collins, at least until after the weekend. But that's only a short-term solution for us.'

'What's happening at the weekend?' Amador asked.

'That doesn't concern you. I want those photographs, Amador. And, believe me, I'll do everything in my power to get them. It would really be in your friend's best interests if *you* were to get them for me.'

'She's not going to give them to me. And if I took them she'd want to know why. What could I say?'

'Make something up. Isn't that what you journalists are good at? Just get those photographs and bring them to me before the weekend's out. Because if I haven't got them by Sunday afternoon at the latest, I'll have to send Peraya over to your house to get them for me. By force, if necessary. You wouldn't want me to do that, now would you?'

'That won't be necessary,' Amador replied nervously.

'I'm glad to hear it. Now, tell me, have you spoken to Lacamara since you met with him last night?'

'No, but he's due to call me later this morning. I said I'd have an answer for him by then.'

'When he calls tell him that your contact's verified the authenticity of the documents. Which means the deal's on. You'll then arrange to meet him and his whore and take them to the safe house. Peraya and several of my men will be waiting for you when you get there. Leave the rest to them.'

'What do I tell Justine?'

'Tell her that you were attacked once you got to the safe house. Peraya will hit you on the back of the head. The blow will be hard enough to knock you out. It'll leave a bruise to give credibility to your story.'

'I don't like it,' Amador said hesitantly.

'It's not open to debate.' Salcido removed a sealed envelope from the inside pocket of his jacket and held it out towards

Amador. 'That's a down payment. You'll get the balance when we've got Lacamara.'

Amador took the envelope and slipped it into his pocket. 'I'll contact you after I've heard from him.'

'See that you do. And remember, I want those photographs before Sunday afternoon. Don't make me send Peraya to get them.'

'You'll get them,' Amador replied, then got out of the car. He waited until the BMW had driven off then slit open the envelope with his finger and began to count the money.

TEN

The headquarters of Ramón Salcido's jewellery empire was a twelve-storey building with a shimmering mirror-glass façade, in the heart of the city. He took great delight in the irony that his own suite of luxury offices, which covered the entire twelfth floor, directly overlooked the Supreme Court of Justice.

He had barely sat down behind his desk, still clutching the messages he had collected from his personal secretary, when one of the phones on his desk rang. It was his secure line and he had already guessed who it was even before he picked up the receiver.

'It's Amador. I've just spoken to Lacamara.'

'And?'

'They've agreed to stay at the safe house tonight. I'm meeting them at four o'clock this afternoon.'

'Where?'

'Outside the National Anthropology Museum – the same place Lopez picked us up earlier this morning.'

Salcido swivelled round in his chair and looked out over the city skyline. 'How long will it take you to get to the safe house?'

'Given the traffic at that time of the afternoon, I'd say about thirty minutes.'

'I'll tell Peraya. He'll be waiting for you.' Salcido severed the connection.

*   *   *

As she entered the hotel Laura wasn't nervous about impersonating Mel – except that Justine might recognize her. She was wearing a wire underneath her baggy T-shirt so that Kellerman, who had driven her to the hotel and was now parked out of sight of the building, would be able to monitor their conversation. He needed to know how much information Justine already had about the photographs. He had told Laura that it was imperative she stall Justine until after the weekend, and if she was in any doubt about any question she was asked, either to feign ignorance or refuse to answer it. She was determined not to let him down. Or herself, for that matter. One slip, and the meeting with Doyle could be in jeopardy.

A porter directed her to the lobby bar and she paused in the entrance to look around her. She saw Justine sitting alone at a corner table. Her eyes lingered on her before she scanned the rest of the room. Mel had never met Justine so it was imperative that she didn't show any recognition in her eyes.

Justine got up and crossed to her. 'Melissa Wade?'

'That's right,' Laura replied.

'I'm Justine Collins. Please, won't you come and sit down? Would you like something to drink?'

'I prefer to choose who I drink with, Ms Collins,' Laura replied coldly. Again she found it easy to slip into Mel's character. Or was it just easier to slip out of her own? It was one way she could distance herself from Justine.

'As you wish,' Justine replied, and led the way back to the corner table. She shook her head at the barman when he looked at them, then she sat down and stared at Laura. 'It's uncanny. If I didn't know better, I'd swear you were Laura.'

Laura? she thought disdainfully to herself. It had always been Dr Wade before. Now suddenly we're on first-name terms. 'Why don't you just get to the point, Ms Collins?'

'Very well,' Justine replied, withdrew the photographs from her purse and slid them across the table to Laura.

Laura picked them up and looked at each one. 'Where did you get these from?'

'I'm afraid I can't tell you that.'

'I didn't think you would. It's not important. We've already got a pretty good idea who gave them to you.' Laura purposely let the sentence hang in the air, knowing that Justine was expecting her to tell her. She didn't. 'So what exactly do you want from me?'

'Your . . . side of the story,' Justine said, wrong-footed by the change in tactics.

'The exclusive confession of a corrupt DEA agent? Is that it? I never realized the *Independent* went in for that kind of tabloid sleaze.'

'I'd hardly call it sleaze, Ms Wade. You're on the take from a drug cartel. And that's a crime.'

'Don't believe everything you see,' Laura said, glancing down at the photographs in front of her.

'What are you saying? That it's a set-up?'

'I can't tell you that . . . at least, not yet. I'm due to fly back to the States early next week for a debriefing at DEA head-quarters in Washington. I can be in New York on Wednesday. Hold back on the photos until then, and I'll give you an exclusive interview. I can't say fairer than that.'

'And how do I know that you're not just stalling for time?'

'You don't,' Laura replied. 'But if you publish those photos without a credible story to accompany them, they're not going to have the same impact, are they? That's my offer, Ms Collins. Take it or leave it.'

'Very well. Shall we say eleven o'clock at the *Independent*?'

'Let's say twelve thirty at Aureole's. I hear their sea-scallop sandwiches are to die for. You can put it on your expense account.'

Justine smiled for the first time. 'OK. But if you don't show, these photos will be on the front page of the *Independent* on Thursday morning.'

'I'll be there,' Laura replied, then pushed the pictures across the table. 'I'd put those away if I were you. I'd hate for them to fall into the wrong hands.'

'They won't,' Justine said, slipping them back into her purse.

Laura got to her feet. 'Well, if you'll excuse me, I've got to get back to work.'

'Ms Wade?' Justine called out after her. 'Have you seen your sister recently?'

Laura looked round slowly, quick to mask her uncertainty behind a frown. 'I saw her when I was in New York earlier this week. Why d'you ask?'

'You do know that her partner, Dr Vasquez, is dead?'

'Yes, I heard. An accident.'

'Do you know that Laura has been missing since Dr Vasquez's body was found?' Justine said.

'Missing?' Laura said, with a quick laugh. 'You're obviously not looking in the right places for her. I've spoken to her twice on the phone since I got back to Mexico. She told me that she gave a statement to the police then went off to the country for a few days. She needs some time to herself. Raquel's death shook her up badly. Which is understandable, considering how close they were. But she'll be back at work next week.'

'Is there any way I can contact her before then?'

'No,' Laura replied. 'As I said, she needs some time on her own.'

'Then maybe I can talk to you both next Wednesday.'

'If you think your expense account is up to it.'

'I'm sure I can stretch it,' Justine replied.

Laura left the hotel and ducked into the adjoining alley, coming out at the back of the building where Kellerman was parked. She got in beside him. 'You did well,' he said, resting a hand lightly on her arm.

'She threw me at the end,' Laura replied. 'I thought you said the police had already issued a statement saying that they were satisfied I had nothing to do with Raquel's death.'

'They did,' Kellerman said, starting up the car.

'Then why did she want to speak to me?'

'To satisfy herself that you're not out here.'

'*What?*'

'Why else would she have come? It wasn't as if she could have known those photos even existed before yesterday. So in a way they've helped us. Now she's got a new angle to work on and she's not going to be so interested in you.'

'You don't think she suspects the truth, do you?' Laura asked.

'If she did, she'd have confronted you with it the moment you entered the hotel. No, she's just fishing about in the dark, hoping to get a bite. And that's fine with me. I bet it really choked her having to agree to hold back on the story until next Wednesday. She wanted an exclusive from you there and then. But she's a professional. She's not going to risk losing the chance of a major scoop just for the sake of a few extra days. And now that we know where she's staying, we can watch her every move. She won't be a problem to us, as long as we can keep tabs on her.'

'And Amador?'

'He'll already know that she went to the embassy this morning and that we'll have tailed her back to his house. That makes her a liability. You can be sure he won't go near her again until he's got Lacamara safely out of the country.'

'Assuming he's already been in contact with Lacamara,' Laura pointed out. 'You've still got no way of knowing that for sure.'

'He's made contact with Lacamara. I'd stake my career on that. How else do you think she got hold of the photos?' Kellerman started up the engine. 'Come on, let's get you home. I've still got a mound of paperwork waiting for me back at the embassy.'

'I'm sorry, none of this was meant to happen to you,' Melissa said, once Laura had explained the latest developments to her over the phone. 'First Doyle. Now this reporter. I just wish I'd been there to take some of the heat for you. But you did well, sis. I'm real proud of you.'

'I'm real proud of me too. I thought I handled Doyle pretty well, even if I say so myself. And, after him, Justine was a cinch. You know, I kind of enjoyed being you. It was a lot more exciting than being boring old me.'

'If I'm not careful, I'll be losing my own identity before long.' Melissa chuckled.

'You won't need to worry about that. I don't intend to make a habit of it. Especially not with Doyle. I was scared before I met him. I honestly didn't think I'd be able to pull it off. But once I'd got the measure of him, I just had to make sure I didn't falter. I can understand how his minions could easily be intimidated by him.'

'Believe me, they are. But they're not in a position to stand up to him. I am. And I've never had any problems with him. I've always given as good as I got. It was the only way to gain his respect. That was essential if I was going to get him to take the bait because he certainly doesn't trust me. Which is understandable. But in this business respect is the next best thing to trust.'

'I don't think I'd ever want the respect of a man like that,' Laura said.

'Do you think I did? It was just something that had to be done.'

There was a pause in the conversation then Laura asked, 'I take it you haven't heard any more about Lacamara?'

'No, he'll have gone to ground after what happened at the hotel last night. And if Amador is babysitting him, as Tom seems to think judging by what you've told me, then he could be anywhere by now. Which is fine by me, as long as he doesn't surface again before Monday. Hell, after that he can shoot his mouth off all he wants because I, for one, won't be around to hear him.'

'Do you know Amador?'

'Only by reputation,' Melissa replied. 'I remember Tom went to see him a couple of months back after he'd written an article for a leading newspaper about a cartel operating out of Tijuana. It was obvious from that that he had access to inside information, but when Tom confronted him about it he refused to give the name of his source.'

'So you never found out who it was?'

'The day after the article appeared in print the decapitated head of one of the senior lieutenants in the cartel was found close to the Mexican–American border. A week later his torso was fished out of a river fifty miles away. His arms and legs have never been found.'

Laura shuddered. 'Remind me never to ask you to tell me any bedtime stories.'

'That's a fairy tale with a happy ending, compared to some of the stories I could tell you about retribution meted out by drug cartels, especially the Cali and Medellín cartels in Colombia.'

'I think I'll pass, thanks.'

'So what are you up to tonight?' Melissa asked, changing the subject.

'Nothing, as far as I know.'

'I thought maybe Tom would be coming to see you,' Melissa teased.

'No, why should he?' Laura retorted. She felt herself flush and was relieved that Mel couldn't see her. It would only have encouraged further ribbing. Of course, she wanted him to come round. More than anything. But she certainly wasn't going to admit it and give her sister more ammunition to use against her.

'You've only got a couple of nights left then you're out of here for ever. You'll never see him again. It's the perfect one-night stand. Fuck him while you can.'

'Mel!' Laura hissed into the mouthpiece. 'That's disgusting.'

Melissa laughed delightedly. 'It's all the more fun when it's disgusting.'

'And you'd know all about that, wouldn't you?' Laura knew it was a tame comeback, but it was all she could muster. Not that she was going to allow herself to sink to Mel's level. She had more dignity than that.

'Oh, sis, what are we going to do with you? All that money and you're still going to be as lonely as ever.'

'Alone. Not lonely. There's a big difference. Have you ever stopped to think that perhaps that's what I want out of this? The financial security to give me my own independence, away from everything and everyone.'

'Sure I've thought about it, but it just makes me depressed. But if that's what you want you gotta do it.'

'Let's worry about that when we're safely out of the country. We've still got two days left. And if these past few days have been anything to go by, who knows what could happen before then?'

'Just make sure you keep me posted, sis, especially if you hear any more on Lacamara. He's the only real obstacle left between us and the diamonds. And I'm damned if I'm going to let him get in our way. Not when we're this close.'

'You know I will.' Laura hung up then headed back to the house.

Lacamara was late, and Amador waited impatiently on the sidewalk in front of the National Anthropology Museum. He had forgotten how many street vendors he'd already waved away since he arrived. They hovered on the large plaza in front of the building peddling their wares to the constant flow of tourists visiting the museum every day. The gullibility of foreigners never ceased to amaze him as he watched them negotiating the price of some catchpenny trinket that wouldn't even survive the trip home in their hand luggage.

'Amador!' a female voice called to him as a car pulled up at the side of the road. Carmen Lopez was behind the wheel. 'Get in.'

He crossed to the idling car, which was different from the one she had been driving the previous night, and climbed into the back. She pulled away even before he had closed the door. 'Where's Lacamara?' he asked.

'I'm going to pick him up now,' she replied.

'You still don't trust me, do you?' he said.

She glanced at his reflection in the rear-view mirror. She didn't need to say anything, the answer was in her eyes. The rest of the journey was conducted in silence. She drove downtown to the Plaza de la República and Lacamara, who had been sitting on a bench in front of the Revolution Monument, hurried across to the car and got in beside her. He looked round at Amador as the car pulled away from the kerb. 'So where exactly is this safe house of yours?'

'It's in Coyoacán. A couple of blocks from the Trotsky Museum.' Amador looked at Carmen. 'Do you know where it is?'

'She knows,' Lacamara said.

'Drive to the museum and I'll direct you from there.'

'Who owns the house?' Lacamara asked.

'A friend. He's out of town on business. Won't be back until next week. I've got a spare set of keys. He used to have a dog, and I'd feed it whenever he was away. It died a year ago, only I never got round to returning the keys. Just as well, really, under the circumstances.'

'Any more news about getting us out of the country?' Lacamara asked.

'Not yet. But I should hear something pretty soon.'

'You're cutting it pretty fine, Amador,' Lacamara said bitterly. 'We've kept our side of the deal—'

'Hey, don't take it out on me,' Amador interjected. 'I'm only the messenger. Justine will call me the moment she hears from her editor. When she last spoke to him he told her that it would be sorted out by tonight.'

'She'd better be right, because I'm damned if Carmen and I are going to hang around here for Doyle to find us,' Lacamara said. 'So if you can't get us out, we'll do it ourselves. And you can forget about the story.'

'And just how far do you think you'd get on your own with a reward of a million pesos on your head?' Amador asked. 'I said we'll get you safely out of the country. And we will. But it has to be done discreetly so that word doesn't get back to the cartel. That's why it's taking so much time. You've got to be patient.'

'That's easy for you to say – you don't have a price on your head,' Carmen retorted.

'Not yet, I don't,' Amador replied, 'but I will the moment the story hits the streets. You don't publicly discredit a major drug cartel and not expect retribution.'

'What will you do?' Lacamara asked.

'What I always do. Be on my guard wherever I go but otherwise carry on with my life as best I can. I've made a lot of enemies over the years and I've already survived two attempts on my life. Maybe the third time won't be so lucky for me. Who knows? But I'm damned if I'm going to hide in the shadows, waiting for them to find me.'

'Will you hand over my files to the police after you've published the story?' Lacamara asked.

'I'll give them to the DEA. I don't trust the local cops. And if the rest of the files are half as incriminating as the ones you gave me, Doyle and the Salcidos will be going to jail for a long time. That can't be a bad thing, can it?' Amador had always found it easy to lie. It came with the job. Most of what he had just said hadn't been true and he knew he would never even get to see the computer files, let alone hand them over to the DEA. Doyle would torture the access codes out of Lacamara, then kill him. The thought left Amador unmoved. He regarded Lacamara as a fool for having done what he had. You don't take that kind of money from a drug cartel and think you're going to get away with it. It had been tried twice in recent months by paymasters of drug cartels in Peru. Lacamara would have known that. He would have also known the fate that had befallen the men when they had been caught. And the money they stole had been only a fraction of what he had embezzled.

147

He would just be glad when this was all over. And it would be, once they reached the house. Peraya had a duplicate set of keys and would be lying in wait with several of his men. What happened to Lacamara after that wasn't his concern. His eyes went to Carmen. Although he didn't like her, he knew much of her abruptness stemmed from her unease at being caught up in the situation. She was a nightclub singer. An innocent. He hoped her death would be quick and painless. It was the closest he could get to feeling any pity for her. It was imperative that he keep his distance from them. He had more than enough ghosts as it was to haunt him every time he closed his eyes.

Not that he could have walked out on Ramón Salcido even if he had wanted to. Salcido had bought his loyalty with the first bribe. Now any article he wrote had to be approved by Salcido who regularly removed sections with which to blackmail his adversaries, leaving the story without any substance and not fit to be printed. Amador kept telling himself that the generosity of the bribes was more than he could get from a newspaper for the original story. What he found more difficult to justify was that he had sold out his journalistic integrity. And no amount of money could ever redress that . . .

'There's the museum,' Carmen said, gesturing to the high stone walls that still enclosed the steel-shuttered house where Trotsky, living in exile, had been murdered on Stalin's orders in 1940.

Amador came out of his reverie and quickly got his bearings. 'Turn left at the stop sign,' he told her. 'Then go straight for another block and a half until you reach a tree-lined driveway. Turn in there.'

She followed his directions, turned into the driveway and continued until they reached a gravel courtyard. The house was old and, from the outside, in need of repair. She drew up in front of the stone steps and was about to switch off the engine when she saw a movement in the bushes directly ahead of her. Instinctively her foot went to the accelerator as a figure appeared, an automatic in his hand. A bullet pierced the windscreen, passing between her and Lacamara, and embedded itself in the back seat inches from Amador's right shoulder. The man sprinted towards the car and she slewed the wheels violently on the gravel as a second bullet thudded into the trunk. Amador ducked as a third bullet shattered the back window, showering him with a fine spray of glass, and he remained prostrate on the back seat as the car sped down the driveway and out into the road. When it stopped he sat up. He saw that they were now parked in an alley, but he had no idea how far they were from the house. His eyes went to the bullet hole in the seat. What had happened? Peraya and his men were supposed to have been waiting for them in the house. That's what Salcido had told him. Unless . . . had he suddenly become expendable as well?

'I think it's time you gave us some answers,' Lacamara snapped.

'I don't . . .' Amador saw the Colt .45 in Lacamara's hand.

'You don't what?'

Amador had to think fast. He looked at Carmen. She stared coldly at him.

'I swear I don't know who that was at the house.' The words had tumbled from his dry mouth before he could stop himself. The fact that they were true helped to make it sound that much more convincing.

She seemed unimpressed. 'You set us up, didn't you?'

'Yeah, sure,' Amador said sarcastically, as he wiped a shaking hand across his clammy forehead. 'I set you up so that some gunman could fire indiscriminately at the car with me sitting in it. Look where the bullet ended up. Another couple of inches to the left and I'd have been dead. Or maybe you think it was all carefully orchestrated so that the bullet would just miss me? He'd have to be some shot to have pulled that off with the car still moving.'

Uncertainty flickered across Lacamara's face as he digested Amador's words. They made sense. But it still left a lot of unanswered questions. 'Who knew that we were coming here today?'

'Only the three of us,' Amador replied.

'And the American journalist,' Carmen added, spitting out the last two words.

'She knew we were going to a safe house but she had no idea where it was,' Amador corrected her.

'Which leaves the three of us,' Lacamara replied.

Amador was now thinking rationally. An idea had taken hold in the last few seconds. He only hoped it would work. 'Unless . . .' he said, massaging the back of his neck. His hand was still shaking. That, at least, was no act. 'No, it can't be,' he added, as if talking to himself.

'Unless what?' Lacamara demanded.

'What if Doyle already knows I'm helping you? I haven't been back to my house since Justine went to the American embassy, so there's no way he could have put a tail on me. So he does the next best thing. He puts a trace on my phone. As I said just now, I told Justine that we'd be staying at a safe house overnight. I didn't tell her where it was because its location wouldn't have meant anything to her. All Doyle would have had to do then was make a few enquiries of his own and deploy men at the houses he thought we might use. And if that's true, I've got to get to a pay phone straight away and warn Justine. Her editor's due to call her some time this evening to tell her about the arrangements to get the two of you out of the country.'

'You don't honestly think we still trust you after what happened back there?' Carmen snapped.

'Then who are you going to trust to get you out of this mess?' Amador sensed he was gaining the advantage. 'Neither of you can risk showing your faces in public. Even I can't, not if I'm right about my phone being tapped. Justine's your only chance. But if you think you can make it on your own, then you've got no more use for me. I'll get out of the car now and you'll never see me again.'

'Then go!' she sneered. 'You're just lucky we don't kill you.'

'Wait!' Lacamara grabbed Amador's arm as he was about to get out.

'You don't honestly trust him after what's just happened, do you?' she said incredulously.

'What would he have to gain by setting us up? He'd be losing out on the biggest story of his career.'

'He could be working for the cartel. Or for the police.'

'Fuck this! I've had enough,' Amador snarled, then flung open the door and got out of the car. He peered in at them through the driver's window. 'I was almost killed back there. But that doesn't seem to bother you. Well, it sure as hell bothers me. I've stuck my neck out for you two. And this is the thanks I get. As far as I'm concerned, you can keep your story. I'm through here. I'll get a taxi back into town. You're on your own now. I wish you luck.' With that he made for the road.

Lacamara scrambled out of the car and hurried after him. 'Amador!'

Amador flicked his hand over his shoulder to dismiss him then emerged on to the sidewalk and flagged down the first taxi he saw. It pulled up beside him and Lacamara grabbed his arm as he opened the door. Amador pulled free. 'I realize that what happened at the house has changed things. And I can understand your concerns. I'd feel exactly the same way if I were in your position. That's why I think it's best if I walk away now.'

'And just how far do you think we'd get by ourselves? For what's it worth, I don't think you had anything to do with what happened at the house.'

'Try convincing your girlfriend of that,' Amador said. 'I'm already guilty as far as she's concerned.'

'You let me worry about Carmen,' Lacamara said, then removed a roll of bank-notes from his pocket, peeled one off and handed it to the taxi driver. 'We won't be needing you.'

The driver looked at Amador, who nodded in agreement then closed the door. 'I've got to get to a pay phone as soon as possible and warn Justine,' Amador said, after the taxi had driven off.

'Then let's go,' Lacamara replied, and began to walk back to the car.

Juan Salcido stood at the window of his twentieth-floor office above the República de Venezuela with its breathtaking view of the Plaza de Santo Domingo, the Dominican church to his left and the eighteenth-century Inquisition Palace to his right. His arms were folded tightly across the chest, his eyes focused on a distant jet that was cutting a white swathe across the bright blue sky, as he listened to his brother's explanation of what had happened earlier at the house in Coyoacán.

'You knew exactly where Lacamara was going to be this afternoon, yet you purposely kept this information from me,' Juan said bitterly, once his brother had finished.

'I wanted it to be a surprise.'

'No, you wanted all the glory for yourself. And because of your ego, we may have lost our last chance of silencing Lacamara before the DEA get to him.'

'It had nothing to do with ego!' Ramón retorted angrily.

'That's the only reason I can think of why you'd let Peraya take charge of such a sensitive operation. He can't even tie his own shoelaces without a diagram.'

'And of course Doyle or Garcia could have done better.'

'My three-year-old daughter could have done better! All Peraya had to do was wait until Lacamara and Lopez were clear of the car then give the order for his men to move and take them. And he couldn't even manage that.'

'It wasn't Peraya's fault,' Ramón said, discomfort edging into his voice. 'Rincón moved too soon. That gave them the chance to get away. Peraya gave chase in his car, but by then it was already too late. He lost them.'

'And why did Rincón open fire on the car? What if he'd killed Lacamara? Then we'd never have been able to recover the files he's hidden in the computer.'

'Rincón disobeyed a direct order. Peraya's already dealt with him.'

Juan sat down slowly behind his desk. 'None of this would have happened if you'd told me what was going on right from the start.'

'It may not be too late to salvage the situation. Amador's still with them. And he'll call me once he knows how Lacamara and his whore are going to be smuggled out of the country.'

'The moment he does you call me and give me the details. Doyle will handle it from now on. And that's not up for discussion.'

'As you wish,' Ramón replied, then stood up. 'Well, if you'll excuse me, I have to get back to my office. I've got to prepare for a board meeting in the morning.'

'Ask Doyle to come in on your way out.'

'I didn't know Doyle was here,' Ramón replied.

'I called him. From what little you told me on the phone, I knew he'd have to be brought in to sort out Peraya's incompetence.'

'Why didn't you just ask him to sit in with us?' Ramón asked, pausing at the door.

'To save you any further embarrassment. You are still my brother, after all.'

'How considerate.' Ramón wrenched open the door and strode out.

ELEVEN

'Tom?' Laura said in surprise, when she answered the front door. 'What are you doing here?'

'Why? Where should I be?' Kellerman replied with a feigned look of uncertainty.

'You know what I mean.' She smiled. 'It's just that you normally ring to say you're coming over.'

'Well, I can call you on my cellular if you want,' he said, patting his jacket pocket.

'Just come in, will you?'

'Have you eaten yet?'

She shook her head then gave him a questioning look. 'You haven't brought any more of those tacos, have you?'

'They're called *quesadillas*,' he corrected her, 'and no, I haven't brought any with me. I thought maybe we could go for a meal tonight. Authentic Mexican food. What do you say?'

'I don't have anything to wear,' she complained.

'That's fine for where I've got in mind,' he said, indicating the jeans and baggy white T-shirt she was wearing. 'The only time I ever eat in swanky restaurants is when I'm entertaining on company time. And even then it's under duress.'

'You could have rung me earlier and told me what you had in mind. Then I could have been ready when you got here.'

'What for? You look great.'

'I don't feel it,' she replied. 'I can't go out in these clothes –

I've had them on all day. I'll have to take a quick shower and put on something clean. Give me half an hour.'

'Half an hour? In other words, forty-five minutes.'

'No, half an hour,' she replied. 'What's made you so cynical about women?'

'My ex-wife,' Kellerman said, but he was grinning. 'I'll call the restaurant while you're in the shower and book a table for . . .' He checked his watch. 'Let's see, it's now six thirty. Say seven thirty for eight? That gives us plenty of time to get there.'

'In other words, it gives me plenty of time to get ready,' she teased.

'Did I say that?' he replied innocently, then disappeared into the lounge.

She went into the spare bedroom and took some clean underwear and a white blouse from her suitcase and unhooked a second pair of jeans from the wardrobe. She wished now that she had brought at least one dress with her, but the last time she had seen Mel in a dress had been at their parents' funeral. She got undressed in the bathroom then switched on the water and stepped into the shower cubicle. She closed her eyes and tilted her head back, allowing the cascade of hot water to explore her body. The water felt like hundreds of tiny therapeutic needles prising open her pores and soon her body was tingling all over. She felt like a teenager again. She smiled to herself as she recalled her first date. What a disaster that had been. She had been sixteen and her academic work had always been more important to her than boys. But then the school dance had come round and at sixteen her parents had felt that she and Mel were old enough to go. She needed a date – only she was too shy to ask any of the boys, most of whom thought she was a geek. She had had a crush on the captain of the football team – but then so did every other girl at the school. And who got to go with him to the dance? Mel, of course. In the end Laura had gone with Cecil Leander, the class nerd. The only person less popular than herself. Glasses. Acne. Halitosis. Wandering hands. She particularly remembered the wandering hands. Enter Mel. She had enticed Cecil behind the toilets then punched him in the face, leaving him with broken glasses and a bloody nose. He never went near either of them again for the rest of the evening and Laura had been left to sit on her own until their father came to pick them up. *Some first date!* How could she equate a creep like Cecil Leander with Tom Kellerman? There was no comparison. No, it was more the anticipation of what might happen . . .

Nothing was going to happen. Period. *Didn't last night's near miss teach you anything?* she asked herself caustically. And she was supposed to be grieving over Mel's death, which meant showing restraint. But there was more to it than that. She didn't want to admit that she had strong feelings for him or that she had not felt that way about any man since . . . no, there wasn't a 'since'. With Jefferson it had been infatuation at first sight. She knew that now. She only wished she had known it then. But with Tom it was different. She had felt at ease with him from the moment they had first met in her apartment. And, under the circumstances, she couldn't have paid him a greater compliment than that. Yet there could never be any future for them. *Had things been different the temptation would have been there to take it further.* The thought jolted her sharply out of her self-absorbed reverie. *Keep it platonic, it's the only way . . .*

She turned off the water then stepped out of the cubicle and began to towel herself down. Ten minutes later she emerged from the bathroom and went through to the lounge where Kellerman was channel-surfing absently with the remote control. He switched off the television and got up when she came in.

'Washed, dressed and ready to go – all in under twenty minutes,' she said, holding out her arms for his appraisal.

'You sound like an ad for a take-out salad,' he replied, smiling.

'Gee, thanks,' she said with a mock scowl. 'You sure know how to flatter a girl.'

'Believe me, it takes years of practice.'

156

'I'd keep practising if I were you,' she said, giggling and picking up her purse. 'Well, shall we go?'

'After you,' he said, and followed her out into the hall.

A barefooted youth directed Kellerman into a vacant parking spot within sight of the restaurant on the Boulevard Dominguez, then hurried over to the passenger door. Laura was alarmed when he tugged at the handle. The door was locked.

'It's all part of Mexican hospitality,' Kellerman assured her. She unlocked the door, which was opened for her, and she climbed out ignoring the extended hand. Then Kellerman got out, activated the car alarm and handed a ten-peso note to the boy.

'How much did you give him?' Laura asked, as they walked away.

'About a dollar fifty.'

'Just for directing you in a parking space?' she replied in amazement. 'That's extortionate.'

'It's more than most locals would normally tip, but at least I know he'll keep an eye on the car while we're eating. That's a small price to pay for peace of mind.' Kellerman put a hand lightly on her arm and pointed out the twenty-storey block a hundred yards further down the street. 'That's the headquarters of Mex-Freight. Juan Salcido's offices are on the top floor. There's a penthouse on the roof where he entertains his guests.'

'And I suppose this restaurant we're going to just happens to be a favourite haunt of his,' she said sharply.

'Do you think I brought you here as part of some stake-out?' He was stung. 'Credit me with a little decency, Laura.'

'I'm sorry,' she said, defensively. 'It's just that I want to have a nice meal and forget about Doyle and the Salcidos, even if it's only for the next couple of hours. They're all I ever seem to think about when I'm at the house.'

'Not another word about them. Promise.'

They walked the short distance to the Hostería de Santo Domingo, built in 1860 and regarded as the oldest restaurant still in operation in the city. Kellerman opened the door for her and as Laura stepped inside her eyes were drawn to the impressive mural, depicting the Plaza Domingo during the colonial era, which covered an entire wall. They were greeted cordially by a waiter who checked the reservation book for Kellerman's name then, armed with two menus, led them to a table close to the mural.

'Ah, Señor Kellerman,' a voice boomed, after they had been seated.

Kellerman looked round at the portly, silver-haired figure in evening dress who was approaching the table. 'Miguel, good to see you.'

'And you, my friend. I haven't seen you in here for a while.'

'You know how it is,' Kellerman replied, with a shrug.

'Still chasing the bad guys, eh?'

'I'm not doing so much of the chasing these days.' Kellerman looked across at Laura. 'This is Miguel,' he said, switching from Spanish to English. 'He owns the restaurant. Miguel, this is Melissa Wade. She and I go back a long way.'

'How do you do?' Miguel said in English.

'*Hablo español,*' she said, with a smile.

'Ah, wonderful,' Miguel said, reverting to his native tongue. He shook her hand gently, but firmly. 'Are you out here on holiday?'

'Yes, she is,' Kellerman answered for her, 'from New York.'

'Ah, New York,' Miguel said wistfully. 'I would love to go there one day but the restaurant takes up so much of my time.' He clasped his hands together. 'You'll have to excuse me. We're filling up fast tonight. I hope you enjoy your meal.'

'I'm sure we will,' Kellerman replied, then watched him weave his way between the tables and disappear through one of the swing doors into the kitchen.

'He obviously knows you work for the DEA,' Laura said.

'And that I'm divorced. I made the mistake of telling him that one night after a little too much tequila. After that he was always wanting to fix me up with some or other single woman he thought would be just right for me. Each time I'd say thanks, but no thanks. He means well.'

'So that's why you asked me here tonight, so that he wouldn't try to fix you up with another of his single ladies,' she said, a mischievous twinkle in her eye.

'You've seen through my little ruse then,' he said, as he opened the menu in front of him. 'A word of warning. The portions here tend to be on the generous side. So unless you're starving, I wouldn't recommend a starter. Just go straight for the main course.'

'As long as there's room for dessert,' she said.

'A dentist with a sweet tooth? That's a good advert for your profession.'

'There's nothing wrong with the occasional indulgence,' she said. 'So, what do you recommend? Something not too spicy.'

'Their speciality's the pork loin. I always have it when I come here.'

'You like spicy food, though,' she said.

'The pork itself isn't spiced. I always have it with a hot *mole* sauce and a side portion of *chilis rellenos* – baked peppers stuffed with cheese, ground beef and raisins. Delicious.'

'For you, maybe, but I'd have heartburn well into next week if I ate that.' She groaned.

He ran his finger down the separate list of sauces. 'Why not try the *pipian* sauce? It's pretty mild from what I hear.'

'Ground pumpkin seeds, nuts and mild peppers,' she said, reading out the ingredients. 'Sounds good. I think I'll go for that.'

'And to drink?'

'Something cold,' she said.

'I know just the thing,' he told her, then raised his hand to get the waiter's attention. He gave the waiter their order and asked him to bring the drinks right away.

'Do you mind if I smoke?' she asked, once the waiter had withdrawn.

'Not at all,' he replied, pushing the ashtray towards her.

She took a pack of cigarettes from her purse and lit one. 'Tell me about your ex-wife.'

The question caught Kellerman by surprise. He sat back in his chair as he pondered his reply. 'Her name's Caroline. We were married for five years. No kids. Amicable split. That's about it.'

'Do you still see her?'

'Yeah, occasionally. She's a lawyer in Washington. We met at a cocktail party at the American embassy in Paris. She'd just graduated from Harvard and she was taking a short vacation before she started work. Her father was a personal friend of the ambassador. Tyrell Hammond. You may have heard of him.'

'Can't say I have,' she replied, then gave him a quizzical frown. 'Should I?'

'No, not necessarily. He's in oil. Very wealthy. We never hit it off, though. He made up his mind from the first day he met me that an intelligence officer with the CIA was never going to be good enough for his daughter.'

'You worked for the CIA?' she said, surprised.

'I started out with Army Intelligence. That's where I learnt to speak Spanish. Then I was recruited by the CIA.' He looked up at the approaching waiter who placed their drinks on the table before leaving again. He indicated the glass in front of Laura. 'Go on, try it. I know you'll like it.'

'What is it?' she asked, picking up the glass to scrutinize its milky contents.

'It's called *horchata*. It's a traditional drink, made from ground rice and almonds. Slightly sweet, but very refreshing.'

She put the glass to her lips and took a sip. 'Mmm, it is nice,' she agreed. 'So how did you make the transition from the CIA to the DEA?'

'I got a desk job at the Pentagon after Caroline and I got married, the idea being that I'd be nearer her. But I wasn't happy behind a desk. I missed the cut-and-thrust of field work. And, inevitably, my frustration spilled over into the marriage. So Caroline and I had a long talk about it and she agreed that I should reapply for a field posting. When I did, I was turned down. So I put out some feelers into other sectors of the intelligence community. The DEA were the first to approach me as a possible replacement for one of their intelligence officers who had been assassinated in Colombia. The CIA got wind of it and offered me the position as head of intelligence at one of their embassies in Central America. It was a tempting offer, but I still saw my future away from the Pentagon. That's when I joined the DEA.'

'What did Caroline think about you being posted to Colombia?'

'She wasn't too thrilled, naturally, but to her credit she never tried to stop me. She knew I wanted to get back in the field. But our relationship was never the same after that. Looking back on it now, I realize that we were both more involved with our careers than we were with each other. That doesn't mean I didn't love her. I just loved my work more. We're still friends, though.'

'At least you could hold on to that.'

'Unlike you and Jefferson?' he replied, reaching for his glass.

'I don't know that we ever were friends in the real sense of the word,' she said, slowly grinding out her cigarette in the ashtray. 'Jefferson only had one friend. Himself. And as long as he was the centre of attention, he was the most charming man imaginable.'

'So why did it take you so long to see him in his true colours?'

'Because when I met him, I knew nothing about men. At school I was the swot with no time for boys. The same at university. Getting my degree was all that mattered to me. Then suddenly I was pushed out into the big wide world to fend for myself. And one of the first people I met was Jefferson. He was a junior doctor at Bellevue at the time and I was flattered to have this dashing young man show such an interest in me. Nobody ever had before. I withdrew under his protective wing. It made me feel safe. There was Mel, the confident young uniformed cop fearlessly riding the streets of Brooklyn. And me, scared of my own shadow. It's pathetic when I look back on it now. But that's how it was.'

'You've come a long way since then,' Kellerman said.

'With a few hiccups.'

'I know that you started to drink as an escape from your ex-husband's infidelity—'

'That's probably what it says in my file,' she broke in. 'No, the real reason I drank was because I felt inadequate. I thought there must be something wrong with me if he was forced to sleep with other women. And I made the mistake of telling him that when I first discovered he was cheating on me. So after that he'd always use my own words against me whenever I confronted him about his womanizing. And every time he did it, it eroded a bit more of what little self-confidence I had left. The only way I could deal with the hurt was to drink more. That's how it got so bad in the end. It was a case of preferring to be miserable with him than miserable without him. Yet despite all the mental torture he put me through, I was still in love with him. That just goes to show you how screwed up I was. What's more, he knew exactly how I felt about him. And that gave him even more ammunition to use against me.' She looked up when the waiter appeared and moved the ashtray to allow him to put the plate in front of her. She waited until he had served Kellerman then whistled softly as she eyed the huge amount of food arranged attractively on her plate. 'You were right. They don't skimp, do they?'

'Just make sure you leave some room for your dessert,' he reminded her, after the waiter had gone.

'You can count on it,' she replied. She took a mouthful and nodded appreciatively. 'Delicious,' she said.

They ate in silence for the next couple of minutes then he said, 'So what finally made you realize you had a drink problem?'

'The death of my parents. I was married to Jefferson for three years. I was an alcoholic for two of them. And in those two years I not only lost my job, but I also turned my back on my parents. They desperately wanted me to get help but I wasn't interested because I didn't believe I had a problem. The standard response of any alcoholic. And the more they tried to reach out to me, the more I pulled back. The last time I saw them was when they came to the house to say goodbye before they left for their annual holiday in Spain. I was drunk, naturally, and I got into a heated argument with my father when he tried to pour my last bottle of bourbon down the sink. I was so desperate I slapped him. To this day I can still remember the look on his face. He just put the bottle down and left the house without another word. My mother was in tears. I guess she just couldn't believe that I'd raised a hand to him. Three days later I got a phone call to say they'd been killed in a plane crash in Andalucía. My first reaction was to hit the bottle even harder to drown my sorrows. Of course, that would have been the easy way out. But I kept remembering the last time I'd seen them. I could never say sorry to them for what I'd done. That's when I decided to get help. I dried out at a detox clinic and I haven't touched a drop now for the last two years.' She smiled to end the sombre conversation, and changed the subject. 'This is wonderful. But filling.'

'Mexico's a hospitable country, particularly when it comes to food,' he said. 'Wherever you go, they love to feed you. And if you've got a problem with your weight, like me, you've got to be careful about how much you eat. That's why I have to work out every day. But I tell you, the older I get, the less enthusiastic I get about working out. One day I'll wake up and decide, that's it, I've had enough.'

'Jefferson had a problem with his weight too but all that screwing around kept him in shape.'

'Do you ever see him these days?'

'Hardly. He's in prison. But you know that.'

'No, I had no idea,' Kellerman replied, surprised.

'I thought that would have been logged in your computer, along with the rest of my life history,' she said, with a hint of disdain.

'No. He's only listed on the computer as your ex-husband. So what's he in jail for?'

'Drugs. A month after the divorce was finalized the cops got an anonymous tip-off that he had half a key of coke hidden in his sports car. He was stopped in New Jersey and the cops found it when they searched the trunk. He got five years. I believe he's due for parole in another six months. I don't know what he'll do when he gets out, though. He's got no future in medicine.'

'Was he dealing?'

'No, he was set up,' she replied, demurely. 'Pity the jury didn't believe him.'

'You mean *you* set him up?' Kellerman said in disbelief.

'And where would I get my hands on half a key of coke? No, it wasn't me.'

'Melissa?' he said, barely audibly, already dreading her reply.

Laura nodded. 'I had no idea that she was behind it until he'd been convicted. That's when she told me. What was I supposed to do? Shop my sister to save Jefferson's butt? Forget it. Not after what he put me through.'

'And what gave her the right to take the law into her own hands like that?' he asked, with such venom that several diners at adjoining tables turned to look at him. He ignored them, his eyes on Laura. 'What if she'd been caught?' he asked, this time in a more composed tone. But the anger was still evident in his eyes.

'She wasn't, was she?' Laura retorted.

'And how did she get the coke?'

'She called in a favour from a couple of dealers in Atlantic City. At least, that's what she told me. I don't know how it was arranged. And I didn't want to know either.'

'I don't believe it.' He shook his head despairingly. 'It just makes you wonder, doesn't it?'

'What?' she asked.

'Whether she was involved in any other illegal deals on the side that the DEA didn't know about. Melissa always sailed close to the wind – hell, we all knew that – but she always gave the impression that she prided herself on staying just inside the law. That way there could be no comebacks. Seems like I under-estimated her.'

'Look, I'm not proud of what she did,' Laura told him, 'but, as I said, there was nothing I could do without getting her into a heap of trouble. I wasn't prepared to do that. You can take it further if you want now that ... Mel's dead. But you won't get any co-operation from me.'

'We look after our own in the DEA.' Kellerman bristled. His voice softened when he continued, 'No, let sleeping dogs lie. I have no intention of dragging the DEA's name into this. It would only reflect badly on the department if it were ever made public.' The waiter returned to remove their plates. 'Just some vanilla ice-cream for me,' Kellerman said, when the menu was offered to him.

Laura took a menu and browsed through the dessert section then looked up at the waiter. 'I'll have the same. Thank you.' The waiter departed.

'You seem to be finding it easier to talk about Melissa than you did, say, a couple of days ago,' Kellerman remarked.

'I have a façade for every occasion,' Laura replied, reaching for her cigarettes. 'It's a trick I learnt as a child. Mel was always the one who craved attention. I didn't. I just wanted to be left alone. So if I had a problem I didn't want my parents to know about, which was just about always, I'd go off and sort it out by myself. I still do, for that matter.'

'Are you hiding behind a façade now?'

'I don't regard it as hiding. To me, hiding implies fear. And if I was so scared of letting you into my world, d'you think I'd have told you anything about myself? Raquel was my best friend, but I never told her about what happened the last time I saw my parents. And I certainly never told her that Mel framed Jefferson.'

'Why did you tell me?' Kellerman asked, his eyes riveted on her face.

'I don't know,' she replied candidly, then lit the cigarette she had been turning around in her fingers. 'I didn't plan to do it. It just kind of . . . happened that way. Perhaps it was a case of *quid pro quo*. You told me about yourself. I told you about myself.'

'Is that you or the façade talking?'

'The only façade I have on right now is the one masking my sorrow. It's the only way I can deal with Mel's death. I don't grieve in public. I didn't for my parents, and I won't for Mel or Raquel. Some people regard me as cold for that. Perhaps they're right, I don't know. But that's how I am.'

Kellerman waited until the ice-cream had been served before he said, 'Stubborn, yes. But cold – no. Melissa was cold. And that's meant as a compliment. It's what made her such a good UC.'

Laura nodded in agreement. 'I used to admire her for that when we were kids. I always wanted to be like her.'

They ate their ice-cream in silence. When Laura had finished Kellerman said, 'You're welcome to have coffee if you'd like, but it's often disappointing in restaurants out here.'

'We can have coffee back at the house.'

'I'd like that,' he said, then raised his hand to get the waiter's attention and made a scribbling motion in the air.

The waiter nodded, disappeared into the kitchen and returned a little later with the bill.

As they walked back to the car Laura slipped her hand into the crook of Kellerman's arm. The youth was sitting on an upturned wooden crate on the sidewalk near the car. He jumped to his feet when he saw them and Kellerman slipped some loose change into his hand. The boy grinned at him and waited until he had unlocked the passenger door before stepping forward and opening it for Laura. She thanked him and got inside. He touched his ragged peaked cap, then retreated to his crate.

Kellerman got behind the wheel. 'We'll drive back via the Plaza de Garibaldi,' he said, starting the engine. 'It's not far from here.'

'What's there?' she asked.

'It's the main gathering place for the *mariachis*.'

'I remember Mel telling me about them. They're musicians, aren't they? And they wear distinctive costumes.'

'That's right. The name is said to have come from the French word for marriage – *mariage*. Originally they were itinerant musicians who would play at weddings during the French occupation of Mexico in the last century. Now they're a major tourist attraction in every city here.'

'Will it be all right for us to be seen together at the plaza?' she asked hesitantly.

'Who do you think's going to see us?' he asked. 'And, anyway, Melissa and I often worked cases together. No, don't worry, we won't attract any unnecessary attention.'

It only took a few minutes to reach the Plaza de Garibaldi where hundreds of *mariachi* bands were gathered within its spacious confines, illuminated by the overhead lights, resplendent in black – tight silver-spangled trousers, ornately decorated jackets, large sombreros and, to add a dash of colour, floppy red and white bow-ties. Each band typically consisted of three or four acoustic guitars, a similar number of violins and a brass section of three trumpeters. The vocalist was normally one of the guitarists and the rest of the band would join in during the harmonies.

Kellerman parked the car and as they got out he was approached by a band member who took him to one side and spoke to him out of Laura's earshot. Kellerman handed him some money then laughed suddenly and shook his head. The man smiled then shot a glance at Laura before beckoning his colleagues towards him.

'What was that all about?' she asked when Kellerman returned.

'A lot of local men – particularly the younger ones – hire one of the *mariachi* bands to accompany them while they serenade their girlfriends. He asked whether I wanted to serenade you. I declined the offer. I told him that we were just friends. I'm not sure he believed me, though.'

The violins started up first, then the guitars were added before the vocalist, who had earlier spoken to Kellerman, began to sing in a rich, mellifluous baritone, which rose effortlessly above the accompanying instruments. Laura began to feel uncomfortable: the sickly-sentimental lyrics were making her squirm. She leant back against the side of the car, her arms folded as if she were trying to put a barrier between herself and the mawkish sentiments of the song. She felt Kellerman's shoulder brush against hers and when she looked up at him she saw that he was smiling gently at her. He swept a loose strand of hair away from her face and kissed her.

Her first thought was to push him away and she got as far as placing the palm of her hand against his chest – but it was as if she lacked the strength to follow through on what her head was urging her to do. Then she slid her hand around the back of his neck where it stayed until she had to pull away reluctantly to catch her breath. Kellerman slipped his arm around her shoulders and she moved closer to him.

It was then that his cellular phone began to ring. He cursed furiously under his breath and walked a short distance away from the band before answering it.

'Tom, it's Bill Walker.'

'This better be good.' Kellerman looked across at Laura. She was watching him. The happiness he had seen on her face moments earlier had been replaced with a resigned acceptance of the inevitable. Work always came first.

'What's that music in the background?' Walker asked. 'You got a hot date there, buddy? Hey, I hope I didn't interrupt anything.' This was followed by a crude laugh.

'What the fuck do you want, Bill?' Kellerman snapped.

'I've just received an anonymous call about Lacamara. I've got it on tape. That's all I can say over the phone. It's best if you come over and hear it for yourself.'

'I'm on my way.' Kellerman switched off the phone then walked back to where Laura was standing. 'That was Bill Walker at the embassy. He's just had a call about Lacamara.'

'Then let's go,' she said.

'*I'm* going to the embassy,' Kellerman told her. '*You*'re going home.'

Laura's eyes narrowed. 'I'm Mel now, remember? She'd be in on this.'

Kellerman stared at her in disbelief. 'You're impersonating her on Sunday but that doesn't mean you're a part of the team now. This isn't some kind of game, you know.'

'You didn't seem to mind the last time I went with you to the embassy,' she pointed out. 'In fact, you complimented me on the way I handled myself.'

'The last time we'd just flown in from New York. There was a driver waiting for us at the airport. I had no choice but to take you to the embassy with me.'

Laura knew that if he blocked her out she wouldn't be able to keep Mel informed on the latest developments. She suddenly felt helpless. And confused. The kiss had seen to that. It was imperative that she get her thoughts together. Quickly. 'I *am* a part of the team now, whether you like it or not,' she told him defiantly. 'I've already had to pass myself off as Mel in front of Walker, Doyle and Justine Collins. Without me you'd never have got this far. And you know it. I think I deserve to be in on this, don't you?'

'No,' Kellerman said bluntly. He looked round sharply when the song came to an abrupt end, forced a smile and nodded to the musicians before he turned back to her. 'I don't know why we're having this conversation. I don't have to explain myself to you. You're not coming to the embassy. That's final.'

'So in other words, I'm just here to impersonate Mel whenever it suits you. You know, there's nothing to stop me from getting on the next flight back to the States.'

'Do you want me to make the reservation for you?' Kellerman countered, then took the phone from his jacket pocket and held it out towards her. 'One call, that's all it'll take. Just say the word, Laura, and you're on your way back home. Is that what you want?'

'I said I'd do this for Mel, didn't I?' she said, angry now with herself. What the hell had possessed her to threaten to fly back home? It had made her sound like a spoilt child resorting to blackmail when she couldn't get her own way.

Kellerman raked his fingers through his hair. 'Look, I gotta go. I'll get you a taxi.'

'I think I can manage that by myself,' she said bitterly.

'This can be a rough neighbourhood, especially at this time of night. I'm not leaving you here by yourself.' He spotted a green and white Datsun taxi for hire and stepped out into the road to flag it down. 'I'll drop by at the house after I've been to the embassy to tell you what's happening,' he said, opening the door for her.

'You can do that on the phone. I think it would be best for both of us if we were to keep this on a purely professional basis from now on. That way there can be no more misunderstandings.'

'Yeah, you're probably right there,' he agreed, then closed the door. He peered at the driver through the open passenger window and gave him the address in San Angel where Laura was staying and was about to reach into his pocket for some money to pay for the fare when he checked himself. No need to cause any more friction. 'I'll call you,' he said to Laura, then took a step back and rapped twice on the roof with his knuckles.

The taxi pulled away and he watched until it had gone then walked the short distance to where his own car was parked, got inside, and drove off in the direction of the embassy.

TWELVE

'You don't like me, do you?'

'No,' Carmen Lopez replied, then parked the car and switched off the engine. Only then did she look at Felix Amador seated beside her. 'And I trust you even less after what happened at the safe house today.'

'You still think I had something to do with that, don't you?' Amador said. 'The fact that I was nearly killed makes no difference to you, does it?'

'Let's just get the food,' she said brusquely, and waved at the McDonald's on the opposite side of the street.

'Just a moment,' Amador said, putting a hand lightly on her arm as she was about to get out of the car.

'Don't touch me!' she snarled, jerking away and getting out of the car.

He climbed out and looked at her across its roof. 'Lacamara trusts me. If he didn't, he'd have ditched me this afternoon.'

'Hector trusts you as much as I do,' Carmen said, with contempt, 'and right now you and the American journalist are our only realistic chance of getting out of the country. But you can be sure that if we walk into a trap, you'll be the first to die.' She patted her jacket pocket, which he knew concealed the Colt .45. Lacamara had given it to her before he had got out of the car several blocks further down the road. He had thought it prudent to keep out of sight while they bought the food.

'I need the rest room,' Amador announced as they entered the restaurant. She stopped abruptly and slipped her hand into her jacket pocket. 'I've been dying to go for the last hour, and I'm going whether you like it or not. But if you want to shoot me in front of all these witnesses, then go right ahead. Alternatively, you could always come in with me and hold my hand.'

'You're disgusting!' she said, taking a step away from him.

He crossed to the men's toilet and, once inside, checked the availability of the cubicles. Two were occupied but the others were vacant. He went into the one furthest from the door and locked it behind him. He unlatched the window above the cistern then climbed on to the bowl, slipped out and jumped to the ground. He was in an unlit alley. Hurrying to the end, he looked around cautiously then ran the short distance to the pay phone he had seen from the car. He dialled a number. 'Peraya, it's Amador. I need to speak to Señor Salcido. And hurry, I don't have much time.'

Moments later Salcido was on the line. 'Amador, it's about time you called. What's going on?'

'That's good coming from you,' Amador shot back then glanced around quickly to check whether his angry outburst had drawn any unwanted attention on himself. Nobody appeared to be looking at him. He gripped the receiver tighter and lowered his voice when he spoke again. 'I was nearly killed at the safe house this afternoon. Whoever shot at the car missed me by inches. I thought the whole idea was to take Lacamara alive. You said that your men would only make their move once we were in the house.'

'One of my men disobeyed his orders. It was unfortunate, particularly for him. Was Lacamara hurt?'

'No, neither of them were. Look, I don't have much time. I'm calling from a pay phone. They confiscated my cellular phone. That's why I haven't been able to contact you before now. I spoke to Justine earlier this evening. Her editor's

173

arranged passage for Lacamara and Lopez out of the country.'

'Where and when?'

'A Guatemalan freighter that leaves Veracruz for Belize tomorrow night.'

'And how will they get to Veracruz?'

'I've booked them seats on a tour bus that leaves tomorrow at midday from the ruins at Teotihuacán.'

'Why a tour bus?'

'It was Lacamara's idea. They've got false passports, so it'll appear as if they're two tourists going back to Veracruz after a visit to the ruins.'

'You've done well. Where are you staying tonight?'

'In the car. They won't go near a hotel in case they're recognized.' Amador glanced at his watch then scanned the road in front of McDonald's. 'I've got to go before I'm missed. You won't hear from me again tonight.'

'That's fine. We'll take it from here. Oh, Amador? Don't forget about the photographs.'

'I haven't. I'll get them for you next time I see Justine. But it won't be before tomorrow.'

'As long as I have them by Sunday afternoon. That was our agreement.'

The line went dead. Amador hung up and ran back to the alley. He hoisted himself back through the window, which he closed behind him. He wiped the sweat from his face then, flushing the cistern, he emerged from the cubicle. He crossed to the door and pulled it open to find Carmen standing directly in front of him.

'What took you so long?' she demanded.

'You want details?' he asked ironically. 'How long have you been standing here?'

'A few minutes,' she said. 'Why are you sweating?'

'Because I don't feel so good,' he replied.

'Then you won't be wanting any food, will you?' she said.

He hadn't eaten all day and the smell of the burgers made

him realize just how ravenous he was. But he had to stick to his story and reluctantly shook his head.

'All the more for us,' she said, with a rare, but cold, smile, then walked towards the main doors. He wiped his sleeve across his sweating forehead and went after her.

'I hope I didn't ruin your evening,' Walker said, when Kellerman swept into his office.

'You didn't ruin anything,' Kellerman replied, pulled up a chair and sat down. 'Let's hear the tape.'

Walker punched the play button on the cassette recorder on his desk.

'I want to speak to the head of the DEA,' said a voice in Spanish.

'My name's Special Agent Walker, I'm the deputy head of the DEA here in Mexico. I'm afraid my superior's not on duty at the moment. Can I help you?'

A lengthy pause followed then, 'If you want Hector Lacamara, he'll be at Teotihuacán tomorrow morning at eleven o'clock.'

'Who is this?' There was a click as the phone was put down. Then silence.

'Did you manage to trace the call?' Kellerman asked.

'Other than that it originated from somewhere in the city, no,' Walker replied. 'You know what the telephone exchange is like out here. We were never going to trace the call in such a short time.'

'What did you make of the voice?' Kellerman asked. 'Male or female?'

'Difficult to tell. I'd be inclined to say female, but it could just as easily have been a guy trying to sound like a woman.'

'Yeah, my initial reaction was that it was probably female. But, as you say, maybe that's what they wanted us to think. It wasn't a CI, though. He'd have made sure we knew exactly who he was so that he could get his hands on the reward money.'

'Are you going to bring in the INCD?' Walker asked.

'What choice do I have? We've got to play this by the book. This is their jurisdiction.'

'Then the Salcidos are going to know too. They've got any number of spies inside the INCD.'

'I'll speak to Colonel Santin. He's the only one I trust. I'll ask him to put together a team of his best agents but not to brief them until they're already on their way to Teotihuacán to-morrow morning. That way we can reduce the chances of the Salcidos finding anything out until after Lacamara's been taken into protective custody.'

'Who are *we* going to use?'

'Just the two of us. The fewer who know about this the better.'

'Why not bring in Melissa? This is her kind of operation.'

'No,' Kellerman said brusquely. He cursed himself inwardly for his impulsive reaction and his voice was more controlled when he spoke again. 'Melissa's working on something else and I don't want to take her off it unless it's absolutely necessary. The two of us can handle it by ourselves. After all, we'll only be onlookers.'

Walker reached for his cigarettes and lit one. 'I still can't figure out why Lacamara would be going to Teotihuacán in the morning. The place is a major tourist attraction.'

'Why not ask him that when you see him in the morning?' Kellerman looked at his watch. 'I'll give Santin a call then I'm going to hit the road. Try to get some sleep.'

'Your date wasn't prepared to wait for you, eh?' Walker said with a sly grin.

'I never had a date!' Kellerman snapped. 'What is it with you and this date fixation? If you really must know, I was meeting with a CI at the Plaza de Garibaldi when you rang me.'

'Get anything useful out of him?' Walker asked.

'As if.' Kellerman snorted. 'I don't know why I keep using him. He hasn't come up with anything substantial for months now.' Which was true of the CI he did meet on occasion at the Plaza de Garibaldi.

'What time do you want me to be here in the morning?' Walker asked.

'The caller said that Lacamara would be at Teotihuacán at eleven, which means that we need to be there by nine at the latest. I'll meet you here at seven. I'll call Santin now. Get him on the line for me, will you?'

Laura sat at the kitchen table, a bottle of Kahlúa in front of her. It was the only alcohol she could find in the house, but it would be more than enough to temper her ragged nerves. She was only too aware of the consequences of that first drink. But at that moment it didn't matter to her. She needed a drink. She wanted a drink. And she was going to have a drink.

Her emotions were as confused as her thoughts as she stared at the bottle. Why had he kissed her? Why hadn't she stopped him? Why had she insisted he take her to the embassy? Why hadn't she just let it drop instead of playing up even more when he'd refused? So many questions. All she wanted to do was forget that any of it had ever happened. And the only way she knew how to do that was with alcohol. As much as she could drink in as short a time as possible.

Although the bottle was within reach she made no move to pick it up. She felt as if two conflicting voices were battling for control inside her head. Good conscience. Bad conscience. *You're stronger than this*, her good conscience told her. *Savour the moment*, her bad conscience told her. *There's a lot more to this guilt than just what happened tonight, isn't there? Forget the analysis and just take a drink – it's what you want. You take a drink now and you'll be insulting the memory of your parents – is that what you want? For God's sake, just take a drink – take it – take it . . .*

She licked her dry lips then reached out a hand and drew the bottle closer. All she had to do now was unscrew the cap. But something was holding her back. She thought of her parents. They would understand. It wasn't as if she was going to slide back into the void of alcoholism again. She was confident she could control it. Of course she could. Only the more she repeated it in her head, the more she began to question why she needed to keep convincing herself. More self-doubt. More guilt. Suddenly the bottle was in her hand, she had removed the cap and dropped it on the floor. This was it. She lifted the bottle to her lips . . .

It had been against his better judgement that Kellerman decided to drive to San Angel. Or, at least, that was what he kept telling himself in the car. He should be going home – he had to be up early the following morning. And, more importantly, Laura had told him that she didn't want to see him again that night. Which was understandable under the circumstances. What had possessed him to kiss her? He had already tried to convince himself that it had seemed the right thing to do at that moment. But it was a hollow excuse, and he knew it. He had taken advantage of her in her time of grief, and that had been unforgivable. The fact that she hadn't resisted was of scant consolation to his conscience. She had been confused. And she wasn't the only one. He had never felt this way about any woman since Caroline. Laura was special. And, yes, he wanted to take it further. But there would be time for that once she was back in the States. Assuming, of course, that she even wanted to see him again after this was over. Even that didn't look hopeful if her parting words at the Plaza de Garibaldi had been anything to go on. She was right to want to keep the relationship purely professional.

When he pulled up outside the house he saw that the lounge was in darkness. Had she gone to bed already? She would be even more angry with him if he woke her up. He got out of the car, made his way to the veranda and was about to climb the steps when he had a sudden thought. He reached a hand over the top of the wooden gate, released the catch, and moved silently to the spare-bedroom window. The curtains were open and the bed was empty. She was probably in the kitchen. He went round to the back of the house. The security light was on, illuminating the small garden. The back door was open and a sudden surge of anxiety pulsed through him when he saw the overturned kitchen chair lying across the entrance. He was unarmed – DEA personnel working abroad were only permitted to draw weapons from the armoury for specific assignments, and then only in conjunction with local law-enforcement agencies. He remained motionless in the doorway, listening for any sound of an intruder, but there was only silence. Then he stepped in over the chair – and saw Laura. She was sitting on the floor, her back against the wall, her legs pulled up tightly to her chest and her arms wrapped tightly around her knees. Her head was lowered and her face veiled by a cascade of black hair.

'Laura?' he said, in a soft, uncertain voice. She jerked her head up sharply. Her eyes were red and puffy from crying and there appeared to be a small bruise on her left cheek. It was then that he saw the bottle of Kahlúa in her hand. He could tell by the angle at which she was holding it that it was empty.

She let go of it and watched it roll across the floor. It came to rest against the leg of the table. 'I didn't drink it,' she said, looking up slowly at him, 'but I was more tempted than you can ever imagine. I already had the bottle to my lips when I managed to stop myself. Another second and I'd have taken a drink. Who knows where it would have led?'

'But you didn't, and that's what counts.'

'I didn't this time. What about the next time? Or the time after that?' She scrambled to her feet. 'I feel like the kid who uses his finger to plug one leak in the dike wall only for another to spring up elsewhere. Eventually it gets to the point where he doesn't have enough fingers to contain all the leaks. And still the pressure keeps building. Sooner or later, something has to give.'

'You know you're stronger than that,' he said.

'No, *you* think I'm stronger than that.' She watched him pick up the chair. 'I kicked it over in a fit of temper after I'd poured the booze down the sink.'

Kellerman touched his finger to his left cheek. 'How did you get that bruise?'

'Bruise?' she replied in surprise, then peered at her reflection in the window and wiped her hand across her face. The mark disappeared and she went to the sink to wash her hands. 'Probably a drop of Kahlúa that splashed on to my face,' she said, drying her hands.

'Did this come about after what happened at the Plaza de Garibaldi earlier tonight?' he asked.

'I guess it started out that way. But then it became more than that. I did a lot of crying tonight, as I'm sure you've noticed. It's helped to clear a lot of the frustration out of my system. And that can't be a bad thing.'

'I'm sorry if I was the cause of it. I know I shouldn't have blown up at you like I did.' He gave her a rueful smile. 'I guess that was my own frustration coming to the surface. I was having a really great night . . . with you. I just didn't want it to end.'

'Me neither,' she said, then picked up the kettle. 'That coffee's still on offer, if you're interested.'

'Thanks.' He pulled out a chair and sat down at the table. 'I was dreading coming here. I half expected you to slam the door in my face. You made it pretty clear that you didn't want to see me again tonight.'

'Then why did you come?'

'To apologize for the way I behaved. I didn't want us to fall out over something like that. It's not worth it.'

'I was the one acting like a jerk. Shouting my mouth off like some spoilt brat when I couldn't get my own way. You had every right to react the way you did. So if anyone should be doing the apologizing around here, it's me. Well, now that we've both had our say, let's leave it at that.'

'Sure,' he replied, with obvious relief.

When she had made the coffee she placed one mug on a coaster in front of him then sat down. 'What did the anonymous caller have to say?' she asked, and grinned at him when he glanced questioningly at her. 'I was just asking, that's all.'

'Let's just say the call was informative and leave it at that.'

'Fine by me,' she said, with a quick shrug to hide her disappointment at not having learnt more. But she knew better than to push it.

'I can't discuss every aspect of the case with you, Laura.'

'Did I say anything?' she asked, putting her hand to her chest.

'As long as we understand each other. Let's change the subject,' he suggested.

'OK, so what d'you want to talk about?'

'Anything,' he replied, getting to his feet and moving to the back door.

'Tell me why you kissed me tonight.'

The question caught him by surprise and he struggled to marshal his thoughts. 'I – I – don't – know – exactly,' he stammered, like some flustered teenager.

'Do you at least know whether you want to do it again?' she asked, having come up behind him silently.

He turned round slowly and met her eyes. 'Only if you do.'

'I want to do a lot more than that,' she replied, then slipped her hands around the back of his neck and drew his mouth down on hers.

'So it's not true.'

'What isn't?' Laura asked.

'That smokers always have a cigarette after sex.'

'Only if the sex was good,' she said, with a teasing smile.

'And there are times when the sex is so good that even the traditional cigarette becomes an irrelevance,' he quipped.

'And there are other times when your cigarettes are in the lounge and you just can't be bothered to get out of bed to fetch them,' she added, then nuzzled closer to him and laid her head on his chest.

'That sounds more realistic,' he said, putting an arm around her shoulders.

'I'm not so sure,' she murmured contentedly.

'By the way, whatever happened to keeping the relationship on a purely professional basis? That was what you said earlier tonight, wasn't it?'

'It's a woman's prerogative to change her mind.'

'I'm glad you did,' he said, running his fingers lightly through her hair.

'Me, too. You know, you're the first man I've slept with . . . well, in a long time. I've kept very much to myself since the divorce went through.'

'You still have feelings for him, don't you?'

'Most of them negative,' she said. 'But we had some good times together. Like when we went to Aspen and he taught me how to ski. That was the best holiday I've ever had. I can't erase those memories. And I wouldn't want to either. But then neither can I ever forget the hell he put me through. He deceived me into marrying him, knowing full well that he wasn't going to be faithful to me. That will always hurt the most.'

'And because of him you got hooked on the booze,' Kellerman added.

'No, I never blamed him for that,' she replied. 'I chose to drink as a means of escape. I wasn't strong enough to face the truth without a bottle in my hand. I chose the easy way out. What frightens me most of all is knowing that I will start drinking again. I came real close to it tonight. It's just a question now of how much longer I can hold out before I crack under the pressure.'

'Somehow I never took you for a defeatist,' Kellerman said.

'I'm a realist. I know myself. I'm not Mel. She was always the stronger one. I was always fallible. And some day that fallibility's going to catch up with me again.'

'You've been off the booze now for the past two years.'

She sat up abruptly. 'And there hasn't been a day when I haven't craved a drink. Not one day. I feel like a criminal who's out on parole desperately trying not to reoffend, but at the same time knowing it's going to happen. It's inevitable, Tom.'

'We can get through this together,' he said, taking her hand in his.

'Hallelujah, my guardian angel's finally arrived to show me the light and save me from eternal damnation.' She jerked her hand free, threw back the sheets, and got out of bed. She pulled on her white towelling robe and secured the belt tightly around her waist then stalked angrily from the room.

Moments later he heard a door slam further down the corridor. He was baffled – and hurt. *What had he said to get her so mad?* He had been reaching out to her, letting her know that he would be there for her if she needed him. He got dressed and when he came out into the hall he heard the sound of the shower. He knocked on the bathroom door.

'Leave me alone!'

'Laura, I need to speak to you.'

'Go away!'

He tried the handle. The door was locked. For a moment his frustration got the better of him and he was tempted to kick it down. Walk away, it's all you can do right now, he told himself. 'I'll call you in the morning,' he said, and left the house without looking back.

Laura was standing in front of the bathroom door, her hand resting lightly on the handle, when she heard the front door bang. She had to force herself not to run after him. She hated herself for what she had done to him but it had been the only way she could push him away from her. *We can get through this together.* That had been the moment when the fantasy had come to an abrupt end, and the reality of her situation had hammered into her with all the force of a battering ram. They had no future together, no matter how much she might want it. But he didn't know that. And he would, when he found out that she had duped him and fled the country with Mel. He would always believe that she had used him. She knew that that thought would haunt her for the rest of her life. And eventually it would probably tip her off the wagon. At least there's one consolation – you can easily drink yourself to death with five million dollars, she thought bitterly.

She felt a tear seep from the corner of her eye and brushed it away. She had never felt so alone. She slid slowly to the floor, her back against the door, and wrapped her arms tightly around her knees as the tears began to stream down her face.

THIRTEEN

Saturday

When the Aztecs arrived in the Valley of Mexico in the fourteenth century to build their capital, Tenochtitlán – which is now Mexico City – they discovered the ruins of a once great city that had already been abandoned for over seven centuries. At its peak, during the fifth and sixth centuries, it had had a population of two hundred thousand and had been one of the largest cities in the world. The Aztecs called it Teotihuacán, 'the place where men became gods'. The name came from Aztec mythology, which told of a place where the gods had met to create the Sun and the Moon. Two pyramids were built so that the gods could cast themselves from the summits into a great fire and be resurrected as the Sun and the Moon. They are now the main features of the ruins of Teotihuacán. Located thirty miles north-east of Mexico City, Teotihuacán is now one of the country's major tourist attractions.

One of the first tour buses to arrive when the complex opened at eight o'clock that morning was registered with a company in Puebla, a city to the east of the capital. The company was fictitious, and its complement of passengers were INCD anti-narcotics agents. All were casually dressed, with an assortment of cameras and camcorders to help them blend in with the tourists. Each agent wore a concealed microphone to

185

stay in touch with the team leader, Colonel René Santin, who had only briefed them on their assignment once they were aboard the bus and on their way to Teotihuacán.

Kellerman and Walker, who had arrived earlier, waited until the last of the team had disembarked before boarding the bus and shaking hands with Santin. 'I wasn't expecting you two to be here so early,' Santin said as they sat down.

'It beats hanging around the embassy,' Kellerman replied. 'Lacamara knows our faces so it's best if we wait here with you until there's been a positive sighting of him. Then we can move in.'

'You know that we can't arrest him,' Santin said to Kellerman, after helping himself to a cigarette from the packet Walker offered him. 'Officially, he hasn't committed a crime. We all know that Lacamara's double-crossed the cartel, but there's been no official complaint against him.'

'Which is hardly surprising,' Walker said, after lighting his own cigarette.

'All the same, we can only offer to take him and the woman into protective custody,' Santin said. 'And if they're not interested, we'd have no option but to let them go.'

'Which means that you're going to have to do a good PR job on them,' Walker said.

'Maybe not,' Kellerman said thoughtfully. 'I've been thinking about that anonymous call you received yesterday at the embassy. How many people would have known that Lacamara was coming here this morning?'

'You mean apart from the two of them?' Walker asked. 'Amador, if he's helping them, and Justine Collins.'

'Exactly,' Kellerman said. 'Four at most. That means one of them must have made the call. And we both agreed that the voice was probably female. Which narrows it down to two. But the caller spoke Spanish, which eliminates Collins. I made some enquiries about her this morning. She doesn't speak Spanish.'

'What are you saying, that Lopez made that call?' Walker replied in amazement. 'It doesn't make any sense.'

'I agree, but if the caller *was* a woman, who else could it have been?' Kellerman wondered.

'If Lacamara is here to meet a contact who's going to help them get out of the country, who's to say it's not a woman?' Santin said.

'It's possible,' Kellerman conceded, 'but whoever is going to smuggle them out of the country will almost certainly know that the cartel would pay handsomely to get their hands on Lacamara. So why sell him out to us for nothing? No, I don't buy it.'

'And I don't buy Lopez being our anonymous caller,' Walker said.

A radio handset on an adjacent seat crackled into life and Santin was quick to answer it. 'It's Hernandez, sir. We've got company.'

'Lacamara?' Santin asked excitedly.

'No, sir. Doyle and Garcia. Do you want us to arrest them?'

Santin glanced at Kellerman, who shook his head. 'We arrest Doyle now and it could jeopardize the deal tomorrow. Tell Hernandez to hold his distance, but keep them under constant surveillance.'

'What if they try to grab Lacamara?' Walker asked.

'In front of hundreds of witnesses?' Kellerman shook his head. 'No, they're only here as observers. Their plan will be to follow Lacamara when he leaves then snatch him when there's nobody around.'

Santin passed on Kellerman's instructions to his agents. 'So much for all that extra security this morning. I should have sent Doyle a personal invitation to join us for the briefing on the bus and be done with it.'

'I'd have been more surprised if he hadn't been here,' Kellerman said.

'At least I can say with complete conviction that I know he couldn't have been tipped off by one of my agents,' Santin said.

'Which means that we've still got the drop on him because if his information came from an outside source he won't know that we've already got the place staked out,' Kellerman said.

'Unless Doyle – or one of his goons – recognizes one of your people,' Walker said to Santin.

'I doubt it,' Santin replied. 'They're all UCs I drafted in from out of town.'

Walker stubbed out his cigarette and looked at his watch. 'If Lacamara doesn't show before eleven, we're going to be in for a long wait.'

'Have you got other plans?' Kellerman asked.

'Are you kidding?' Walker laughed. 'The in-laws flew in from Boston yesterday afternoon to spend the week with us. As far as I'm concerned, this assignment's a godsend. I don't even have to make up an excuse to get out of the house. So if you've got any more stake-outs planned for the next week, put me down for as much overtime as possible.'

'I'll be sure to bear it in mind,' Kellerman said, with a smile.

Walker lit another cigarette, then swung his legs up on to the two adjoining seats and leant back against the window. 'I got a feeling I'm going to get through a lot of these in the next week. Family, eh? Fuck 'em.'

'I'll be glad to get home, change out of these clothes and soak in a hot bath.'

'Not half as glad as I'll be to see the back of you,' Carmen retorted, eyeing Amador in the rear-view mirror.

'I can see why you fell for her,' Amador said to Lacamara. 'She's such a charmer, isn't she?'

'Can't you two ever stop bickering?' Lacamara said, impatiently.

'He's always the one—'

'That's enough!' Lacamara cut angrily across her words. He immediately regretted his outburst and squeezed her arm gently. 'I'm sorry. I'm just on edge.'

'We're almost there,' she told him. 'Another few minutes, that's all.'

'Are you sure your contact will be waiting for us at Teotihuacán?' Lacamara asked Amador.

'He's not my contact. This was all set up by Justine's editor in New York. You should know, you were both there when I spoke to her on the phone last night. She said that the contact will be waiting for us in front of the Pyramid of the Sun with a holdall containing your false passports, some toiletries and change of clothes. Once you've freshened up, he'll take you to the bus. Then you'll be on your way to Veracruz – and freedom.'

'You make it all sound so easy,' Lacamara said.

'That's because it will be,' Amador said. 'Once you're aboard that bus, you're on the home stretch. In twelve hours you'll be at sea. Justine will be waiting for you when you reach Belize. She'll handle everything from then on.'

'In return for an exclusive exposé on the cartel,' Lacamara said.

'That was the understanding,' Amador replied. 'You're not having second thoughts, are you?'

'A deal's a deal,' Lacamara said indignantly.

'But what's to stop us from backing out of it once we reach Belize?' Carmen asked Amador. 'It's not as if there's anything you could do about it.'

'Officially, no,' Amador replied. 'After all, there's no written contract between us. But that could work equally in our favour. There's nothing to stop us giving the cartel an anonymous tip-off as to your whereabouts. They'd send in a team of assassins to kill you and we'd be on hand to monitor their every move once they arrived. That would certainly make some story, wouldn't it?'

'I don't believe that even you would stoop to that,' she said.

'And I don't believe you'd renege on the deal,' Amador replied.

'I told you we won't!' Lacamara wiped the sweat nervously from his face.

'No, I don't believe you will,' Amador agreed.

'Look, there's Teotihuacán ahead,' Lacamara said, grateful to be able to change the subject.

'Where do you want me to leave the car?' Carmen asked.

'There's a parking lot close to the Pyramid of the Sun,' Amador said. 'When you leave the highway, keep to the periphery road. Don't take the turn-off to the Great Compound, otherwise we're going to have a long walk to get to the meeting point.'

A short time later she was on the peripheral road, which encircled the whole complex, and drove past the huge, rectangular *ciudadela* – the citadel – a sunken square surrounded by the dwellings where the omnipotent priests and governors once resided, across the bridge spanning the San Juan river, which ran the breadth of the once magnificent city before finally reaching the Pyramid of the Sun. She parked the car, switched off the engine, and handed the keys to Amador. The car was his ride home. Lacamara was the last to get out. His shirt was drenched with sweat and clung to him uncomfortably. He wiped a damp handkerchief across his face then slipped on a pair of dark glasses.

'It's going to be OK,' Carmen said softly to him, and squeezed his hand reassuringly.

'I'll start to believe that when we're at sea and on our way to Belize,' he said, then forced a smile. 'I know I'm being paranoid but I worked long enough for the cartel to know that they've got eyes and ears everywhere.'

'If you didn't trust Amador—'

'No, you're the one who's got the problem with him,' Lacamara interrupted, and looked across at Amador who was standing a little apart from them. 'If I didn't trust him, don't you think I'd have dumped him after what happened at the safe house? Of course I'd have preferred to have made the arrangements myself. But that's not possible. Not with the cartel looking for us. We would never have made it by ourselves. Amador's our only chance now of getting safely away. And if we don't take it, we're not going to get another chance.'

'I know,' she said, then took his hand and they crossed to where Amador was waiting for them. 'Are you ready?' she asked, a harsh edge creeping back into her voice.

'I've been ready ever since we got here. You were the ones who went off for a team talk.'

'We're ready now,' Lacamara told him.

They walked in silence to the Calle de los Muertos – the Street of the Dead – around which the entire city of Teotihuacán had been built. The Pyramid of the Sun was on the west side of the city: at over two hundred and ten feet tall, it was the most prominent landmark at Teotihuacán and the obvious place for them to meet their contact.

Although the area around the pyramid was seething with tourists, Amador spotted the man from the description Justine had given him. He crossed to him and repeated the phrase Justine had made him memorize earlier. The man responded, then handed Amador the fax Ethan Byrne had sent him from New York. Amador read it and, satisfied it was genuine, beckoned Lacamara.

'Everything's been arranged,' the contact assured Lacamara, once they had been introduced. 'Are you ready to go?'

'I'm ready,' Lacamara replied, and gave a thumbs-up sign to Carmen.

'This is where I get off,' Amador said, then extended a hand to Lacamara. 'Good luck.'

'I hope we won't need it. Thanks for everything. We couldn't have made it this far without you.'

'Try telling that to Carmen,' Amador said. 'I think it's best if

I don't say goodbye to her in person. The parting might just prove too emotional for her.' With that he was gone, swallowed up by the tourists milling excitedly around the base of the pyramid. Lacamara was about to walk over to where Carmen was in conversation with their contact when a hand clamped his shoulder firmly from behind. His body stiffened in fear. He turned round to face a Japanese tourist who extended a camera towards him and made a tapping gesture with his finger. Lacamara took the camera and the man moved back to where his wife was standing at the foot of the pyramid. As Lacamara raised the camera he caught sight of a familiar face. He turned his head sharply but the man was gone. Then a small girl ran across his field of vision, breaking his concentration. He wiped his sleeve across his forehead. Had he imagined it? Then he noticed the Japanese couple watching him closely, looking uncertain. He took their picture then returned the camera and went to the spot where he thought he had seen the man. He looked down a narrow alley that led off from the Calle de los Muertos. There was no sign of him among the tourists.

'What are you doing?'

Lacamara swung round, startled. 'Carmen, you scared the life out of me. I – I thought I saw a face I knew. It's just my nerves getting the better of me.'

'Who did you think you saw?' she asked.

'His name's Ortez. He's an enforcer for the cartel.' Lacamara gave a nervous laugh. 'I must have been wrong. It couldn't have been him.'

'You're normally pretty reliable when it comes to remembering faces,' she reminded him.

'Under normal circumstances, perhaps. But right now I'm a wreck. Look at me! I'm sweating. My hands are shaking. My legs are trembling. I just want to get out of here. I feel so vulnerable in the open like this.'

'Come on then, let's go,' she said, taking his hand.

'I'll be all right once we're at sea,' he said, but he sounded as if he were trying to reassure himself.

'I know you will,' she said. 'You'll feel a lot better after you've had a chance to wash your face and put on some fresh clothes.'

'I'm sorry that I'm being so . . .' His eyes widened with fear as he looked past her. 'It's him. Look!'

She followed his gaze. 'Where?'

'He's – he's gone again,' Lacamara stuttered. 'But he was standing there. He looked – straight – straight at me. I swear it was him, Carmen!'

'I believe you,' she said. 'That means they're on to us. And Amador's the only person who could have sold us out.'

'But that's impossible. We didn't let him out of our sight after he'd contacted Collins last night. How could he have passed on any information to the cartel? No, there has to be another explanation.'

'Fine, have it your way,' she said. 'But we still have to assume that Doyle already knows our escape route, so we can forget about taking the bus to Veracruz.'

'We don't know that for sure,' Lacamara said, more in desperation than anything else.

'Do you want to take that chance?' she asked.

'What choice do we have?'

'We can do it my way,' she said.

'Your way?'

'Do you trust me?' she asked.

'You know I do,' Lacamara replied.

'I need to make a call.' She took Lacamara by the arm and led him away from the tourists to an area of open ground adjacent to the pyramid. Then she took Amador's cellular phone from her shoulder bag and dialled.

'I've got a call on hold for you,' Walker was told by the duty officer at the embassy when he answered his phone. 'It's a woman. She specifically asked to speak to you. She says she spoke to you yesterday about Lacamara.'

'Patch her through,' Walker said, then put his hand over the mouthpiece and looked at Kellerman. 'It's the anonymous caller from yesterday.'

'You mean Lopez,' Kellerman said.

'Yeah, well, we don't know that.' Walker removed his hand from the mouthpiece when he heard a female voice on the line. 'Hello, who is this?'

'This is Carmen Lopez. The name means something to you?'

'You're Hector Lacamara's girl,' Walker replied, his eyes flitting between Kellerman and Santin.

'I made that anonymous call to you yesterday.'

'Yeah, I guessed it was you,' Walker replied smugly.

'It was obvious. I assume you're here at Teotihuacán.'

'Yes. We've got undercover agents working the place. You're under surveillance as you speak.'

'We believe we've been compromised and that the cartel have men watching us as well.'

'Yes, you have – and yes, there are,' Walker said.

'Then we want to be taken into protective custody,' she told him.

There followed what sounded like a scuffle at the other end of the line, as if the phone had been yanked from her hand, then Walker heard a man's voice – 'What are you doing?' To which he heard her reply, 'Do you have a better idea?' This was followed by silence. 'Hello? Hello?' Walker shouted anxiously into the mouthpiece.

'I'm here!' she snapped back at him. 'Well, can you offer us protection?'

'Stay where you are. I'll get some of our people to you. They'll be carrying INCD badges. They'll remain with you until we get there.'

'How long will you be?'

'A few minutes. We're in the parking lot next to the Great Compound.'

The line went dead. Although Kellerman and Santin had got the gist of the conversation, Walker briefed them quickly.

'We'll go in our car,' Kellerman said. 'It'll be quicker than taking the bus.'

Santin issued orders over the radio for those agents already near the pyramid to make contact with Lacamara and Lopez then escort them to the adjoining parking lot and wait with them there until he arrived.

'You made a deal with the DEA behind my back, didn't you?' Lacamara said furiously, after she had switched off the phone.

'I didn't make any deal with them!'

'But you called them yesterday, without my knowledge or my—'

'Permission?' She finished the sentence for him. 'Is that what you were going to say?'

'I still can't believe you did that.'

'I did it merely as a precautionary measure because, unlike you, I wasn't taken in by Amador and his protestations of innocence after what happened yesterday. You were so sure that he was on the level and nothing I said would convince you otherwise.'

'And what if you'd been wrong about him?' Lacamara asked sharply.

'I wasn't, was I? But I only wish I had been because then we could have got on the bus and been on our way to Veracruz by now. The DEA couldn't have stopped us. They must know about the money you took from the cartel but they don't have any proof. It's all just hearsay.'

'And you think we'll be safe if the DEA take us into protective custody? I hate to disillusion you, Carmen, but all you've done is made it that much easier for the cartel to get to us. The DEA can put us in an impenetrable fortress and surround us with as many heavily armed guards as they want but it won't make any difference, because you can be sure that at least one of those guards will be working for the cartel. And there are many ways to kill someone without making it look suspicious.'

'You said the Salcidos would want you alive because you were the only one who can lead them to their money.'

'Ideally, yes.' Lacamara glanced past her as four men approached them. 'But they wouldn't hesitate to sacrifice the money if it meant preventing me from testifying against them.'

'Hector Lacamara?' one of the men said, holding up his laminated ID card. 'We're with the INCD. Would you come with us, please?'

'Where are we going?' Lacamara demanded.

'We've been asked to take you to the parking lot and wait with you there until Colonel Santin arrives.'

'Forget it!' Lacamara retorted. 'We're not going anywhere with you. I don't know you.'

'I told you—'

'That you're with the INCD. Yes, so you said. But I only have your word for it. For all I know you could be working for the cartel. Those ID cards aren't difficult to forge. We're staying right here until I see a face I know.'

'I'd have thought you'd have known which agents were on the take,' the agent replied.

'I was the paymaster. Names I know. Not faces.'

'OK. We'll wait here with you until Colonel Santin arrives.'

'You can stand over there,' Carmen said, flicking her hand towards the edge of the clearing. 'We were in the middle of a private conversation and we'd like to finish it, if you have no objection.'

The man conceded with a nod and retreated with the others.

'The way I see it, we've got two choices,' she said to Lacamara. 'Either we take our chances with the DEA or we try to get out of here on our own. But if the place is already crawling with the cartel's men, I don't think we'd get very far, do you?'

'I thought you said we had two choices.'

'Then you agree – we take our chances with the DEA?' she said.

'I guess so,' he replied dejectedly, then noticed three men hurrying towards them. 'Now these faces I do know. The one on the left is Colonel René Santin – he's the head of the INCD in Mexico City. Totally incorruptible. He's been a real thorn in the cartel's side for years. The one in the middle is Tom Kellerman. He's the DEA's top man here in Mexico. Like Santin, untouchable. And it's not as if we – the cartel haven't tried to recruit them.'

'And the one on the right is Walker,' she concluded.

'Yes. Officially he's Kellerman's right-hand at the DEA. Unofficially Kellerman's known to favour his other senior aide. I'm surprised she's not here.'

'*She?*' Carmen said, astonished.

The three men reached them before Lacamara could elaborate further. Lacamara looked at each face in turn, then smiled faintly at the irony of the situation. 'I never thought I'd see the day when I'd have to turn to the DEA for help. Not that it's going to do me much good now that the cartel knows where I am.'

'We can talk about this in the car.' Kellerman looked around him. 'You're exposed out here. We don't want to take any unnecessary risks.'

Santin had his men escort Lacamara and Carmen to the car. They both got into the back and Kellerman closed the door. 'I want to speak to them alone,' he told Santin.

'Suits me, I want a word with their contact anyway,' Santin said.

Kellerman got into the front passenger seat. He turned to face them. 'We can take you both into protective custody. You'd be perfectly safe.'

'And in return I would be expected to testify in court against the Salcidos, is that it?' Lacamara asked.

'You've got it,' Kellerman said.

'You don't think that the Salcidos would let me testify, do you? They'll have me killed at the first opportunity. You know that.'

'Not if we were to keep you on the move until after you'd testified. They can only get at you if they know where to find you.'

'Except that it would be an inside job,' Lacamara replied. 'They have a lot of influence within the INCD. They've even managed to penetrate the DEA. One of your senior aides is already on the payroll.'

'Interesting,' was all that Kellerman said.

'So you see, even if you were to keep us on the move from day to day, we still wouldn't be safe.'

'Not if your movements were known only to a select few within the DEA and the INCD. We'd also let you vet the list of agents in advance that were assigned to protect you. After all, you're in the unique position of knowing exactly which members of the INCD work for the cartel.'

'That's true,' Lacamara said. 'What would we get in return if I took the stand against the Salcidos?'

'New identities and relocation anywhere in the world,' Kellerman replied. 'You'd also get to keep the money you skimmed from the cartel.'

'What if Hector refused to testify?' Carmen asked.

'Then we'd cut you loose.'

'Knowing full well that the cartel would track us down within hours and kill us,' she said.

'This is a sweetheart deal, Ms Lopez,' Kellerman told her. 'You help us, we help you. If you don't like it, you're welcome to walk away now. We can't hold you against your will – as far as we're concerned, neither of you has committed a felony.'

'And what's to prevent you from throwing us to the wolves after Hector's testified against the cartel?' she asked.

'Our reputation. Word would spread quickly if we reneged

on our part of the deal and that would make it harder for us to convince others to go down the same road.'

'Can we have a few minutes alone to talk about this?' Lacamara asked.

'Take as long as you want,' Kellerman replied. 'But stay in the car. I don't think Doyle would be foolish enough to make a move against you here, but let's not give him any ideas.'

'Doyle's here?' Lacamara's face paled.

'Doyle and Garcia. And an assortment of their goons. But don't worry, you're safe in here. The windows are bulletproof and the bodywork's reinforced. They can't get to you, even if they wanted to.'

'Why don't you arrest Doyle?' Carmen demanded.

'On what charge?' Kellerman replied.

'It's obvious why he's here – to have us killed,' she said.

'Except no one can prove it,' Lacamara told her.

'If we were to hold Doyle, we'd be sued for false arrest,' Kellerman said, 'and with the kind of slick lawyers the Salcidos have at their disposal, he'd have every chance of winning. We don't need that kind of bad publicity, especially if we intend to press charges of our own against the Salcidos.'

'Assuming that Hector agrees to testify,' Carmen pointed out.

'I'll leave you to discuss that between yourselves. Call me when you've come to a decision.'

'Are you going to arrest Amador?' Carmen asked, as Kellerman reached for the door. 'He's the one who set us up. It's obvious he's working for the cartel.'

'Is he?' Kellerman asked Lacamara.

'Do you think I'd have trusted him if I'd known he was on the cartel's payroll?' Lacamara snapped. 'Credit me with some intelligence, Kellerman.'

Kellerman got out of the car and saw that Santin had returned. He was talking to Walker. 'Well?' Santin asked, as Kellerman came up to them.

'I put our cards on the table. They asked for time to think it over.'

'You think they'll go for it?' Walker asked.

'What choice have they got?' Kellerman replied. 'René, have a couple of extra cars brought in to escort them to the embassy. I don't want to take any chances.'

'Where are you going to take them from there?'

'We'll discuss that at the embassy,' Kellerman said. 'Did you find out anything useful from their contact?'

'He doesn't appear to know much – other than his own limited part in the operation to smuggle them out of the country. I've had him taken into custody anyway so that he can be questioned further. I don't think we'll get much out of him, though.'

'Kellerman?' Lacamara called. 'You've got yourself a deal.'

'Good,' Kellerman said, crossing to the car. 'We can leave as soon as the escort cars get here from INCD headquarters. It's an added security precaution, that's all.'

Santin came over and put a hand on Kellerman's arm. 'Can I have a word? In private?'

'What is it?' Kellerman asked, once they were out of earshot.

'You're not going to believe this. Doyle wants to speak to you.'

'Where is he?'

'At the Pyramid of the Sun.' Santin held up his radio. 'I've got one of my men waiting to give him your reply. Do you want to speak to him?'

'Sure, let's hear what he has to say,' Kellerman replied. 'It should be interesting, if nothing else.'

Kellerman waited until Santin had given the order to let Doyle through the cordon, which had been set up between the pyramid and the parking lot, then walked back to the car. 'Doyle's asked to speak to me,' Kellerman told Lacamara. 'I've agreed to see him.'

'Just make sure you keep him well away from us!' Carmen blurted out.

'He may ask to speak to you,' Kellerman said to Lacamara. 'If he does, do you want to see him?'

'Didn't you hear what I just said?' Carmen shrieked.

'I wasn't asking you,' Kellerman told her.

Lacamara rubbed his hand anxiously over his face then shook his head. 'No, I don't want to speak to him.'

'That's all I need to know,' Kellerman said, then went to the edge of the clearing where Doyle was being frisked. He was clean.

'Agent Kellerman, isn't it?' Doyle said, and proffered his hand.

'What do you want, Doyle?' Kellerman replied, ignoring it.

'I believe you've arrested Hector Lacamara,' Doyle said.

'He hasn't been arrested. He's asked to be taken into protective custody.'

'Protective custody?' Doyle exclaimed. 'You must realize that Hector's unwell, Agent Kellerman. He's been under a lot of strain these last few months. In fact, he's on the verge of a breakdown. At least, that's what two of the country's leading psychiatrists concluded when they examined him last week.'

'And I'm sure you've got their diagnoses in writing,' Kellerman replied coldly.

'I would assume they each have a case file on him – after all, it's not the first time he's been to see them. I take it his request for protective custody has got something to do with the money he embezzled from the company.'

Kellerman was caught off guard by Doyle's frankness but recovered quickly. 'So you admit that he's skimmed money from the Salcidos?'

'It's no secret.'

'Why didn't you press charges?' Kellerman asked.

'Hector and Juan Salcido go back a long way and Mr Salcido felt that the amount involved didn't warrant bringing in the police. He doesn't want to press charges – not only to avoid any bad publicity but also because of their friendship. He just wants the money returned, that's all.'

'I'll bet he does,' Kellerman retorted. 'Fifty million's a lot of money to write off as a bad debt.'

'Fifty million?' Doyle replied in apparent disbelief. He laughed heartily. 'I'm sorry, Agent Kellerman, but if you knew the truth you'd realize why I find that so funny. Where did you get a figure like that from?'

'So you're saying that he didn't skim fifty million dollars from the cartel?'

'Cartel?' Doyle replied with a frown. 'I'd hardly call Mex-Freight a cartel, would you? From what we can gather from an independent audit, Hector's embezzled in the region of three hundred thousand. If he'd taken fifty million Mex-Freight would be financially crippled and unable to continue operating.'

'We both know where that money came from, Doyle, so you can drop the act.'

'I really don't know what you're talking about, Agent Kellerman.'

'Have it your way, Doyle, but you won't be laughing when Lacamara's testimony puts you and the Salcidos behind bars for life.'

Doyle's smile faltered. 'Obviously it was a mistake trying to reason with you, Agent Kellerman. I'd like to speak to Hector.'

'He doesn't want to speak to you.'

'Then let him tell me that himself.'

'I think it's time for you to leave.'

'Or what? You'll have me arrested. Just as you had Hector arrested.'

'He came to us of his own free will,' Kellerman said.

'Then let him tell me that himself because I only have your word for it.' Doyle raised a finger to silence Kellerman before he could respond. 'I've already explained to you that Hector's been under a lot of strain these past few months. And we have experts who will publicly verify that if necessary. I don't want to tell the press that the DEA have taken advantage of a man who's in a confused state of mind to use him in their ongoing vendetta against the Salcidos. A vendetta which, as far as the public is concerned, has no foundation. Can the DEA afford that kind of negative publicity?'

'Is that a threat?' Kellerman said icily.

'I'm merely asking you to let me speak to Hector to help clarify the situation,' Doyle replied evasively. 'And if he tells me that he doesn't want to speak to me, then I'll leave. That's not an unreasonable request, is it?'

'And go straight to the press?' Kellerman said.

'Not if I'm satisfied that Hector's not being held against his will. If that's so then our lawyers will challenge any allegations Hector might make against either Juan or Ramón Salcido.'

Kellerman knew that Doyle had trapped him. If he refused to let him speak to Lacamara, the press would have a field day at the DEA's expense – which would be especially harmful if they were able to quote expert medical opinion. But Doyle would almost certainly have some spiel lined up to try to get Lacamara to leave with him. And as Lacamara was not under arrest, there was nothing he, or the INCD, could do to stop him. 'Very well,' he said at length, 'I'll let you speak to him. But if he tells you he doesn't want to speak to you, you leave. And if you don't, I'll have you arrested.'

'That's fair enough,' Doyle agreed, then followed Kellerman to the car.

'I know that you said you didn't want to speak to Doyle, but he wants to hear it from you,' Kellerman told an apprehensive Lacamara. 'Then he'll leave.'

'Hector, it's good to see you again,' Doyle said quickly, before Lacamara had a chance to say anything. 'Juan's been worried about you. He asked me to come here in person to talk to you. He has a proposition which I'm sure will interest you.'

'Hector doesn't want to talk to you!' Carmen snapped. 'Now leave.'

'I didn't realize that you let your woman speak for you,

Hector,' Doyle said, without taking his eyes off Lacamara's face. 'I can't believe that you of all people would allow yourself to be pussy-whipped like that.'

'How dare you—'

'Shut up, Carmen!' Lacamara turned on her.

'That's more like the old Hector I know,' Doyle said. 'So what do you say, Hector? Will you at least hear me out? I think you'll find the offer more than generous.'

'I'll be the judge of that,' Lacamara replied.

'Can we talk?' Doyle said, then looked at Carmen. 'In private?'

'Forget it,' Kellerman said behind him.

'So you're speaking for him as well now, Agent Kellerman?' Doyle said, and shrugged helplessly at Lacamara. He looked round at Kellerman. 'Is Hector under arrest?'

'I've already told you he's not.'

'Then let him speak for himself!' Doyle turned back to Lacamara. 'Juan specifically asked that we discuss his offer in private. I think at least you owe him that, don't you?'

'Whatever you have to say to Hector, you can say in front of me,' Carmen told him. 'We don't have any secrets from one another.'

A faint sneer touched the corners of Doyle's lips and Lacamara glared at Carmen. Then he shoved open the door with such venom that Doyle had to step back smartly. Lacamara got out and slammed the door. Doyle led him away from the car and stopped only when he was satisfied that they could not be overheard by the others. 'Here's the deal. You return the money you stole from us, together with the codes for the files that you've hidden in the computer, and the contract on you and your girlfriend will be lifted immediately. Neither of you will be harmed.'

'And of course I have your word on that,' Lacamara said contemptuously.

'You have Juan Salcido's word on that,' Doyle countered, 'and you know as well as I do that he never goes back on it.'

'Why the sudden change of heart? Yesterday I was being used as target practice, today I'm being offered a lifeline. It doesn't make any sense.'

'That was Ramón's doing. He's since had his wings clipped. I've been put in charge of recovering the money and the computer codes. And I'm answerable only to Juan.'

'Supposing I did go for this deal. What would happen to me after I returned the money? I could never go back to accounting. Who would trust me after what I've done? I'd be lucky to get a job sweeping the streets. It's not much of an incentive, is it? Thanks for the offer, but I think I'll take my chances with the DEA.'

'What have they promised you? That in return for testifying against the cartel, they'll let you keep the money you stole? And that they'll give you and your girlfriend new identities and relocate you in a country of your choice. Sounds good, doesn't it? I guess two out of three wouldn't be bad.'

'What do you mean?' Lacamara asked uneasily.

'What do you think would happen if you were to take the stand against the cartel? The defence would paint you as an embezzler who walked out on his family and who only agreed to testify against the Salcidos to keep the money he stole from them. By the time they'd finished with you, your credibility as a prosecution witness would be in shreds. And the money would be impounded by the authorities as evidence. And do you really believe they would just give it back to you at the end of the trial? Because if you do, you're living in a fantasy world.' Doyle smiled at Lacamara's obvious unease. 'But I wouldn't worry about that. It's all hypothetical. You'd never live long enough to testify against the cartel. Oh, I know Kellerman will have given you assurances that the DEA can protect you until the trial. I'm sure he means well, but we'll get to you. And we'll get to your girlfriend. You have *my* word on that.'

'We'll see about that,' Lacamara said defiantly, but the bravado was as false as the tone of his voice.

'It looks like the reinforcements have just arrived,' Doyle said, looking across at two approaching cars. 'None of this is necessary, Hector. The offer is on the table.'

'I've got nothing more to say to you,' Lacamara snapped and walked off.

'You will,' Doyle said softly to himself, as he watched Lacamara get back into the car. 'Believe me, you will.'

FOURTEEN

'He didn't go for it,' Doyle said, when Juan Salcido answered the phone in his office on the twentieth floor of the Mex-Freight building.

'I can't say I'm surprised,' Salcido replied, sitting back in his chair. 'It was always going to be a long shot. Have you found out yet how the authorities knew Hector would be at Teotihuacán today?'

'Not yet. I didn't ask Lacamara. Somehow I don't think he would have told me even if I had.'

'No, probably not,' Salcido said. 'Have they left Teotihuacán yet?'

'Yes, they were driven in convoy to the American embassy. I'm parked outside the embassy now. The DEA will assume that we're watching the place, which means they're going to take every precaution when it comes to moving Lacamara. Assuming, of course, that they haven't already smuggled him out.'

'Any ideas where they might take him?' Salcido asked.

'I've already got all the INCD safe houses under surveillance,' Doyle told him. 'So far nothing. But the DEA may have a safe house of their own that I don't know about.'

'I assume that will be rectified soon?'

'I'm working on it,' Doyle assured him.

'Good.' Salcido lit a cigarette. 'We've got another little problem which needs to be handled quickly – and discreetly. I had a word with Ramón a short time ago and it seems that Hector gave Justine Collins several incriminating photographs of you with Melissa Wade. Amador was supposed to have got them back for us by tomorrow afternoon but with Hector now in protective custody, she has no reason to stay in Mexico any longer. My guess is that she'll want to get back to New York with the photographs so that she can write up a story about Wade and salvage something from her trip out here. Frankly, I don't care what happens to Wade after tomorrow, but until then we can't afford to have those photographs in the wrong hands. Get them back.'

'Is she still staying at Amador's house?' Doyle asked.

'Yes. The INCD have got it under twenty-four-hour surveillance. You'll have to get past them first.'

'What about Amador?'

'The INCD may not be able to prove that it was Amador who tipped off Ramón that Lacamara would be at Teotihuacán this morning, but they're going to reach that conclusion anyway. Which means that his cover's blown. He's become a liability.'

'I'll get on it right away,' Doyle told him.

'I want to know the moment you get any information on Lacamara's whereabouts. Call in as many favours as you want. Money is no object. But I want him found before the authorities start to debrief him.'

'For all we know, they may have already started,' Doyle pointed out.

'Then why are you still talking to me?' Salcido snapped and slammed down the receiver.

Laura hurried through to the lounge to answer the phone when it rang. 'It's Tom,' a familiar voice announced. 'How're you doing?'

'Good.' She had been waiting all morning for him to call. Now that he was on the other end of the line, she felt self-conscious. Especially after her performance the previous evening. It had been unforgivable, and she knew it. 'Tom, about what happened last night . . .' Her voice trailed off when she remembered Mel telling her never to use the phone in the house if she wanted to contact her. Was it bugged? She flushed, embarrassed that an eavesdropper may have read something into what she had been about to say.

'Laura, are you still there?' Kellerman asked, after an uneasy silence.

'Yes. I'm sorry, I didn't mean to mention . . . you know . . .'

'The phone's not tapped if that's what you're worried about.' Kellerman chuckled. 'We can talk quite freely.'

'That's a relief,' she said lamely.

'What made you think it might be?'

'I remembered Mel once telling me that she thought her phone was being tapped,' Laura said, blurting out the first thing that came into her head.

'Why would she think that?' Kellerman replied in surprise. 'We don't tap our agents' phones without reasonable cause – any suspicious calls would show up on the weekly print-out we receive from the phone company. Melissa knew that. And we'd know straight away if an outside source ever tried to put a wire on any of our phones.'

It had been a bad blunder and Laura knew it. She had thought Mel had meant the phone was being tapped when she had told her never to call her from the house. Only she hadn't said it in so many words. Laura gripped the receiver tighter. 'I guess I must have misunderstood her,' she said, hoping that would put an end to the subject.

'I guess so,' came the reply. A pause. 'Any chance of us getting together later?'

'I'd like that,' she replied.

'I can't give you an exact time right now. It'll probably be early evening before I can get away. We took Lacamara and his girlfriend into protective custody earlier this morning. He's agreed to testify against the cartel.'

Laura almost dropped the phone, such was the devastating impact of his words. She sat down slowly on the edge of the nearest armchair and struggled to regain her composure. If the DEA found out that Mel had been helping herself to a cut of every bribe she had received from the cartel over the past eight months, it would put the meeting with Doyle in jeopardy. No meeting, no diamonds. No diamonds, no way out . . .

'That's great news,' she said, having to force the enthusiasm into her voice.

'With Doyle and Lacamara as the two main witnesses for the prosecution, we can finally smash the cartel once and for all. The Salcidos can hire as many fancy lawyers as they want but it won't do them any good. I tell you, Laura, it's a good feeling knowing that the net's finally closing over them. A real good feeling.'

'I can believe it,' she said.

'Doyle will see Melissa now as his best chance of getting to Lacamara. So don't be surprised if her beeper goes off in the next few hours. If it does, call me. We can take it from there.'

'Sure,' she said absently, then replaced the handset. She tried to console herself with the thought that the DEA's initial debriefing would centre on the Salcidos, and not on the payments made to Mel. But what if it came up in discussion and the discrepancies were uncovered? She knew the chances of it happening were remote to say the least, but not impossible . . .

Suddenly the beeper went off. She could feel her heart pounding frantically as she stared at the device lying on the coffee table, then she silenced it. Her breathing was ragged and uneven. She picked up the receiver again and had already punched in the first two digits of Kellerman's cellular phone, which he had written down for her on the memo pad beside the telephone, when she disconnected the line. 'What the hell are you doing?' she asked herself aloud. It had been an instinctive reaction to call him, she tried to tell herself, but she had no intention of going through with it. At least, not until she'd had a chance to talk to Mel. And, depending on how Mel wanted to handle it, perhaps not at all.

Laura didn't bother to set the alarm when she left the house and hurried to the pay phone at the end of the street to call her sister.

'The DEA have got Lacamara,' she told Melissa.

'Well, at least now we know where he is,' Melissa replied.

'You're taking it very calmly,' Laura said. She had expected a volley of expletives down the line.

'There are only two safe houses they would use, at least until they can get him safely out of the country – which I assume they will do within the next couple of days anyway. Both are funded by the DEA. One's ten miles north of Mexico City. The other's in the south of the country. Near Zenzontepec. Only that one's being renovated so they won't take him there. Which doesn't leave them with much choice.'

'You seem very sure of that,' Laura said.

'It's my job, sis.'

'What are you going to do?' Laura asked uncertainly.

'You let me worry about that.'

'Doyle's already tried to contact you. Your beeper went off just before I left the house to come here to phone you.'

'He certainly didn't waste any time.'

'Tom said I was to phone him if the beeper went off—'

'You haven't, have you?' Melissa cut in sharply.

'No, of course not!'

Melissa exhaled deeply down the line. 'Thank God for that. You really had me worried there.'

'Your trust in me is touching, Mel,' Laura said.

'You're right. I'm sorry. It's just that we've got a lot riding on this. One mistake now could prove costly.'

'What do you want me to do about Doyle?' Laura asked.

'Nothing. I'll contact him.'

'You're going to tell Doyle how to get into the safe house so that he can kill Lacamara, aren't you?'

'Like I said, sis, you let me worry about that. And remember, as far as Tom's concerned, the beeper never went off. He's got no reason to doubt your word.'

'And that's what hurts most of all after what happened last night,' Laura replied, and immediately regretted what she had just said.

There was a pause. 'You fucked him, didn't you?'

'Why do you always have to be so crude?'

'Oh, I forgot, sis, you always hear the Mantovani Strings playing in the background when you have sex. Well, I hate to interrupt the violins, but you'd better snap out of your daydream. We're here to do a job. Professionally, and impartially. You go soft on me now and you could blow everything just by saying one wrong word in a moment of weakness.'

'I can handle it,' Laura said angrily, but knew she sounded as if she was trying to convince herself. 'And anyway,' she continued quickly, 'you were the one who said to me yesterday that I should sleep with him.'

'It was only said as a joke, for Christ's sake. I didn't think for one moment that you would. But I should have seen it coming, shouldn't I? You only sleep with a guy once you've developed real feelings for him.'

'And is that such a crime?'

'Oh, sis, you can be so naïve at times. Tom's wanted to get me into bed for as long as I can remember. Now he has. Don't you see? It wasn't you he was fucking, it was me.'

'You're sick, you know that?'

'It's true,' Melissa said, her voice softening. 'I know I should have told you this before. I'm sorry.'

'I don't believe it!' Laura yelled. 'He said that you two were nothing more than platonic friends.'

'We were, but that doesn't mean it's what he wanted. And he was hardly going to say that to you, was he? That would have been real tactful, considering that I'm supposed to be dead.'

'I can't believe he could have used me like that,' Laura said, but there was no self-pity in her voice. Just anger and bitterness.

'Me neither. Not Tom. Are you going to be OK?'

'I'm not going to hit the bottle if that's what you mean. As you said, we've got a job to do out here. And, what's more, we're going to pull it off without a hitch.'

'Good on you, sis, but whatever you do, don't say anything to Tom about what I've just told you. He mustn't suspect a thing. All you have to do is keep him at arm's length for another twenty-four hours. Then we're home free.'

'I think I can manage that,' Laura said. 'After all, I've had enough practice over the years. If anything, I'm something of an expert on that score.'

'I'm going to have to meet with Doyle in the next couple of hours, but I should be back at the hotel later this afternoon. So if you want to come over – or if you just want to talk on the phone – I'm here for you. Remember that.'

Laura hung up then walked home. The man in the house opposite was washing his car in the driveway. He gave her a friendly wave but she slammed the gate behind her and strode up the path to the front door without acknowledging him.

'Cigarette?'

'Thanks,' Jorge Alvarez said, taking one from the packet.

Roberto Carranza pushed a cigarette between his lips and lit it, then Alvarez's, before tossing the spent match through the open window. Both were experienced INCD agents and neither welcomed the tedium of surveillance duty. Especially not on a Saturday afternoon when they could have been at home with their families. Sitting in the blue Ford Topaz parked in the mouth of an alley, they could monitor the comings-and-goings from Amador's house on the corner of the street. Carranza had radioed in to headquarters an hour earlier to say that Amador had returned to the house. But apart from that, everything was quiet. And they still had three hours to go before their relief team took over . . .

'Shit!' Alvarez muttered when a white Transit van pulled up in front of the alley, blocking the view of Amador's house. The logo of a national courier service was printed on the side of the vehicle. The passenger door opened and a man got out, carrying a large padded envelope. He was wearing a blue tunic and a peaked cap, tugged down over his head, which with the sunglasses partially concealed his face. He stood with his back to them, apparently in discussion with the driver, then turned towards the Ford Topaz and pulled a silenced Glock automatic from inside the padded envelope. They were still clawing frantically for their holstered pistols when he dispatched them, each with a single shot through the head.

Doyle's eyes lingered on the double-dimpled windscreen, now spattered with blood, then he slipped the automatic back into the envelope. He glanced fleetingly at Garcia, who sat stone-faced behind the wheel of the van, pulled on a pair of black gloves and crossed the road to Amador's house. He rang the bell then slipped his hand into the padded envelope. As the door swung open he brought out the gun and pressed the tip of the silencer firmly against the centre of Amador's forehead. He entered the house quickly and kicked the door shut.

'What – do you want?' Amador stammered fearfully.

'I'm here for the photographs.'

'I – I told Mr Salcido – that – I'd – get them—'

'I don't give a shit what you told him,' Doyle barked. 'I want them. Now.'

'I don't know where they are,' Amador blurted out. 'Justine's got them. They're probably somewhere in her room.'

'Then you're no use to me any more,' Doyle said disdainfully, and shot him.

'Felix, what's going on out there?' a woman called from a room further down the hall. Doyle followed the sound of the voice and found Justine sitting in an armchair, writing on an A4 pad balanced on her knees. 'Felix, what . . .' She trailed off as she raised her head and saw Doyle standing in the doorway, the silenced automatic in his hand. 'Who are you? Where's Felix?' she asked shakily.

'I'm surprised you don't recognize me. But maybe I wasn't wearing these in the photographs,' he replied, then removed his sunglasses and slipped them into his breast pocket. 'There. Is that better?'

'Doyle,' she whispered in horror.

'Very good,' Doyle said sarcastically.

She shrank back further into the armchair when he entered the room. 'Where's Felix? What have you done to him?'

'What do you think?' Doyle said. 'But I wouldn't waste any sympathy on him, if I were you. He was a snitch. He worked for Ramón Salcido.'

'I don't believe it.'

'How do you think we knew that Lacamara and his whore would be at Teotihuacán this morning? How do you think we knew about the freighter in Veracruz? How do you think we knew that you had the photographs?'

She stared at Doyle with a mixture of anger and disbelief as she struggled to come to terms with the realization of Amador's treachery. 'Why kill him if he was one of your own?'

'He was never one of us. He was an outsider. A paid informer. His cover was blown this morning at Teotihuacán. That made him a liability.'

'You're going to kill me as well, aren't you?' she asked, and was surprised by the calmness in her voice. It was almost as if she had resigned herself to her fate.

'Yes,' he replied, 'after you've given me the photographs.'

She laughed. Only it came out as a choked cough. 'That's hardly much of an incentive for me to get them for you, is it?'

'It all depends on how you want to die. Give me the photographs, and I promise it'll be quick. Hold out on me, and you'll die very slowly. A bullet in the belly. And as you're slowly bleeding to death you'll have time to reflect that you were responsible for killing your own baby.'

She launched herself out of the chair and lunged at him in a fit of sheer rage. Her pace and agility caught him by surprise and before he had a chance to react she had lashed out at him with her fist, striking him across the face. He stumbled backwards but kept his balance and, sidestepping her flailing arms, slammed the base of his palm painfully into the small of her back. Her momentum carried her forward and she landed in an ungainly heap on the sofa. It took her a few seconds to catch her breath but by then Doyle had already retreated a safe distance and had the automatic trained on her as she sat up slowly. She noticed, with some satisfaction, the red mark on his cheek where she had caught him with her fist. It was a hollow victory. But a victory all the same. Not that it was over . . . yet.

'So much for the foreplay. Now maybe we can get down to business.' Doyle tilted the angle of the automatic until the barrel was aimed at her belly. 'Where are the photographs?'

'In my room.'

'Ladies first,' Doyle said, gesturing to the door. He followed her out and kept his distance when she paused to look down dispassionately at Amador's body. Then she continued on to the spare bedroom and as she stepped inside she slipped a hand around the edge of the door, ready to slam it in Doyle's face when he was in range. But he anticipated the move. 'Right idea, wrong pigeon,' he said. She let her arm drop to her side then entered the room and crossed to the chest of drawers by the window. 'That's far enough! Where are the photographs?'

'They're in that folder.'

Doyle could see a folder lying in front of a row of cosmetics on the chest of drawers. 'Get it, and put it on the bed,' he ordered.

She had never believed in fate before, but now she was beginning to have second thoughts. The previous evening she had cleared out her purse and placed the contents on the chest of drawers. The mace she always carried was partially concealed behind a can of deodorant spray. Of course, she still had to get it without him seeing her. She already had an idea in mind and as she picked up the folder she caught the edge on the deodorant spray, knocking it over. As she righted it, she slipped the mace surreptitiously under the folder, holding it against the inside of her fingers. She turned away from the chest of drawers, almost expecting Doyle to have seen her, but from his expression he suspected nothing. She knew she would have only one chance. If she missed, he would kill her and her baby. That was enough to boost her confidence.

She crossed to the bed then hesitated as if she was about to drop the folder and Doyle took a step forward intending to pick it up. Then she let go, brought up the can of mace and sprayed it into his face. He had only seen it at the last moment but even then he could still have got off a shot before she sprayed him yet all his instincts were telling him to protect himself. It felt as if his body were moving in slow motion as he turned his head away from the nozzle and raised his hands to cover his face.

He took the brunt of the spray on the side of his face and cried out in anguish as it seared painfully into his skin, temporarily blinding him in one eye. He stumbled back against the wardrobe, tears streaming down his face, and was vaguely aware of Justine darting past him and disappearing into the hall. He screamed in fury and, still disoriented, went after her. He clamped his hand over his blinded eye in an attempt to realign his impaired vision and saw her running towards the front door. His first shot went wild, slamming harmlessly into the wall. He fired again. And again. Both bullets were also wide of the mark but one shattered a vase on the hall table, spilling the flowers across the carpet. The sound of breaking glass startled Justine and she caught her foot on the door mat, lost her balance, and had to slam her hands against the wall to prevent herself falling. Valuable seconds lost. She was still clawing frantically for the latch when the first bullet took her between the shoulder blades. She was slammed forward against the door and lost all sensation in her legs as they buckled underneath her. She knew then that she was going to die and clamped her hands protectively over her belly to protect the child she would never know . . .

Doyle stood over her then pressed the automatic against the back of her head and squeezed the trigger. He felt for a pulse and, finding none, staggered back to the bedroom where he sat down on the edge of the bed, trying to clear his head. It felt like a hot poker was being ground savagely into his eye. All he wanted was to be rid of the excruciating pain. He knew it would fade in time and that there would be no lasting after-effects. There never were with tear gas. Forcing himself to concentrate, he slipped the automatic and the folder into the padded envelope then, getting to his feet, he moved unsteadily into the hall. Putting on his sunglasses and his peaked cap, he opened the front door and stepped out on to the small patio. He almost lost his footing as he went down the three steps to the path then walked as purposefully as he could towards the gate.

Garcia had realized that something was wrong the moment Doyle emerged from the house. He pulled away from the mouth of the alley, drew up in front of the gate and pushed open the passenger door. Doyle got in beside him.

'What happened?'

'It's done,' Doyle said, through clenched teeth. 'I've got the photographs.'

'Are you OK?'

'Do I look OK?' Doyle snarled. 'Just get us the fuck out of here. Now!

'I still don't see why you can't arrest him? He threatened to kill us.'

'We've been through this all before, Ms Lopez,' Kellerman said. 'It would come down to Doyle's word against Lacamara's. And in view of what Doyle told me about the psychiatric reports on Lacamara, his lawyers would have every right to sue us for false arrest.'

'But Hector's never seen a psychiatrist in his life,' she replied, clenching her fists.

'The fact remains those files exist,' Kellerman told her. 'And that's what any judge would go on, particularly as they were prepared by two of the country's leading psychiatrists.'

'Is there anybody the Salcidos can't buy?' she snapped.

'Ask your boyfriend. After all, he was their paymaster.'

'We couldn't buy you,' Lacamara said to Kellerman.

'You obviously didn't make the right offer,' Kellerman replied.

The three were sitting on wooden chairs in an otherwise empty office at the rear of the American embassy, nowhere near the DEA's basement sanctum.

They had been there for the past hour, and were still waiting for the INCD helicopter. Lacamara had remained in his seat in the corner of the room ever since they arrived, his head bowed in thought. Carmen had paced the room incessantly and it had only been in the last few minutes that she had finally sat down. She'd had a lot to say in that time, much of it critical of the DEA and their handling of the situation. Particularly for allowing Doyle to walk at Teotihuacán. They had been over the same ground several times, but nothing Kellerman had said placated her. Not that it bothered him. He regarded her as nothing more than a passenger along for the ride.

Kellerman liked to think of himself as a tolerant person, but he had taken an instant dislike to her. She was petty, vindictive and thoroughly unpleasant. What Lacamara saw in her was beyond him. But that wasn't his concern. All that mattered to him was ensuring that Lacamara survived long enough to testify against the cartel. After that he couldn't care less what happened to either of them. That was purely on a personal level, though, knowing as much as he did about Lacamara's past involvement with the cartel. The man had as much blood on his hands as the Salcidos. That said, though, he would keep to his side of the deal and have them relocated, together with new identities, to a country of their choice. Assuming, of course, the country would take them. Chances were that Lacamara would choose a Spanish-speaking country where they could blend into their new community – more than likely somewhere in South America. But that was still way off . . .

'How much longer are we going to have to wait in here?' Carmen demanded then got up and began to pace the floor again.

'Until the helicopter gets here,' Kellerman replied.

'You keep saying that!'

'And I'll keep saying it every time you ask me,' Kellerman said irritably.

'It's not good enough,' she retorted.

'If you don't like it, feel free to leave. I certainly won't try to stop you.'

'Carmen, sit down,' Lacamara said, and pointed at the vacant chair in the centre of the room.

'I can't just sit around—'

'Sit down!' Lacamara bellowed. He sighed heavily. 'Please, just do it,' he asked her, more calmly. His eyes went to Kellerman. 'This waiting game's starting to get to me too. A lot of it's down to not having slept properly in days. All I want to do is soak in a hot bath then stretch out on a soft mattress and get a good night's sleep. I hope you'll allow me that luxury once we get to the safe house.'

'The debriefing can wait until tomorrow,' Kellerman replied.

The door swung open. 'The chopper's on its way,' Walker announced. 'It should be here within the next ten to fifteen minutes.'

'About time too,' Carmen said tersely.

'You go with them to the safe house,' Kellerman said to Walker. 'I've got a backlog of calls waiting for me in my office. Starting with Braithwaite in Washington. That should be fun.'

'When do we start the debriefing?' Walker asked.

'Tomorrow,' Kellerman replied. 'See that they get settled in, then you can leave.'

'Is there a cook on the premises?' Carmen said.

'This is a safe house, Ms Lopez, not the Sheraton,' Kellerman snapped. 'The fridge is well stocked, but speciality dishes can be brought in for you if necessary. Our people are there to protect you, not to cater for you. And now, if you'll excuse me, I'll leave you in the capable hands of Agent Walker. See you both in the morning.' With that Kellerman got up and left the room.

'Nice bruise.'

'Sit down.' Doyle kicked the chair towards Melissa.

Melissa put out a hand to stop it then sat down. She had called him after her conversation with Laura and agreed to a meeting at the usual place. 'Shades as well?' she remarked. 'It must have been some fight.'

'It had its moments,' Doyle replied, then reached for the bottle of beer in front of him. 'I didn't bother getting you a drink. Not after the last time.'

Although Melissa had no idea what he was talking about, she knew he must be referring to when he had met Laura in the same bar two days earlier. 'I didn't come here to reminisce,' she said shortly, knowing it was best to change the subject before she could be drawn in any further. 'So to what do I owe the pleasure of your company this time?'

'An hour ago a helicopter put down on the roof of the American embassy then took off again. I imagine Lacamara was on board.'

'It could have been a decoy,' Melissa suggested.

'It's possible, but it doesn't really matter, the point being that we've no idea where he's likely to have been taken. That's why you're here. Where is he?'

'Just like that?' she replied, with a bemused smile. 'OK, so assuming I do know where he's been taken, what's in it for me?'

Doyle took a drink from the bottle then leant forward. His voice was low, but still audible above the sound of the rowdy drinkers around them. 'Lacamara was our chief paymaster. That meant he was responsible for all payments made by the cartel. Including all monies paid to informers. And one of the first things the DEA will want to know when they start to debrief him is which of their agents are working for the cartel. Your name's sure to be one of the first to crop up. In which case you'll be suspended with immediate effect, pending a full inquiry. But maybe they won't find out about your treachery until after we've concluded our little deal tomorrow morning. In which case you've got nothing to worry about. But if they do, you can kiss those diamonds goodbye.'

'And you can kiss the disk goodbye,' she responded.

'Right now, that's the least of our worries. Lacamara's our main priority. We need to get to him before he has a chance to talk to the authorities and do some serious damage to the cartel. So, you see, we're in the same boat, albeit for different reasons.'

'I wasn't told where he's been taken – I'm not part of the security detail – but my guess would be the DEA's safe house on the outskirts of the city,' Melissa said.

'A DEA safe house on our doorstep? Well, you learn something new every day.' Doyle sat back slowly in his chair. 'I guess it's impregnable?'

'That all depends who wants to get in,' she replied, with a knowing smile.

'Go on,' Doyle prompted.

'I think I'll have that drink after all. Make it a double.'

FIFTEEN

The name of the farm had once hung proudly at the entrance to the dirt road. That had been before the DEA had bought the property and converted it into a safe house. The sign was long gone, but the support post and projection beam were still in place, rotting like some abandoned gibbet and made all the more macabre by the length of rusted chain that hung there. The dirt road was riddled with potholes and flanked by thick, overgrown shrubbery, which wound a lifeless trail through the desolation for several hundred yards before reaching a grove of trees. Beyond, the shrubbery had been levelled in stark contrast to what had come before and even the potholes had been filled in and smoothed over. A brick wall was visible from the edge of the grove. Behind it lay the farmhouse.

There were no guards patrolling the grounds outside the wall, no dogs straining at their leashes. Instead infra-red sensors were concealed strategically among the trees, which would trigger off an alarm the moment the beam was broken. The entrance was a wrought-iron gate with a closed-circuit television camera mounted on the adjacent wall. Any approaching vehicle could be kept under constant surveillance from a control room in the basement of the farmhouse. The gate could be opened only by a double command: a switch in the control room as well as a security card, which had to be swiped through the scanner built into the wall at the side of the gate. Only senior DEA agents, and selected INCD personnel, were issued with these cards.

The closed-circuit camera monitored the approaching car and when it drew up in front of the gate the driver activated the window and pressed a communications button at the side of the gate, which was linked directly to the control room. 'Special Agent Melissa Wade,' she announced.

'We weren't expecting you this afternoon, Agent Wade,' a voice replied.

'Agent Kellerman asked me to bring over some documents for Lacamara to look at tonight,' she replied. 'I'm surprised you weren't expecting me. Agent Kellerman said he was going to phone ahead and clear it with the duty officer before I got here. Who is the duty officer here this afternoon?'

'Captain Hidalgo, although Agent Walker's here too.'

Her first thought was that the debriefing had already begun. But she discounted the idea – Tom Kellerman and René Santin would have been in on it as well. Both were senior to Walker. Then another thought came to her, which sent a cold chill through her whole body. Walker was one of the few people who knew about her clandestine meetings with Doyle over the past eight months and that they had been set up as an element of Operation Checkmate. If Doyle discovered that he had been duped, he would kill them both. She knew the chances of him finding out were remote, because he intended to kill all the agents at the safe house before taking Lacamara away for interrogation. But the possibility still remained, and she knew she would have to take the necessary action to protect herself should the need arise.

'I didn't realize Agent Walker would be here,' she said.

'He should have been long gone but the Lopez woman has been giving him the runaround ever since they arrived.'

'Well, I'll leave just as soon as I've dropped off these documents,' she replied.

'My orders are not to let anyone in without prior authorization so I'll have to clear it first with Captain Hidalgo. I'm sure you understand.'

'Of course. I don't know why Agent Kellerman didn't call to say that I was on my way.'

'I'm sure he did, but as I said the Lopez woman has been driving everybody crazy ever since she got here. One moment, Agent Wade, I'll call Captain Hidalgo.'

A short time later a second voice came over the intercom: 'Melissa, it's Carlos Hidalgo. I haven't heard anything from Agent Kellerman. I've just tried to get hold of him at the embassy, but his line's engaged.'

This news didn't surprise Melissa. She already knew that his line was engaged. She had called him shortly before arriving at the safe house and when he had answered she had asked for a fictitious person only to be told that she had the wrong number. She had waited for him to hang up – but hadn't severed the connection at her end, effectively blocking any incoming calls to his phone. But it was imperative that she stick to her cover story. 'Shit!' she snapped. 'He was supposed to have called you before I got here. I'm already running well behind schedule as it is. I still have to drive back to town for an important meet with a CI. Only I'm never going to make it at this rate. I'd have shoved the files under the gate and let you give them to Lacamara, only my orders were to deliver them to him in person. How long am I supposed to sit out here like this?'

'I can understand your frustration,' Hidalgo replied. 'Let me have a word with Agent Walker, see what he says.'

'You do that,' she replied tersely.

A minute later Hidalgo's voice came over the intercom again. 'Melissa, Agent Walker's cleared it for you to enter the compound. Run your card through.'

'Thanks, Carlos, I owe you,' Melissa said, with a quick smile in the direction of the closed-circuit camera. That was the difficult part over. She had successfully breached the system. Not that she had ever doubted she could. When she stroked her security card through the scanner the light changed from red to green and a moment later there was a metallic click as the gate slid open. As Melissa withdrew the card from the scanner she let it fall surreptitiously from her fingers before engaging gear and driving into the compound. The gate closed behind her.

Walker was a problem she could have done without. She had more than enough to worry about as it was. Her main concern, at least initially, was to avoid him and with that in mind she drove to the back of the building and parked in front of the old barn. On the opposite side of the yard was the back door, leading into the kitchen. She had been the duty officer enough times to know that the INCD agents liked nothing more than to congregate in there and play a few hands of poker to relieve the boredom. More often than not she had joined in. Walker, on the other hand, preferred to keep his distance from the rank and file, which meant that he rarely ventured into the kitchen. She switched off the engine and retrieved a spacious shoulder-bag from the passenger seat. Then she got out of the car and walked to the back door. It was ajar. She pushed it open and broke into a wide grin when she saw the four men seated around the wooden table, cards in hand and bank-notes scattered haphazardly across the table. Hidalgo was among them. They greeted her in chorus and one waved her to an empty chair. She declined the offer then slipped out into the hall and closed the door behind her. To her right was the lounge. She moved silently along the carpeted hallway until she reached a pillar and, pressing herself up against it, peered cautiously into the room. Her instincts had been right. Walker was sitting in an armchair with his back to her. His hair was dishevelled and she could see an empty glass and a bottle of bourbon on the coffee table beside his chair. She had never seen him drink on duty before – Lopez had got to him. She took a perverse pleasure in that thought.

Doubling back the way she had come, she continued past the closed kitchen door to a flight of stairs at the end of the hall.

She removed the Smith & Wesson from her shoulder holster, screwed a silencer on to the barrel, then moved to the door at the foot of the stairs. The control room lay beyond it. She went in. 'We've got a major security breach on our hands,' she announced to the agent seated at the control desk.

'What?' he replied in disbelief, and frantically scanned the row of black and white screens in front of him. 'The perimeter sensors haven't been activated and I've got nothing showing on the monitors.'

'That's the beauty of it,' she replied, then shot him through the back of the head. She pulled the body off the chair then sat down and secured the door behind her. It was a fail-safe mechanism that was only meant to be used in an emergency, should the building ever come under attack. That way the controller could isolate himself from his attackers and bring into play any of the numerous security measures already in place around the compound, as well as having direct radio contact with both DEA and INCD headquarters. The only reason she had locked herself in was to ensure that she wasn't disturbed while she carried out the next phase of the operation.

She unclipped a two-way radio from her belt. It was already tuned into a prearranged frequency. 'Doyle, come in.'

'Doyle here. Are you in?'

'I'm in and running the show. Come and join the party.'

'Did you drop your security pass at the gate?'

'That's what I said I'd do, wasn't it?'

'OK, we're on our way. Over and out.'

She focused her attention on the screen, which was relaying pictures of the approach road, and moments later a black BMW came into view. Although she couldn't see behind the opaque windows, she knew that Doyle was seated up front with Garcia. Peraya was in the back. The BMW stopped in front of the gate, Doyle got out and retrieved her security pass. He looked up directly into the lens of the overhead closed-circuit television camera, held up the card for her to see, then swiped it through the scanner. A green light appeared on the console in front of her. She pressed a button and a second green light appeared beside it. She watched as the gate slid open, Doyle got back into the passenger seat and Garcia drove the BMW into the compound. She left the gate open.

She turned her attention to the computer terminal integrated into the main frame of the control desk. She fed Walker's personal ID number into the computer to access a file linked directly to the card scanner at the main gate. It contained a list of all personnel who had entered the compound that day. She deleted the entire file. Then she scanned the row of VCRs on a shelf above the control desk – each was connected to a closed-circuit television camera. After switching them all off, she ejected those tapes which might have incriminated her and slipped them into her shoulder-bag. Now there was no record of her ever having been at the farmhouse that day.

'Wade, we've parked the car.' Doyle's voice came over the radio.

She sat down again and checked the screens in front of her. 'OK, the backyard's clear. Keep close to the barn as you approach the farmhouse. It'll give you added cover.'

'Where are the guards?'

'In the kitchen. Four of them. All seated. Bill Walker's in the lounge.'

'I didn't realize he'd be here. Not that I mind, though. I've got a few old scores to settle with that bastard anyway,' Doyle said.

'I didn't set this up for you to settle old scores.'

'No, you set it up to save your own ass. What about weapons?'

'Handguns, that's all,' she replied.

'OK, we're coming in. Maintain radio silence until we're inside. Over and out.'

The three men came into view on one of the screens. They were dressed in camouflage fatigues and armed with silenced

Heckler & Koch MP5 machine-pistols. Doyle was wearing a lightweight communications headset. They ran across the yard to the side of the building then, with their backs pressed against the wall, edged their way silently to the back door. Doyle motioned them to stop and nodded to Garcia who slipped past him and took up a position beside the door. Garcia swung round, kicked open the door and fired on the four men seated at the kitchen table.

It was over in seconds. Chairs lay overturned, bodies were scattered across the floor. All handguns still sheathed in their shoulder holsters. Melissa felt strangely unmoved as she stared at the carnage on the screen. It was a similar feeling to the one she'd experienced when she killed Raquel. Would the guilt come later? And, if it did, could any amount of money buy back her conscience?

A movement caught her eye and she saw that Walker was now on his feet in the lounge. He must have heard the chairs clattering in the kitchen. Drawing the Smith & Wesson from his shoulder holster, he crossed the room, up the three steps, and she had to switch screens to continue monitoring him when he entered the hall.

'Doyle, Walker's coming your way,' she said into the radio. 'Take him out quickly.'

'I didn't know you cared,' Doyle said facetiously.

'He's DEA.'

'And that makes him even more valuable to us alive,' Doyle replied.

'That wasn't part of the deal!' Melissa shouted into the radio and saw Doyle wince sharply then gouge out his earpiece as her voice reverberated through his head.

He glared furiously at the wall-mounted closed-circuit camera then directed Peraya to stand at the side of the door. Only then did he push the earpiece back into his ear. 'Where's Walker?'

'Why don't you ask your pet gorilla to open the door and

take a look for himself?' she shot back angrily then activated the door from the control desk.

'Wade?' Doyle hissed into his microphone, unable to raise his voice for fear of Walker hearing him. 'Wade, are you there?'

She put down the radio, retrieved her Smith & Wesson, then hurried to the door. Easing it open, she slipped outside, then began gingerly to climb the stairs towards the hall. It was imperative that she silence Walker before he could incriminate her. And he would if he discovered that she was working in league with them. Yet there was more to it than just that. She may never have liked Walker, but he was still DEA and she was damned if she was going to let Doyle torture any information out of him. Walker deserved better than that. So did the DEA. *Well, well, maybe you do have a conscience, after all,* she thought. Either way, she was going to have to kill him.

As she reached the top of the stairs she heard a cry of pain, followed by a dull thud. She swung round into the hall, the Smith & Wesson held at arm's length, and saw Peraya standing over the prostrate figure of Walker, who was lying face down on the floor. Her first thought was that he was dead, then he rolled over on to his back, his hand clutching the back of his head. For a moment she was tempted to shoot him, but dismissed the idea. It would be too risky from where she was standing – and wounding him would accomplish nothing. She lowered the gun then ducked down the stairs before Walker could see her. She would have to rethink her strategy. Returning to the control room, she heard Doyle's voice calling to her repeatedly over the radio. 'What is it?' she snapped at him.

'What the hell happened to you?' Doyle demanded.

'Those two goons may be answerable to you, I'm not. What do you want?'

'Where's Lacamara?'

'Presumably in the master bedroom. Top of the stairs, second door on the right.'

'What do you mean "presumably"?' Doyle snarled. 'You've got a view of every room in the house down there.'

'I've got a view of every room being monitored by a camera. The master bedroom isn't one of them.'

'How many other places could he be?' Doyle demanded.

'The only other rooms that aren't on camera are the toilets and the two smaller bedrooms on either side of the master bedroom. But we mainly use those bedrooms when we're doing shift work. The witnesses are normally put up in the master bedroom.'

'Is the door reinforced?'

'Naturally. And it also has several dead-bolt locks for added protection. If it has been locked from the inside, you'll only break your foot if you try to kick it down. So I guess that leaves only diplomacy. Hardly your strong point.'

'I've come this far, I'll find a way to get in. Maintain radio silence until further notice. Over and out.'

Doyle's main concern as he climbed the stairs was that Lacamara might have heard the commotion in the kitchen and, even if he didn't know what was going on, had barricaded himself inside the bedroom. The sound of the television emanating from behind the door gave him encouragement. He gestured for Garcia to take up a position on one side of the solid oak door and was about to try the handle, then thought better of it. If the door was locked, Lacamara might become suspicious. Instead he rapped on the door. No answer. He knocked again. Louder.

'Who is it?' a male voice called.

'Special Agent Kellerman,' Doyle replied, changing the pitch of his voice. He knew he didn't sound like Kellerman, but Lacamara had only spoken to him for the first time earlier that day. He wouldn't know the difference – but he would have recognized Doyle's voice. 'I need to talk to you.'

'We agreed that the debriefing would start tomorrow.'

Doyle smiled triumphantly at Garcia then leant his face closer to the door. 'I know we did, but I've got something here I need you to look at. It'll only take a minute, but it really is important.'

'Door's open,' Lacamara shouted back.

Doyle entered the room. Lacamara was lying on the double bed, dressed in a white towelling robe. He reached for the remote control on the bedside table and muted the sound of the television. 'Now what's so . . .'

'We were in the neighbourhood and thought it only good manners to drop in and see how the DEA were treating you,' Doyle said, and stepped away from the door to let Garcia into the room.

'Well, by the looks of it,' Garcia said, helping himself to a sandwich off the tray on the edge of the bed.

'I don't – how did you – the guards—' Lacamara stammered incoherently, his face masked with terror.

'We're here and that's all that really matters,' Doyle replied.

'It's all – been a – misunderstanding,' Lacamara said, getting to his feet. He laughed nervously. 'I – I – I would never have – testified against – the cartel. You – you know that, Doyle.'

'You had your chance at Teotihuacán,' Doyle replied. 'Not only are you going to tell me exactly where you hid the money that you stole from us, but you're also going to tell me how to retrieve those incriminating files you tucked away in the computer before you ran off with your whore.'

'Yes – anything,' Lacamara replied.

'Where is the whore?' Garcia asked. Lacamara's eyes flickered past Garcia to the bathroom door behind him.

'She doesn't know anything,' Lacamara moaned as he watched Garcia make for the bathroom door. 'I swear she doesn't.'

Doyle clamped his hands underneath Lacamara's chin and jerked his head round to face him again. 'If you've got something to say, say it to me.'

'She doesn't know anything,' Lacamara repeated, still monitoring Garcia's reflection in the mirror. 'Please don't hurt her. I beg you, Doyle. Please.'

'Do you want to take her as well?' Garcia asked Doyle.

'What for? If Hector says she doesn't know anything, that's good enough for me.' Doyle glanced round at Garcia. 'Kill her.'

'No!' Lacamara screamed, but when he tried to get past Doyle he was shoved back violently on to the bed.

Garcia opened the door, raised his machine-pistol, and fired a short burst into the bathroom. Lacamara ran to the bathroom and froze in the doorway when he saw the splashes of blood spattered across the white tiles above the bath. Then his eyes went to the arm that hung limply over the side of the bath. The rest of Carmen's body had slipped beneath the rich lather of foam that covered the surface of the water. The glass of champagne he had taken in to her minutes earlier still stood untouched on the side of the bath. He knelt beside it and put her lifeless hand gently to his lips as the tears spilled down his cheeks.

'You had the chance to save your whore at Teotihuacán,' Doyle said, from the doorway. 'But I guess you needed the money to stop her straying like a bitch on heat.'

Lacamara grabbed the champagne glass and hurled it at Doyle. It shattered harmlessly against the wall behind him. Then he lunged at Doyle, his anguish now turned to rage. Doyle easily blocked his wild punch, twisted his arm savagely behind his back, and shoved him back through the doorway into the bedroom. Lacamara swung another punch which was so far wide of the mark that Doyle didn't have to move to avoid it.

'Sedate him,' Doyle snapped. Garcia's punch caught Lacamara flush on the jaw. He was already unconscious when he hit the floor.

'*Patrón?*'

Doyle looked round to find Peraya standing outside the bedroom door. 'What are you doing here? You're supposed to be downstairs guarding Walker.'

'You'd better come and see, *patrón*,' Peraya said nervously.

'Come and see what?' Doyle demanded.

233

'Please, *patrón*,' Peraya said, gesturing towards the stairs.

'Bring Lacamara,' Doyle told Garcia. Then he left the room and followed Peraya down the stairs and into the hall. It was then that he saw Melissa sitting on the top stair leading down to the sunken lounge, the Smith & Wesson in her hand. She looked up slowly at the two men, but there was no recognition in her eyes.

'I couldn't stop her, *patrón*. It happened so quickly.'

'What did?' Then Doyle followed Peraya's pointing finger and saw Walker lying on the lounge floor, the carpet around his head soaked with blood. He brushed past Melissa, who made no move to get out of his way, and crouched beside Walker. There was no pulse.

'She shot him through the back of the head,' Peraya said. 'I didn't see the gun until it was too late. I'm sorry, *patrón*.'

'So am I,' Doyle said, then looked across at her. 'Why?'

'I told you earlier, this wasn't part of the deal. Bill Walker and I may have had our differences over the years, but he was still DEA to the core. Incorruptible. And I was damned if I was going to stand by and let you take away the last of his dignity by forcing him to sell out the DEA while you tortured him to death. That was what you had in mind, wasn't it?'

'It really doesn't matter what I had in mind any more, does it?' Doyle replied, then turned to Peraya. 'We're done here. Let's move out.'

'*Sí, patrón*,' Peraya replied, and hurried from the room.

Doyle paused in front of Melissa and returned her security pass to her. 'We couldn't have done it without you. And for that you have my gratitude. We make quite a good team, don't you think?'

'I'll tell you what I think,' she replied, holding his stare. 'After tomorrow I'll be in a position to hire a top hitter to take you out. Only you won't know where or when it'll happen.'

'As long as he doesn't mind standing in line,' Doyle said, eased past her and walked towards the kitchen. He called cheerily over his shoulder, 'See you in the morning, Agent Wade.'

Shortly afterwards she heard the sound of the BMW start up and drive away. Then silence. From where she was sitting she could see only Walker's legs. When she shot him she had made no sound, given no warning. A single bullet to the back of the head. At the time she had convinced herself that she had no other choice. Not only did she have to protect her own interests, but she also had to protect him from a slow, agonizing death. But she knew it was sheer hypocrisy to think that both arguments held equal sway. If getting her hands on the diamonds had meant watching Walker being slowly tortured to death, she would have been in the front row. The diamonds had become an obsession with her, and she would willingly sacrifice anyone – or anything – to get her hands on them.

She got up and, as her eyes lingered uncomfortably on the body, she was overcome with an intense sensation of nausea. She shuddered and stumbled down the corridor on unsteady legs. As she burst into the kitchen she almost slipped on the bloodstained floor. When she had witnessed the murder of the four agents from the sanctuary of the control room it had almost seemed as if she were watching a movie. Viewing it through the psychological barrier of the screen had helped to desensitize her and diminish the effect it had had on her at the time. Now there was no escape. This was the reality of the aftermath.

Unable to bring herself even to look at the bodies, she tiptoed through the blood, struggling to hold back the rising bile in her throat. As she emerged into the yard her body heaved and she threw up violently into the bushes at the side of the building. She barely had time to draw breath before she vomited again. She continued to retch uncontrollably – her body doubled over, her hands clutched tightly to her stomach, sweat pouring down her face. Then she straightened up and looked into the kitchen, her eyes lingering on each body in turn. Not because she wanted to, but because she needed to prove to herself that she could. Now there was a mixture of anger and contempt in her eyes. Anger that these deaths had managed to expose a weakness in her character she had wanted to suppress; contempt for allowing that weakness to manifest itself in the way it had. She took a last look round then walked back to her car.

SIXTEEN

Had Tom only slept with her because he had never been able to get Mel into bed? Had he fantasized about Mel when they made love? Could he really have duped her like that? No. No. No. Same questions. Same answers. Yet Laura knew that if she was so sure of the answers, she wouldn't have been torturing herself with the questions ever since she had spoken to Mel. She wanted to believe that Tom had wanted her and not Mel. But the doubts lingered. Perhaps Mel was right. Perhaps she was naïve. All those years in the celibate wilderness and when she did return to the sexual fold she had to fall for a guy who fancied her twin sister! *You sure know how to pick 'em, girl.*

Yet there was another side to the equation that she could use to her advantage. She did have feelings for Tom – strong feelings – but if she could convince herself that he had been using her, it would make it that much easier for her to walk away from him, when the time came. Not that she had ever had any intention of hanging around after they had got the diamonds. No man was worth that. Not even Tom. *Not even Tom – listen to yourself. You've only known him a few days and already you're talking like some guileless sap . . .*

She was startled out of her thoughts by the doorbell. She wasn't expecting anyone. Tom had said he would call her before he came over. Pushing back the kitchen chair, she got to her feet, moved cautiously down the hall and peered through the spy-hole in the door. Kellerman stood on the patio. She wasn't ready for him. Not yet. Perhaps she could pretend she was out. That would give her time to prepare herself to face him.

'Laura, it's Tom,' he called.

'Oh, the hell with it,' she muttered, and opened the door.

'Hi,' he said, forcing a smile.

'You said you were going to call first,' she said, making it sound like an accusation.

'I've been kind of busy these last few hours. I just needed to see a friendly face to cheer me up. Naturally I thought of you.'

'How nice.'

'I'd say that judging by the sound of your voice I've caught you at a bad time. Consider me gone.'

'No, wait,' Laura said, as he was about to turn away. 'I'm sorry, I didn't mean to snap at you like that. I guess I've just got a lot on my mind at the moment.'

'Yeah, me too. Can I come in?'

'Of course,' she said, stepped aside to let him enter and followed him into the kitchen. He had already removed his jacket and slipped it over the back of the nearest chair. 'Coffee?'

'That would be great,' he said, and sat down. 'Justine Collins is dead.'

Laura froze. Then she looked at Kellerman. 'What happened?' she asked.

'She was shot in the back of the head at close range. Felix Amador was also killed, along with the two agents who'd been watching his house. They were both good men.' His eyes flashed in anger when he looked up at her. 'When we found Justine's body her arms were wrapped around her stomach, as if she were trying to protect her unborn baby. The last thought she probably had was that she'd somehow failed her child. What kind of way is that to die – to take that kind of guilt with you to the grave?'

'Do you know who did it?'

238

'Doyle. Who else? Only I don't have any proof.' He banged his fist on the table in frustration then stood up and began to pace about restlessly. 'You know what the best part of it is? After we've taken that bastard into custody tomorrow I'm going to have to make all kinds of concessions to get him to testify against the cartel. New identity. New life. Not to mention a generous financial package just to set it up. Who said that crime doesn't pay?'

'He can change who he is, but never who he was,' she replied. 'Nobody can run from their conscience for ever, no matter how much they try.'

'It helps if you have a conscience to begin with,' he said.

'Everybody has a conscience. It's just that some are able to hide it better than others.'

He sensed that the conversation had drifted away from Doyle and that her last remark had been aimed at him. Did it have something to do with what had happened the previous evening? That made no sense. It had been a mutual attraction. If anything, she had made the first move. Admittedly, he hadn't pushed her away. Was she regretting it now? Suddenly it all seemed so complicated.

'Milk. No sugar. Right?'

'Right,' Kellerman said.

'Same as Mel,' Laura said, sat down at the table and held her mug between her cupped hands. 'What else did you have in common with her?'

'Not a lot really, apart from work,' he said. 'Why do you ask?'

'No reason,' she replied, with a shrug.

'If something's bothering you, I wish you'd tell me what it is.'

'Why should anything be bothering me?'

'Because you've been on edge ever since I got here.'

'Tomorrow's the big day, isn't it? Sure I'm on edge.' She thought she handled that rather well.

'You've already met Doyle. You know what to expect. All you

have to do is hand over the disk. We'll take it from there. There's nothing for you to worry about.'

'Thanks. Being patronized makes me feel so much better,' she replied coldly.

'Time for me to make a tactical withdrawal, I think.'

'No, don't go. Please,' she said, a sudden vulnerability in her voice.

'I wasn't being patronizing, but if it came across that way I'm sorry.'

'You've got nothing to apologize for. It's me.'

He waited for her to elaborate. When she didn't he asked, 'Has this got anything to do with what happened last night?'

'It seemed right at the time. I think I even heard the Mantovani Strings playing in the background,' she said, wistfully.

'The Mantovani Strings?' he said, bewildered.

'It's something that Mel . . . used to say to me, that I had to hear the Mantovani Strings playing when I make love. I guess what she was trying to say—'

'I think I get the idea,' he interrupted with a smile, 'and I take it as a compliment that you heard them last night.'

'They weren't that loud.'

'Ouch,' he said, wincing. 'You sure know how to kill a moment.'

'I don't want you getting any ideas, that's all.'

'And exactly what kind of ideas would those be?'

'That last night was the start of something between us. It happened, and I have no regrets. I hope you feel the same way. Only that's where it ends.'

'And I thought it was Melissa who was into the one-night stands.'

'Is that from personal experience?' Laura asked, holding his gaze.

'You already know that Melissa and I had a purely platonic friendship. The closest we ever came to having sex was a kiss on the cheek at the annual Christmas party.'

'Was that by choice?'

'From my side, it was,' he said.

'Are you saying that Mel wanted to get you into bed?' Laura asked.

'Melissa had more than enough admirers on hand to keep her entertained.'

'That's not an answer, and you know it,' Laura said, propping her elbows on the table. Her eyes remained fixed on his face. 'Did Mel want to sleep with you?'

'I didn't sleep with you as some kind of substitute for Melissa. That's what you want to know, isn't it?'

'I want to know whether Mel ever wanted to sleep with you! Yes or no?'

'Yes. Now are you satisfied?' He shoved back his chair with such force that it clattered to the floor, unlocked the back door and stepped out on to the patio. He drew in several deep breaths to calm himself.

'Tom?' she said softly behind him. When he looked round she was standing in the doorway, her eyes filled with tears. 'I'm sorry, but I had to know. You do understand, don't you?'

'Yeah, I think I do,' he replied, and reached out for her.

She drew back, her hands raised defensively in front of her. 'I meant what I said about last night being a one-off. It's best if we keep our distance.'

'So when this is over, you're just going to walk away and I'm never going to see you again?'

'It's for the best,' she replied, wiping away a tear that trickled down her cheek.

'I'm not another Jefferson, Laura. I could never hurt you.'

'But I could hurt you, and I don't ever want that to happen. You deserve so much better than that.'

'You sound like my mother. She always thought she knew what was best for me. Come to think of it, she still does.'

'I just know what's best for me,' Laura said.

'Yeah?' he drawled sceptically.

'Your coffee's getting cold,' she said. 'Why didn't you tell me before that Mel had tried to hit on you?'

'It happened a long time ago,' he said. 'Some things are best left in the past.'

'I can take a hint,' she said, and they lapsed into a silence that was only broken when Kellerman's phone rang.

He answered it. 'Excuse me,' he said to Laura, his hand over the mouthpiece, then he left the room.

Although she didn't know what was being discussed, she could hear that he was agitated, which made her think that the conversation could have something to do with the safe house. Had Mel tipped off Doyle as to its location? Was Lacamara dead? Then another thought struck her. What if Doyle was dead – or injured? She was still contemplating the options when Kellerman appeared in the doorway, the phone clenched in his hand.

'What is it?' she asked, frightened by his expression.

'The safe house has been hit. Lacamara's gone. Six of our agents were killed. Bill Walker was among them.'

'Oh, my God.' Laura was appalled. 'Doyle?'

'You can be sure he was there. Only he couldn't have got in by himself, not without breaching the security system. Which means that he must have had someone with him who was able to get in without raising the alarm. The cartel have got an insider we don't know about. At least not yet. But I'll find him. And God help him when I do.' Kellerman slipped the phone back into his pocket. 'I gotta go. I don't know how long I'll be at the safe house. Probably most of the night.'

'Could this affect the meeting with Doyle tomorrow morning?' she asked.

'I don't know yet. And I won't know until I've had a chance to assess the situation in more detail.'

She waited until she heard the front door close behind him then went through to the lounge and watched discreetly from the window as he started up his car and drove away. After a few minutes she went to the pay phone at the end of the street. 'You

242

were the one who duped the guards and got Doyle into the safe house, weren't you?'

'So you've heard about it, have you?' Melissa replied calmly. 'We were in and out of there in under fifteen minutes.'

'You said that you were only going to tell Doyle how to bypass the security system, not hold his hand when he went in.'

'No, that was *your* assumption. I told you to let me worry about how I'd get Doyle into the safe house.'

'And I suppose killing Walker and the other agents was also part of the deal.'

'Are you sure you don't want a bullhorn in case someone on the other side of town didn't quite hear what you said?' Melissa asked. 'Keep your voice down, for God's sake.'

'When you first outlined your plan to get the diamonds, you told me that nobody was going to get killed. At this rate, it's going to end up with a body count straight out of a Schwarzenegger movie. It's got to stop, Mel. Do you hear me? It's got to stop!'

'And had it run according to my original plan, nobody *would* have got hurt, let alone killed. But how was I to know that Raquel would confront me in your apartment? How was I to know that Lacamara was going to choose this week to run off with the cartel's money? These were situations I couldn't possibly have anticipated when I put the plan together. Don't you see that, sis?'

'All I can see is that this has spiralled out of control. I wish I'd never got involved.'

'In which case you'd still be pulling teeth in Spanish Harlem and sleeping with a loaded gun under your pillow every night. It's still not too late to pull out, sis. Is that what you want?'

'Did you know that Doyle was going to kill Bill Walker?' Laura asked, purposely not answering the question.

'I didn't even know that Walker was going to be there. And Doyle didn't kill him. I did.'

'What?' Laura gasped.

'I had no choice. Doyle would have tortured as much information out of him as he could before he killed him. I wasn't about to stand by and let that happen. Strange as it may seem to you, I do still have some scruples left.'

'Tom said he wasn't sure whether what had happened at the safe house would have any bearing on my meeting with Doyle tomorrow morning.'

'None whatsoever.' Melissa was quick to reply.

'You seem very sure of that,' Laura said.

'Tom's obviously worried that Walker may have compromised my – I mean, your – cover before he died. The fact is he never got a chance to say anything. Only Tom doesn't know that. Having said that though, Tom knows he's now only one step away from nailing Doyle and bringing down the cartel. He's got to take that chance.'

'Even if it were to put my life in danger?' Laura said in surprise.

'But your life won't be in any danger, will it?'

'We know that, but he doesn't,' Laura said.

'Let him worry about it.'

'I'm not sure whether it will worry him, not after I gave him the brush-off this afternoon,' Laura said.

'You did the right thing, sis.'

'Under different circumstances I think we could have made it work,' Laura said.

'Under different circumstances you'd never have met him,' Melissa reminded her.

Laura considered telling her that Tom had admitted, albeit under pressure, that it had been Mel who had come on to him and not the other way round, but Mel would only have denied it. Laura had a sneaking suspicion that Mel had only made the claim out of spite. It was certainly the first time a guy they had both fancied had chosen her over Mel. And the fact that Mel had actively gone after him, without success, made it all the more satisfying.

'We probably won't talk again until after I've got the diamonds. Good luck for tomorrow, sis,' Melissa said.

'Considering that you'll be doing all the hard work, I think it
should be me wishing you luck,' Laura replied.

'Your role is just as important to the overall success of the
operation. We're a team, sis. I know it can't have been easy for
you these past few days, but you've done so well. You've more
than earned your share of the spoils, so don't go selling yourself
short.'

'Sure,' Laura replied absently.

'As you can see, no structural damage,' Colonel René Santin
said to Kellerman, who had just arrived. They were inspecting
the main gate, which was still open but now guarded by an
armed policeman. 'All indications point to the killers having had
someone on the inside to let them in. Which would narrow it
down to two possibilities. Hidalgo, who was the duty officer
for the night, and Walker, who was supposed to have handed
Lacamara and Lopez over to Hidalgo once the helicopter got
here. Which raises the question, what was Walker still doing
here two hours later?'

'So you've already got yourself a scapegoat. How convenient.'

'Hidalgo was only informed an hour before the helicopter was
due to arrive at the safe house that he was being drafted in as a
member of the protection detail. You should know that, you
specifically asked for him.'

'That's because I had Lacamara vet all the names on the list
I drew up for the protection detail. Bill Walker was one of the
first to be cleared. So it looks like you've got to find yourself
another scapegoat.'

'Why wasn't I told about this list?' Santin demanded.

'I assumed you already knew. I discussed it with Lacamara at
Teotihuacán.'

'Well, I didn't know,' Santin snapped.

'That's my fault, I should have made sure you were told,'

245

Kellerman said, in an attempt to pacify him. 'But the fact still remains that someone tricked your agent in the control room. Someone with a security pass. And there aren't many of us around with those kind of passes. You've already checked the surveillance tapes in the control room for any clues?'

'All the relevant tapes are missing. And the computer file that would have contained a list of all persons who had accessed the card scanner over the past twenty-four hours has been erased. Whoever it was knew exactly what they were after and where to find it.'

'I know one face that will definitely be on those missing video tapes,' Kellerman said. 'Doyle's. Lacamara would have been regarded as far too big a catch for him not to have been here in person.'

'You'll get no arguments from me on that score. But without the tapes we've got nothing on him. Just like we've got nothing to link him with the murders at Amador's house this afternoon. You know as well as I do that he's got a watertight alibi for every day of the year. He leaves nothing to chance.'

'That's all going to change tomorrow,' Kellerman said.

'And in return for testifying against the cartel he walks away with a new identity and enough money to set himself up for life in some luxury beach condo in the Bahamas.'

'I don't like it any more than you do!' Kellerman thundered, and caught the policeman at the gate casting a startled glance in his direction before looking away quickly when their eyes met. 'I'm just as frustrated as you are about letting him walk, René, but that's the deal the suits in Washington told me to put to him. And now that we've lost Lacamara as a potential witness, Doyle's our last realistic chance of bringing down the cartel. It's a once-in-a-lifetime opportunity. You know as well as I do that we can't afford to pass it up.'

'You just make sure that part of the deal is giving up the name of the person who got him in here today,' Santin said, stabbing a finger at Kellerman.

'You can count on it,' Kellerman replied.

'How many of your people have security passes?' Santin asked.

'In theory, only Bill Walker, Melissa Wade and myself. As the three senior special agents at the embassy, we have our own personal passes which we carry with us at all times. Having said that, though, special passes can be issued on request. As the duty officer, Hidalgo would have been supplied with a twenty-four-hour pass.'

'Could a pass have been forged?'

'Anything can be forged with the right equipment. But if the pass was forged, whoever did it would have needed certain technical data to replicate it successfully. And that kind of information could only have come from inside the DEA – though not necessarily from one of my team. The technicians back in the States who make these passes know more about the procedure than anyone else. One of them could have been compromised into handing over the relevant information. I'll have a check run on all of them as soon as I get back to the embassy.'

'You said that Lacamara insisted on vetting all agents who were going to be brought in on the protection detail. Walker was cleared. You must have been too, or he wouldn't have gone along with it in the first place. Which throws up an interesting thought. As far as he was concerned, Melissa was working for the cartel so she couldn't have been considered for this detail anyway, not without him being told the truth behind Operation Checkmate. And Operation Checkmate has been kept tightly under wraps ever since its conception. Apart from my superiors at DEA headquarters in Washington, the only other people who knew about it were you, me, Bill and Melissa. Hidalgo knew nothing about it. Neither did the agent in the control room. So if Melissa turned up unexpectedly at the gate neither of them would have had any reason not to admit her.'

'It wasn't Melissa,' Kellerman said.

'You seem very sure of that,' Santin replied, his eyes lingering on Kellerman's face as if trying to read something into his expression.

'I was at Melissa's house when I got the call to come here,' Kellerman said.

'I've already spoken to the police pathologist. He puts the time of death for all the victims between three and five this afternoon. We were both at Amador's house from two thirty till about four fifteen. What time did you get to Melissa's house?'

'It wasn't Melissa,' Kellerman reiterated, this time more forcefully.

'So you said. Only I haven't heard anything to corroborate it. I have to brief the chief of police later this evening. He's going to want to know what I've come up with so far. What am I supposed to tell him?'

'Give me twenty-four hours, then I'll be in a position to explain everything,' Kellerman said.

'This has got something to do with Operation Checkmate, hasn't it?'

'Trust me on this, René,' Kellerman replied. 'Twenty-four hours. That's all I ask.'

'Seven of my best agents have been killed today. And now I find out that you've been holding out on me. I don't like the conclusions I'm being forced to come to, right now.'

'I had nothing to do with their deaths – and neither did Melissa.' Kellerman was furious at the insinuation.

'Then tell me what's going on,' Santin said. He touched Kellerman's chest lightly. 'Operation Checkmate may be a DEA deal, but this is still my jurisdiction. I have the authority to pull the plug on it at a moment's notice and there's not a damn thing either you or the DEA could do to stop me. Now don't you think it's about time you levelled with me?'

Kellerman knew he was cornered. And there was no way out unless he came clean. He doubted whether Santin would deliberately sabotage Operation Checkmate at such a late hour, but if his superiors ever got wind that the DEA had been holding out on them, they might just decide to make the decision for him. He couldn't take that chance. 'Walk with me awhile,' he said, then took Santin's arm and guided him away from the gate. He glanced back to ensure they were out of earshot of the policeman before he spoke again. 'What I'm about to tell you is known only to Braithwaite and myself and can't go any further than you, at least not until after Doyle's been taken into custody. I want your word on that, René.'

'First I have to hear—'

'Your word, René!' Kellerman cut in, then turned to face Santin. 'I know you're an honourable man who prides himself on keeping his word. That's why I need to hear you say it.'

Santin exhaled deeply then nodded. 'Very well. You have my word.'

'Melissa's dead.'

'*What?*' Santin exclaimed.

'She was killed in a car crash in New York on Monday night.'

'Then . . . who . . .' Santin was flummoxed.

'Melissa had a twin sister. Her name's Laura. I managed to persuade her to take Melissa's place at the meet tomorrow morning. All she'll have to do is hand over the disk, take the diamonds, then leave. Your guys will do the rest.'

'And what happens when the truth comes out?'

'Why should it? Laura will fly back to New York tomorrow night, on her sister's passport, and on Tuesday morning the DEA will issue a statement saying that Melissa was killed in a car crash the previous night. It's not as if it's a lie. It's just a week late, that's all. So as far as the authorities are concerned, it *was* Melissa who met with Doyle.'

'It certainly explains why Melissa's been so conspicuous by her absence this last week. At the time I was surprised when you didn't put her on Lacamara's trail.'

'Not that it would have done any good. Doyle would still have got to him.' Kellerman took a step back as an ambulance swept into the grounds and drove past them towards the farmhouse. 'Are you OK with Laura meeting Doyle tomorrow morning?'

'I guess so,' Santin said, after a thoughtful pause.

'You don't sound too sure.'

'I'm as sure as I can be, considering what you've just off-loaded on to me,' Santin replied. 'I'd have preferred it if you'd levelled with me from the start, but I can understand why you'd want to keep the deception under wraps. You've obviously got a lot of faith in her. I hope it's justified.'

'She'll keep her head. She's already had to impersonate Melissa when she met with Doyle earlier this week. She pulled it off brilliantly. Doyle didn't suspect a thing.'

'Is she a lot like Melissa?' Santin asked.

'Only in appearance. Their personalities are complete opposites. Laura's very reserved, keeps to herself, although she has opened up to me as she's got to know me better. I still find it strange when I see her. It's as if it's Melissa, only without the aggravation.'

Santin laughed. 'I know exactly what you mean by that. But I still had a lot of time for Melissa. She knew what she was about and that's what mattered. She was the best. I'll certainly miss her.'

'Me too.'

'Come on, we'd better go to the house and see what Forensics have come up with so far,' Santin said, patting Kellerman's shoulder.

'Somehow I doubt it'll be much,' Kellerman muttered, then dug his hands into his trouser pockets and went after Santin.

'I thought you were supposed to be at the dinner-dance with the Salcidos tonight?' Doyle said, when Garcia arrived unexpectedly at the Workshop shortly before ten o'clock that evening.

'Fortunately Mr Salcido decided to leave early,' Garcia replied, closing the door behind him.

'That bad, huh?' Peraya said, with a grin. 'Is he here?'

'He's upstairs making a call. He'll be down shortly.' Garcia looked across at the naked, blindfolded figure crucified against the wooden board on the opposite side of the room. Had he not already known who it was, it would have been impossible to recognize Hector Lacamara beneath the mask of blood that obscured his features. All of his fingers had been severed – one at a time – with a variety of implements, his kneecaps shattered by a hammer drill, the layers of skin on his chest and stomach buffed raw by a sander and his manacled feet grotesquely blistered and disfigured from the prolonged exposure to a hot air gun. To his surprise he saw that Lacamara's genitals had been left untouched.

'We left them especially for you,' Doyle said, with a knowing smile as he followed Garcia's lingering stare.

'Sounds like the perfect way to round off a frustrating evening,' Garcia replied. He noticed that Doyle and Peraya were still dressed in the fatigues they had worn during the raid on the safe house, except that Peraya had since stripped to the waist and his muscular chest was splattered with Lacamara's blood. Garcia picked up the discarded tunic and tossed it at Peraya. 'Put it on. Mrs Salcido's here as well.'

Peraya buttoned up his tunic and was still tucking it into his trousers when the door opened and Juan Salcido entered the room with his wife on his arm. 'Good evening, gentlemen,' he said, nodding to Doyle and Peraya. 'We thought we'd drop in on the way home and see how you were getting on.'

'I believe the dinner-dance turned out to be a disappointment,' Doyle said.

'It was an absolute nightmare,' Katrine replied. 'We couldn't wait to get away. The food was awful. The band was terrible. And as for the hostess – well, the less said about her the better. Twice she mistook Garcia for a waiter.'

'A waiter?' Doyle said, unable to stop himself smiling. He stepped forward and took Katrine by the arm when her husband made his way to Lacamara. 'Careful, Mrs Salcido. There's a lot of blood around. You don't want it on your shoes.'

'I think I'll just stay here,' she said, then looked at Lacamara for the first time. There was no revulsion in her eyes at what she saw, just a cold disdain for the way he had dared to betray her husband.

'Doyle?' Salcido called over his shoulder.

'Excuse me,' Doyle said to Katrine, then crossed to where Salcido was standing in front of Lacamara.

'Is he still alive?' Salcido asked, lighting a cigarette.

'He's passed out, that's all,' Doyle replied. 'Do you want him revived?'

'Yes, and take off that blindfold. I want him to see me.'

Doyle snapped his fingers at Peraya, who hurried forward with a bottle of smelling salts which he wafted under Lacamara's nose until he got a reaction. Doyle removed the blindfold then grabbed Lacamara by the hair and lifted up his head until Salcido could see his bloodied face. 'You've got a visitor, Hector,' Doyle said, but the only response was a faint flutter of the eyelids. Doyle slapped Lacamara viciously across the face. 'Open your eyes, Hector, otherwise I'll let Peraya continue practising his dental skills on you.' The sound of Peraya snapping shut a pair of pliers had the desired effect and Lacamara abruptly opened his eyes. They were glazed, as if he were somewhere else, trying to block out the excruciating pain that racked every sinew of his broken, tortured body. 'You can talk to him now, he can hear what you're saying. Unfortunately he won't he able to reply – we've already cut out his tongue.'

'Hector, I just wanted to let you know that we've recovered all the money you stole from us and returned it to our own accounts in the Cayman Islands. We've also found all the incriminating files you hid in the computer. Doyle told me that you were very co-operative when it came to revealing the whereabouts of both the money and the files, and for that I am grateful. We've been through a lot together, haven't we? Good times.

Bad times. But, then, that's what friendship's all about, isn't it? I always considered you a good friend. And, despite what you did to me, I still wish you'd taken up my earlier offer because if you had both you and Ms Lopez would still be together and none of this would have been necessary. But obviously the money meant more to you than her life. Or your own life, for that matter. And why did you steal fifty million dollars? What could someone like you have done with that amount of money? I could have understood it if you'd stolen, say, five million. That kind of money is still manageable. But fifty million? It was greed, Hector. Sheer greed. You never wanted for anything when you worked for me and this is how you repaid me. That's really the saddest part of it all, as far as I'm concerned.' Salcido dropped his half-smoked cigarette on to the floor and ground it out underfoot. 'That's all I wanted to say to you, Hector. I'll let you get back to your dental treatment.'

Doyle let go of Lacamara's hair and took Salcido to one side. 'How much longer do you want us to work on him?'

'How much more can he take?' Salcido replied.

'He's already lost a lot of blood. Probably another few hours at the most.'

'Well, it's up to you,' Salcido said. 'Don't forget, you've got an important day ahead of you tomorrow. It's imperative that the deal goes down without any hitches.'

'I don't foresee any problems,' Doyle replied.

'So you still intend to go through with the deal in the morning?' Katrine asked, her eyes flitting between Doyle and her husband.

'Yeah,' Doyle replied hesitantly. 'Why do you ask?'

She gave a quick shrug and addressed her husband. 'I just thought that perhaps you might delay it after everything that's happened these past few days. After all, you've got your money back and you've also secured the computer files. Surely the deal could wait. Let the dust settle first. It's not as if a few more days would make any difference.'

'You almost make it sound as if you know something we don't,' Salcido said.

'I'm just looking at the situation as an outsider, that's all,' she replied.

'Maybe Katrine's got a point,' Salcido said, looking at Doyle.

'I say we go through with it,' Doyle replied firmly. 'If we stall Wade now, she might get suspicious. We can't afford to take that chance. Not at this late stage.'

'Yes, you're probably right,' Salcido said, after a thoughtful pause. 'Tell you what, I'll send Garcia back here after he's dropped us off at the house. He can take over from you. That way you can get a good night's sleep, and he gets to join in the fun. He deserves it after tonight. The next time we get an invitation to dine with the Oliveiras, I'll give it to Ramón. He can take one of his whores and get drunk. That way we can be sure we won't be invited back again.'

'Who are these Oliveiras?' Doyle asked. 'I've never heard of them.'

'They've just moved here from Monterey. He's something in construction, I believe. Not that I took much notice of what he had to say. I have no use for him or his company.' Salcido turned to his wife. 'Shall we go?'

'Whatever you say, darling,' she replied sweetly, then beckoned Doyle over to her. Her eyes hardened as she cast a last disparaging glance at Lacamara. She lowered her voice when she spoke. 'When you do come to castrate him, you can tell him that it's with my compliments. And make sure you do it slowly. I want him to suffer for what he did to Juan.'

'You can count on it, Mrs Salcido,' Doyle assured her.

'What are you two whispering about?' Salcido asked, with a good-humoured scowl.

'Now, that would be telling, wouldn't it?' Katrine winked at Doyle. Then she slipped her hand into the crook of her husband's arm and they left the room, followed by Garcia who closed the door behind them.

Ramón Salcido prided himself on having one of the country's finest collections of black-and-white gangster movies from the thirties and forties. Bogart. Cagney. Raft. He had them all. He always viewed them alone in the specially designed soundproofed room, with its precision acoustics, in the basement of his mansion in the heart of Chapultepec Park.

That evening he was watching *Little Caesar*. But that was hardly surprising as he watched it at least once a week and could recite the dialogue word for word. Not that he ever did, though. He never uttered a sound as he watched Edward G. Robinson's Rico Bandello, the small-time crook who rises from the gutter to become a big-time hoodlum in Chicago, only for his greed and ambition to destroy him. Yet it was the immortal exit line, 'Mother of mercy . . . is this the end of Rico?', which always got to him. No matter how many times he heard it, it always brought a tear to his eye. It always felt as if a part of him was dying along with Rico.

When the phone rang beside him, breaking his concentration, he cursed and paused the film before answering.

'Salcido, it's me.'

'Ah, my very own Lieutenant Flaherty.' Salcido poured a measure of Chivas Regal into the tumbler beside him.

'What?'

'Have you never seen *Little Caesar*?' Salcido asked.

'Not that I can recall.'

'Flaherty's a smug, pretentious cop in *Little Caesar*. He reminds me a lot of you.'

'I didn't ring to get a movie review,' snapped the caller.

'No, you called to give me some information. That is what an informer is for, isn't it? And my star informer no less.'

'Don't call me that!'

'But you are. Nobody else knows that you work for me.

Lacamara used to say that you were incorruptible. I have to admit that always made me smile. There he was, trying to recruit you to work for the cartel while all the time you were working for me.' Salcido took a sip from the glass, replaced it on the table, then sank back into his armchair. 'So what have you got to tell me, Colonel Santin?'

SEVENTEEN

Sunday

Laura had spent most of the night tossing and turning restlessly in her bed, and when she finally drifted off to sleep in the early hours of the morning she found herself drawn into the vortex of her own troubled conscience, like an innocent child being lured into darkness by the sound of a familiar voice. And the further she ventured, the more frightened and alone she became. She wanted to go back, return to the reassuring comfort of the light, but the voice enticed her deeper into the unknown. And still she went, as if caught in a trance.

Suddenly a face appeared before her, close enough to touch, illuminated by a flame that flickered uneven shadows across the smooth, pale skin. A face she didn't recognize. A face without eyes. A face without expression. Yet she knew instinctively that it was Raquel. Then a second face materialized beside the first. Identical. Again she knew who it was. Bill Walker. A third face appeared. A fourth. A fifth. All identical. Then she felt something grab her arm. She looked down and saw a skeletal hand locked around her wrist. She tried frantically to shake it loose, but to no avail. A second skeletal hand grabbed her other wrist. More bony fingers clawed at her arms and she screamed in sheer terror as she felt herself being dragged down . . .

She was awake in an instant and sat bolt upright in bed. It

took a few seconds for her to realize where she was, then she wiped a trembling hand across her cold, clammy face and looked at the alarm clock on the bedside table. Any lingering anxieties she may have had about the nightmare were immediately forgotten when she saw the time: 8.19. She was due to meet Kellerman at the embassy at nine o'clock. The meeting with Doyle was scheduled for ten. She remembered setting the alarm the previous evening for 7.30 a.m. – she must have switched it off and gone back to sleep. She hurried through to the bathroom and took a quick shower then, wrapping a towel around her naked body, returned to the bedroom to get dressed. She was desperate for coffee but with less than half an hour to get to the embassy she reluctantly pushed the idea from her mind, set the alarm and left the house. She walked to the main road, and a minute later she was sitting in the back of a taxi.

It was the first chance she'd had to collect her thoughts since she woke up. She chose not to dwell on the nightmare – she had a feeling it wouldn't be the last time those faces would haunt her sleep. Instead she concentrated on what lay ahead. In twelve hours' time she and Mel would be airborne, clear of Mexican airspace, and on their way to a new life with ten million dollars' worth of diamonds to share. She knew she was jumping the gun – they still had to pull off the scam, or at least Mel did. Her own involvement amounted to little more than a cameo. But, in its own way, it was just as important . . .

The taxi arrived at the embassy with five minutes to spare. She showed her pass at the entrance and was admitted into the building where she went straight to Kellerman's office, having already memorized the diagram he had drawn for her. She *was* Melissa as far as the rest of the embassy staff were concerned, and it had to appear that she knew where she was going. She knocked lightly on the door, then opened it and peered inside. Kellerman, who was seated behind his desk, beckoned her in.

'Sorry I'm a bit late – I overslept,' she said with a sheepish grin.

'Come in and close the door,' he said gruffly.

She did as she was told and sat down in front of his desk, her eyes never leaving his face. 'Is something wrong?' she asked.

'You could say that.'

She waited for him to elaborate. When he didn't, she asked, 'Doyle hasn't pulled out of the meeting today, has he?'

'It's us who may have to pull out,' Kellerman replied. 'It really depends on you.'

'I don't understand,' she said.

'Do you remember me telling you about Colonel René Santin, the head of the INCD here in Mexico City?'

'Yes,' Laura replied.

'He was due to meet me here at eight o'clock this morning. Only he never showed, so I contacted INCD headquarters to see if he'd been delayed. He hasn't been in his office at all this morning. They thought he was here. That's when the alarm bells began to ring. I called his wife but she told me that he hadn't returned home last night. She'd assumed he was working. But he left the safe house a good hour before I did last night. And nobody's seen him since. It's as if he's just vanished into thin air.'

'Maybe he had an accident,' Laura suggested.

'The INCD have checked every hospital and mortuary within the city limits. Nothing. Which means we've got to face the real possibility that he's been kidnapped – or even assassinated and his body dumped in some out-of-the-way place.'

'I still don't see what this has to do with me,' Laura said.

'I had to tell him the truth yesterday about Melissa. I had no choice. He knows you're not her. And if he has been taken, it's almost certain that the Salcido cartel would have been behind the kidnapping. Mexico City is their stronghold. He could have been tortured into telling them everything he knows. And who knows what anyone might say to stop the torture if only for a few seconds?'

'So he may have told them the truth about Operation

Checkmate,' Laura said softly, revulsion in her voice at the thought of what might have become of Santin.

'It's possible, and that could put your life in danger were you to show up at the meet this morning.'

'But surely they'd call it off if they knew it was a set-up?' she asked.

'And throw away the chance of getting their hands on the disk? The names on it would give them the edge in any future power struggle between the main drug cartels here in Mexico. With so much at stake it may be a risk they'd be willing to take. Having said that, though, it's all speculation. We don't have any proof that Santin has been taken by the cartel. And if not, Doyle will show up as planned at the hotel this morning, none the wiser that it's a set-up. That's why I said earlier that it really depends on you, whether you still want to go through with it after what I've told you. I'd fully understand if you wanted out.'

'I'm not backing out now,' she replied.

Kellerman got to his feet and moved round to the other side of the desk. He opened the cigarette box on his desk and held it out towards her. She took one and he lit it for her. 'We'll wire you so that we can monitor the situation and be ready to move in at the first sign of any trouble.'

'And what if he were to find the wire?' she asked. The last thing she needed was to be wired up: Doyle could incriminate both her and Mel just by mentioning Mel's presence at the safe house the previous day. But she knew that was just speculation. And it was the least of her worries.

'He's got no reason to frisk you, unless he already knows it's a set-up,' Kellerman told her. 'That's why you need to wear the wire.'

'I don't know Doyle like you do, but common sense tells me that if he already knows Mel's dead, he's not going to go anywhere near the hotel this morning. On the other hand, if he doesn't know, he's going to turn up as planned. And what if he decided to search me for wires? If I refused to let him, he'd be suspicious and call off the deal. If he found it, he'd call off the deal and probably kill me too. What chance would you have of reaching the room before he pulled the trigger?'

'We can conceal the wire in such a way that he wouldn't find it,' Kellerman said.

'He'd know exactly where to look. Forget it, Tom, I'm not wearing a wire.' She raised a hand before he could argue. 'Let me put it another way. If you insist that I wear a wire I'll toss it the moment I enter the hotel. If you don't like it, then we can call the whole thing off right now.'

'OK, no wire. Satisfied?'

'I'm only looking out for myself. It's my butt on the line when I go in there this morning.'

Kellerman removed a sealed envelope from the wall safe then closed the door and relocked it. He used the paper-knife on his desk to slit open the envelope, then removed the contents – a micro floppy disk. 'This is what it's all about,' he said, holding up the disk. 'The names of every narcotics agent and every known CI both here and in Colombia. It arrived in the diplomatic bag from Washington last night.'

'Couldn't you have used a disk with false names? What if Doyle were to slip through the net and get away?'

'The INCD already have agents in place around the hotel and the moment you appear with the diamonds they'll move in and grab Doyle,' he replied. 'Of course, we'd have preferred to give him a list of fictitious names but Doyle's going to check that list carefully before he hands over the diamonds. It's fair to assume that he'll already know several agents on the disk and those are the names he's going to look for first to verify the authenticity of the document. Only we don't know which names he already knows. If they aren't on the disk, he'll pull out of the deal. And if he doesn't have the disk on him when he's arrested, the charges won't stick. He'll walk, and Operation Checkmate will have failed. I know it's far from ideal, but what choice do we have?'

'How will I know if the diamonds are genuine?'

'We've drafted in a local jeweller to act as your evaluator. He's worked for us before. He'll check the quality of the diamonds, and that they're worth ten million dollars. He'll be waiting for you in a car outside the hotel. Call him once you've made contact with Doyle. This is the number.'

'You didn't say anything about this before,' Laura said, taking the sheet of paper from him.

'I didn't think it was important. It's no big deal. Melissa didn't know anything about diamonds either. It only adds to the credibility of your cover. Once he's authenticated the diamonds he'll leave so that you and Doyle can complete the deal.' Kellerman handed her a second sealed envelope. 'That's the jeweller's fee. Pay him before he leaves.'

Laura slipped the envelope into her purse. 'How long will it take me to get to the hotel from here?'

'Ten minutes at most,' he replied.

'Any chance of coffee before I go? I was in such a rush this morning that I didn't get a chance to have any.'

'I'm sure we can arrange something,' he said, reaching for the telephone.

'D'you think Doyle will show?' she asked.

'Your guess is as good as mine,' he replied, putting his hand over the mouthpiece. 'All we can do is set the trap and hope he takes the bait. The rest is out of our hands.'

Doyle used a remote control to activate the security grille at the mouth of the ramp leading to the underground car park beneath the Mex-Freight building. He drove his Mercedes to the lower of the two parking levels, which was deserted except for the Salcidos' BMWs. He pulled up beside them, killed the engine, then got out and pressed the button for the elevator. The doors slid open and, stepping inside, he inserted a security card into a slot at the foot of the control panel. The doors closed and he was transported to Juan Salcido's roof penthouse.

He emerged into a pale blue carpeted hallway where Garcia

was waiting to escort him to the lounge. Juan and Ramón Salcido were seated together on a large sofa facing the door. Peraya was sitting at the semicircular bar in the corner of the room. 'Ah, Doyle, come in,' Ramón Salcido said, then snapped his fingers at Peraya who picked up an attaché case off the bar and placed it on the coffee table in front of the brothers. Salcido released the catches then lifted the lid. Inside were two velvet pouches, both secured with a drawstring. 'Each of these contains fifteen hundred small, cut diamonds,' he told Doyle. 'Total weight, six hundred grams. Total value, ten million dollars. That was the deal you agreed with Wade?'

'Yes,' Doyle replied.

Salcido closed the lid, secured the locks, then pushed the case across the table towards him. 'Personally, I'd have preferred it if Peraya or Garcia had accompanied you to the hotel. After all, ten million dollars in untraceable diamonds could prove a serious temptation to a lot of people.'

'If you don't trust me, take it yourself,' Doyle said.

'I don't trust anybody outside my immediate family, Doyle. You've worked for me long enough to know that. But Juan has complete confidence in you. And I would never question his judgement.'

'But you would question my loyalty,' Doyle said coldly.

'When it comes down to it, Doyle, we all have our price. You've bought enough people over the years to know that.'

'But I also know that some people can't be bought at any price,' Doyle replied.

'Only because we haven't been willing to pay them what they thought they were worth. Vanity and greed always go hand in hand.'

'So do suspicion and fear,' Doyle said, then grabbed the attaché case and headed for the door.

'Doyle,' Juan Salcido called after him, 'as soon as you've completed the deal, bring the disk straight back here. We'll be waiting for you. Garcia, see him out.'

Garcia followed him out into the hall. 'You know he was only trying to wind you up back there,' Garcia said, catching up with Doyle as he strode towards the elevator.

Doyle stopped abruptly. 'You know as well as I do that he meant exactly what he said. I've worked for the cartel now for four years and in that time I've never once given him any reason to question my loyalty. I've helped launder millions of dollars' worth of cash and not one lousy dollar has ever gone missing. And this is how I'm treated in return. I don't have to take that kind of shit. Not from him. Not from anyone. Someone needs to teach him a lesson.'

'You're not going to do anything stupid, are you?' Garcia said, grabbing Doyle's arm as he reached for the elevator button.

'Don't think I'm not tempted,' Doyle snarled, then saw that Peraya had come out of the lounge and was standing by the door, hands behind his back, watching them. How much had he heard? Whatever he had picked up would be reported back to Ramón Salcido. That unnerved Doyle. He hadn't meant anything by his last remark. It had just been said in a moment of frustration. He would never do anything to hurt the cartel. Quick to limit any damage he might have already caused, he broke into a grin and patted Garcia on the arm. 'Don't take any notice of me, I'm just letting off steam. See you later.'

He returned to the underground car park then got back into his car and wound his way to the top of the ramp where he used the remote control to raise the security grille. As he turned left into the República de Venezuela, heading towards the Canada Hotel, a car started up further down the street and began to tail him at a discreet distance.

Melissa had been up early that morning and after a continental breakfast in her room she had left the hotel shortly after seven thirty and had driven the hired car to Chapultepec Park and parked within sight of Doyle's spacious bungalow. It had been another hour before Doyle's Mercedes swept out through the gates and she had followed him to the Mex-Freight building where she had waited until he emerged from the underground car park before continuing the pursuit.

To be on the safe side, she kept at least two vehicles behind Doyle – not that he would have recognized her with her blonde wig and dark glasses, but there was no point in taking any unnecessary risks. When they stopped at a set of traffic lights two blocks away from the hotel, she dialled a number on her cellular phone.

'Doyle, it's Melissa Wade,' she said, injecting a tone of anxiety into her voice.

'What is it?' Doyle demanded, and she heard him curse as the taxi behind him hooted when he failed to respond to the green light.

'Where are you?' she asked, easing her foot on to the accelerator as the car in front of her pulled away.

'I've just passed the junction of Donceles and Brasil—'

'Don't go any further!' she shouted into the mouthpiece. 'Chances are they won't have seen you yet.'

'What are you talking about?' Doyle asked uncertainly. 'Who won't see me? What the hell's going on, Wade?'

'Don't go any further!'

Doyle swung the wheel violently and pulled over to the side of the road. The taxi braked hard behind him and the driver gave Doyle the finger before driving off. Melissa drove past him and turned into the next side-street where she parked, but kept the engine idling. She had his attention and knew he wouldn't be going anywhere until she had explained. 'OK, I've stopped,' Doyle told her. 'Now what the fuck is going on?'

'I've just driven past the hotel. I saw Tom Kellerman in an unmarked car parked close to the entrance. I also saw an INCD agent in a taxi. There's sure to be more of them around. They're on to us, Doyle.'

'How, for Christ's sake?' Doyle demanded.

'I was hoping you could tell me that,' she replied, with equal acerbity.

'What's that supposed to mean?'

'It means that the tip-off came from your end.'

'Impossible!'

'Well, I'm not going to argue with you. There's probably an APB out on me as we speak. I'm getting out while I still can. The deal's off, Doyle.'

'Wait!' Doyle shouted frantically down the line.

She had him rattled, and now he was at her mercy. Not that she was going to let him off lightly. This was her moment, and she was going to play it for all it was worth. 'Who knew about the meet today?'

'The Salcidos, naturally. Garcia. Peraya. Myself.' Pause. 'That's all. Only the five of us. But, then, you know that.'

'I only know that's what you told me,' she replied.

'Nobody else knew about it. You have my word on that.'

'Right now, your word means jack shit to me, Doyle. I'm getting out of the country. I'll find another buyer for the disk once the dust has settled.'

'Wade – Melissa – listen to me,' Doyle said desperately, 'don't hang up. We can still resolve this. Let's at least talk about it. Please.'

'You've got sixty seconds, Doyle. Talk.'

'OK, so the authorities are on to us. I'm not disputing that. And neither am I disputing the possibility that they were tipped off by ... someone from this end. But that doesn't mean we have to scrap the deal. We can rearrange—'

'I'm not hanging around Mexico City while you rearrange your schedule to fit me in at your convenience,' she cut in angrily. 'Either we do the deal now at a different location or I find myself another buyer. I'm sure I won't have too much difficulty there. After all, the names of most of your snitches are on the disk as well. That alone would boost the price considerably on the open market.'

'OK, you've made your point. Where do you want to meet?'

'I haven't even thought about it. Somewhere quiet. You know

this town a lot better than I do. Where do you suggest?'

'There's a multi-storey car park on Juárez Avenue, a couple of blocks up from the Revolution Monument opposite the National Lottery building.'

'Which level?'

'Make it the second.'

'It's now nine forty-two. I'll meet you there at ten fifteen. If you're not there, the deal's off. If I see anyone else there other than you, the deal's off. And it goes without saying that you keep this to yourself, at least until we've made the trade and gone our separate ways. You can't trust anyone – not even the Salcidos – until you've found out who's been playing footsie with the DEA.'

'Ten fifteen. Don't be late.' The line went dead.

Melissa switched off her phone and smiled. She had manoeuvred Doyle into her lair, exactly as she had planned. But before she helped him tighten the noose around his own neck, she had first to return to the hotel to meet Laura. Starting up the engine, she edged her way to the mouth of the side-street and saw that Doyle's car was no longer parked at the side of the road. She swung out into the República de Brasil and drove the short distance back to the hotel.

As the taxi pulled up outside the Canada Hotel Laura recalled Kellerman's parting words to her before she had left the embassy: *Remember, Doyle's sure to have his own people watching the hotel and if they were to suspect for one moment that everything wasn't right they'd pull him out without a second thought. It's imperative that we have the element of surprise on our side so that we can take him completely unawares when he leaves the hotel with the disk . . .*

Only he wouldn't be leaving the hotel with the disk. In fact, he wouldn't be showing up at the hotel. And while she acted as the decoy at the hotel, Mel would conclude the deal with Doyle at a rearranged location without the authorities being any the wiser. And when they finally unravelled the truth both she and Mel would be long gone . . . with the diamonds.

Laura paid the driver, then got out of the taxi and entered the hotel. She knew the INCD had the lobby under surveillance and it was imperative that she continue the pretence for their benefit. The room Doyle had booked was on the third floor. She rode the elevator and when the doors parted she stepped out into the corridor. It was deserted. She used the stairs to go down a floor and then made her way to Melissa's room at the end of the corridor. She rapped sharply on the door. It swung open. Melissa grabbed her wrist and pulled her inside.

'Santin's disappeared,' Laura said, once her sister had closed the door.

'Santin's dead,' Melissa replied, and saw the look of uncertainty flash across her sister's face. 'No, I had nothing to do with it.'

'How do you know he's dead?'

'I have my sources,' Melissa replied.

'So why haven't the DEA found out about it yet?'

'I guess I just have better sources than them. But they'll find out soon enough.'

'He knew about me being out here,' Laura said.

'Who told him?'

'Tom,' Laura replied, then added quickly in his defence, 'but he said he had no choice. He thinks that if the cartel kidnapped Santin, they may have tortured the truth out of him before they . . . killed him, and that they would call off the deal this morning.'

'I'm reliably informed that it was a clean hit,' Melissa replied. 'Don't worry, the cartel don't know anything.'

'So the deal's still on?' Laura asked.

'It certainly was when I spoke to Doyle a few minutes ago. We're in business, sis,' Melissa replied, with a broad grin. Laura gave a whoop of delight and they hugged each other. Then Melissa disengaged herself. 'We'll have plenty of time to celebrate later,' she said. 'Where's the disk?'

Laura took it out of her purse and gave it to Melissa, who

switched on the laptop computer on the bed. She fed the disk into one of the two internal drives, checked the first few pages to authenticate the program then slipped a blank disk into the second disk drive and copied the original document. She made a second copy before ejecting the master disk and returning it to Laura.

'You said you were only going to make one copy to give to Doyle.'

'The second copy is my – sorry, *our* insurance policy,' Melissa told her. 'When the DEA realize what's happened, it won't take them long to work out that I was involved in the attack on the safe house yesterday. Then they're going to come looking for me. That's why I posted a letter to the embassy earlier this morning. Addressed to Tom. He should get it in the next couple of days. I've told him that should anything happen to us the disk will be sent to the Cali cartel in Colombia. Their methods of retribution make the Salcidos look tame by comparison. Everyone UC on that list would be marked for execution. Without exception.'

'It's a bluff, right?'

'I don't bluff, sis. The DEA know that. Which is why they're going to have to take the threat seriously.' Melissa smiled in an attempt to put Laura at ease. 'If they leave us alone, they've got nothing to worry about. I'm merely taking extra precautions to cover every eventuality, that's all.'

'You never mentioned this before.'

'That's because I didn't plan it this way. If our only crime had been to steal the cartel's diamonds then ride off into the sunset, the authorities wouldn't have lost much sleep. But the events of the last few days have changed all that. We have to adapt to those changes, sis, and make sure we stay one step ahead of the DEA at all times otherwise we're going to get caught. I don't know about you, but I sure as hell don't fancy spending the rest of my life rotting in a Mexican jail.'

'Me neither,' Laura replied, then gestured to the first disk lying on the bed. 'Is that the one you're giving to Doyle?' Melissa nodded. 'And it's rigged, right?'

Melissa picked it up. 'You don't "rig" a floppy disk, sis. You corrupt it with a virus. Doyle's going to be in for a big surprise.'

'They all are, aren't they?'

'You could say that,' Melissa replied, then slipped the disk into her pocket and moved to the door. 'You'd better get back up to the third floor before someone notices that you're not there.'

'How long should I wait outside the room?'

'Half an hour at the most, although the INCD will probably pull you out before then when they realize that Doyle isn't going to show.'

'And you're still going to pick me up from the house this afternoon?' Laura asked.

'Yeah. It'll be some time around one. One thirty at the latest. Make sure you're ready, sis. We'll be going straight to the airfield to meet the plane.'

'I'll be ready.'

Melissa hugged her briefly then opened the door. 'Now go on, I'll see you later.'

'Good luck, Mel.'

'Who needs luck when I've got this?' Melissa replied, tapping the disk in her pocket.

As soon as Laura left the room the door closed abruptly behind her. She took the stairs back to the third floor, knowing that all she had to do now was wait . . .

It was already ten fifteen when Melissa turned off the Paseo de la Reforma, the main thoroughfare running through the heart of the city, into Juárez Avenue. She drove the short distance to the multi-storey parking lot – which she noted wasn't as close to the National Lottery building as Doyle had claimed – then took a ticket from the machine at the entrance, which automatically activated the boom gate, and wove her way up the spiral ramp to the second level. Half a dozen cars were parked there, including Doyle's Mercedes with its opaque windows. She cruised past the other cars to check that they weren't occupied. She was far more concerned about being spotted by a witness than she was of being set up by Doyle. That thought had not crossed her mind until now and she dismissed it out of hand. Doyle was in the mould of Juan Salcido: both were men of their word. To the best of her knowledge neither had reneged on a deal. Loyalty was always rewarded. It was a code of honour that seemed somehow anachronistic in their violent world of drugs and death.

She pulled up two spaces from the Mercedes and switched off the engine. A moment later the Mercedes' passenger window slid open and Doyle acknowledged her with a cursory nod. She removed a holdall from the back seat, got out of her car and, after looking around her slowly, walked over to the Mercedes.

'Back seat,' Doyle said.

She opened the door and got in. Doyle pressed the button to close the passenger window.

'You're late,' he said, looking at his watch. It was ten eighteen.

'I'm allowed to be late,' she replied. 'I made the rules.'

'Have you brought the disk with you?' Doyle asked.

She took it from her pocket but pulled back her hand when Doyle reached out to pluck it from her fingers. 'You give me the diamonds. I'll give you the disk. That way we can authenticate each other's merchandise at the same time. Unless you've got a problem with that.'

In reply, Doyle unlocked the attaché case, which lay beside a laptop computer on the passenger seat, removed the two velvet pouches and handed them to her. She gave him the disk, and took an electronic diamond tester from the holdall.

'If this is a set-up, I'll kill you,' Doyle said, looking at her in the reflection of the rear-view mirror.

'You took the words right out of my mouth,' she replied, then pulled her Smith & Wesson from the concealed holster at the back of her jeans and placed it within easy reach on the seat beside her.

'Then I suggest we get on with it,' Doyle said, and switched on the computer.

'No problem,' she replied, pulling the drawstring of one of the pouches to check its contents.

Laura knocked lightly on Kellerman's open door. No reply. That surprised her – she had been told he was waiting for her in his office. She peered round the door. He was sitting at his desk, hands behind his head, staring at an imaginary spot on the opposite wall. 'Tom?' she said.

He looked at her without moving his head. 'Come in,' he said, in a hollow voice. She closed the door and sat down. 'I guess I shouldn't be surprised that Doyle didn't show at the hotel this morning. Not after Santin's disappearance last night. I told you that the cartel would have had something to do with it. And I was right. He must have told them what I confided in him yesterday at the safe house. I know he'd have held out for as long as was humanly possible under torture, but right now that's of little consolation. We'll never get another chance like this. It was a once-in-a-lifetime shot. And we blew it.'

'You can't blame yourself, Tom.' *No, it was my fault*, she told herself bitterly. *Mel and I, partners in crime. We're to blame. We're the guilty ones.* She hated herself for what she had done to him.

'You try telling that to the suits in Washington. They don't like loose ends. It doesn't look good in their reports to Congress. And, as the senior agent out here, I'll be taking most of the flak for the failure of Checkmate.'

'But that's not fair,' she said, helping herself to a cigarette from the box on his desk.

'Maybe not, but that's the way it works. It was the most important deal set up by the DEA in the last twelve months. Not only did Melissa and I have to sell it to our superiors, but also to a group of senior White House advisers because, as I've already told you, the President had to make a secret deal with the Mexican government to agree to extradite Doyle back to the States after he was arrested. The White House went out on a limb to accommodate us. And in return they wanted guarantees that nothing could go wrong. I had to give them those guarantees, which was one of the main reasons why I asked you to help us out at the eleventh hour. Now that the deal's collapsed, the White House will want a fall guy so that they can walk away without appearing to have dirtied their hands. No prizes for guessing who that's going to be.'

'I – I had no idea,' she stammered. *This wasn't how it was supposed to have been.* Mel had never said he would have to take the rap for their deception.

'Why should you?' he replied dejectedly. 'It doesn't concern you. You shouldn't have been involved in any of this as it is. Having said that, though, we couldn't have got this far without you. And I know I'll never forget what you did to help us.'

The telephone rang. He sat forward and grabbed the receiver. His eyes never left Laura's face as he listened to the caller. 'I'm on my way,' he said, hung up and got to his feet. 'Santin's body's been found in a ditch on the outskirts of the city. Sounds like a professional hit – a single bullet to the back of the head. Strange thing is, there are no signs that he was tortured before he was killed, which throws up a lot more questions than answers.' He pulled on his jacket then patted his pocket to check that he had his car keys. 'I guess this is where the inquest into Operation Checkmate really begins.'

'What do you want me to do?' she asked.

'You may as well go back to the house. But first you'd better give me back the disk. All we need is for that to go missing on top of everything else that's happened today.' She took the disk from her purse, as well as the money he had given her earlier to pay the evaluator, and handed them to him. He put them in the wall safe. 'I'd have given you a ride, only I'm headed in the opposite direction.'

'I think I can manage to get myself a taxi, don't you?' she said, but the thinly veiled sarcasm was accompanied by a smile.

'Come on, I'll walk you out.'

They went up to the lobby then out into the parking lot at the rear of the building. He paused beside his car and fished the keys from his pocket. 'I doubt I'll get a chance to see you before tonight. But I promise I'll drop by at the house on my way home.'

'That would be great,' she replied, without expression.

'Don't sound so enthusiastic,' he said good-humouredly.

She just smiled. What could she say? She already knew she would never see him again. That hurt enough. But what made it unbearable was that he would never know just how much she cared about him. And she would have to live with her betrayal of him and her own feelings for the rest of her life. More guilt. More pain.

The sharp blast of the car horn startled her and she stepped aside to let him reverse out of the parking space. He gave her a quick wave then drove to the gate, which was raised by the guard. The car swung out into the road and disappeared from sight. She slipped on her sunglasses. She was damned if she was going to let anyone see the tears in her eyes.

EIGHTEEN

'Where have you been?' Juan Salcido demanded, when Doyle returned to the penthouse. 'Why didn't you go to the hotel? And why haven't you been answering your phone?'

'Because I switched it off,' Doyle replied, and added quickly, 'but I had my reasons. You'll understand why once I've explained what happened.'

'This better be good, Doyle,' Ramón Salcido warned him.

Doyle detailed the events after he had left the penthouse to go to the hotel, careful not to omit anything, starting with the call he got from Melissa through to the deal he had finalized with her less than fifteen minutes earlier. He took the disk from the attaché case. 'I checked the document carefully in the car. It's authentic.'

The brothers exchanged glances, then Juan took the disk from Doyle and fed it into the laptop computer on the coffee table. His eyes remained riveted on the screen as his fingers danced across the keyboard. Then he looked up slowly at Doyle. 'Somehow I expected better than this after the spiel you've just given us. That part of it was good. Really good. Well rehearsed, and very convincing. If I didn't know you better, I could have almost believed you.'

'What are you talking about?' Doyle replied in bewilderment.

'That's what you authenticated, is it?' Juan growled, then

swivelled the computer until the screen was facing Doyle. It was blank.

'That's impossible!' Doyle gasped. He ejected the disk, checked that it was the one he had been given in the car, then fed it back into the computer. The screen remained blank. 'There were hundreds of files on here. I know, I saw them. I tell you, *I saw them!* They were here.' He reeled off a dozen names that had been on the disk.

'Every one of them works for us,' Ramón said. 'We'd be a lot more impressed if you gave us the names of some UCs that we didn't already know about.'

'I can't remember any of the other names,' Doyle said, wiping his hand nervously across his mouth. 'Like I said, there were hundreds on file. The only way I could verify the disk's authenticity was by checking the names I already knew. They were there. I swear it!'

'Then why aren't they there now?' Ramón demanded.

'The bitch obviously put a virus in the program to crash the file,' Doyle replied. 'It's the only logical explanation.'

'I've heard enough!' Juan snapped. 'We already know that Wade arrived at the Canada Hotel this morning at nine fifty-six. She didn't leave again until ten thirty-two.'

'That's impossible. I told you, I met with her at the parking lot on Juárez. And I can prove it.' Doyle took the ticket from his pocket. 'There. It's got the time punched on the card. Ten thirteen a.m. She arrived about five minutes later.'

'That only proves you were there,' Ramón replied.

'She was there too,' Doyle insisted.

'I've got half a dozen witnesses who say otherwise,' Juan told him. 'Not only did they all positively identify her, but they also logged her arriving at the hotel at exactly the same time. We had a man inside the hotel who was dressed as a room-service waiter. He went to the third floor on three separate occasions between ten and ten thirty. And each time he saw Wade waiting outside the room where you were supposed to have met her. So, we have seven independent witnesses who put her in the hotel at the exact time you claimed she was with you and we also have your story that you met her at a parking lot on Juárez where the two of you concluded the deal. You return here with a blank disk and no diamonds.' He picked up the computer and flung it against the wall. 'Don't insult my intelligence, Doyle! Where are the diamonds?'

'I told you—'

'A stream of lies from the moment you entered the room,' Juan cut in furiously. 'You never met her at the parking lot. You took the diamonds for yourself, didn't you?'

'If I'd taken the diamonds I'd have been on the next plane out of the country. I sure as hell wouldn't have come back here, knowing what would happen to me. I didn't take them. I would never betray you, you know that. My loyalty to the cartel has always been beyond reproach.'

'The same could have been said about Hector until his greed got the better of him. You know what hurts the most, though? The two people I trusted most in this organization have now both betrayed me within days of each other.'

'I never betrayed you. I didn't take the diamonds,' Doyle said. 'How can I make you believe that?'

'Prove that you met Wade at the parking lot, and I'll believe you,' Juan replied.

'I can't,' Doyle said despairingly. 'I've been set up. I don't know how or why, but I've been set up.'

'Prove it.'

'I can't,' Doyle shouted back. 'You know I can't.' Then he managed a weak laugh of relief. 'Of course. She had a double posing as her at the hotel.'

'Double?' Juan said scornfully.

'Double – as in twin sister,' Doyle replied. 'Melissa Wade's got a twin sister. I remember that now from her DEA file. It must have been her twin our people saw at the hotel this morning.'

'And what would she have to gain by sending her twin sister to the hotel in her place?'

'She said on the phone that the DEA had the hotel under surveillance,' Doyle replied. 'She could have been using her as a decoy.'

'Except that, according to your story, she only found out the DEA were watching the hotel minutes before the two of you were due to meet there. So what you're saying is that she flew her sister all the way out here to act as a decoy on the off-chance that the hotel may be under surveillance.'

'There's one way to find out whether it was her twin sister at the hotel this morning,' Ramón said. 'What's her name? Where does she live?'

'All I know is that she's a dentist in New York. I don't remember her name.'

'Peraya, call international enquiries,' Ramón said. 'There can't be that many dentists called Wade in New York.'

'*Sí, patrón,*' Peraya replied, then crossed to the telephone on the bar. He gave the operator the details and drummed his fingers impatiently as he waited for her to come back to him. When she did he put his hand over the mouthpiece and turned to Ramón. 'There's only one dentist called Wade listed in the New York directory. Laura Wade.'

'That's her,' Doyle said, nodding his head. 'Laura Wade.'

'Get her home and surgery number,' Ramón said, then took the receiver from Peraya after he had written down the two numbers.

'What if there's no answer?' Juan asked, as his brother dialled. 'That doesn't prove anything. She could be out for the day. It's Sunday, after all. The whole idea's ridiculous.'

'But if she does answer it proves—' Ramón stopped abruptly when the receiver was lifted at the other end. 'Good afternoon,' he said, switching to English. 'Dr Wade?' Pause. 'One moment, please.' He beckoned Doyle towards him.

Doyle took the receiver hesitantly from him. 'Is that Dr Laura Wade?'

'That's what I've just said. Who is this?'

'And you're a dentist in New York?'

'Yes. Look, who is this? What do you want?'

An ashen-faced Doyle slowly replaced the receiver. 'It doesn't make any sense. It had to be her at the hotel this morning. That could have been someone impersonating her on the phone. A DEA agent. It could have been anybody . . . I don't know.' But there was no conviction left in his voice.

'Take his gun,' Ramón said to Garcia.

'And if he resists, kill him,' Juan added tersely.

Doyle extended his arms away from his body when Garcia approached him. Their eyes met momentarily then Garcia shook his head sadly before easing the Glock from Doyle's shoulder holster and placing it on the table. 'You think I stole the diamonds as well, don't you?' Doyle said, grabbing Garcia's arm. 'You, of all people, should know me better than that.'

'Let go of my arm,' Garcia hissed.

Ramón was quick to remove the Glock before his brother could pick it up. He deposited it on the bar, then eased himself up on to a stool. 'Those diamonds came from my personal stock. And if we can't have the disk, then I want them back. You can do what you want with him if it turns out that he did steal the diamonds from us. Only right now we don't know that for sure. And until we find out what really did happen this morning, he has to be given the benefit of the doubt.'

Juan sat down on the sofa. 'I'd have thought that you, of all people, would have wanted to see him punished, whether he was guilty or not.'

'I'm the first to admit that I don't like Doyle any more than he likes me, but that doesn't mean I don't respect him for his professionalism. And right now I'm not as convinced as you are that he did take the diamonds. As he pointed out, why would he have come back here if he was guilty? He's well aware of the penalty for stealing from the cartel.'

'All I know are the facts as they stand,' Juan said. 'Doyle didn't show at the hotel this morning. Wade did. When he returns here he gives us some story about them changing the rendezvous to a parking lot at the last moment and making the trade there instead. Only the disk conveniently turns out to be blank, which he puts down to some virus which didn't show up when he originally checked it. As far as I'm concerned, the conclusions speak for themselves.'

'Check Doyle's car,' Ramón told Garcia.

'You don't really think the diamonds are there, do you?' Doyle said, scornfully.

'Give Garcia your keys!' Juan snapped.

Doyle bit back his anger then tossed his keys to Garcia, who caught them deftly and left the room.

'You say there were no witnesses who could have verified this meeting with Wade at the parking lot?' Ramón asked Doyle.

'Not as far as I'm aware, no,' Doyle replied.

'Didn't she have anyone with her to evaluate the diamonds?'

'No, she came alone,' Doyle replied.

'So she checked the diamonds herself?' Ramón said in surprise.

'Not all of them. Just a random selection to verify they were genuine.'

'What did she use to verify them?' Ramón asked.

'She had one of those electronic diamond testers.'

'What else did she use?'

'That's all, as far as I know,' Doyle replied.

'And how did she use it?'

'I wasn't watching her. I was verifying the disk.'

'What did she use to cool the diamonds she tested?' Ramón asked.

'I don't understand,' Doyle replied hesitantly.

'A diamond has to be cool before it can be checked with an electronic diamond tester. The easiest way of cooling them is by putting them under cold water then wiping them clean with a dry cloth. But obviously she wouldn't have had access to running water. Another way is to spray the diamond with a canister of freon, or some other type of compressed air. Did she do that?'

'Not to my knowledge, no,' Doyle replied, sensing that each answer he gave was manoeuvring him further into a corner. But he was only telling the truth. What else could he do? If he started to lie now, he would only incriminate himself further down the line. Stick to the facts, it was all he had left going for him.

'If a diamond's warm, chances are it won't test genuine on an electronic diamond tester,' Ramón said. 'And considering that these diamonds had been in two sealed pouches inside an attaché case ... well, let's just say I wouldn't have trusted a reading under those conditions. I would certainly have cooled the stones first. How many of the stones did she test?'

'I don't know. We must have been there for about twenty minutes.'

'So what you're saying is that every stone she tested, at random, must have given a positive reading otherwise she'd have called off the deal.' Ramón shook his head. 'I'd say the chances of that happening, under those conditions, would be similar to winning the state lottery with the same numbers every week for a whole year. It's just not feasible.'

'I'm telling you, that's how she did it,' Doyle said, the desperation returning to his voice.

'And how did she weigh them?'

'I don't know,' Doyle replied.

'You don't know *how* she weighed them, or you don't know *if* she weighed them?' Ramón pressed.

'I didn't see her weigh them,' Doyle replied, wriggling out of a direct answer.

'You're certainly not helping your case, Doyle,' Ramón told him. 'Everything you've told me so far goes against the very basics of diamond testing. If you had met Wade at the parking lot as you claimed, she'd have come a lot better prepared than you made her out to be. She may not be an expert in gemstones, but neither is she a fool. She'd have known exactly how to use the electronic diamond tester. But from what you've said, it sounds to me as if she didn't know one end of it from the other. I don't believe she would have been that irresponsible with ten million dollars' worth of diamonds at stake, do you?'

'I can only tell you what I know,' Doyle said.

'You can only tell us what you made up,' Juan interceded. 'Ramón knows more about gemstones than anyone else in the country. Did you honestly think you could deceive him with something so basic as authenticating a diamond?'

'Don't you think I'd have had the sense to get my facts right if it had been my intention to steal the diamonds?' Doyle retorted. 'Can't you see that she's set me up?'

'Maybe she was working in league with this mysterious DEA informer that she mentioned to you on the phone,' Juan said sardonically. 'I'm surprised you haven't made more use of him in your defence.'

'What's the use? You've already made up your mind that I'm guilty and nothing I say will make the slightest bit of difference,' Doyle said, slumping into the nearest armchair.

'What would you think if you were in my position?' Juan asked.

'I would weigh up the situation impartially and not let my emotions get the better of me,' Doyle said, sitting forward. 'I've negotiated numerous multi-million-dollar drug deals with the Colombians and you know as well as I do that not one dollar – not one gram of coke – has ever gone missing. You asked me personally to handle those deals because you trusted me.'

'I trusted Hector as well,' Juan said bitterly. 'Not only that, but Hector was a close family friend. And while I foolishly thought that he had only the cartel's best interests at heart, he was systematically skimming off millions of dollars from our accounts to satisfy his own personal greed.'

'I'm not like Lacamara,' Doyle replied.

'That remains to be seen,' Ramón said, turning the Glock around slowly on the bar.

'Garcia's back,' Peraya announced from the doorway when he heard the familiar *ping* as the elevator reached the penthouse. He stepped away from the door to allow the other man to enter the room.

'I found these hidden in the back of Doyle's car,' Garcia said, dropping the two pouches on to the coffee table.

'No!' Doyle yelled, but as he jumped to his feet Garcia pulled his Colt automatic from his shoulder holster and swung it on him to prevent him from approaching Juan. 'Please, you've got to listen to me,' Doyle begged. 'I didn't take those diamonds. I didn't take them. You've got to believe me.'

'Take him to the Workshop and dissect him piece by piece,' Juan ordered.

Doyle realized then that the time for reasoning was over. Whoever had set him up had succeeded in turning Juan against him. Once his closest ally in the cartel, now his bitterest enemy out for revenge. All that mattered now was his own personal survival. He knew that the odds were stacked heavily against him, but he had to do something. Chances were that he would be killed in the process, but he was ready to take a bullet if necessary. It would be infinitely more preferable to a slow, agonizing death at the hands of Garcia and Peraya in the Workshop. No, this was his last chance. He had to take it.

He lunged at Garcia, his fingers clawing frantically for the automatic. He got his fingers around the stock but as he tried to force the barrel away from his body a shot rang out. He stumbled backwards, as if he had just been punched viciously in the solar plexus, and felt a sharp pain spear through his stomach. Then he looked down and saw the dark blood stain on the front of his shirt. It was spreading rapidly, seeping on to his trousers. He clutched a hand to his stomach, as if that might somehow stem the bleeding. His eyes began to blur. Then he lost all sensation in his legs. They buckled awkwardly underneath him and he made a desperate grab for the armchair as he fell. He missed it and landed heavily on the ground. He suddenly felt cold. He was shaking. Or trembling. He didn't know which. Then he began to cough. He could feel the blood bubbling in his throat. In his mouth. On his lips. Down his chin. He was dying. He knew that. Yet he wasn't scared. He actually felt relief. Relief that he had cheated the Workshop. There had to be some irony in that. He coughed again. Only in his confused state of mind it sounded like a laugh. The last laugh . . .

'He's dead,' Garcia said, finding no pulse. He straightened up and looked round uncertainly at Juan. 'I'm sorry, *patrón*. He caught me by surprise. I was trying to take my finger off the trigger when the gun went off. I didn't mean to kill him.'

'Regrettable,' Juan said, making no effort to conceal his bitterness as he stared coldly at Doyle's body.

'On the contrary, it's worked out perfectly,' Ramón said, then picked up the Glock off the counter and shot Garcia twice through the chest. Garcia was punched back against the wall by the force of the bullets, the Colt spilling from his hand. There was a look of complete disbelief on his face as he slowly slid to the floor. He tried to speak but no words came out. Then he toppled sideways against the armchair and his head lolled forward on to his chest, his vacant eyes still open in death.

'You've killed him,' Juan exclaimed, as he stared at Garcia's body.

'I didn't kill him,' his brother replied. 'Doyle did. It's his gun. They shot each other. At least, that's the conclusion the police will come to when they find the bodies.'

'I don't understand,' Juan said, bewildered.

'I believe it's called a coup. I've just taken control of the cartel, brother. Actually, Melissa Wade was instrumental in helping me put it all together. She works for me.' Ramón grinned triumphantly when he saw the look of incredulity flash across his brother's face. 'I knew that would get your attention. She's been my main source inside the DEA for the last eighteen months.

All your sources are paid by the cartel. That's why Lacamara didn't know about her. Or about Santin for that matter. Or about any of my other sources who work solely for me.'

'René Santin works for you as well?' Juan said in amazement, struggling to marshal his confused thoughts.

'Worked. Yesterday he found out a little too much about the intricacies of the operation for his own good. That's when he decided he wanted money to buy his silence. Peraya met with him last night. Now his silence is assured.'

Juan rubbed his hands slowly over his face. 'Doyle's been played for the patsy all along, hasn't he?'

'Everything he said was true. We had to use him as the bait. It was the only way that the DEA would go for it. She had to involve them to get the disk as she didn't have the necessary security clearance to access the file herself. Their plan was for her to give Doyle the disk in exchange for the diamonds. Then he would have been arrested by the INCD and put on the next flight back to the States and offered immunity from prosecution if he agreed to testify against us.'

'So who was at the hotel?'

'Her twin sister.'

'But you rang her in New York? Doyle even spoke to her on the phone.'

'No, I rang Melissa Wade. She just pretended to be her sister. It was really very simple. She faked her own death in New York earlier this week, which forced the DEA to bring in her twin sister to take her place. Her sister's in on it as well, I believe. They're sharing the diamonds between them.'

'And the diamonds Garcia found in Doyle's car?'

'Paste. Only he didn't know that. It was all part of the plan to frame Doyle and make it look as if he'd stolen them. So when the police get here, they'll find the bodies and the two pouches of fake diamonds. The DEA will assume that Doyle switched the paste for the real diamonds, which would explain why he didn't show at the hotel this morning, and that's what caused the altercation which so tragically led to their deaths. Of course, they can't prove anything because, as far as they're concerned, the deal never went down. Only the DEA don't know that Wade made a second copy of the disk to sell to me in exchange for the real diamonds. I'm due to meet with her later to conclude the deal.'

'If it was your intention all along to make it look as if they had fallen out over the diamonds, why didn't you just let me shoot Doyle when I had the chance?' Juan asked.

'With his own gun? That could have thrown up a lot of awkward questions. And anyway, I was enjoying myself. Doyle actually thought I was on his side, but all I was doing was prolonging his agony by constantly raising his hopes only to dash them again. Very gratifying.'

'You still haven't said why you want control of the cartel.'

'Why? Because you've become complacent. You're more interested these days in how your precious Mex-Freight shares are doing on the stock market than you are in the cartel.'

'That's not true!' Juan shouted.

'You were the one who insisted that Lacamara handle all the cartel's finances. You were the one who insisted that Doyle negotiate all the deals with the Colombians. And the more responsibility you delegated to those around you, the more you were able to distance yourself from the day-to-day running of the cartel.'

'I didn't hear you raise any objections at the time.'

'What good would it have done? You had Lacamara and Doyle to back up every decision you made. I was always on the periphery, and any suggestions I ever made about expanding the cartel were always dismissed out of hand.'

'Only because they were unworkable.'

'That's where you're wrong, because while you were busy off-loading your responsibilities on to Lacamara and Doyle I was holding secret talks with the leaders of the main cartels in both Bolivia and Peru. I've already made deals with them to handle a significant percentage of their product *en route* to the streets of America. The Salcido cartel will finally become the most powerful cartel in the whole of Central America.'

'And what do you think the Cali cartel are going to do when they find out that you've reneged on the deal I made with them? We had an understanding that we would only do business with them.'

'You made the deal, not me. This is a competitive business. If the Cali cartel want to renegotiate, I'll be more than willing to listen to any offer they may want to put on the table.'

'The only offer they'll put on the table is to the person they send to kill you,' Juan said. 'You've got no idea what you've done, do you?'

'I've finally stepped out of your shadow, Juan, that's what I've done,' Ramón said then levelled the Glock at his brother.

'What are you doing?' Juan exclaimed in horror, and stumbled backwards until he was pressed against the wall.

'You didn't think I'd let you retire gracefully from the cartel, did you? Your reputation would always be a threat to me as long as you were still alive. Don't worry, though, I'll see to it that Katrine and the kids never want for anything. After all, they are family.' Ramón shot his brother through the heart then put the Glock in Doyle's hand, aimed it at the wall, and fired off another round.

'Why did you do that, *patrón*?' Peraya asked.

'It has to appear as if Doyle shot them. That means there would have to be some discharge residue on his hand, no matter how minute. If Forensics don't find any traces of lead and nitrate on his skin, it could raise some awkward questions later. I'm not taking any chances.'

'I wouldn't have thought of that, *patrón*,' Peraya said in admiration.

'I can believe that,' Ramón muttered to himself, then followed Peraya from the room.

*   *   *

'Good morning,' the receptionist said with a friendly smile.

'Morning. I'm here to see Mr Salcido.'

'He's just this minute checked in. I'll ring his suite and see if he's there. Could I have your name please?'

'Melissa Wade.'

She looked around the lobby of the Sheraton Hotel as the receptionist called the suite. She had discarded the wig and sunglasses. This time she wanted to be seen.

'Excuse me, Ms Wade,' the receptionist said. 'Mr Salcido asked if you'd go straight up. He's expecting you.'

Melissa was given the suite number and took the elevator to the appropriate floor where she alighted, then made her way to the room and knocked on the door. Peraya opened it and gestured for her to enter.

'Perfect timing, as always,' Ramón Salcido said, getting up from the armchair by the window.

'You're armed?' Peraya said, blocking her progress into the room.

'Naturally, but then so are you,' she replied.

'Your weapon,' Peraya said, holding out his hand. She made no move to comply with his request. 'If you don't hand over your weapon voluntarily, Agent Wade, I'll be forced to take it off you.'

Melissa raised a finger in warning. 'You so much as touch me and I'll break your fucking arm. And if you don't believe me, just try it.' Her eyes went to Salcido. 'I'll make a deal with you. If he's prepared to surrender his weapon to me, then I'll surrender mine to him. That's only fair, isn't it? Or we could just leave the situation as it is. But if you've got a problem with that, then I guess I'll just have to go find myself another buyer for the disk.'

Salcido waved Peraya away from her. 'You'll have to excuse him. He's overprotective. But he means well.'

'Maybe now we can get down to business,' Melissa said.

'By all means,' Salcido replied then gestured to the telephone. 'Call your man. He's in room six-o-five.'

Melissa rang the room, had a brief conversation, then hung up. When she had originally made the deal with Salcido she had insisted that she be allowed to bring in an independent jeweller to value the diamonds before she handed over the disk. He had concurred. She had then made some discreet enquiries about a possible evaluator and found that one name seemed to crop up more than any other. A jeweller called Fuentes, based in Acapulco. Fuentes was willing to take on the job, as long as all his expenses were met by her. She persuaded Salcido to agree to pay for Fuentes to be flown to Mexico City, his overnight accommodation and his valuation fee. Fuentes had arrived in Mexico City the previous day and shortly after he had checked into the hotel Peraya had personally delivered the diamonds to his room. She had decided against telling Fuentes in advance the estimated value of the diamonds. Best to let him put his own price on the diamonds and see if it matched Salcido's valuation. If it did, they were in business . . .

'You don't mind if I order something from room service while we're waiting for Fuentes, do you?' she asked, picking up the menu that lay beside the telephone. 'I'm starving. I haven't eaten anything today. And as I'll be going straight to the airfield from here, I don't know when I'll get the chance to eat again. I just want something light to tide me over, that's all.'

'Help yourself,' Salcido said uninterestedly.

'Do you want anything?' she asked, picking up the receiver.

'No,' Salcido replied tersely.

She placed an order for a club sandwich and a Diet Coke, then hung up. Moments later there was a knock at the door. Peraya peered through the spy-hole and opened the door to admit a middle-aged man carrying a black attaché case. 'Good afternoon, Ms Wade,' the man said cordially to Melissa.

'Mr Fuentes,' she replied. 'I don't think you know Ramón Salcido?'

'Only by reputation. It's an honour to meet you in person. I had no idea that you were personally involved in this deal.'

'Give the case to my associate,' Salcido said, gesturing to Peraya.

Peraya took the case from Fuentes then placed it on the table, opened the catches, and lifted back the lid. Inside was a velvet pouch, secured with a drawstring. Salcido nodded to Peraya who then closed the lid. 'I believe that you and Ms Wade have some business to conclude?' Salcido said to Fuentes. 'There's an adjoining room if you'd prefer to talk in private.'

'No need,' Melissa replied, then addressed Fuentes. 'Well, how much are the diamonds worth?'

Fuentes was horrified by her bluntness and fidgeted with the knot of his silk tie as he eyed her, with distaste, over the rim of his glasses. 'I did as you requested. I authenticated each diamond, then I priced them individually—'

'Just give me the bottom-line figure,' she cut in.

He bristled, then removed an envelope from the inside pocket of his jacket and placed it on her upturned palm. Melissa slit it open and unfolded the single sheet of paper inside. The figure had been written neatly in fountain pen in the centre of the page: *$10.2 m.*

'The figure represents what I would pay for those diamonds, were I to buy them in individual parcels of, say, ten or less,' Fuentes told her. 'That was the assumption you asked me to work on. If they were sold in bulk you'd probably lose about twenty-five per cent on that figure.'

'Are we in business?' Salcido asked Melissa.

'We're in business,' Melissa replied, then folded the sheet of paper and slipped it back into the envelope.

Salcido snapped his fingers at Peraya, who removed an envelope from his pocket and handed it to Fuentes. 'That's the fee you agreed with Ms Wade. It includes a full reimbursement for your airfare as well as your accommodation here last night. Feel free to count it before you leave.'

'That won't be necessary,' Fuentes replied, pocketing the envelope. 'If you'll excuse me, I've got a plane to catch back to

Acapulco this afternoon. It's been a pleasure doing business with you, Mr Salcido.'

'You never did any business with me,' Salcido told him. 'You were never in this room. You never met me. You never met Ms Wade. I'm sure we understand each other.'

'Perfectly,' Fuentes said, with a smile. 'Good day to you both.'

Salcido waited until Peraya had escorted Fuentes to the door then held out a gloved hand towards Melissa. 'I believe you have something for me?' She gave him the disk, which he fed into the laptop computer he had brought with him. He spent the next few minutes scrutinizing the screen, occasionally pressing a key to roll the page as he sought to authenticate the document to his own satisfaction. He finally clapped his hands together and smiled contentedly.

'Well?' Melissa asked.

'I think I've got a real bargain here,' he replied smugly.

'We can always renegotiate the price,' she said, then looked round on hearing another knock on the door. Again Peraya peered through the spy-hole before he unlocked the door and admitted the waiter into the room. 'Ah, food,' she said, crossing to where the tray had been placed on the sideboard.

'Peraya, sign for it,' Salcido said, without looking up from the screen.

'There's no charge,' the waiter replied.

'I don't understand,' Peraya said, with a frown.

'Compliments of the Cali cartel,' the waiter replied, already pulling a silenced automatic from the back of his trousers. Peraya was still clawing frantically for his holstered weapon when he was shot through the head. The assassin swung the automatic on Salcido, who stumbled away from the table, his hands raised in front of his face. 'Please, don't kill me. Please,' he implored, his face twisted in terror.

Melissa ejected the disk, pocketed it, then switched off the computer. The deal with the Cali cartel had been to set up Ramón Salcido. They knew nothing about the disk. She looked down at the figure cringing fearfully against the wall. 'It's nothing personal, you understand. The Cali cartel and I go back a long way. I'd come to owe them a few favours over the years. Now we're quits. I'll leave the two of you to get better acquainted. I've got a plane to catch. I don't want to be late.'

She helped herself to a segment of the club sandwich and as she walked to the door Salcido called out desperately to her not to leave him alone with the assassin. This was followed by the muffled sound of the silenced automatic. She didn't know whether Salcido had been executed, or merely wounded to prolong his inevitable death. Not that it bothered her either way. She left the room without looking round and walked to the elevator.

She knew it wouldn't be long before the bodies were found. And when they were, she would be the prime suspect. Or, at least, Laura would. Laura who had no alibi. Laura who was still waiting for her at the house. It would be Laura who was arrested on suspicion of the double murders. Of course, she would protest her innocence and deny any knowledge of what had happened at the hotel, until she realized that she had been duped by her own sister. Then she would talk, if only to limit the damage of her own part in it. By the time the authorities finally unravelled the truth Melissa would be safely out of the country, with the diamonds, leaving Laura to take the fall.

The last piece of the jigsaw had finally slotted into place, exactly as she had planned it right from the start . . .

NINETEEN

It was the first time that Melissa had been back since leading the night raid on the private airfield fifteen miles south of the capital – which had proved to be her first success against the Salcido cartel – barely a fortnight after she had arrived in Mexico to take up her new position with the DEA. Several tons of coke had been seized as they were being unloaded from a Beech Sierra, which had flown in from Colombia. The pilot had been shot and killed when he tried to resist arrest. Three others were arrested and the airfield shut down with immediate effect. It had never reopened.

At the time the raid had proved little more than an irritation to the cartel, but it had brought her to the attention of Ramón Salcido. Six months later, after having her thoroughly investigated, he had recruited her to work for him – without the knowledge of his brother – on a retainer equal to three times her normal salary. She had proved a rich source of information . . . or so she'd had him believe. The truth was that most of what she had passed on to him had only exposed local anti-narcotics agents who were already on the take from rival drug cartels. Retribution was always swift, and often brutal. Yet she prided herself that her clandestine duplicity – both in Mexico and Colombia, where she had allowed herself to be recruited by a senior figure in the Cali cartel – had never once endangered the life of a fellow DEA agent. It had been the perfect way to eliminate the corrupt element within the local law-enforcement agencies, who were always well protected by equally dishonest superiors which invariably put them beyond the reach of the law. That was one aspect of the job she was certainly going to miss . . .

Turning off the highway, she followed the slip-road until she reached the perimeter fence that had once enclosed the airfield. Much of it had since been torn down by vandals, and what remained was beyond repair. The main gate was open, hanging precariously off a single rusted hinge. She drove inside and followed the road to an abandoned wooden hut on the edge of the neglected, overgrown airstrip.

She parked at the rear of the hut, retrieved the attaché case from the back seat and got out of the car. Although she could hear the monotonous rumble of traffic on the highway, which ran parallel to the airfield, she was isolated from view by the trees that bordered the site on all sides. An ideal blind spot for smuggling. Or for slipping unnoticed out of the country. She scanned the length of the deserted airstrip. The pilot had assured her on the phone that morning that he would be waiting for her when she got to the airfield. So where was he? Only one way to find out. She opened the attaché case, removed her cellular phone and rang the number he had given her for emergencies.

It was answered after the second ring. 'Hello?' A female voice.

'Can I speak to Aguirro?' Melissa said.

'He's busy.'

'Just get him!'

There was a pause. 'One moment,' came the reply, followed by the sound of the receiver being put down.

Melissa heard the woman's raised voice in the background, then silence. It was another minute before the receiver was picked up again. 'Aguirro,' a male voice said testily.

'What the hell's going on, Aguirro?' Melissa demanded.

'Señora Wade, is that you?'

'Yes, and you'd better have a damn good reason why you're not here.'

'I'm sorry, señora. The engine has been playing up. I had the plane refuelled early this morning, ready to fly to Mexico City, but as soon as I started her up I could hear that the engine wasn't right. I've been trying to locate the problem all morning. I think I've found it.'

'Am I supposed to be grateful for that?'

'You have every right to be angry with me, señora, but I couldn't risk taking off with the engine not a hundred per cent. You do understand that, don't you?'

'What I don't understand is why you didn't check the engine last night.'

'I did, señora. It was fine. But, as I said, I'm sure I've found the problem. It shouldn't take very long to fix.'

'If you've known about this problem all morning, why didn't you arrange to get another plane?'

'It's not that simple, señora. I've already logged a flight plan for this plane with air traffic control in Guatemala. It would have been difficult to make the necessary changes at such short notice.'

'What you mean is you bribed some corrupt official to let you enter Guatemalan air space illegally and that you'd have had to give him another bribe to make the necessary changes at such short notice,' she retorted disdainfully.

'You have to understand that these officials don't come cheap, señora,' Aguirro whimpered.

'You were given generous funds to cover those eventualities, on top of your own exorbitant fee.'

'My expenses were—'

'I don't want to hear it, Aguirro,' she cut in angrily. 'I expect you here within the hour.'

'I can't guarantee that, señora.'

'Then I'll find someone else to fly me to Guatemala. And you'll lose the balance of the money still owing to you. Only that will be the least of your problems because, in case you've forgotten, you were recommended to me personally by Ramón

Salcido. You are, after all, one of the cartel's more experienced fliers, aren't you? But I don't think he'd be too pleased if I were to tell him that you'd let me down. In fact, he'd probably see it as a personal affront. And I don't have to tell you what happens to people who displease him.'

'I'll be there in one hour, señora.'

'I hope so, for your sake,' Melissa said then severed the connection.

It was far from ideal, but what could she do? She sought comfort in the knowledge that even if Aguirro was late, she still had time on her side. Two, three hours. Probably more. OK, so it was a hitch she could have done without but it was no big deal. Yet a sense of uncertainty lingered in the back of her mind. She tried to shake it, but to no avail. This only angered her more and, finding the door to the hut secured by a flimsy padlock, she slammed the heel of her boot furiously against the frame. The wood splintered but the door held firm. She delivered a second kick. Harder. The door swung open and banged against the inside wall throwing up a cloud of dust, which she waved away from her face.

She waited until the dust had settled before going inside. It brought back more memories of the raid. She looked across at the cobwebbed filing cabinet in the corner of the room. The empty drawers were still hanging open, the contents confiscated at the time by the INCD. A desk was pushed against the wall, directly beneath the single window that overlooked the airstrip. Her eyes settled on the two gouges in the wall to the right of the window. A stain was still visible on the floorboards beside the desk. Blood. She had chased the pilot into the hut where he had foolishly gone for a gun that had been lying on the desk. She had shot him. A double-tap. Two shots in rapid succession. Both to the centre of the chest. He'd been dead before the paramedics arrived.

She righted the chair, brushed the dust off the seat, and sat down. Good memories, she thought. But, more importantly, they had helped take her mind off her own self-doubts. She swung her legs up on to the desk then clasped her hands behind her head and allowed herself to think over her years with the DEA. It was one way to keep her mind occupied and pass the time until the plane arrived.

Laura knew that something must have gone wrong. Mel had said she would pick her up from the house no later than one thirty. It was now two o'clock. She had tried not to dwell on what might have happened by trying to convince herself that Mel had merely been delayed, and that she would still turn up. But each passing minute had chipped away a little more of her brittle defences until she was now beginning to fear the worst. She knew it was unlikely that Mel would have been arrested, especially as neither the DEA nor the INCD were even looking for her. But what if Ramón Salcido had reneged on the deal? Mel had always assured her that the Salcidos were as good as their word. Had Mel been over-confident? No, she refused to believe that. Mel was a professional. She never left anything to chance. So where was she? Why was she late? What had happened to her? Questions that had no answers. At least not yet.

She stopped pacing the lounge floor, moved to the window once again and craned her neck to scan the road in both directions. She saw nothing. She looked at her watch: 2.03. Her eyes went to the phone. She had already tried to get through to Mel's but it had been switched off. But, then, Mel had told her it would be while she completed the deal with Ramón Salcido. Had she forgotten to switch it on afterwards? Unless something had happened to her when she met with Salcido. No, she refused even to entertain the idea that Mel might be . . . dead. Not Mel. She had always been a survivor.

What she would give for a drink to settle her frayed nerves. Just one. She pushed the thought angrily from her mind. But it wasn't the first time in the last hour that she had found herself thinking about a drink to calm herself. Initially it had been nothing more than a fleeting thought. But then it had slowly, almost insidiously, taken hold in her subconscious until it was now returning with increasing regularity. Not that it surprised her. She was already riddled with guilt over Raquel's death, and now she had the added uncertainty about her own future to erode what little self-belief she still had. The last time she had felt as low as she did now she had turned to the bottle to counter Jefferson's adultery. The vicious cycle had almost come full circle. She knew that whatever happened in the next few hours, it was now only a matter of time before her resolve broke . . .

She heard the sound of an approaching car and hurried to the window just in time to see it pull up outside the house. Her excitement was replaced by an overwhelming sense of dread when she saw that it was Tom Kellerman's. The driver's door opened and he got out. She stumbled away from the window, stricken by panic. Why had he come to the house? Had Mel been arrested? Or worse?

The doorbell rang. She was in two minds what to do. If she ignored him, he might go away – but what good would that do? If she answered the door, would she be strong enough to deal with the worst possible scenario – that Mel was dead? No, probably not. But she also knew that if she avoided him, she was only delaying a further visit. And by then she would have worked herself into a feverish state of worry.

The doorbell rang again. This was followed by a sharp rap on the door. She took a deep breath then walked the short distance to the front door. Another deep breath. Then she opened it. 'Tom, what are you doing here?' she said, trying to sound surprised. She wasn't convinced by her own performance. *Drop the act*, she told herself.

'We need to talk,' he said sombrely.

Has something happened to Mel? she wanted to ask him. *For God's sake, whatever you do, don't pre-empt him.* Instead she said, 'Of course. Come in.'

He brushed past her and went through to the kitchen. She

closed the front door and followed him. He was sitting at the table, facing the kitchen door. 'Sit down,' he said.

Has something happened to Mel? The voice was now screaming inside her head. 'What's wrong?' she asked, sitting down opposite him.

'Where were you between twelve and one this afternoon?'

'Here, of course,' she replied. 'Where else would I have been?'

'So you deny that you were at the Sheraton Hotel?' he enquired.

'Yes,' she replied forcefully. Mel had told her that she was meeting Ramón Salcido at midday. Only she hadn't told her where. Had it been at the Sheraton? Had Mel been seen there? And, if so, by whom? She knew that, irrespective of what he asked her, it was imperative that she remain calm. It sounded easy when she said it to herself in her head. Putting it into practice would be quite another matter.

'A woman claiming to be Melissa Wade went to the reception desk at the Sheraton Hotel shortly before midday and asked for the number of Ramón Salcido's suite, which he'd only checked into a few minutes earlier. Shortly after one o'clock Salcido and his bodyguard, Peraya, were found dead in the suite. Both had been shot through the head.'

'You don't think I killed them, do you?' Laura replied in disbelief.

'I showed the receptionist a photograph of Melissa,' he continued, ignoring her outburst. 'She was in no doubt whatsoever that it was the same person who had asked her for Salcido's suite number. She's prepared to swear to that in court, if necessary.'

'It wasn't me!' Laura exclaimed, the first sign of fear infiltrating her shaky voice.

'Melissa's dead. Who else does that leave?' Kellerman shot back.

'It wasn't me,' Laura repeated, this time stressing each word in turn. 'I came straight back here after I left the embassy. I haven't been out again.'

'You could have easily got a taxi back into town, gone to the Sheraton—'

'You're not listening to me, Tom!' she cut in frantically.

'And you're not listening to me.' Kellerman banged his hand on to the table. He sat forward and clasped his hands in front of him. 'For what it's worth, I don't think you killed them. Salcido had been shot through the back of the head at close range. It had all the signs of a professional hit. We also found some food in the room. Only room service has no record of any order being received from – or delivered to – the room. But an identical order was sent to another room around twelve fifteen. Single occupant. A man who arrived last night. He checked out at twelve forty this afternoon. Paid cash. The name he gave turned out to be false, as did the address. It's my guess that he was the shooter. What better way of getting into the room than to pose as a waiter? But he would have needed an accomplice to get him into the room.'

'I wasn't his accomplice, Tom. Why would I want to kill Salcido? I don't know anything about him other than what you've told me. The closest I've ever got to him was the photograph you showed me back in New York. How many more times must I tell you? I wasn't at the Sheraton this afternoon. End of story.'

'That's where you're wrong. A warrant's already been issued for your arrest for the murders of Ramón Salcido and his bodyguard. And if you were found guilty, even as an accomplice, you'd be looking at twenty-five years to life in a Mexican jail. I'd only wish that on my worst enemy. I'm trying to help you, Laura. Can't you see that? You've got to level with me. Tell me what happened. I'm your only chance now.'

Her head was pounding. There were so many unanswered questions. Why had Mel gone to the reception desk instead of getting Salcido's room number over the phone? Why hadn't she given the receptionist a false name? Why hadn't she been in disguise? Why had she been so unprofessional? It was so unlike her ... so unlike *her* ...

'The police wanted to arrest you straight away. I had to call in a lot of favours to hold them off. They've given me an hour to talk to you. Then I've got to take you in myself. That was the only way I could swing this. You've got to tell me what happened at the hotel, Laura. It's the only way I can help you.'

Laura was vaguely aware of him talking, but she was no longer listening to what he was saying. *So unlike her.* Her mind was now solely focused on those words. Three words that suddenly brought everything sharply into focus. So unlike Mel. But Mel was officially dead. The DEA had the pathologist's report to verify that. It had allowed Mel to move around Mexico City unhindered while *she* played the decoy ... and now seemingly the fool as well. Mel had double-crossed her and taken off with the diamonds. If the bodies had been discovered in the room at one o'clock, it meant that Mel had already left the hotel. That would have given her an hour at least to make the fifteen-minute drive to the house. And if the man who had checked out of the hotel at twelve forty was the shooter, as Tom seemed to think, that would have given her an extra twenty minutes. But not content to sneak away unnoticed, which she could have easily done, Mel had seen it necessary to announce herself to the receptionist, knowing that it would lead to Laura's arrest. And by the time the truth came out, Mel would be long gone.

It was only then, in the cold reality of her own despair, that the full force of Melissa's treachery hit her with all the savage ferocity of a hammering body blow to the stomach. She was struggling for breath, as if suddenly overcome by a terrifying sense of claustrophobic self-recrimination that seemed to be closing in on her. She was suddenly so alone. Unable to speak. Unable to comprehend what her mind was trying to force her to accept. Yet as she continued to fight against the inevitability of the truth, she kept telling herself that she could never have believed Mel capable of doing something like this to her. Did that make her naïve? Was it naïve to trust her own sister? Her own twin sister? No. But the fact remained that Mel had duped her. She had never had any intention of splitting the diamonds with her. Never. It had all been a sham from the start . . .

'Laura, are you listening to me?'

Kellerman's voice infiltrated her thoughts and she raised her head slowly to look at him. 'It wasn't me at the hotel, it was Mel,' she said, her voice now hollow and unemotional.

'I came here in good faith, but you obviously aren't interested—'

'Mel's alive!' Laura interrupted savagely, the anger in her voice levelled as much against Melissa as it was against herself. 'She's alive, Tom. Do you hear me? She's alive.'

'Except that I've got a report from one of New York's top pathologists on my desk, which says otherwise,' Kellerman replied.

'And how did the pathologist identify the body? Dental records. And who's been Mel's dentist for the past ten years?'

Kellerman held her unflinching stare for several seconds as her words slowly sank in. Then he slumped back in his chair and exhaled sharply as if he, too, had just been caught by a jarring blow to the pit of his stomach. 'Tell me everything. From the beginning.'

She did.

'She's certainly played you for the fool – just as you did me,' he said, once she had finished, making no attempt to conceal the bitterness in his voice.

'You must really hate me after what happened between us,' she said softly.

'Forget it. It happened. Let's leave it at that.'

'No, I want you to know—'

'I said forget it!' he rapped, then pushed back his chair and crossed to the door where he stared out over the small lawn. 'My head's already on the block after the fiasco with Doyle this morning. Now I've got Ramón Salcido lying in the mortuary with the back of his head blown away, executed by – or else on the orders of – a rogue DEA agent, who's been carrying out an elaborate scam right under my nose for the past week without me ever suspecting a thing. The same DEA agent who admitted to murdering Raquel Vasquez in New York as well as helping Doyle break into one of our most secure installations then cold-bloodedly executing Bill Walker to ensure that her cover remained intact. The same DEA agent who's now gone on the run with ten million dollars' worth of diamonds that she stole from the Salcido cartel, and which she acquired by using a classified document as bait.' He swung round to look at Laura. 'Imagine how well that's going to go down in Washington. I'll be busted right out of the DEA. Anything that happens to me after that will be a bonus. But that's nothing compared to what will happen to you if Melissa gets away with this. The authorities will need a scapegoat to minimize the damage she's already caused and they'll make sure that you're charged as an accessory to everything she's done. You can forget about the luxury of ever standing trial back home because by the time they've finished with you out here you'll be spending the rest of your life in a Mexican jail without the possibility of parole. Is that what you want?'

'I didn't realize I had a choice,' Laura whispered.

'I think you'd find that the authorities would be a lot more tolerant towards you if they had Melissa in custody as well. After all, she was the mastermind. And if you were to co-operate fully with the investigation, they'd take that into consideration when you were sentenced. I need to find Melissa before she can flee the country.'

'She'll be long gone by now,' Laura said. 'She probably went straight to the airfield from the hotel. You won't see her again.'

'What airfield?' Kellerman demanded.

'I don't know. She never said. Not that it would have meant anything to me even if she had told me. It could be anywhere. She set me up by giving her name to the receptionist at the Sheraton, knowing that I'd be arrested as soon as the bodies were found. She would have made sure she was safely out of the country, or at least airborne, by the time you came knocking at the door.'

'I think I know which airfield she'd use. It's not far from here. About ten minutes by car.'

'I still say you're too late,' she told him. 'Mel planned this down to the last detail. She's not going to make a mistake at this stage.'

'For your sake, I hope you're wrong. Let's go.'

'You want me to go with you?' she said suspiciously.

'I'm not letting you out of my sight until I've handed you over to the local police. That was the deal I made with them, and that's how it's going to be.'

'And what makes you so sure that I won't try to warn Mel if she's there?'

'After what she's already done to you, I think I can risk it, don't you?'

He led her out on to the porch and locked the door behind them then, keeping his hand lightly on her arm, escorted her to his car. Once inside he removed a pair of handcuffs from the glove compartment and she didn't resist when he snapped them around her wrists. He laid his jacket across her lap, concealing the handcuffs. She noticed then that he was armed, the butt of a Smith & Wesson protruding from the top of his shoulder holster. He started up the car and pulled away from the kerb.

'I never meant to hurt you, Tom, you have to believe that,' she said softly, breaking the lingering silence between them. She got no response from him as he kept his eyes focused on the road. It didn't surprise her. But she was determined to say her piece, to try to make him understand. That was all that mattered to her now. 'Do you honestly think that I set out to seduce you? I'm not cynical, not like Mel. She uses men. I could never do that. Especially not . . . someone I care about as much as I do . . . about you.' Still no response. She managed a weak smile. 'Mel always used to tease me about having to have strong feelings for a man before I slept with him. But it's true. You're the first . . . since Jefferson. Yet none of this was ever supposed to happen. And I'm not saying that out of spite. Or even remorse for that matter. I don't regret sleeping with you, Tom. I never will. I care so much about you. My only regret is that I've hurt you. I'm sorry. I'm so sorry.' She looked down sharply as tears welled in her eyes. She didn't notice his eyes flicker towards her. Just for a fleeting moment. Then he fixed his eyes back on the road again.

Neither of them spoke for the remainder of the journey, although Laura glanced several times at him, hoping for some response from him. Nothing. It was as though she wasn't there. She was sure that he still thought she had just used him when they had slept together. If only that were true it would have made it so much easier to reconcile with her own tortured conscience. But that was something she would have to live with for the rest of her life. And considering that the rest of her life was going to be spent behind bars, she would have a lot of time to reflect on her mistakes. Maybe, with luck, the cartel would put a contract on her and end her misery. She would have welcomed it, after what Mel had done to her.

Her initial feelings of hurt, disbelief and devastation had since been replaced by an intense bitterness that was now slowly eating away inside her. She remembered her father telling her as a child that it was pointless to bear a grudge towards someone else because the only person it affected ultimately was yourself. She thought back to her feelings for Jefferson. And her feelings for Mel. The two people she had trusted most in the world had betrayed her by first using, then discarding her. Maybe she was too naïve. Maybe she was too trusting. Maybe she was just a damn fool. Her father had been right, after all. But, then, he usually was. She wondered what he would make of her now. She had always been his favourite daughter and she knew he would have been devastated that she could have allowed herself to become mixed up in anything like this.

The car stopped. She had been so caught up in her own thoughts that it was only then that she realized they had left the highway and were now parked on the lip of a slip-road with a view of the airstrip below. Kellerman removed a pair of binoculars from under his seat then got out of the car and scanned the airfield before focusing his attention on the wooden hut. He got back into the car and phoned INCD headquarters and told the duty officer to have an armed response unit dispatched to the airfield.

'Is she there?' Laura asked, after he replaced the phone on the dashboard.

'There's a car parked close to the landing strip, but there's no sign of Melissa, or of a plane,' he replied, starting up the engine again. 'That doesn't mean she's not there. She could be in the hut. I couldn't see inside.'

'You seem very sure that this is the airfield she was talking about.'

'I am,' was all he said.

They followed the slip-road until they reached another crescent in the road, at which point he cut the engine and coasted the next hundred yards before stopping the car. Taking a key from his pocket, he unlocked one of the cuffs from her wrist then secured it to the steering wheel.

'If you wanted me to stay here, all you had to do was ask,' she said, with a weak smile.

'It's for your own protection,' he told her.

'You mean it's for your protection in case I were to side with Mel in the event of a confrontation.'

'On the contrary. I think, given the opportunity, you'd confront her yourself. And who knows what she might do in that situation?'

'What are you saying? That you think she'd kill me?'

'What I'm saying is that you'd be no match for her in a fight. I doubt I am, for that matter, but it's my job to stop her.'

'Assuming she's still here,' Laura pointed out.

'There's only one way to find out,' he replied, then unholstered his Smith & Wesson and climbed out of the car.

'Tom?' she said, as he was about to close the door. He peered in at her. 'Be careful,' she said softly.

Briefly his eyes softened. Then he closed the door and moved silently down the road, his body doubled over as he used the long grass as cover to keep out of sight of the hut. He paused every few yards and peered cautiously through the grass to get his bearings until he was directly in line with the hut. It was less than twenty yards away from where he was crouched, but he was still unable to see whether anyone was inside. He tightened his grip on the Smith & Wesson and waded through the grass to the edge of the clearing. He crossed the clearing noiselessly and pressed himself against the side of the hut. He was on the blind side. The door was around the corner and the window on the opposite side, looking out across the deserted airstrip. Wiping his sleeve across his sweating forehead, he took a deep breath then pivoted round, the Smith & Wesson extended away from his body. Nothing. He kept his back pressed against the side of the hut as he inched his way to the door. Then he swung round into the doorway and fanned the interior of the hut with the automatic. It was empty. His eyes settled on the attaché case lying on the desk. It was open. Stepping into the hut, he made his way cautiously to the desk, ever mindful to keep out of sight of the window. Inside the attaché case was a passport, a computer disk, a bulky, sealed envelope and a velvet pouch. He opened the drawstring and looked inside. Thousands of small, glinting diamonds winked back invitingly at him, caught in the reflection of the sun. He picked up the pouch and held it in the palm of his hand. It was remarkably light.

'That's ten million dollars you've got in your hand, Tom,' a female voice said behind him. 'And don't even think about trying to fire on the turn. I know all your little tricks, remember?'

He held the Smith & Wesson away from his body and replaced the pouch in the attaché case. Only then did he turn his head to look at Melissa, who was standing in the doorway, her Smith & Wesson trained on his back. He had to keep her talking until the INCD arrived. Unless, of course, the plane turned up first. That would certainly complicate the situation. But all he could do was play it by ear, for the moment.

'Put the gun down on the desk, Tom. Then step away. Do it slowly.' She chuckled softly to herself when he didn't move. 'You don't think I'd shoot you, do you?' Her voice hardened. 'Just try me. Now put the fucking gun down.'

Kellerman knew her well enough to gauge just how far he could push her. The tone of her voice was enough to tell him not to hold out any longer. He put the gun down then took a step away from the desk. Only then did he turn to face her. 'Why, Melissa?'

'I don't think you're in any position to be asking me questions, do you?' she asked, then stepped back from the doorway and cast a furtive glance up at the sky.

'We thought you'd be long gone by now. Your pilot let you down, has he?'

'We?' she said, with a frown, then nodded to herself. 'Of course. Laura with her sad little dreams of getting away from the monotony of her dead-end life in New York. She was so easy to fool. It was like luring a gullible kid into a dark room with the promise of a few sweets. God, she's pathetic.'

'And the fact that she's your twin sister means nothing to you?'

'She was a means to an end, nothing more,' Melissa said, with contempt. 'The fact that she's my sister, twin or otherwise, made no difference. She was always going to take the fall. I guess that was her with you in the car.' No reply. 'I saw the car the moment you turned off the highway. I know you've got no backup with you, although you must have called in the INCD by now. It'll take them a good twenty minutes to assemble a unit. And another half an hour on top of that to get here. I'll be long gone by then.'

'If your ride turns up in time,' Kellerman replied.

'That's all in the bag, but thanks for your concern anyway,' she said. 'If only that fucking asshole of a pilot had turned up when he was supposed to, none of this would have been necessary.'

'Meaning that you're going to have to kill me?'

'It's not by choice.'

'Is that supposed to make me feel better?'

'You've been a good friend to me over the years, Tom.'

'Spare me the bullshit, Melissa.'

She laughed. 'Yeah, you're right. Sentimentality was never my strong point . . .' She had heard the sound of an approaching plane. 'He's here.'

'I don't hear anything,' Kellerman lied, taking a step towards the door as he cocked his head, pretending to listen for the sound of the plane's engine.

'Listen . . . there,' she said then stepped back through the doorway and peered up at the sky.

There was still several feet between them, but he knew it would be his only chance to take her. She intended to kill him anyway, so what did he have to lose? He took two bounding steps to the doorway and lunged at her. She pulled the trigger as he hammered into her, knocking them both to the ground. The gun spun from her hand and landed out of reach of both of them. He was the first to react but as he tried to get up a sharp pain shot through his side and when he looked down he saw a dark stain forming around a small tear in his shirt. He had been hit. Then he felt blood running down his back. The bullet had passed straight through him. At least it was a clean shot. Better that way. But painful. He was about to make a grab for the gun when Melissa, who had landed under him, brought her elbow up sharply into his midriff, winding him. It gave her enough time to scramble to her feet and retrieve her fallen weapon.

She saw the movement out of the corner of her eye and was

still turning when Laura hammered into her with her full body weight. The gun catapulted out of her hand and their combined momentum propelled them both against the side of the hut. Melissa took the full brunt of the impact and cracked her forehead on one of the wooden struts. She collapsed to the ground without a sound. Laura stumbled back, her hand clasped to her mouth, fearful that she had killed her. Kellerman struggled to his feet and crossed to where Melissa lay. Blood was streaming down her face and on to her neck from a deep gash above her left eye. He winced as he got down on one knee and checked for a pulse.

'Is she . . . ?' Laura asked.

'She's out cold, that's all, but she's going to have one hell of a headache when she comes round,' he said, then picked up Melissa's Smith & Wesson and looked across at the Piper Cherokee Cruiser, which had already turned at the end of the runway and was now taxiing back towards the hut.

'At least she's alive. I thought . . . I'd killed her.'

'How the hell did you get out of those cuffs?' he asked.

'I used a hairpin,' she said, giving them to him. 'Mel once showed me how to do it.'

'Well, I'm sure glad she did,' he replied, then turned Melissa on to her back, pulled her arms behind her, and snapped the handcuffs around her wrists.

'Are you all right?' Laura asked anxiously, reaching out a hand to steady him as he got to his feet.

'It looks a lot worse than it is.' He returned to the hut where he retrieved his own Smith & Wesson and pushed it back into his shoulder holster. After pocketing the computer disk he closed the attaché case and took it outside with him.

'Are you going to arrest the pilot as well?' Laura asked, looking across at the Piper Cherokee Cruiser, which had finally come to a halt fifty yards from the hut.

'Then who's going to fly you out of here?'

'What are you talking about?' she asked, confused.

'You told me back at the house that you only came into this as a way of escaping your old life. A chance to start again. There's a passport and ten million dollars' worth of diamonds in here. This is your chance.' He held out the attaché case towards her. Her eyes went to where Melissa lay motionless by the side of the hut. 'You can't help her now. She's going to jail for the rest of her life. It's up to you whether you want to join her. Personally, I wouldn't recommend it.'

'But you'll . . . need me to testify . . .' she stammered.

'You said Melissa admitted she killed Bill Walker. Once we prove that the slug taken from his body came from her gun, she's already looking at life without the possibility of parole. And I'm sure we'll turn up a lot more evidence once we've searched her hotel room. Who knows? I might even have saved my job. But, then, I guess I'll just have to wait and see, won't I?'

'Letting me go isn't going to help your cause, is it?'

'You almost sound as if you want to go to jail.'

'I don't know what I want any more,' she replied.

'You don't need to go to jail to punish yourself. Your conscience will do that for you. As for letting you go, I didn't. You got away in the confusion after Melissa shot me. I think you'll find that the authorities won't exactly be falling over themselves trying to find you once I've briefed them on what you told me back at the house. Melissa was the mastermind. Let her take what's coming.'

'Hey, Wade, come on,' the pilot shouted from the cockpit, and beckoned her towards the plane.

'Well?' Kellerman said, proffering the attaché case. Still Laura hesitated. 'Take it, before I change my mind.'

She took the attaché case from him. 'Tom, I know that . . . well . . .'

'No speeches. Just go.'

'Thank you,' she said, and kissed him lightly on the lips.

'I hope you find what you're looking for. Now go on.'

She hurried towards the plane and only looked round once she reached the open cockpit door. Kellerman was gone. She got inside and closed the door behind her.

'I'm sorry I'm late, señora, but like I said to you on the phone, I had to be sure that the engine was running properly before I could take off. You do understand, don't you?'

'Let's just get out of here,' she said tersely.

'You have the balance of my money?' the pilot asked.

Laura opened the attaché case and removed the bulky manila envelope. She assumed it contained the money owed to him. He slid open the envelope. Inside were bundles of hundred-dollar bills. He extracted the first bundle and fanned it with his thumb. 'You can count the money once we reach our destination,' she told him. 'It's not as if I'm going anywhere until then.'

The pilot stuffed the money back into the envelope, which he slid under his seat. Laura looked across at the hut again as the plane began to move. There was still no sign of Kellerman. She thought about the diamonds as she placed the attaché case at her feet. Ten million dollars. Double what she had expected. But was it what she really wanted? Had it all been worth it? The deception. The greed. The loss. Yet she knew it would be the loss that would affect her most. The loss of her past. The loss of her identity. The loss of her dignity. Gone for ever.

The diamonds would buy her the anonymity she had so desperately craved, but she knew she would have to find a way to reconcile herself with her guilt-ridden conscience.

'You got any booze on the plane?'

'I never drink when I'm flying,' the pilot said briefly.

'That's not what I asked.'

'In the bag behind you,' the pilot said, jabbing a thumb over his shoulder. 'I was going to have it later tonight. Take it. I can buy more.'

She unzipped the holdall on the seat behind him and pulled out an unopened bottle of brandy. The plane lifted slowly off the ground. She cast a last look down at the hut. For a moment she thought she saw Kellerman standing in the doorway. Then the plane banked, and the hut was gone. She remembered what she had said to him the previous day: *Nobody can run from their conscience for ever, no matter how much they try.*

She broke the seal on the bottle. There was no turning back.